THE

SCAPEGRACE AT SEA ;

OR,

THE ADVENTURES OF DICK LIGHTHEART.

BEAUTIFULLY ILLUSTRATED.

VOLUME COMPLETE.

LONDON :

"BOYS OF ENGLAND" OFFICE, 173, FLEET STREET, E.C.,

AND ALL BOOKSELLERS.

" Off with his head !" cried Dick.

DICK LIGHTHEART;

or, The Scapegrace at Sea.

"AN ARM ENCIRCLED HIS WAIST AND DICK FELT HIMSELF DRAGGED DOWN."

No. 1

DICK LIGHTHEART;

OR, THE SCAPEGRACE AT SEA.

His Adventures

On the Sea, Under the Sea, On the Earth, and in the Centre of the Earth.

CHAPTER I.

"AFLOAT ON THE OCEAN WAVE."

"I'M afloat, I'm afloat, and the ro-o-over is free! I'm a——"

"Stop that noise, or I'll make you!" shouted a second voice, which was raised louder than the first.

"I'm a——" began the first voice again.

"I'll tell you what you are when I get hold of you," interrupted the second voice, which was that of the first mate of the "Indiana," Mr. Prentice.

The form of Dick Lightheart was perceived amidships, and it was he who had been singing with his accustomed gaiety.

"Beg your pardon," said Dick; "did you address your remarks to me?"

"I did."

"Who are you, may I ask?"

"My name's Prentice, and I'm first mate of this ship."

"Sorry for the ship, then," said Dick, coolly. "What on earth did they make you first mate for?"

"I'll teach you a thing or two before I've done with you!" shouted the mate angrily.

"Thank you, I'd rather not. I've left school."

"Have you?"

"Oh, dear, yes. It was yesterday afternoon when I started for a cruise. You ran me and my friends down, and you very properly picked us up. I have recovered from the effects of my ducking, and have come on deck to look about me," said Dick.

"You'll have to work, my lad, and I don't allow singing," said the mate.

"Don't you? That's a pity. I can't help it."

"You'll have to."

"Can't. It runs in the family. I'm a——"

"Stop it!" said the first mate; "you'd better. I'm boss on board this ship when the captain's below."

"So you don't allow singing," said Dick reflectively.

"No."

"Perhaps you're not musical?"

"What's that to you?"

"Just try the first bar of 'I'm afloat.' It goes like this. Tum-te-rum, tum-te-rum, tum-te-ray!"

The mate was speechless with rage.

"Go ahead, old cock; don't be afraid of it," said Dick. "It won't hurt you."

The mate made various ludicrous contortions of the face in the vain attempt to speak.

"Got a stomach-ache?" asked Dick, feelingly.

The only reply was a shake of the fist.

"Ah, that's bad," said Dick. "I can feel for you. Perhaps you have been eating measly pork. Take a pill or two when you go to bed by-and-bye."

"I'm all right in my inside," said the mate at last, with an effort; "it isn't that."

"Glad to hear it. Now let's see what you know about singing. I'll lead, you follow me. I'm a——"

Mr. Prentice rushed upon Dick, and seizing him by the arm, said, "You drop it. I won't have any more of your cheek, youngster."

"All right, let go," said Dick; "if singing isn't allowed, why don't you chalk it up, as they do smoking on board the penny boats from London Bridge, and put it like this, 'No singing abaft the funnel?'"

"Look here, my lad," said the mate. "No doubt you think you're very clever, but it won't wash."

"Won't it?" said Dick, looking at the mate's necktie; "you shouldn't have bought it then. It isn't a fast colour."

"I'm not talking about that. It's not neckties. It's your performing; drop it, or else you and me will be bad friends."

"Can't help that," said Dick. "I consider myself a passenger on board this ship."

The first mate forgot his anger, and began to laugh.

"What," he said, "you a passenger?"

"Yes. I'm the son of a gentleman, and my father can pay for me."

The mate laughed louder than ever.

"That's a good try on," he answered; "you're an old soldier, but you don't perform on me. You and your friends will have to work, and precious hard, too; we're short-handed with apprentices, and these decks want swabbing."

"Very well, swab 'em," said Dick.

The mate stared at him in amazement.

"I shall have to make you acquainted with a rope's end, my lad," he said.

"Who's he?" asked Dick.

"You're not such a fool as you look; take my advice, and don't try it on with me, that's all," shouted the mate, walking away in high dudgeon.

"I'm afloat, I'm afloat," sang Dick, "and the mate is a bully-ee; I'm afloat; I'm afloat; and I don't care a rap for he."

It will be remembered that Dick Lightheart, Messiter, and the boy Ted, who was deeply attached to Dick, had gone out for a cruise in a sailing boat from Brighton.

They had met with bad weather, been run down by an outward bound, and fortunately rescued by the ship that caused their disaster.

The captain, whose name was Simpson, had undertaken to convey them to his destination, which was the Cape of Good Hope, but he could not land them anywhere as it was out of his power to make for any nearer port.

A night's rest restored Dick to his accustomed good temper, and high spirits.

He and Messiter had been out sailing so much that they were never seasick.

As for Ted, he was a young sea lion, bred and born, as it were, on the stormy ocean.

Dick's encounter with the mate, which we have just described, took place during his first appearance on deck, on the morning after his accident and rescue.

He strolled along with his hands in his pockets, until he came to the cook's galley.

The cook was a young fellow, named Tom Wildey, who had run away to sea a year before.

"You're nice and warm in here," exclaimed Dick, inhaling an agreeable smell of ham and eggs, which were being prepared for the captain's breakfast.

"Nothing much to complain of," answered the cook, liking Dick's looks. "You keep your sea-legs well. Been afloat afore?"

"A little," replied Dick.

"It was a mercy you wasn't drowned yesterday," said the cook.

"Perhaps I'd better have been, than be on board with a first mate like yours," rejoined Dick.

"Ah! he's a caution, but he isn't a patch on the captain, who's a fiend when he's got you all to himself."

"Is he?"

"You haven't shipped from London before, or you would have heard of Captain Simpson. He's pretty well known,

I can tell you, and the owners have some difficulty in manning the ship."

"Why do they keep him?" asked Dick.

"Because he's clever. He may be out in all weather, but he's never lost a ship."

"This seems an old tub," observed Dick, looking round him.

"Yes, she isn't up to much. She pitches and tosses in a gale awful. It's the oldest ship the firm's got. It's a long time since she's been A. I. But since the 'Merican war, the English have done all the carrying, and any old ship's good enough for merchandise."

"Is it insured?" asked Dick.

"Yes. I know the insurance was very heavy, and it wouldn't be a bad job for the owners if she went down," replied the cook.

"Bad job for us, though," remarked Dick. "I don't want to be drowned."

"Have you had any breakfast?" asked Tom Wildey, good naturedly.

"Not a bit."

"I don't expect the apprentices will give you a chance of getting much. There's Sam Jolly and Jerry Coward. Jolly's a bully and Coward's a sneak."

"I haven't seen them yet," remarked Dick.

"Fight shy of both of them. They're no good. They'll make you and your pals do all the work now you've come on board."

"I'll bet a sovereign they won't get a stroke of work out of me," exclaimed Dick.

"You will?"

"Yes, and post the money."

"Well, you're a plucky un," exclaimed the cook, admiringly; "and from your size and looks, I should think you could slog."

"Just a little bit," answered Dick, smilingly.

"The captain favours Jerry Coward, and listens to all he says. He's a regular sneak," said the cook. "You look out for him."

"I will," said Dick.

"Will you have a bit of breakfast along with me?" said the cook. "I can give you a nice bit I've cut off the skipper's ham, and it's hard if I can't sneak a couple of eggs."

"I'm with you," said Dick, readily, "and I'll return your kindness on the first opportunity."

"Cut in then; we'll have ours first. Here's a prime bit, cut off a real Yorkshire ham—take this egg, it's yolky."

"Thanks—I like yolks; frizzle up the white a bit."

In a moment Dick was supplied with a good breakfast, which was washed down with a cup of coffee.

The sea was rather high, as there was a heavy swell in the Channel, although the wind had gone down.

It was not difficult to perceive, when Dick came to examine her, that the "Indiana" was a very old ship, and had seen her best days.

It did not matter much to him, however; he had meant to go to sea, and the accident which took him to the Cape of Good Hope was just what he would have wished for.

At the same time he did not mean to be the captain's slave.

Or the first mate's either.

He had not shipped with them, and they couldn't legally make him work, though he did not mind lending a hand if he was asked in a friendly manner.

His father would pay for his passage if he was asked.

But there was some difficulty in making the officers believe in the truth of his story.

They evidently took him, Messiter, and Ted, to be three sons of fishermen, and had made up their minds to treat them accordingly.

When he left the galley, Dick went into the cabin where the apprentices slept and messed, and where he and his companions had slept.

There was a great outcry as he came in.

Messiter was exclaiming—

"Leave off, I say—I won't have it. Two of you on to me at once isn't fair."

In a moment Dick was there.

He found the two apprentices, Sam Jolly and Jerry Coward, standing over Messiter with two ropes' ends with which they were hitting him.

"What are you licking him for?" asked Dick, his eyes flashing.

"Because he won't get the breakfast," said Jolly.

"He's not your servant," said Dick; "why should he?"

"He'll have to do it, or you will," said Sam Jolly, the bully, setting his arms akimbo, and staring impudently at Dick.

"My good fellow," said the latter, "don't you make any error. Neither my friend nor myself mean to do anything on board this ship unless we're asked civilly."

Jerry Coward laughed.

Dick immediately gave him a box on the ears, which sent him rolling over a bunk.

"You'll know what you're laughing at next time, my hearty," said Dick.

The boy Ted grinned with intense delight.

"I'll go and tell the captain," said Jerry. "We can't have the ship upset like this."

"I shan't call you Jerry Coward, I shall call you Jerry Sneak," said Dick. "If I catch you sneaking about me, watch it, that's all."

Sam Jolly, who was a thick-set, heavy-looking fellow, turned to Dick and said—"I have had enough of this nonsense. Do you mean to do your work or not?"

"Certainly not," said Dick. "Do it yourself."

"Do you want a tarnation good hiding?"

"You can't give it me."

"I can try, can't I?" said Jolly.

"So can any other fool, but it doesn't follow he will do it."

"Look here," said Sam Jolly. "I've been two voyages before this. You're a green hand compared to me, and I'm cock of this loft. We are short handed. Do the work, and I'll make things easy for you; if not——".

"Well?" ejaculated Dick.

"If not, it will be the worse for you."

"I'll chance that," said Dick.

"Do you mean a dust-up with fists?"

"Oh, yes, I'm game for a rough and tumble. It's sure to come sooner or later, and we may as well get it over at once."

"Mind your eye then, I'm on," said Sam Jolly.

"Ted," said Dick.

"Yes, sir," said the boy.

"Just stand near the hatch, and don't let that Jerry Sneak get out. I don't want this mill stopped."

"Right, sir."

"Messiter," said Dick, again.

"Well?" said Harry.

"Get a sponge and a basin of water ready for this cock of the loft, will you? He may want it presently."

Messiter grinned.

"More likely you'll want it yourself," growled Sam Jolly, who was getting very savage.

His ugly face glowed with passion, and his great, stupid-looking ears seemed to stick out like cabbage leaves.

"Come on," he said.

"I'm ready," said Dick.

The fight commenced in the little cabin, and it was evident that the combatants were in earnest.

They knew it was a battle for the mastery of their man, and that the one who won would keep the other in subjection as long as the voyage lasted.

CHAPTER II.

BILL BUNG DOESN'T LIKE IT.

DICK found his opponent as strong as a young pony, but he had not very much skill.

Parrying his blows, and hitting hard when he had a good chance, Dick punished him severely.

But he was knocked down first.

"Will that do for you," said Jolly, "or do you want any more? I learnt something when I was on board the 'Chichester.' It isn't a bad training ship, anyhow."

"Oh!" exclaimed Dick, getting up, "I suppose they picked you out of the gutter. That's generally how you get into training ships like the 'Chichester,' isn't it? How's your father?"

Sam Jolly foamed with rage.

"Perhaps you never knew him. Poor fellow. It's bad not to know your father.

isn't it?—and to get picked up out of the streets, and sent on board the 'Chchester?'"

"Come on!" exclaimed Jolly in a husky voice.

This time Dick Lightheart was more careful.

His arms were longer than Jolly's, and he kept him at a distance.

Every now and then he hit him hard, and darted back again.

The fight continued for ten minutes, with varying success.

At last Dick saw a good chance, and pretending to strike Jolly's face, he dropped his hand, and hit him in the stomach.

Jolly doubled himself up with a groan.

In an instant Dick kicked up his knee, and struck him under the chin, making his teeth rattle, causing him to bite his tongue badly, and half stunning him.

As Jolly fell back, gasping for breath, and spitting out blood, Dick exclaimed—

"That's how we do it, where I come from. How do you like it now, cock of the loft? Do you want any more?"

"Not this voyage," rejoined Jolly, dismally; "you're best man."

"It's a pity you didn't find that out before," remarked Dick. "However, it's never too late to learn. Perhaps you will get our breakfast ready. I'm cock of the loft now. Do you understand that, Mr. Sam Jolly?"

"Don't crow, if you are cock," exclaimed Jolly; "I'm licked this time, but my turn may come. Sit down, and have your grub."

Dick was quite satisfied with his victory.

He shook hands with Jolly, and they all sat down together, making a comfortable breakfast, though the fare was not luxurious.

Messiter and Dick went on deck afterwards, and hearing an altercation forward, ran in that direction.

Captain Simpson was beating a sailor with a marlinspike for some breach of discipline.

The crew looked on without interfering.

The sailor was a fine, handsome fellow, and in vain begged the tyrant to desist.

"Take that, Bill Bung," cried the captain, at each stroke, "and let us have no more of your mutinous conduct. I'll let you all know I'm captain, and will string

you up to the yardarm, if you don't behave yourselves."

"I've done nothing," said Bill Bung; "it wasn't my watch, if——"

"You'll argue with me, will you?" interrupted the captain, recommencing his ill-treatment.

The poor fellow's face was streaming with blood, and Dick's blood began to boil.

Rushing forward, he seized the captain's arm and exclaimed—

"Stop that—I won't have it!"

The next moment he was alarmed at his rashness.

What had he done?

Turning upon him with incredible fury, the captain exclaimed—

"How dare you speak to me, youngster! I'll break every bone in your skin!"

"No, you won't," answered Dick; "I've got a knife here, and if you touch me, you shall feel it. Knifing isn't my usual style of fighting, but it's fair with a man like you."

"He's threatened me with a knife; you heard him," said the captain. "Put him in irons—I'll have him flogged."

At a sign from the first mate, on whose face sat a smile of malicious satisfaction, four men fell upon Dick, whose arms were pinioned, and he was thrown on his back, where he lay helpless.

"Take him away," continued Captain Simpson, "I will deal with him presently. It's a pity I took the young whelp on board; he should have drowned if I'd have known what he was made of."

Strong arms lifted him up, and he was forced into a dark hole, near the cook's galley, where he was half stifled with the heat and a smell of tar.

Everything had passed so quickly that he could scarcely realise what had happened till it was all over.

"I've done a nice thing," he reflected; "offended the captain, and the men are too much cowed to help me. It looks cheerful, I must say."

There was the prospect of being flogged, which was not pleasant, as he did not doubt the captain would keep his word.

In a miserable state of mind, but still very angry, Dick sat down in his gloomy prison, and wondered what would happen next.

The captain went moodily to his cabin, as if afraid to trust his temper any farther.

Bill Bung got a bucket of water, and washed the blood off his hands and face, grumbling to himself all the while.

While he was thus engaged, Messiter came up to him.

"What cheer?" said Messiter.

"Bad enough; I don't like it, my lad," replied the sailor.

"You took it quiet enough."

"Cos I couldn't help myself. The skipper's always going on like that with some of us."

"More fools you to put up with it; I wouldn't. There is my friend, Dick Lightheart, going to be flogged till he's half dead, perhaps; none of you seem inclined to raise a hand to save him."

"I wouldn't stand it, boy, if the others would hang with me," replied Bill Bung, thoughtfully.

"Did you ever ask them?"

"Can't say as ever I did," said Bill, with a shake of the head.

"How can you tell, then? The crew musters about thirteen men, I suppose?"

"Fourteen and all told."

"What's to prevent you fellows taking your own part? You call yourself a man, and let yourself be beaten about the head like a hound. I am ashamed of you," cried Messiter.

"I'm a bit ashamed of myself; that's the truth, master."

"Talk to the men, and save Lightheart. If you are altogether, you can easily bind the captain and the mates."

"And get brought up before the British consul at the first port as mutineers," said Bill.

"You needn't hurt them. State your case to the consul, and no one will blame you. Lightheart stuck to you, and it would be cowardly in you to desert him now. If he is tied up, say you won't have it," urged Messiter.

"I'll talk to my messmates about it," rejoined Bill, "for blow me if I like it."

Messiter watched him go to a knot of seamen and begin to harangue them, and with a smile of satisfaction he said to himself—

"I thought the worm would turn at last. Dick must be got out of this somehow, if it's possible."

Ted came up, and looking very much concerned, asked Messiter what they were going to do to Master Dick.

"Cob him," answered Messiter

"What for?"

"Interfering with the captain, who was behaving like a brute to one of the sailors."

"Will they hurt him?" asked the boy, with tears in his eyes.

"If they don't, it will be a very good imitation of it."

"They shan't," exclaimed Ted, boldly; "I'll run at them and bite their legs first, if I can't do anything else."

Messiter laughed, but Ted thought it no laughing matter.

"I'd rather ever so much they'd lick me instead. Do you think the captain will let me take the licking instead of Master Dick?" he went on.

"It isn't likely. What have you done?"

"Nothing, but if he wants to lick somebody, I'll bear a lashing as long as I can stand to save my young master," answered Ted.

"You're a good fellow, Ted," exclaimed Messiter. "In this case, though, you can't do any good. The captain's a tyrant, and too strong for us."

"Are we to stand by and see it done?" asked Ted indignantly.

"Perhaps it won't come to that."

"If it does, I'll do something desperate, that I will," said Ted. "It wouldn't matter thrashing me much—I'm nobody—I've been kicked and beat ever since I was two feet high. I'm used to it; but Master Dick's a gentleman, and he's been kind to me. If he hadn't saved me, I should have drownded myself. They shan't hurt him."

"Hush," whispered Messiter. "Here comes the captain."

In fact, Captain Simpson had just come upon deck.

He had gone into his cabin to solace himself with a dram.

The spirits, however, only served to increase his agitation.

He saw that his control over his crew was becoming gradually weaker; like, and all tyrants, he fancied the only way to secure his power was by taking a high hand, and increasing his brutality.

"Mr. Prentice," he cried.

"Sir," replied the first mate, touching his cap.

"Let the prisoner be brought forward, and tell off the hands for punishment; muster them all. I mean to make an example."

The mate summoned the crew, all of whom trooped forward with a sullen and discontented air.

"Bung, step forward," continued the captain.

Bill Bung did so.

"Take this rope's end, and wait for my further orders."

He handed a thick tarred rope to him, which, as an instrument of punishment, was very formidable.

A rope's end will bruise and tear a man's back like a cat o' nine tails, and inflict more lasting pain.

"Bring out the prisoner," said the captain.

The first mate went to Dick, and personally conducted him on deck.

"Now, my lad," said the captain, with a brutal air, "I'm going to let you know what discipline is. Strip!"

Looking around him defiantly, Dick, whose arms were unbound by Mr. Prentice, did not move.

"Do you hear me?" thundered the captain. "Strip!"

"Captain Simpson," said Dick, quietly, "I protest against this treatment. You saved my life and those of my companions, for which I thank you.

"We would leave your ship at once if we could. As it is, we are unwilling passengers."

"You are part of the crew, and must work out your passage."

"Not at all. We have not signed articles, and you have no power over us so long as we conduct ourselves properly."

"Why did you interfere between me and one of my crew? But I'll waste no words with you," replied the captain. "Tie him up to the foremast."

"You will repent this," said Dick, turning pale.

"I'll risk that. Make him fast," replied the captain, with a reckless laugh.

Mr. Prentice, and Slowman, the second mate, seized Dick, and, despite his struggles, stripped him naked to the waist. Then they fastened him with a rope to the mast in such a way that he could not move.

Captain Simpson took out his watch, and, holding it in his hand, looked at it,

"Now, then, Bung," he said. "Lash away, and keep on until I tell you to stop."

Bung hesitated.

Dick's back shone in the noontide sun

Messiter could have cried with vexation, but was powerless to interfere.

As for Ted, he could have flown at the captain like a wild cat, and strangled him.

Perhaps he would have done so, if Messiter had not held him back.

"Wait," he said; "something may turn up yet."

"One—two—three. Start!" said the captain.

Bill Bung raised his stalwart arm, and the rope flew up in the air; but it fell down as suddenly.

"I can't do it, sir," he said; "it would break my heart, cappen, to hurt the lad. He interfered for me, and I ain't a brute beast."

"That is just why I selected you to punish him; it is a double punishment; so you will feel every blow you give him as he will. Go on, you fool! I'll have his back in a jelly before I've done with him."

Loud murmurs arose among the crew at this ferocious speech.

Bill Bung threw the rope on the deck, and walking away, joined his messmates.

"You won't obey orders!" shouted Captain Simpson. "Seize him, two of you, and put him in irons."

Not a man stirred.

"Mr. Prentice," said the captain, aghast, "what is this?"

"Mutiny, sir, I think; it looks like it," replied the first mate.

"If no one will flog him, I'll do it myself!" exclaimed the captain, grasping the rope's-end.

He made it describe a circle in the air, and it descended on Dick's back with crushing violence.

The flesh was discoloured, and became blue and swollen.

But not a cry broke from the courageous boy.

The captain was about to repeat his cruel treatment, when the men advanced in a body, and formed a line between him and Dick.

"Back, you scoundrels! Back, mutinous dogs!" exclaimed the captain, foaming at the mouth.

The solid line remained immovable.

Both mates put themselves by the captain's side, as they feared a crisis was approaching, and they determined to side with the skipper.

"Look'ee here, cappen," said an old, grizzled sailor; "I've shipped aboard o' many vessels, and I've seen a few skippers, but never the likes o' you. We don't want to do you no harm, but we ain't a-goin' to stan' by and see that poor lad flogged half to death acos he interfered for one o' us."

"I'll have you all tried at the first port I come to," exclaimed the captain.

"That ye may do, and welcome, but we'll all see as Bill Bung has his action agin you first, for hitting of him brutal," said the old seaman.

Mr. Prentice caught hold of the captain's arm.

"For Heaven's sake, go below, and leave them to me," he said.

"Not I. Where are my pistols? I'll shoot some of the dogs."

"Be guided by me, sir. Let them alone this time, and tackle them one by one. If you don't, they'll do something desperate."

The captain mumbled something which was inaudible.

He was almost speechless with rage.

"They are just in the humour to seize the ship," continued the mate.

"You will stand by me?"

"To the death, and so will Mr. Slowman—but we are only three against so many."

"I did a nice thing, it seems to me, in picking up this youngster. Cut him loose. You are right, Mr. Prentice. I will bide my time."

Captain Simpson, though a passionate man, did not lose his senses.

The first mate obeyed the order with the greatest joy.

In a few moments Dick was free, and began to scratch his back with a ludicrous air, which made the men laugh.

"Something's been biting me, hasn't it?" he said.

The crew roared again.

"It's only a sting," said Dick. "Wonder what it was."

He began to put on his clothes leisurely.

"My lads," said the captain, "I forgive the boy this time, and look over your misconduct. Perhaps I was hasty, but don't do it again. Mr. Prentice."

"Sir."

"Send out a double allowance of grog to the men."

"Yes, sir; it shall be done directly."

So easily are sailors managed or mismanaged that the men broke out into a hearty cheer.

"Have you done with me?" asked Dick, putting on his jacket, and coolly regarding the captain.

"For the present I have. Beware how you cross me again," was the reply.

"You've given me a great deal of trouble for nothing," said Dick. "It's a bore, dressing and undressing, this hot weather. The sun is strong in these latitudes."

Suddenly the voice of the look-out man rang out clearly—

"A strange sail."

"Where away?" asked the captain.

"On the larboard bow, sir."

The captain took his telescope, and began to reconnoitre the strange sail.

Everyone crowded to the side to have a look, and every eye was soon searching the horizon.

Even Dick shared the excitement.

He had a pocket glass, and brought it into use.

Messiter came to him and shook his hand.

"I am so glad you got off," he said.

"Don't worry me, Harry," exclaimed Dick. "I'm looking at the strange sail. One must have a little excitement now and then, or one couldn't live."

"You are a cool fish," said Messiter.

"Why not? What's the use of flurrying your fat? Take it easy, that's my motto. 'Free and easy, free and easy, I'll be free and easy still,'" sang Dick. "But look," added Dick, excitedly, "the strange sail is bearing down upon us!"

CHAPTER III.

THE STRANGE SAIL ON THE LARBOARD BOW.

AFTER a minute spection, the captain of the "Indiana" handed the glass to the first mate.

"I can't make it out, Mr. Prentice," he said.

After a momentary pause, the mate replied—

"Seems to me, sir, like a raft with a shipwrecked person on board."

"That occurred to me."

"Shall we bear down, sir?"

"I've had enough of picking up people," said the captain, with a grim smile. "But I suppose that common humanity suggests such a course."

The necessary orders were given to the ship's crew, and the "Indiana" bore down upon the strange sail.

It was soon discovered that the sail was nothing more or less than a man clinging to a hen-coop, who had taken off his shirt and hoisted it on high to attract attention.

When he was neared, a boat was lowered, and the unfortunate man picked up and brought on board.

He was a little, wiry man, about forty-five years of age, with a sharp, intelligent face, and an expression of anything but good temper.

As he stepped on deck, he exclaimed—

"Which is the captain of this vessel?"

"I am," replied Captain Simpson.

"You've been a long time picking me up. What do you mean by it?" said the little man.

"That's a cool remark," said the captain, "considering we have, in all probability, saved your life."

"And if you have, you only did your duty. Where is your cabin? Give me some fresh clothes immediately, and something to eat and drink."

"You've got a nerve," said the captain, inclined to be angry. "I've a good mind never to save anyone again."

"That will not matter much to me. You are not likely to save me twice."

"Why not?"

"It will be your turn next," said the little man.

"What do you mean?"

"What I say, sir. My name is Crawley Crab, sir. Do you hear? Crawley Crab."

"You speak loud enough," replied the captain.

"Bah!" said Mr. Crawley Crab; "it's evident you ar not a man of science, or you would have heard of me. I have written books, sir—books!"

"What then?"

"Why, sir, I am a famous man. My position in life is that of Secretary to the Society for the Exploration of the Unknown Parts of he World, sir, and I am making my third voyage."

"How were you wrecked?"

"That is the strangest thing. But give me to eat and drink, clothe me, and you shall hear."

"Speak first, and then I'll think of it, Mr. Crab," said the captain.

The conversation was audible enough to be heard by all on board, who crowded round the speakers in a way that showed how severely discipline on board the "Indiana" had been interfered with by the late occurrence.

"Well, well, well," cried the little man, irritably, "what a boy you are. I left England last week, on board the 'General Johnstone.'"

"I know her," said the first mate "Government ship, isn't she?"

"Be good enough, my dear sir, not to interrupt me," rejoined Mr. Crawley Crab. "I cannot tell my story, if I am interrupted. W at does it matter to the cause of science whether an insignificant individual like you knows or doesn't know the 'General Johnstone?'"

"Go on, sir. Sorry I spoke."

"So you ought to be. Don't do it again. Well, sir, this ship was fitted up at a great expense, in order that I and other scientific men might make discoveries. Do you see?"

"Not clearly as yet," answered the captain.

"Tush, tush! be quiet," exclaimed the irritable little man; "don't interrupt me. This morning, about eight o'clock, we were struck amidships, but below the water line, by a wonderful sea monster, which nearly cut us in two."

"Did the ship sink?"

"She did almost directly afterwards. I seized a hen-coop, and here I am."

"A monster cut you in two!" exclaimed the captain, opening his eyes. "What sort of a monster? Did you see it?"

"We did for a few minutes. It was black and long, like a gigantic eel, and threw out phosphorescent light."

"Then there was something electric about it?" remarked the first mate.

"Undoubtedly."

"That's a strange yarn," observed the captain.

"It may be strange, but it's true, and I will tell you that in all my travels, and all my reading, I never heard of such a creature before. Never, as sure as my name is Crawley Crab."

"Is he cruising still in these latitudes?" asked Captain Simpson.

"Of course he is. He can't be far off."

"Bill Bung," cried the captain.

"Sir," said Bill, reporting himself.

"You have been in a whaler, I think?"

"Yes, sir; two years, when I was a lad."

"Can you harpoon?"

"Show me a whale or a shark, and try me. I've got my 'poon with me, in my chest, and should like to have the chance," replied Bill.

"Get it ready, then—it may soon be wanted," said the captain.

He took Mr. Crawley Crab, the Secretary of the Society for the Exploration of the Unknown Parts of the World, into his cabin, gave him dry clothes, and provided him with the best dinner the resources of the ship could afford.

Dick had listened curiously to the conversation between Captain Simpson and Mr. Crab.

Taking Messiter's arm, he said—

"That's a wonderful yarn of that fellow who has just come on board."

"Very," replied Messiter.

"I don't know what to make of it, exactly. A fish is a fish, and unless it has a big horn, it can't sink a ship."

"Perhaps he's cracked," said Messiter.

"Not he. There is something in it. The man is sane enough. He has been wrecked, and he has told his story plainly enough, only I don't believe in the strange animal."

"What is it, then?"

"That's the mystery. There can't be any rocks in the middle of the sea. It isn't a rock," said Dick.

"Then it must be a wonderful fish."

"I hope we shall see it," exclaimed Dick.

"I hope it won't sink us," replied Messiter.

At this moment Ted approached, and said—

"Glad you wasn't hurt, Master Dick."

"Hurt, you young rascal," answered Dick. "If you had a rope's end laid across your back, wouldn't you feel it?"

"I suppose so, sir."

"So did I: but I wasn't going to make a song about it; all I know is, I was very glad there was only one of them."

"If Mr. Messiter would have let me, I'd have bit the captain's legs," said Ted.

"And very likely got your teeth kicked out. I'm much obliged to you, Ted, for your kind intentions," replied Dick, "but you was best out of it."

A couple of hours passed.

Mr. Crawley Crab came on deck, arm in arm with Captain Simpson.

Dick saw at a glance that Mr. Crab was a character, and meant to study him.

After a time, Mr. Crawley Crab left the captain, and met Dick.

"Nice weather, my lad," he exclaimed.

"Who are you calling 'my lad?'" asked Dick.

"You're one of the crew, I suppose, and you needn't be so snappish."

"I'm a passenger," replied Dick, "and my name is Lightheart. Sorry I haven't got a card, but I was wrecked yesterday, and that will account for it."

"Indeed! I presume you were picked up as I was? Did you meet with the singular animal that destroyed my ship?"

"Can't say I did. What was he like?" asked Dick.

"A huge long thing, covered with scales, half in, half out of the water," replied Crawley Crab.

"Are we likely to meet with him again?"

"I should think so," answered Mr. Crab.

Suddenly he exclaimed—

"Look there!"

"Where?" exclaimed Dick.

"To the right. There. There. I don't understand those confounded sea rms, and I don't know larboard from starboard, but on my right is the creature."

"The dreaded animal?" asked Dick, with a laugh.

"Yes. Look!"

Dick followed the direction of the out-stretched arm, and beheld a curious sight.

Not far from the ship, was a long, black-looking thing, lying like a log on the water.

No phosphorescent light came from it.

It seemed silent and motionless.

"Sort of sea serpent, I should think," he continued.

"Can't tell," answered Mr. Crab. "Where's the captain? We must fire at it, harpoon it, or do something, or else I shall be wrecked again."

"Try another hen-coop, sir!"

"Not if I can help it, my young friend. Four hours in one day, on a floating hen-coop, on the bosom of the briny deep, is quite enough for any ordinary man," replied Mr. Crab, with a grim smile.

Bill Bung came by, and Dick said—

"Pass the word for the skipper."

"Aye, aye, sir," replied Bill. "Glad you got out of that scrape, sir," he added.

"Thanks to you,"

"It was tit for tat. You did as much for me."

"And would again. Call the captain. We have the monster on our lee," exclaimed Dick, who was strangely excited about the marvellous thing he saw floating down to them.

"The what, sir?"

"The monster."

Bill Bung took one glance at the sea.

It was quite enough for him.

"There is a curse on the ship," he exclaimed. "I knew how it would be. We sailed on a Friday, and the first mate shot an albatross the second day we were out. We're doomed, we're doomed!"

And he went aft, repeating the sinister words, "We're doomed! we're doomed!"

CHAPTER IV.

"A MONSTER OF THE DEEP."

CAPTAIN SIMPSON at once came on deck, and was soon busily engaged in looking at the wonderful creature which Crawley Crab declared had sunk the ship in which he had been sailing.

The crew were much agitated.

Seamen are at all times superstitious, and never having heard of such a strange monster, they fancied its appearance boded them no good.

The weather, which had hitherto been favourable, now changed.

Dark, heavy clouds flew up from the south.

The sea hissed and boiled in an uneasy manner, and the wind whistled funereally through the straining cordage.

It was evident to the practised eye of the captain that a violent storm was at hand.

In a clear and collected voice he quickly gave orders to make all taut, and was soon riding snugly under close-reefed top-sails.

Suddenly the storm burst in all its fury.

The thunder crashed, while the forked and vivid tongues of lightning played round the vessel in streams of bluish fire, and the darkness was intense.

The monster, which had been perfectly inert up to this time, threw out a marvellous light, which illuminated the depths of the sea.

The magnificent irradiation was evidently the result of electricity, and it revealed the shape of the strange fish, if fish it was, very distinctly.

Its form was what we may call a lengthened oval, tapering off at the head and tail, which were under the water, only part of the scaly back being exposed to the air.

With a strange hissing noise it all at

once sank to the bottom of the sea, and was seen no more.

"It has disappeared," exclaimed the captain.

The sailors breathed a sigh of delight.

"I would have given a hundred pounds," said Crawley Crab, "if we could have captured it."

"For my part," replied the captain, "I am glad it is gone. No good ever comes of meddling with such singular things. What do you, Mr. Crab, as a scientific man, take it to be?"

"I fancy, sir," answered Mr. Crab, "that it must be some extraordinary species of electric eel. That there are huge deep sea snakes I have never doubted."

"Ah! we know very little of what lives at the bottom of the sea," answered the captain.

The storm was not of long duration.

Heavy torrents of rain succeeded the war of the elements, and towards night the sea calmed itself, the wind went down, and a placid moon, beaming from the serene, star-studded sky, shed its silvery light upon the still heaving waves.

The mutinous spirit of the men had died away.

Captain Simpson did not attempt to tyrannise over the crew any more, and the boys were left to themselves, doing very much as they pleased.

Out of good nature and a love of activity, they gladly lent the apprentices a hand, when there was any work to be done.

Dick was looking over the side, soon after the moon had risen, and to his astonishment he saw something rise in their wake, making a splashing noise, and then laying perfectly still.

It was undoubtedly the monster, which had risen again from the depths of the ocean, now that the storm was over.

He uttered a shout.

Crawley Crab, who was on deck, was astonished at the cry, and hastened to his side in a moment.

"Is it the strange creature again?" he asked nervously.

"Yes, sir; there she lies," said Dick.

As he spoke, the marvellous light broke out around him, quite dazzling in its brilliancy.

Crawley Crab called the captain.

"Sir," he said, "the monster is again close to us. I ask you, in the interests of science, to capture it."

"Who's going to do it, and how is it to be done?" said Captain Simpson.

"This thing is a scourge of the ocean. It destroys ships, therefore it is your duty to destroy it," persisted the man of science.

"We will harpoon it, if you like, though I do not know why I should risk the lives of my crew. Where's Bung? Pass the word for Bung," said the captain.

When Bill Bung made his appearance, he was trembling like a leaf.

He was a brave man, and had faced death many a time, but he, in conjunction with his messmates, had again beheld the monster, which they thought must be something supernatural.

"Get your harpoon, my man," said the captain.

"Not me, sir," said Bung, firmly. "I wouldn't harm a scale of the critter's back was it ever so. We shall all be sent to the bottom of the sea, if I do."

Turning to Mr. Crab, the captain said—

"You see the feelings of my men; what can I do?"

"I'll do it myself," said the man of science, grandly. "If no one will attack this chimera, sir, the honour and the glory of the task shall belong to me, sir."

"You, Mr. Crab?"

"I, sir. Give me a boat and loaded guns. It will be hard, indeed, if I cannot put a bullet in him, and lay the mighty brute low. Who will volunteer for this splendid task?"

There was no response.

"What! Are you all cowards? Will no one volunteer?" continued the man of science, scornfully.

Dick stepped forward.

"I'm on, sir," he exclaimed. "Can't stand by and see a gentleman left alone. I'm not afraid of the creature."

Messiter, as a matter of course, took his place by Dick Lightheart's side.

So did Teddy.

Where Dick went, his devoted friend and equally attached follower felt bound to go as a matter of duty.

"Three of you. Bravo?" cried Mr. Crab. "Now, sir, we are four, and we shall triumph. Lower a boat, if you please."

The order was given to put the ship about, and a spot favourable for the enterprise being selected near the monster, a boat was lowered, into which the volunteers descended.

Messiter and Teddy took the oars, Dick grasped the tiller, and Crawley Crab stood in the bows with a loaded gun under each arm.

"My four troublesome customers," said the captain, in a low tone to the first mate, "stand a very good chance of never returning."

"It will be a cheap get rid of them, if it costs us the boat," said the mate in the same tone.

Bill Bung was much impressed with the bravery of the little party, though he would not have joined them for the world.

"Give 'em three cheers, my lads," he said. "Shiver my timbers, but they deserve it for their pluck."

Three hearty cheers broke out, and travelled, as it appeared, to the ears of the sleeping monster, for in an instant the bright electric light went out, and the creature was almost imperceptible in the darkness of the night.

The moon, however, served to indicate his whereabouts, and the boys pulled steadily towards him.

"Steady, my lads," said Crawley Crab. "Easy all; keep the head before the wind, Mr. Lightheart, if you please."

"Steady she is, sir," answered Dick.

The boat stopped at a short distance from the monster.

Crawley Crab stood up, placed a gun to his shoulder and fired.

The ball struck the huge slumbering beast, but glided off its back, as if it had struck a piece of polished steel.

"Hard as the hide of a rhinoceros," said the man of science; "we must try again. Steady, boys."

The monster, however, did not seem to approve of being shot at.

It seemed to tremble violently for a moment.

Then with incredible velocity it darted past the boat, which was upset in a moment, and proceeded to strike the "Indiana."

It struck the unfortunate vessel amidships.

The crash was distinctly audible, and amidst the noise of falling masts and flapping sails, were heard the cries of the sailors and the moans of the dying.

After the concussion the monster retired as it had come.

A cloud obscured the surface of the moon, and it was difficult to tell where it had gone, or what had become of the "Indiana."

Dick found himself struggling in the sea, and wondered what had become of his companions.

"Bother those monsters of the deep," he said to himself; "I don't like them."

Swimming gently, he got hold of one of the oars of the boat, and so kept himself afloat without much exertion.

It was not a hopeful position to be in.

Struggling alone in the middle of a vast ocean, ignorant of the fate of his companions, and doubtful of succour, it was not to be wondered at if he felt inclined to despair.

CHAPTER V.

AFLOAT ON THE OCEAN.

DICK little imagined at that moment what a strange influence over his career the marvellous monster that had broken up the boat was to have.

Such creatures of chance are we, that we never know one moment what may happen to us the next!

He thought of his home, of the girl he loved, of his school at Brighton, which he had so lately quitted.

"Well," he said, aloud, "I like adventures, and now I have met with a beautiful one. Perhaps I shall be picked up. Perhaps not. No matter. One must die some day. Still it is uncommonly hard to die so young."

As one is emerging from youth to manhood, the world seems so beautiful and enticing; we have so much to see, to learn, to enjoy.

"Hullo! Hi! What cheer? Ship ahoy!" he cried.

He had scarcely closed his lips, after this appeal for help, when he felt his arm seized vigorously.

"Who are you?" he asked.

"If you will lean upon my shoulder, sir," was the reply, "you will soon gain strength and swim better."

"Is it you, Ted?" said Dick, recognising the voice of his faithful servitor.

"At your service, Master Dick. I have been swimming about everywhere looking for you ever since that submarine beast swamped us. Ugh! What a terrible brute it is. It laughs at bullets, and cares no more for a ship than I should for kicking over a stool."

"Is no one saved?"

"I can't tell any more than you, sir; all I thought of was to swim after you."

"Why," said Dick, "you are more like a Newfoundland pup than anything else."

"I've been brought up to it, sir. That's it. Water's my native element, I may say."

"Take one end of my oar and hang on. Do you think the 'Indiana' will pick us up?"

"I'm afraid, sir, from the way in which she cracked up when the monster charged her, that she is either floating a helpless wreck, or gone down with all hands aboard her."

"Then it's all up with us," said Dick dismally.

"Perhaps," replied Ted; "but we shan't give in for some hours, and lots of things may turn up in that time."

Dick felt cheered by the philosophic spirit of his companion.

Nevertheless, the situation was as terrible a one as can well be imagined.

Those on board the "Indiana" were in too much trouble, if they were yet living, to think of the perils of the others who had courted destruction by going in the boat to attack the monster.

Nor would Captain Simpson feel very friendly disposed towards them, because it was Crawley Crab's shot that caused the slumbering creature to rush madly upon the vessel.

Dick began to calculate the chances of safety.

If the "Indiana" had not foundered, the crew might lower another boat in the morning to search for them.

The sun would not rise for about eight hours.

Could they exist so long in the water without fainting or becoming cramped by the sluggish circulation of the blood?

In vain he tried to pierce the dense darkness which surrounded them, for now the moon had disappeared, and bad weather seemed imminent again.

The luminous waves broke up against his chilled hands.

About two o'clock in the morning Dick was seized with extreme fatigue; his limbs were a prey to an agonising cramp.

Ted put his arm round him, but he drew his breath with difficulty, and evidently required all his strength for himself.

"Let me go, Ted," said Dick; "save yourself."

"Certainly not, sir," said Ted; "you won't refuse my last wish, and that is to be drowned with you, if it comes to that."

At that moment the moon appeared again from under the edge of a thick cloud which had concealed it for a time.

The surface of the sea sparkled under its rays.

This fortunate light put new strength into the boys.

Dick searched the horizon, with eager, careful gaze.

He saw the "Indiana," or what appeared to be her, about five miles off, looking like a sombre, inert mass, but there was no sign of a boat.

At first he was inclined to cry for help, but of what use would it have been at that distance?

His lips, moreover, trembled and his teeth chattered, so that he could scarcely speak.

Ted had more power left.

He exclaimed—

"Here, this way! Hi! help, help!"

Was it one of those delusive sounds which the anxious mind sometimes conjures up?

Or did an answer really come to the lad's cry for help?

"Did you hear anything?" he asked.

"Yes, I thought so," said Ted.

He began to cry out again.

"Help, help!"

This time there was no mistake.

"'AH!' EXCLAIMED CRAB, 'WE ARE NOT SO MISERABLE AFTER ALL.'"

A human voice clearly responded to his.

Ted lifted himself as high out of the water as he could, and taking a look, fell back exhausted, clinging desperately to the oar.

"Did you see anything?" asked Dick, anxiously.

"Yes; don't talk, sir; we want all our strength," answered Ted.

There was a hopeful ring in his voice which inspired Dick, who, however, fancied he heard the boy sigh almost directly afterwards.

He thought of the monster.

Was it still near them? But, if so, whence came the voice?

They began to swim with all the strength they had left, and after some minutes of continued exertion, for moving was a painful task in their state, Ted spoke again.

"Are you far off?" he said.

"Not far—push on," replied the voice, which Dick fancied he knew.

Dick's strength was leaving him fast.

He was very cold.

Had it not been for Ted he must have sunk.

Suddenly an outstretched hand seized him; he was pulled violently out of the water, just as his senses were going, and, after some one had rubbed his hands vigorously, he opened his eyes and murmured—

"Ted."

"Here, sir," replied the lad.

By the rays of the moon, Dick saw a figure which was not that of Ted, but which he recognised easily.

"Mr. Crab?" he said.

"Right, my lad," answered the man of science. "Crawley Crab, as you see me, safe and sound."

"Where is Messiter?"

"Here, Dick," answered Messiter. "Mr. Crab and I stuck together, and our only concern has been for you."

"Where the deuce are we?" asked Dick, puzzled; "this thing I am sitting on seems firm enough."

"It's a floating island," answered Mr. Crab.

A horrible thought crossed Dick's mind, to which he could not give expression.

"To put you out of your misery at once," continued Crawley Crab, "we are

on the back of the gigantic creature at whom I shot, and I know now why I did not kill him."

"Why?"

"Because he is iron-clad, or something very like it. I can make no impression upon the scaly monster with my knife."

These words produced a strange feeling in Dick's mind. He found that he was really with his friends on the back of the monster, which continued to float on the surface, after causing the partial destruction of the "Indiana."

He got up and stamped his foot.

It was certainly a hard, impenetrable body, and not the soft substance of which all the marine inhabitants that he had heard of were made, such as whales, sharks, walruses, and the like.

If anything, it more resembled a tortoise or an alligator.

A hollow sound was emitted when it was struck, and it appeared to be made of cast-iron plates secured together.

"What is your opinion of the creature, sir?" asked Dick.

"You want my candid opinion as a man of science," said Mr. Crab.

"Certainly, sir."

"I should say then, that this peculiarly constructed monster is the result of humanhands and ingenuity."

"In that case, it is not a monster at all."

"By no means," said Mr. Crab. "I am very much in the dark at present, but I am positive that there is some wonderful mystery about this thing, which to my mind is a sort of submarine ship, ingeniously constructed to sail under the water for a time, and to come to the surface for a supply of fresh air from time to time."

"If that's so, sir," said Dick, "there must be some internal mechanism to make it work about."

"Evidently."

"It gives no sign of life."

"Not at present," answered the man of science. "But we have seen it move. It has appeared and disappeared. Consequently, it must have hidden machinery."

"Of course."

"So that we come to the conclusion, which is inevitable, there must be a man or men inside to direct the ship."

"Hurrah!" cried Dick; "I didn't

think of that. We are saved if that is so, and it must be as you say."

" Hum !" muttered the professor; "I don't know so much about that.

" The fact is this," he continued. " If, when it makes a start, it glides along the surface of the water, we are all right; but if it goes down we are lost."

" I've got an idea," said Dick, after a pause.

" Let's have it."

" We must knock at the door, and see if we can find any one at home."

His companions laughed.

" I have searched carefully," said Messiter, " but I can't find even a man-hole. Oh, I wish I was back again at school."

" So don't I," said Dick. " Shut up snivelling, Harry; don't show the white feather."

" I can't help it. When I meet with things I understand I am all right, but when I come across things like this, it is enough to frighten any fellow," said Messiter.

There was nothing for it but to wait until morning.

Dick wanted to keep his feet warm, so he amused himself by kicking his heels upon the body beneath him.

" I'll wake 'em up," he said. " They shan't sleep if they won't let me in."

Their safety depended absolutely upon the caprice of the mysterious steersman who inhabited the iron-clad, fish-shaped machine.

It seemed to the professor that before they descended again they would have to open some hole to obtain air.

If so, they could communicate with them and would be saved.

But saved for what fate ?

He scarcely dared to ask himself.

The beings who inhabited that singular structure clearly had a secret to guard, and might not shrink from murdering their captives, or dooming them to a life-long imprisonment.

All were now very tired, wet, and hungry.

A raging thirst began to attack them.

Dick fancied he heard vague sounds beneath him, but could not be sure.

Who were the strange beings that lived in the floating iron shell ?

Kicking angrily upon the iron surface, Dick said—

" You are very inhospitable inside. I am hungry and thirsty. Do you want me to die up here ?"

He had no sooner spoken than a flap beside him opened.

Half the body of a strong, wiry, thick-bearded man appeared.

An arm encircled his waist, and Dick felt himself dragged down into the interior of the iron shell.

A cry of terror broke from his companions.

This was answered by a smothered cry from Dick, as the flap fell back and shut out any further view of the interior.

Dick had vanished.

CHAPTER VI.

INSIDE THE MONSTER.

THIS removal, so brutally executed, was accomplished with the rapidity of lightning.

Crawley Crab felt his hair stand on end.

As to Messiter, he was chilled to the marrow of his bones with fear.

" What have they done with him ?" he asked.

" Your friend Lightheart is the first victim," replied the professor. " Perhaps they mean to eat him. For my part, they may eat me as soon as they like ; anything is preferable to this."

" I wish I could get at them," replied Teddy. " I'd soon have my young master out."

The words were scarcely out of his mouth when the trap-door opened again, and Teddy was dragged down below in a similar manner.

" Really this is very extraordinary," said the professor; " two of us are gone.

Just as if we had been swallowed by a whale."

"Can this be a monster after all, and the trap-door his mouth, through which he takes in his food?" asked Messiter.

"No, my boy," replied the professor; "we are no doubt in the hands of pirates, wretched rovers of the sea, who have brought science to their aid. It is to be hoped that they will respect the person of the Secretary of the Society for the Exploration of the Unknown Parts of the World. If not, I threaten them with the vengeance of all civilised Europe, for my learned books have been read every-whre, and——"

The door opened while he was speaking and a long arm twining round his waist, dragged him too into the heart of this floating prison.

His legs kicking up ludicrously in the air attracted the attention of Messiter, who could not refraim from laughing, miserable though he was.

"My turn next," muttered Messiter.

He was not long kept in suspense.

The long arm twined, snake-like, round him, and he too descended into the bowels of the infernal machine.

Dick's experience was that of all of them.

He had descended an iron ladder, was pushed into a room, the door of which shut to with a heavy bang.

In ten minutes they were altogether in the same compartment.

The darkness of their prison was so intense as to prevent Dick seeing his hand before his face.

Thus it was impossible to guess where they were, or even to tell if they were alone or not.

"This is an outrage," said Mr. Crab. "I protest against it. Is the author of a dozen immortal works to be treated like a naughty schoolboy?"

"We're up a tree," remarked Dick, "and it's no use hallooing. They're not going to eat us. This isn't an oven, and I think we are better here than up above."

"At least we had our liberty," continued Crawley Crab, who was never satisfied or happy unless he was at work or grumbling.

"I've got a knife," said Ted, boldly, "and I'll stick the first that comes near me. It's a regular pig-sticker, my knife, and I'll bet they feel it."

"Don't you do anything of the sort, Ned," cried Dick. "You might get us all killed."

"It's very hard, sir, if a poor bloke can't do something."

"You'll get it hot if anyone is listening to you," continued Dick. "If you don't care for yourself, think of us."

Ted grumbled inaudibly, and Dick began to take the dimensions of the prison in which they were.

This he did by walking about, and he made it twenty feet long by ten wide.

The walls were of iron, made of plates riveted together.

Half an hour passed.

At the expiration of that time, the cabin was illuminated by a flood of light so vivid and blinding, that it was difficult to bear the intensity.

Dick recognised the electric light that had floated round the ship when he first saw it.

When he got used to its clear white-ness, he looked up and saw that it proceeded from a globe which hung from the ceiling.

"Light at last; our captors are becoming more civil," said Mr. Crab, rubbing his hands gaily.

"It's about time, I think," answered Dick.

They were not much better off, how-ever, for the cabin only contained a table and five wooden stools, but the light was refreshing, and made them more cheerful.

Not a sound reached their ears; every-where reigned the silence of the grave.

Perhaps the ship had sunk to the bottom of the ocean, for it seemed to have the power of going where its strange owner wished.

In a short time the door opened, and two men appeared.

One was a negro of the Southern States of America type, with intelligent but flat face, and short woolly hair.

The other was a tall, handsome white man, with keen, searching eyes, that looked into the very soul.

He wore a thick moustache, whiskers, and beard, and appeared to be an Eng-lishman.

His expression was sad in the extreme.

It gave the beholder the idea that he

was the victim of remorse, either for some great crime, or for some awful calamity which had befallen him.

Evidently proud, and born to command, he was to all appearance the captain of the vessel, for the negro treated him with the utmost respect.

He regarded the prisoners with a fixed gaze and said something to the negro in an unknown language, which was so sweet and soft that it seemed to be all vowels and no consonants.

At length he fixed his eyes upon Mr. Crab, who, as the eldest of the party, seemed to be the leader of it. The professor made a low bow.

"I presume," he said, "that I am in the presence of the proprietor of this singular machine, and, as I am a man of science, I respect one who could conceive and carry out the idea of a submarine ship."

There was no answer.

"Permit me to tell you our history," continued the professor.

Still no reply.

"He's remarkably polite," remarked Dick. "Perhaps he don't understand our language."

"Leave him to me," said the professor; "my name may have an effect upon him. I am, sir, Mr. Crawley Crab, professor of natural history, and Secretary to the Society for the Exploration of the Unknown Parts of the World. I have written valuable books, sir, which have been translated into foreign languages, sir."

The professor paused to look proudly around him.

Nothing in the sad man's face indicated that he understood one word.

Undaunted by this silence, Crawley Crab continued—

"This, sir, is my friend, Mr. Lightheart. This my friend, Mr. Messiter, both of Brighton, and sons of gentlemen. The lad is their servant."

There was still no answer.

The professor grew cross.

He spoke in French, then in German, finally in Greek and Latin; but with the same disheartening effect.

"I have recounted our Odyssey in five languages," said the professor, in despair, "and he does not understand a word. Where could he have been educated?"

"Leave him to me," said Dick. "I'll speak to him in the universal language."

"What may that be?"

"Wait a bit and you'll see."

Dick went up to the man with the sad but aristocratic and commanding face.

"Look here, governor," he said, pointing to his stomach; "see that. It's empty. Look at this," he added, pointing to his mouth. "That wants filling—twig? If it's only a bit of tommy and a glass of water, I shan't say No to it."

Not a muscle of the stranger's face moved.

Turning to the right, he muttered some words in his incomprehensible language, and, without making any reassuring sign to the prisoners, turned on his heel and walked away.

The door closed after him.

"Well, I'm blowed!" said Dick. "This is a queer go, and no mistake. If he doesn't speak English, French, German, Greek, or Latin, what does he speak? Is it the king of the sea?—is he Neptune himself?"

"What a face! What intelligence! What spirit!" said the professor, clasping his hands together admiringly. "I never saw such a man."

"I don't want to see another like him," answered Dick. "One cove like that in a lifetime is quite enough for me."

"It's my opinion," remarked Messiter, "that he's kidding."

"What do you mean?" asked Dick.

"I believe he understood us all along, but he didn't want to say anything, because he has not yet made up his mind what to do with us."

"I know one thing," said Dick, "that is, I am dying with hunger."

"If they would only give me a saucepan and some fire, Master Dick," said Ted, "I'd make some soup."

"How?"

"I've got my boots, and the swell cove who came in, let his sealskin cap fall. I picked it up and sneaked it. The two together wouldn't make bad soup."

While he spoke, the door opened again, and another negro entered with a tray upon which were four plates.

A savoury smell issued from them. Knives and forks were provided, and having placed the plates on the table, the negro raised the covers.

"Another nigger," said Messiter. "They seem to grow here."

"Grub," said Dick, "that's good."

"Not up to much, Master Dick, I'll bet," observed Ted.

"What do you know about it?"

"What can they give us? Porpoise stew, fillets of dog-fish or stewed shark. I'd rather have some salt junk on board the 'Indiana.'"

The negro disappeared with the covers, and all but Teddy sat down.

"Fire away, Teddy," said Dick, looking at the dishes.

"After you, sir; I can wait," replied Teddy.

"Sit down, I tell you. When people are shipwrecked, they are all equal. Pitch in," answered Dick.

Teddy sat down. There was no bread and wine, but a bottle of water supplied its place.

It was difficult to say what the dinner consisted of. It was a mixture of fish and vegetable matter, but not an atom of meat.

Delicately cooked, and its flavour was good and pleased the palate.

On each plate, each knife and fork, was stamped this sinister motto—

DEAD TO THE WORLD
N.

This was peculiarly appropriate to the life the inhabitants of this remarkable vessel lived.

Dead to the world!

That they seemed to be in fact, while the letter N was doubtless the first letter of the proprietor's name.

For some time no one spoke. The business of eating was all-absorbing, for one must eat, especially after a shipwreck.

It was consoling to reflect they were not destined to die of hunger.

"I think," exclaimed Teddy, when he had finished his plate, "that they mean to fatten us before they kill us."

"Hold your tongue, Ted, till you are spoken to," said Dick.

"Yes, sir. I know I'm only an odd boy, but——"

"Shut up, I tell you. I want to go to sleep," exclaimed Dick.

"Certainly, sir. Sorry I took the liberty, but if I don't talk to somebody, I must talk to myself."

"Try it on, that's all, and if you wake me when I'm asleep, I'll give you something for yourself. I'm just getting dry, and shall sleep like a top," answered Dick, throwing himself in a corner.

The professor, who was worn out, had already chosen his corner.

Messiter followed his example, and soon they all slept.

Teddy, however, was the last to lie down, and before doing so, he, with a devotion that was quite touching, took off his jacket, and folding it up, laid it under his young master's head.

"It will make him a pillow," he muttered, "and I shan't miss it."

CHAPTER VII.

CAPTAIN NEMO.

HOW long he slept Dick did not know.

He woke first, and saw his companions snoring like most boys.

Nothing was changed in the apartment, except that the remains of the dinner had been removed.

It was with difficulty that he managed to breathe, and he guessed that he had consumed all the oxygen in his prison. His lungs were oppressed, and the heavy air was not sufficient for proper respiration.

How did the commander manage?

Did he obtain air by chemical means, manufacturing it by means of chlorate of potash, and absorbing the carbonic acid by caustic of potash, or did he compress air in large reservoirs?

While Dick was revolving these questions in his mind, a valve opened in the side of the room, and a fresh current of sea air swept into the cabin.

Evidently the vessel had ascended to the surface of the ocean, and taken in a fresh supply of air.

The others, influenced by this invigorating atmosphere, woke up, and rubbing their eyes, started to their feet.

Teddy looked at Dick, and said, "Have you slept well, sir?"

"Pretty well," replied Dick. "How are you, Mr. Professor?"

"I breathe the sea air, sir, and I am content," answered Crawley Crab. "How long have we slept? It must be four-and-twenty hours, at least, for I am hungry again; I cannot tell to a certainty, for my watch has stopped."

"There is one comfort," replied Dick, "we are not in the hands of cannibals, and we shall be well treated."

"I don't know that, sir," replied Teddy. "They've got no fresh meat on board; all they gave us yesterday was fishy stuff, and four fine, fat, healthy fellows——"

"Shut up, Teddy," cried Dick; "how often am I to tell you to hold your tongue?"

"I know I'm only an odd boy, sir, but——"

"Will you be quiet?" exclaimed Dick, taking up a stool threateningly.

"All right, sir," replied Ted, "I won't say anything more."

"Say your grace," observed Messiter: "open your mouth, and wait for what Providence will send you."

Mr. Crawley Crab was very silent and thoughtful.

Dick remarked this, and said—

"How long do you think they will keep us here, sir?"

"I can't tell any more than you, Lightheart," replied the professor.

"But what is your opinion?"

"Not a very encouraging one. We have by chance become possessed of an important secret. If the secret is worth more than our lives, we shall either be killed or kept prisoners."

"For ever?"

"Yes, for ever," answered the professor, gravely. "If the secret is not very serious, we may be landed on some island. I advise that we remain perfectly quiet, and take things as they come."

"May I say a word, sir?" exclaimed Ted.

"Well?" asked Dick.

"I'll get out of this," replied Ted.

"How? It is difficult to break out of a prison on earth, but to get out of one under the sea is impossible."

"Suppose we kill our gaolers, and take the key? If four Englishmen aren't a match for a lot of niggers, and one cove who can't speak any language, and doesn't belong to any country at all, it's time we shut up shop, and cried a go," replied Ted.

At that moment the door opened, and the negro who had before appeared entered.

Ted instantly threw himself upon him, and, seizing his throat with his two hands, held him so tightly as almost to strangle him.

But being a powerful man, he soon disengaged himself, and a fearful struggle ensued between them.

"Help, help!" cried the negro, in excellent English.

Ted let go his hold at this, and fell back laughing.

"So you can talk English!" he cried; "that's all right. I only flew at you to see what countryman you were. Now, then, tell us all about this ship, or I'll give you another dose."

Putting his finger to his lips, the negro gave a peculiar whistle—prolonged and shrill.

This was evidently a signal.

He had scarcely finished, when the captain appeared on the threshold.

His sad face was lighted up with an expression of anger, before which even the impetuous Ted recoiled.

"Go!" he said to the negro, who immediately departed.

Sitting down on the edge of the table, with his arms crossed on his powerful chest, this strange being seemed plunged in deep thought.

Our heroes regarded him with expectation, not unmixed with awe.

They were entirely in his power.

Was he about to punish them for the indiscretion of one of their number?

At length he spoke in English.

"Gentlemen," he said, "you see I can speak your language. I did not answer you at first, because I was undecided what to do with you. I am well acquainted with the scientific works written by Professor Crab, and I esteem it an honour to have made his acquaintance."

The professor bowed in acknowledgment of this compliment.

"I am also glad to see two intelligent young gentlemen like Mr. Lightheart and Mr. Messiter."

"You've forgotten me, sir," said Ted. "I'm only an odd boy, but——"

The captain extended his arm, and Ted was silent.

"I'm a man," he continued, "who has broken with society, and renounced humanity. In a word, I am dead to the world, as all those who are associated with me, must be. I have my history, which, however, does not concern you. Had you not molested me, and fired at my vessel, I should not have crippled your ship, and upset your boat. The attack came from your side."

"But, sir," answered the professor, "we took your ship to be some unknown creature."

"Possibly, but this creature had done you no harm. I saw you all take refuge outside, and I hesitated a long while what to do with you. I knew nothing of you. What were you to me? Why should I extend my hospitality to you? All that was necessary to break off our connection, was to give a signal to my engineers, and the 'Enigma,' which is the name of my vessel, would have sunk to the bottom of the ocean. I had the right to do it."

"No," said the professor, with a smile, "allow me to contradict you; it would have been the act of a savage, and not of a civilized man."

"Sir," interrupted the captain, hotly, "I am not what you call a civilized man. Society and I have nothing in common. I do not recognise your laws, and I forbid you to speak to me again of them."

An air of anger and disdain lighted up the features of the unknown, and it was clear that his past life had been unutterably bitter.

"At last," he went on, "I took compassion upon you, and have saved your lives. You shall be well cared for, and a cabin to sleep in placed at your disposal. You may go about this ship as I and my slaves do, but I warn you not to intrude upon me without permission. There are times when I have my black hours, when it is not safe for any human being to come into my sight."

His hearers shuddered at this avowal.

"It seems to me that we are to be prisoners?" observed the professor.

"Certainly."

"But this is an outrage," exclaimed Dick. "I demand to be put on shore at the nearest port, or given up to the first ship we meet."

"You will none of you ever see the earth again, or set foot upon it," replied the captain.

"This floating prison is then our tomb—our coffin in which we must live and die?"

"Call it what you will," replied the captain, "you have surprised the secret of my existence. Do you think I could ever allow you to revisit the world, to let it be known through every newspaper how I pass my life? There are those who think me dead. I wish them to think so, in order that some day they may have a terrible awakening."

"Death would be preferable to a life such as you propose to us," said the professor. "Am I to be cut off in the prime of life, in the midst of my scientific labours?"

He spoke indignantly, and with great animation.

"Perhaps," answered the captain, "you will not find your captivity so arduous as you seem to imagine. As a scientific man, you can study the animal life of the ocean. My library shall be open to you."

"You have a library!" cried the professor, astonished.

A smile passed over the commander's face.

"The 'Enigma,' Mr. Crab, is fitted up as luxuriously as was my palace," he said.

"Your palace! Were you a king?" asked Dick, sharply.

The shade of displeasure crossed the face of the unknown again. He raised his arm threateningly, but dropped it directly.

"Ask me no questions," he said in a harsh voice. "Those who do so will suffer for their rashness."

"Sir," said the professor, "we are poor, helpless, shipwrecked travellers, entirely in your power, and therefore at your mercy, but we have only one wish, and that is our liberty."

"It is impossible."

At these words Dick felt his heart sink within him.

"It's a crying shame, that's what I call it," said Teddy Larkin; "and the first chance I get of stepping it, my name will be Walker."

"Silence, Teddy," cried the professor, adding—

"How are we to address you, sir?"

"My name to you is Nemo."

"That in Latin means nobody," said Dick.

"You are right. Since I have quitted society, I have become nobody."

"Very well, Captain Nemo, of the 'Enigma,' dead to the world," said Dick, "we must make the best of our situation, but I will never give my word that I will not attempt to escape."

"I like you, boy, for your honesty," said Captain Nemo, "though I warn you that if you are caught in the attempt, you will be instantly put to death."

"To death? You dare not."

The captain laughed in a wild, weird manner.

"Dare not!" he said. "Foolish lad, there are no laws for me. I am the sole master here. My black slaves only live to do my bidding. What is your life or death to me? I have no more to say at present. Follow this negro into another cabin, where a repast awaits you."

He called to someone outside, and bowing politely, went away, while the four companions were conducted to a dining room handsomely furnished and lighted by an electric lamp.

Various preparations invited their attention. The dinner service was of silver, and everything denoted immense wealth on the part of the owner.

The negro waited upon them attentively, and Dick said to him, "I suppose you may speak to us now, my black friend."

"Yes, massa, me speak now," answered the negro, with a grin.

"What is this I am eating? It tastes like meat."

"That, massa, a turtle steak. Very good meat, but all fish here. Never have no flesh—all fish."

"How do you catch it?"

"Put out nets sometimes," was the answer. "Other times, Cappen Nemo,

he go out shoot, at the bottom of the sea."

Dick laughed.

"Shoot at the bottom of the sea! How does he do that?" he asked.

"That one of um secrets, massa," answered the black. "Great many secrets on board this ship. P'raps you know all some day; if Massa Nemo he tell you."

"What's your name?"

"Me name One, massa."

"One!"

"Yes, massa. There twelve slaves on board this ship, and all have figure names, me one, other nigger two, other three, four, five, six, seven, eight, and so on, up to de twelve."

"That's a rum idea," said Dick; "fancy calling out for your servant, and saying, 'Here, nine, I want you,' or, 'I say, three, do this.'"

"It is my opinion," exclaimed the professor, "that Captain Nemo is a very remarkable man—the most remarkable, in fact, that ever lived. He has invented a singular ship which can go under the sea at will, but why not? Was not the invention of steam engines laughed at, as well as the invention of gas? Who, a hundred years ago, would have believed in the electric telegraph, by means of which we send a message to the end of the earth in a minute?"

"Very true," replied Dick. "It's a pity a man of such genius should shut himself up like this, though."

"It is a pity," answered the professor.

"What's worse, though," remarked Messiter, "is that he means to keep us as prisoners."

"If he can," said Ted.

"Don't you be so fast, Master Ted," said Dick. "Keep your mouth shut, or you may get into trouble."

"Very sorry, sir. I know I'm only an odd boy," replied Ted; "but I don't like such goings on, and wish I was back again on the beach at Brighton."

The negro handed the professor a fresh dish.

"Will massa have some American oysters stewed in whale's milk," he asked; "or some jam, made of sea anemones?"

"I'd rather you would not tell me what the dishes are; it will set me against them if you do," answered the professor, with a wry face.

When the repast was ended, Dick jumped up. "I feel better," he said.

"Stop!" cried the professor, "if we are prisoners in a submarine ship, if we are removed from civilization, let us not forget that we are Christians. Allow me, as the elder and the leader of our little party, to return thanks."

Dick sat down again.

The boys bowed their heads, and the professor said grace in a simple, reverent and touching manner.

When he had ended, he rose, and said—

"Now, my lads, I am going to make a little speech. I'm not an old man, but I am older than you, and my experience goes for something, and I tell you that you never lose anything by repeating those prayers you learnt at your mother's knee. We are in a position of danger; an awful position, and each night and morning you should invoke the protection of Providence. Never be ashamed of saying your prayers. Let us pray for a happy issue out of all our troubles and perils. That is all. Now let us pull our chairs together, and enjoy an after-dinner chat."

The words of the professor cheered the drooping spirits of the boys.

He was calm, brave, confident.

"Mister No. 1," said Dick.

"Massa call me?" asked the black, who was clearing away.

"Yes. Where are we now?"

"We gone down, massa, and now we lie at the bottom of the sea."

Dick regarded him with undisguised astonishment.

CHAPTER VIII.

THE MYSTERIES OF THE "ENIGMA."

THE negro entered the cabin again, bearing a decanter containing a light liquid, richly-cut glasses, and some cigars on a dish.

Mr. Crab jumped up delightedly.

"Ah!" he exclaimed, "wine and tobacco. We are not so miserable, after all."

He tasted the contents of the decanter, and continued—

"This is not wine, but it is very good. How do you get it, my friend?"

"Massa cappen, um distil it from a certain seaweed, and from another sea-leaf he make the cigar," replied the negro.

"A very remarkable man, indeed," observed the professor, lighting a cigar, which was rich in nicotine.

Many days elapsed.

The life of the captives was unvaried by any incident.

They saw nothing of Captain Nemo; were well attended to, slept comfortably, and had nothing to complain of but their imprisonment.

Books were freely supplied them.

They were not allowed, however, to leave their cabins.

At the expiration of a fortnight or thereabouts, as well as they could reckon, No. 1 entered their cabin after breakfast.

Addressing Dick, the negro observed—

"Massa Lightheart to come to cappen's cabin."

"Does he want me?" inquired Dick. "All right. I'm game. Good bye, my friends," he added, "perhaps you will never see me again. I may be the first victim."

"No fear," exclaimed Messiter. "We shan't be hurt if we keep quiet."

"I'll suggest that you're the fattest, Harry, if there is any question of cooking one of us."

"Then it won't be true, for you're as fat as a mole. Go on and be cooked first! I'll have a bit of you," answered Messiter.

Dick went away laughing.

He was not really alarmed, for although he did not like Captain Nemo, he fancied he was safe as long as he did not irritate this strange being.

The negro conducted him along a passage which opened into a magnificent library, full of books, which gave admittance to a drawing-room, furnished with all the taste that could be found in Paris or London.

The space within the iron-clad shell had been made the most of, and no expense had been spared to make the cabin luxurious and well appointed.

The walls were richly papered, and covered with valuable paintings.

The ceiling was frescoed, and works of art were everywhere to be seen.

Rich couches and chairs invited rest, and the foot sank in the soft pile of a Turkey carpet.

Captain Nemo rose as Dick entered.

"Take a seat," he said, as the negro retired, closing the door after him. "I have taken an interest in you, Lightheart. Your presence soothes me. I once had a son who resembled you."

"Is he living now, sir?" asked Dick.

The black frown crossed the captain's face.

"Did I not warn you that I would have no questions asked respecting my former life?" he said. "I wish to forget it."

"Your past must have been a fearful one," said Dick, boldly, "or you never would have quitted the world to live like this, with your slaves."

"My object was to begin life anew, and forget utterly that I had ever lived before," said the captain, more mildly than Dick had expected.

"And you find that you were mistaken."

"Why?"

"Because you feel remorse, or you wouldn't be so upset at my asking a few innocent questions," said Dick.

The captain was silent for a moment.

"You are right," Captain Nemo answered at length. "It remained for a boy to teach me wisdom. I cannot forget; but at least I have quitted the scene of horror, which was dyed with the blood of— —"

He paused suddenly, and bit his lip, as if he had said too much.

"Yours is a sort of madness," said Dick, with his usual coolness. "I don't believe you are quite right in your upper story, clever though you may be."

"You talk boldly," replied the captain, angrily.

"Why should I not?"

"Your life is in my hands."

"I know that; but you might as well kill me as keep me shut up here. Besides, you sent for me, and I did not begin the conversation," answered Dick.

"If anyone else had dared to speak as you have spoken, I would have killed him with this hand," cried Captain Nemo, savagely.

"Perhaps I should not be the first you had disposed of."

The captain rose and came close to him.

"How do you know there is blood on my hand?" he cried.

"I don't know; I only guessed it," answered Dick. "It was a fluke; but I don't think I'm far out."

"Do not provoke me too far," said the captain. "Let us change the subject. I should not like to harm one so young. I wish you well; in fact, I have taken a fancy to you. You are a fine specimen of a brave young English boy. Come, I will explain all the mysteries of this ship to you, and show you how I have managed to escape from the world, and exist under the waves, for in no other place could I be safe from terrible enemies!"

In spite of his reserve, the captain kept on making admissions which roused Dick's curiosity.

"Your history must be a strange one, sir," he said.

"Ah! you would indeed say so, if you knew all. Perhaps some day I may tell you. Not now."

He approached the end of the room, and drawing back a curtain, revealed a splendid organ.

"Do you like music?" he asked.

"Very much," answered Dick. "Play us something. It will enliven me a bit. I feel awfully low, and I'll give you a game at dominoes or crib afterwards, if you like."

Captain Nemo smiled, and sitting down, played Mozart's Twelfth Mass with great skill.

"Thank you," said Dick, when he had finished. "Very fine. Now, will you tell me how you manage for air?"

"I will not trouble you with chemical details," answered the captain, "which you would not understand, but when I do not take in air at the surface, I have some compressed in a reservoir, which, by means of an apparatus, is wafted all over the ship."

"And about light and moving about?"

"That is the result of electricity, which I make myself. My motive power is electricity, and I can attain a speed of thirty miles an hour. The men of the world have not yet discovered half the value of electricity. My machinery is of the finest kind. If I want to sink to the bottom of the sea, I fill certain reservoirs I have with water; when I want to rise, I lighten the ship, by letting out the water. In short, I have invented everything that is necessary for my safety and comfort."

"Wonderful!" ejaculated Dick.

"Your friend, the professor, would understand me, if I were to explain to him how everything is managed, but to you, it all seems as strange as the first railway train did to the country people through whose districts it passed. Engineering science is yet in its infancy. The world has great discoveries to make. You are at present only on the threshold of the great unknown."

"You work your ship with a screw, I suppose?"

"Exactly. The helmsman sits in a cabin with a glass front, and the electric light illumines the sea for some distance so that all is clear to him."

"Where did you build this extraordinary vessel," continued Dick.

"On a desert island in the Pacific. I had the various parts brought in a vessel that belonged to me from various parts of the world, and the twelve negroes who are now with me were my only workmen."

"You are rich, then?"

"Money was never any object to me," replied the captain. "If I wanted gold even now, could I not obtain millions from the bottom of the sea out of ships that have sunk? The treasures of the deep are mine; I am the King of the Ocean!"

He spoke proudly, and his eyes dilated with rapture.

"You like the sea?"

"I love it; I revel in it. Look at the solitude and the freedom I enjoy! What life can be comparable to mine?"

"But you must feel weary at times," said Dick.

"Never. I read, I think; and when I want diversion, I shoot."

"Where?"

"In the submarine forests. I have invented a square case to strap on the back, which is attached to a mask covering the head, and this will contain enough compressed air to last for several hours' consumption, so that I can walk under the waves with ease and comfort."

"And your guns?"

"Are air guns, also my own invention. I have several, and each is prepared to fire twenty shots by a mere movement of the trigger, the requisite force of air being placed in a hollow of the butt end; but all these mysteries will become plain to you before you have been long with me," answered Captain Nemo.

"What time is it?" asked Dick.

Looking at his watch, the captain answered—

"A quarter to twelve, or nearly midday."

"If you want to give me a treat," said Dick, "I wish you would go up to the surface and let me have a look at the sea, and breathe the fresh air."

"Certainly. Come with me to the engine room."

Dick rose, and followed his conductor through several iron passages to the place where the machinery was fitted up.

It was vast and complicated.

An unpleasant odour rose from various gases, which was unavoidable.

A negro saluted the captain.

"Number twelve," exclaimed the latter, "I wish to ascend."

The engineer touched a valve, and a rush of water escaping was heard.

The pumps were forcing out the water from the reservoirs.

The "Enigma" began to ascend.

After a time she stopped suddenly.

"We have arrived," said the captain.

He led the way up a central spiral staircase, and, raising a small door, they emerged upon what may be called the deck, or what Dick had taken to be the back of the monster.

Touching a spring, an iron railing sprang up, about five feet high.

This prevented any danger of falling into the sea in rough weather, for it made a small enclosure about twenty feet by ten.

Dick saw that the shape of the ship was something like a long cigar.

The sea was calm and the sky clear; a light breeze fanned their cheeks as Dick opened his lungs to take in the inviting atmosphere.

There was, however, nothing to be seen.

Not even a passing ship or an island.

All was one vast desert.

The captain proceeded, armed with a sextant, to take the height of the sun, which would give him his latitude.

He waited some minutes until the sun attained the edge of the horizon.

Having calculated the longitude chronometrically, he said—

"We are in 137 degrees and 15 minutes west longitude, and 30 degrees 7 minutes north latitude, that is to say, at about three hundred miles from the coast of Japan."

"Then you have been travelling while we slept," said Dick.

"Certainly; we have gone several thousand miles. To-day I start again, and we shall commence a voyage of exploration under the waves."

"When you like," replied Dick; "anything for a little excitement."

The captain conducted him downstairs again, the iron railing fell, the trapdoor closed overhead, and with a bow, the strange being left him to join his companions.

One thing Dick remarked.

Never did Captain Nemo shake his hand or offer to take his when he stretched it out.

This was singular.

"He's done something awful in his time, I'll bet," was Dick's thought. "Wonder what it is. I'll have it out of him some day."

When he entered the cabin, Ted and Messiter crowded round him.

Even the professor evinced the liveliest interest.

"How do you like him?" asked Messiter.

"Oh, he's a stunner," said Dick. "We are great pals and get on swimmingly."

"Really."

"I think he showed bad taste in not sending for me," said Professor Crab. "I could have talked to him scientifically, which a chit of a boy could not do."

"He knows more than you could teach him; don't you make any error, sir," answered Dick.

"What did you see?" asked Mr. Crab, hiding his annoyance.

"Saw the swell drawing-room and heard him play the organ, told me all about the electric force that moves the ship, and the electric light for the cove to steer by. Saw the engine room; made him go up to the surface; went on deck and had a look round; took our reckoning, and, in fact, I can do what I like with him," said Dick grandly.

"Where are we?" cried the professor.

"We have been travelling, and we are now three hundred miles from Japan, and we start to-day for a long voyage under the sea."

"By Jove!" said Messiter, "they wouldn't believe us at home, if we were to tell them, would they?"

"Not much. We are going out shooting, that's another thing," exclaimed Dick.

"Shooting. Then we shall go on land, and have a chance of escaping," exclaimed Teddy, rubbing his hands gleefully.

"No, we shan't. We are going to shoot at the bottom of the sea. Shoot strange big fish and monsters."

"Beg your pardon, sir," exclaimed Teddy, with a curious expression. "I know I'm only an odd boy, but I can't stomach that."

"You needn't pull a face as long as a farthing kite," answered Dick. "It's true."

"How is it to be done, Lightheart?" asked Mr. Crawley Crab. "I am a man of science from my youth up, but I must confess I am staggered."

"Nothing staggers me on board this ship," rejoined Dick.

"But explain."

"The captain has invented air guns."

"Ah! that is possible. How about breathing, however?"

"That's another invention. He condenses air in a box strapped on the back, which communicates with a mask like a diver's helmet, and this will last some time, so we can get out and walk about rippingly."

"I shall be glad to do something. Why don't they have windows, and give us a view of the sea, and all the strange things that swim in it?" asked Messiter.

It appeared as if their conversation was overheard, for at that moment, a panel in the wall slid back.

A large sheet of very thick plate glass, quite transparent, was revealed to view almost immediately; a flood of electric light lit up the sea for some distance, and everything was clear as daylight.

It was as if they were looking at an immense aquarium.

"The captain is giving us a surprise," remarked the professor; "this is charming."

Innumerable fishes of various kinds, most of which were unknown, even to a naturalist of Mr. Crab's standing, passed before them.

Strange, wild, fierce-looking things, with wonderful tails and heads.

Some looking unmistakably voracious, others being long and slimy, like hideous snakes.

They were doubtless attracted by the electric light.

For two hours the four companions gazed at the ever-changing procession, without the least abatement of their delight.

"This licks the Brighton aquarium into fits," exclaimed Dick, who was the first to speak.

The light became suddenly extinguished, the sliding panel slid back into its place, and the sight was over.

"The show's closed," remarked Messiter.

"It's as good as a pantomime," observed Dick. "You couldn't have had a better bob's worth in the pit of a theatre at Christmas time."

"Ah," observed the professor, "this strange man's life is not so miserable as we are inclined to think it. He is lord of the sea, and can enjoy its mysteries."

The door opened, and a negro handed the professor a letter.

He opened it, and read its contents aloud.

"Captain Nemo presents his compliments to Professor Crab, and will be glad if he and his companions will accept an invitation to shoot in the weed forests under the sea, to-morrow morning at ten o'clock."

"I'll be blowed if I go!" exclaimed Ted. "Not if I know it. I'm safe here, but I don't want to be chawed up by some strange reptile."

"Silence, Ted," said the professor.

"All right, sir," answered Ted. "I know I'm only an odd boy, but——"

"Will you shut up," said Dick; "or do you want a prop under the ear? Because you can have it if you do."

Ted was silent.

"Tell Captain Nemo," answered the professor, "that we are much obliged to him for his invitation, which we gladly accept."

The negro bowed and retired.

"We are in for an adventure now," said Messiter.

"Suppose we get lost," remarked Ted, "and can't find our way back, and the air in our cases gets exhausted, and a great big fish thing comes to chaw us up! Oh, Lord! oh, Lord! I wish I was back on the beach at Brighton."

"You're always croaking since you've been here," said Dick. "I'll have you put outside if you don't mind."

"Very sorry, sir," replied Ted. "I'm only an odd boy, but I have my feelings. It wouldn't be very nice to be lost, now, would it?"

"We must stick together. We shall have electric lamps, I expect, to light us; and, for my part, I like anything new."

"And I," said the professor, "would do anything in the cause of science. If I ever return to the world, what a wonderful book I shall be able to write."

The rest of the day was passed in various animated discussions as to the sort of game they would meet with, and the chances of their coming back alive to the ship from their marvellous excursion.

CHAPTER IX.

LOST IN THE OCEAN WILDS.

AT the time appointed the professor and the boys were conducted to a cabin, which may be called the dressing-room, or arsenal, of the " Enigma."

Hanging on the walls were numerous helmets, such as divers wear, and a number of guns reposed on hooks.

Ted had determined to accompany the party, as it was his duty to follow and attend upon his young master wherever he went.

Captain Nemo was already there, and received them graciously.

" I wish you good day, professor," he said; " and you too, my boys. I think we shall enjoy some excellent sport among the sea otters and other animals worth killing. You, Mr. Crab, will be able to add to your knowledge of natural history, for we are about to traverse a forest of remarkable seaweeds and plants, in which you will find all kinds of submarine life."

" I am obliged for your kindness, sir, and put myself entirely at your disposal," replied the professor.

At a signal from the captain, two negroes assisted our heroes to put on their apparel, and clothed them in thick waterproof made of india rubber, which formed trousers and vest, the trousers terminating in a pair of shoes with lead soles; a cuirass of leather protected the chest from the pressure of the water, and allowed the lungs full play.

Supple gloves covered the hands, the helmet was then put on, and the knapsack of compressed air adjusted on the back.

To each one was given a gun, the butt of which was of brass and hollow.

Here was stored the compressed air which discharged the electric bullets, one of which fell into its proper place just as the other had been shot away. The whole mechanism was perfect.

When all was ready they stepped into an empty cabin, the door closed behind them, and, touching a knob, the captain allowed the room to fill with water.

Then he opened a door, and they walked out into the sea.

Each had an electric lamp fastened to the waist, which made their path clear and distinct, enabling them to see every object through the glass holes in their helmets.

The captain walked in front with the professor.

Messiter and Dick were side by side, and Ted brought up the rear.

Walking was not very difficult, and the supply of air, well charged with the oxygen necessary for prolonged respiration, was all that could be wished. It entered as it was required from the knapsack reservoir, and escaped when used through a turret at the top of the circular helmet.

They proceeded along fine sand, covered with a variety of shells, for at least a mile, when they came to some rocks covered with beautiful anemones.

Innumerable fish sported round them; long, writhing eels, of a prodigious size, with ugly, flat, snake-like heads, glided away at their approach; and thousands of jelly fish danced about their heads.

They were not at a great depth, and presumably were near some island, for Dick, looking up, saw the sun overhead, guessing the depth to be about thirty or forty feet.

The sun's rays easily penetrated the waves, and made a kaleidoscope of colours inconceivably beautiful.

If the party could have spoken, they would have given vent to their admiration in no measured terms.

The least sound was transmitted easily, showing that the sea is a better conductor of noise than land.

By degrees the depth increased, and they must have been a hundred yards from the surface, as the pressure of the water increased.

Dick suffered no inconvenience, except a slight tingling in the ears and fingers.

He moved with ease, and was intensely delighted with the wonderful bed of sea

"Forward!" cried Dugard, waving his sword.

"THE CAPTAIN CLUBBED HIS GUN, AND WITH ONE BLOW BROKE ITS BACK."

flowers which gave place to the fine sand they had been traversing.

A dark mass extended itself before them: and Captain Nemo, extending his hand, indicated the beginning of the forest.

It was composed of large seaweeds and plants, which extended in a straight manner, having no drooping branches; all were erect and motionless.

When displaced by the hand, they resumed a perpendicular position.

They scarcely had any roots in the sand, and were evidently nourished by the water and not by the earth.

Some were long and slender, others short and bushy, covered with blossoms of various colours; others, again, reached a height equal to our forest trees.

They had not proceeded far through this dense jungle of weeds, amongst which it was difficult to pick a path, when the captain halted.

In front of him was a huge sea spider, over three feet in height, with long terrible claws, and a scaly back like a crawfish.

It endeavoured to seize the professor, who, sinking on his knees, presented his head to it as the least vulnerable part of his body.

The captain, however, clubbed his gun, and, with one blow of the butt, broke its back and left it convulsed in its dying agonies.

As they continued to descend into a valley, bounded on each side by high rocks, the darkness increased, for the sun's rays could not penetrate more than a hundred and fifty yards.

It was now that the electric lamps became of importance.

As they got lower and lower, Dick felt an oppression about the head, and a great desire to sleep overcame him.

He lagged behind the others, and with difficulty kept up with them.

Several fine sea otters were seen in front, playing about amongst the weeds.

The captain fired, and the others followed his example.

Three fell dead, one of which Ted took up and threw over his shoulder.

Suddenly Dick sank down on the ground and immediately fell asleep.

His companions, in the eagerness of their chase after the game that had escaped, did not notice his absence.

They had proceeded fully half a mile before Messiter, looking back, was unable to discover any trace of Dick.

He at once ran to the captain, and made signs, pointing to himself, the professor, and Ted, and pointing in different directions to intimate that Dick was lost.

Captain Nemo at once comprehended his meaning.

He retraced his steps, going carefully over the ground they had trodden.

It was without success.

Nowhere could they find the slightest trace of their unfortunate companion.

Messiter would have given worlds to be able to speak.

He was profoundly agitated.

It was horrible to think that Dick was lost under the sea, not knowing his way back to the "Enigma," for they had come a roundabout way.

Captain Nemo was also annoyed.

If Dick chose, he could climb up the rocks, and reach the summit.

There he might take off his helmet, and breathe the free air of heaven.

But would he think of this?

Perhaps in his confusion he would wander about in the effort to meet his companions, and at last be suffocated miserably.

The supply of air with which each was provided was not sufficient to last more than five hours.

Two of those hours' supply had been already consumed.

It was necessary that Captain Nemo and those with him should think of returning to the ship.

Making a sign, he led the way back.

Messiter felt inclined to stay, and die in the attempt to find his friend.

It would have been an immense relief to him to have said something, but not a sound could he make audible outside his helmet.

With sad and weary steps, they traversed the lovely valley, which had lost all its former attractions for the party.

The forest was passed, and the sand regained.

They were not more than two miles from the "Enigma."

Messiter determined to make a last effort.

He seized the captain's arm, and pointed pathetically, almost imploringly, to the dense mass of vegetation behind them.

His mute appeal to go back after Dick was comprehended.

But it was disregarded.

Their own lives would have been in jeopardy had they turned back.

The air in the reservoirs was becoming weak and impure.

Shaking his head in a negative manner, the captain pursued his way.

With a heavy heart, Messiter followed him, and in time the ship was reached.

They entered the water room, closed the doors, and the captain touched a bell.

Directly it sounded within the vessel, the pumps were heard at work, the water gradually lowered, and when it was all out, they opened the inner door, and regained the dressing room.

It was indeed a pleasure to have the helmets removed, for they had retained them so long that they were oppressed and ill.

The captain was the first to speak.

"I am very sorry for the misfortune that has happened," he exclaimed ; " you must not think me hard-hearted because I returned."

"But Dick will die," answered Messiter; " he is lost, and does not know his way back."

"His supply of air will last another hour and a half. There is yet hope."

"What can we do?"

"I will send out a party to search for him, and I will head it myself," replied Captain Nemo.

At this generous offer, Messiter's heart was filled with fresh hope.

"Will you let me come, sir?" asked Ted. "I'm only an odd boy, but my master is very dear to me."

"No; I must refuse, as you are already tired. If you were overcome with sleep, you would only be in the way."

The captain gave orders for three negroes to accompany him.

They were soon dressed and supplied with air, Captain Nemo himself taking a fresh reservoir.

Then the ceremony of going out was repeated, and as the exploring party quitted the ship, all Messiter could do was to pray fervently for its success.

He, the professor, and Ted, were very languid, and, in spite of their anxiety they could not shake off the somnolent effects of their long walk.

Each sank down on the floor of their cabin, and was soon fast asleep.

How long they remained there, they did not know.

Messiter awoke, feeling a hand laid on his shoulder.

It was Captain Nemo.

Springing to his feet in an instant, he said—

"Have you found him? Where is Dick?"

"Unhappily," said the captain, "we could find no trace of him."

"Why did I let him go last? I ought to have had him in front of me," cried Messiter, angrily. "Poor Dick! he is lying at the bottom of the sea, and I shall never see him again. Never, never."

He covered his face with his hands, and the salt tears trickled down his fingers.

"I have dispatched another party to seek for him," exclaimed the captain; " I am too worn out to go with them this time. If they find the body, we may restore him to consciousness."

"There is no hope," said Messiter, sadly; " you are the cause of his death. Why did you enclose us in this tomb, and then take one of us in the sea to die?"

"Was it my fault? You are hasty, my boy, and do me an injustice. I am as much grieved as yourself, for I had begun to love that lad," said the captain feelingly. "We will mourn for him together; there is a silent friendship in grief. We are friends, for we have the same sorrow."

In a few hours the searching party came back, weary and unsuccessful.

They could see nothing of Dick.

Everyone gave up all hope, and Dick was mourned for as one dead.

CHAPTER X.

FACING DEATH.

AFTER about an hour's sleep, Dick was aroused by an acute sensation of pain in his right leg.

Stretching out his hand, he encountered a slimy substance, and withdrew it very quickly.

Leaning on his elbow, he saw by the light of his lamp, that a strange fish, with a head like a frying pan, and a body resembling that of a codfish, was biting through his waterproof covering and trying to eat part of his leg.

In an instant he seized his gun, and, firing at its eye, wounded it grievously, causing it to splash about and retreat into a mass of weeds, where its struggles continued for some time.

For a moment Dick forgot where he was.

But as his senses came back to him, he recollected everything, and rising, looked about for his companions.

He could see nothing of them.

A horrible fear took possession of him, and he trembled from head to foot.

They had lost him in the depths of the ocean.

Without an experienced guide like Captain Nemo, it was impossible for him to find his way back.

The dangerous and perhaps fatal sleep which had overcome him must be fought against.

For if it came on again he knew he must die.

How much precious air had he not consumed already?

To him, in his condition, air was life.

He knew that he had only a supply for a limited period.

The only course that remained open to him was to march as quickly as the dense mass of water would let him, and try to regain the " Enigma."

But though he turned round he could not find the sandy plain they had first traversed on leaving the ship.

The forest of sea-weeds, rising straight as arrows on all sides of him, erect and motionless, grew dense; animal life was everywhere.

Strange fishes glared at him and seemed to mock his misery by the quick, darting movements and sportive gambols.

He pushed his way fiercely through the vegetable growth, but only to become more entangled.

Despair settled on his soul.

All at once the ground became hilly, and it seemed as if he had come to the end of the valley and was ascending one of the sides.

He pushed on, thinking he would give the world to be able to rise to the surface.

If he could only penetrate that thick water and float on the top of the waves, breathing the free air of Heaven, he would have gladly done so, even if he were to die an hour afterwards.

Gradually he quitted the forest and the sun's rays began to be visible again.

Decidedly he must be getting higher.

All at once a great black mass appeared at his side.

He could see that it was a ferocious shark, whose huge mouth seemed capable of engulfing him.

Instinctively he threw himself on his back.

The voracious creature had made a dart at him, but shot past, disappointed of its prey.

If it had seized his arm or his leg, or even his head, one snap of its mouth would have been sufficient to cut off either.

As the animal swam about him, Dick pointed his gun and fired.

The shot entered its stomach, but was not mortal.

Another and another followed, and at last the vast mass floated slowly upwards.

It was dead.

Thanking Providence for this narrow escape, and congratulating himself on his presence of mind, Dick continued the ascent.

The path became steep and rugged, and it was with difficulty he made way.

He was evidently ascending the side of a rock, which became more precipitous as he went on.

Where did it lead?

Was it raised above the surface or did it fall short of it?

If so, he would have his trouble for nothing.

He breathed with an effort, and his breath grew shorter every moment, for he was making a great demand upon his reservoir of air, while undergoing strong exertion.

At length he had to stop.

It seemed as if his strength was failing him.

The sleepy feeling overtook him again, and he leant back against the shining rock, which reflected the sun's rays.

He was face to face with death.

Not much longer would his lungs be supplied with breathing air.

Suffocation threatened Dick with a painful end, yet he was so weak and prostrate that he seemed unable to make another effort.

Every moment was of priceless value.

Will nothing move him?

Is he to lie there like a senseless log and perish in the pride of his youth?

Added to the dizziness of his head, was a singing in his ears.

All his past life was before him, and passed through his mind with the vividness of a panorama.

A serene expression of resignation crossed his mind as he prepared for death.

When, suddenly, he thought he saw the face and figure of his old enemy, and afterwards friend, Armond, who had died at Mr. Simcox's school at Brighton.

Armond was dressed in white, and, to Dick's fancy, had a circle of light round his head.

He was standing above him, and beckoning him to move, extending a shadowy hand.

Impelled to follow him, Dick rose.

And this phantom hand seemed to have the power of helping him over the rough places, and pulling him up the ascent.

How he did it he never knew; but he managed to climb the almost perpendicular rocks, which afforded little or no footing.

At last the sun's rays were more vivid and, with a feeling of wonder, Dick found himself moving with comparative ease.

This was because he had reached the summit of the rock, after climbing nearly two hundred and fifty yards.

He was out of the water.

With nervous hands he tore off his helmet, and, lying on his side, inhaled the air for a few minutes.

He looked out for his supernatural conductor, but could not see him.

Was it then a delusion?

He could not tell.

Anyhow, had it not been for his spirit guide, he would never have lived to again see the golden sun, the blue, fleecy clouds, and feel the breeze which caressed the bosom of the slumbering ocean.

"I am saved, saved!" cried Dick delightedly.

But what a fate was in store for him.

He rose at length, and looked around him.

The rock on which he was standing was a narrow, barren peak, which just rose above the surface and that was all.

The remainder of the ledge was under water.

If he had not ascended in that place he must have died.

It was singular that the guiding spirit which had saved him should be that of Armond.

Afar off was what appeared to be a small island.

But whether it was an arid desert or not he was unable to tell.

"Perhaps I shall die of hunger and thirst," he muttered; "but death is better here than in the forest under the sea."

Sleep again overcame him, and he passed several hours in a deep slumber.

With wakefulness came a horrible sensation of hunger and thirst.

While he was gazing around him, with despair again attacking him, he saw something rise in the sea a short distance off.

He thought he recognised the black back of the "Enigma."

Nor was he mistaken.

The trap-door opened, and two men appeared on the platform.

They were Captain Nemo and Professor Crab.

Dick tried to cry out, but only a feeble sound came from his lips.

He, however, waved his hands, and the signal was seen.

Soon the "Enigma" floated gently to the rock.

He stepped on the platform, which was by this time crowded with the crew, Messiter, and Ted.

The next moment he was in the arms of kind friends.

But the reaction was too much.

He sank fainting at their feet, and was carried below, where he remained some days before he entirely recovered his strength.

Captain Nemo had entertained an idea that Dick might reach the surface by climbing up the rocks, although he scarcely dared to hold this opinion as a certainty.

But when nothing could be seen of him below the surface, he resolved to look for him above.

Consequently, the " Enigma " rose under his orders, with the happy result we have described.

Messiter's joy on recovering Dick was as intense as Ted's.

The poor boy danced and sang, and was never tired of listening to the account of his adventures.

When he was fully recovered, the negro, No. One, announced that they were going a long voyage.

" Massa say him start for um Pole," he said. " In one hour, we be off, and travel for many week. Travel to the Pole."

In effect, they soon heard the motion of the machinery, and the " Enigma " began her long submarine cruise.

For some weeks they saw nothing of the captain.

This mysterious man shut himself up, and sought intercourse with no one.

Every day, for some hours, the panel in their cabin slid back, and they enjoyed the treat of looking at the sea lighted by electricity.

The direction of the " Enigma " was south-east, and she kept at a depth of a hundred to a hundred and fifty feet.

It was the 13th of October, when the ship crossed the tropic of Cancer, in longitude 177°.

On the following day, she sighted the Sandwich Isles, where Captain Cook was killed in the year 1779.

She had travelled about 4,860 leagues since her departure.

After that, she passed the Equator, and when occasionally she remained some time stationary on the surface, and the captives were allowed to go on the platform, they beheld large and fertile islands at a little distance, volcanoes in action, and many other wonderful things.

One day, while the " Enigma " was stopping to replenish her electric power, a curious incident happened.

The electric fire was composed of elements extracted from the sea itself, which was found better than zinc, the sea containing chlorates of sodium, of magnesia, and of potash, but the sodium was the great agent.

Ted was looking out of the window and he suddenly exclaimed—

" What is that, sir ?"

Everyone went to examine, and a ship dismantled was seen slowly sinking to the bottom.

It had foundered a short time before with all hands.

Several men were lashed to the riggings, and their agonised faces testified to their late sufferings.

A shoal of sharks followed the sinking wreck with distended eyes, anticipating a feast of human flesh.

As the hull passed the window, Dick read her name, which was the " Sir John Burgoyne," London.

This was not an isolated case, for they frequently saw wrecks, and remains of wrecks, such as cannons, anchors, chains, and decaying hulls.

" Well, this is a lively existence," exclaimed Dick; " we eat nothing but fish, and see nothing but fish."

" And wrecks," put in Messiter.

A heavy step was heard behind them, and all turned round.

It was the captain.

He placed his hand upon a map, and exclaimed—

" Do you see this island—Vanikova? It is where the gallant French explorer, La Perouse, perished. We are close to it, and, if you please, gentlemen, you shall land, and explore it for yourselves."

This was good news.

" But," said the professor, " if I remember rightly, it is inhabited by savages."

" Certainly."

" Shall we not be in danger ?"

" I fear nothing," said the captain. " I have braved danger among civilized nations, and I can afford to despise savages. If you do not wish it, however, I will continue my voyage."

"Don't do that, sir," replied Dick. "I'll chance the niggers. Let us land. I know Messiter and Ted would like it."

"And you, Mr. Professor?" said the captain.

"I, sir, will go anywhere in the interests of science," replied Mr. Crab, with a nervous tremor in his voice, which showed he did not like savages.

The news raised the boys' spirits to the highest pitch.

After so long a confinement on board the "Enigma," the prospect of going on land was enchanting.

No matter what danger they might encounter they were ready.

Ted whispered that they might have a chance of escaping.

Dick said nothing.

But he was of the same opinion.

CHAPTER XI.

CAUGHT IN A TRAP.

THE party were allowed to go on shore without even promising to return, and the hearts of each beat high with the prospect of liberty before them.

Professor Crab explained that they might traverse the country of New Guinea, and so get to some port, but the journey would be perilous in the extreme.

His advice was to camp in the wood, obtain fresh provisions, and wait the course of events.

Messiter alone was in doubt.

"The captain," he remarked, "is a wonderful man, and knows perfectly well what he is about. He has told us we shall never again set our feet on civilized ground. Has he not?"

"Yes. Everyone knows that," answered the professor.

"He'll keep his word, and I'll bet a new hat we are on board again to-morrow, or perhaps to-day."

"I'll take you," replied Dick. "Down with you, though how the bet is to be paid I don't know, as there are no hat shops on board the 'Enigma.'"

"I'd give something to find out all about our skipper," said Messiter. "He is the most curious beggar I ever met. All four of us are not a match for him."

"Speak for yourself, my young but still intelligent friend," answered the professor. "Time will show."

"We'll have some fresh meat soon," observed Ted. "I'll take my davy about that, and if you'll trust the cooking to me, Master Lightheart, you shall have a dinner fit for a king in half an hour after running down the game."

"A little venison or wild boar, which is pork, would be very acceptable," answered the professor; "and my knowledge of natural history enables me to tell you that we shall find both on this island which we are about to visit."

"Roast pork, lovely. It makes my mouth water," said Ted.

"Do you want to have the jaw all to yourself?" asked Dick.

"No, sir; I know I'm only an odd boy," exclaimed Ted, repeating his favourite phrase; "but——"

"Chain up, and go and ask when the boat will be ready to take us ashore."

Ted departed on his errand and found the boat already prepared for them.

It was made of various pieces of wood, which were easily put together when it was wanted, and taken apart when it was not required.

It would hold half-a-dozen men, and floated by the side of the "Enigma."

Each of the four companions was provided with an electric gun, containing the usual twenty shots.

"A pleasant excursion, gentlemen," said the captain, as they emerged on the platform; "I hope you do not intend to deprive me for any length of time of the pleasures of your society."

"Wouldn't do such a thing for worlds, sir," answered Dick.

"You needn't return to-night, if you prefer camping out."

"We didn't mean to," replied Dick.

A peculiar smile crossed Captain Nemo's expressive face, as if he divined what was passing in his mind.

'Remember one thing," he said; "be very careful of your ammunition."

" Why ?"

"You will find out in time. All I have to say is, recollect my advice," was the answer.

They got into the boat and rowed ashore, picking their way carefully through the coral reefs, and in five minutes the bottom of the boat grated upon a sandy beach.

"Hurrah!" cried Dick, throwing up his cap, "land once more!"

Ted, who was thoroughly familiar with all the tricks of boys who have been accustomed to pick up halfpence in the streets, put down his hands and did a wheel, after which he stood on his head, to give expression to his delight.

Huge forests stretched far inland, and raised their mighty heads a hundred feet from the earth.

Palms, shrubs, and creepers were mingled with the trees in grand confusion, and this scene, in the glowing sunshine, was indescribably beautiful.

The professor saw a cocoa-nut palm, and knocking off some of the fruit, gave it to the boys, who pronounced it delicious.

"Now," he said, " we will shoot something and dine as we have not dined for a long time."

"I've some salt in my pocket, and Ted has knives," remarked Messiter.

"It looks to me," said Dick, " as if we were likely to have a sirloin of tiger for dinner; that forest ought to be chock full of wild beasts."

"No matter," answered Messiter, "anything's better than fish. Come on."

They skirted the forest, fearing to enter it lest they might lose themselves in its dense interior.

Keeping their guns ready for instant action, they proceeded about half a mile, when the professor held up his hand.

In front of them was a large bread-fruit tree.

Under its branches was a wild boar, engaged in eating the tender fruit which had fallen to the ground.

"Approach gently, and fire all together," said the professor.

They did so, and four shots were discharged at the same time.

The wild boar uttered a ferocious grunt, ran a few paces, and fell down dead.

"What is it, sir?" asked Dick.

"A wild boar; do you not see his tusks? Now, Ted, set to work, and cut a leg of pork off piggy. You, Lightheart, make a fire with the dry wood; it will kindle when I rub two sticks together. You, Messiter, gather some of this fruit?"

"Is it good to eat, sir?"

"You will find it excellent. I recognise it as the bread fruit of the tropics, and, cut up in slices and toasted over the fire, nothing could be better for us with our roast pork," answered the professor.

They were quickly all at work.

The fire was lighted, the leg of pork cut off, and fixed to a tripod, the bread-fruit toasted, and plates supplied by large palm leaves.

Presently a delicious odour of roast pork spread itself around.

After living so long on the peculiar fare provided by Captain Nemo, they enjoyed their dinner immensely; and, when they had satisfied their appetites, they sat down under the shade of a tree, sheltered from the noontide heat.

"Now, sir," said Dick, " what are we to do ?"

"I have no wish to return to our floating prison," replied the professor. "The question is, shall we go back, or shall we try to make our way to some port, risking the dangers of the way, the chances of starvation."

"That does not appear likely," answered Dick, thinking of the roast pork and the bread-fruit.

"When our guns are empty, we may not find it so easy to kill game, however abundant it may be. The savages are another danger."

"Put it to the vote, sir," said Dick.

"Certainly; all you who wish to make an effort to escape from the thraldom in which we are held, hold up your hands."

Every hand was extended.

" To the contrary?"

There was no response.

"Not a hand," said the professor. "I may, then, conclude, that we are unanimous in our wish for freedom, and it is decided that we do not return to the 'Enigma.'"

"Hurrah!" cried Ted, proceeding to stand on his head again.

"If you don't cut those street Arab tricks," remarked Dick, "you'll have a fit, after a bellyful such as you've got."

Ted resumed his natural position.

"There's no kid, sir, about my having had a tightener of pork," he replied. "But though I'm only an odd boy, I've got my feelings, and I'd as soon be a convict as in that there blessed ship."

"Ted is right," observed the professor, mildly; "to live and die in that ship is an awful prospect, and I would rather herd with savages in their wilds than do it."

And as if it was intended as an answer to his speech, an arrow flew over his head.

Fortunately it missed its mark, and stuck quivering into the bark of the tree under which they were sitting.

Every one sprang to his feet, and stood, gun in hand, on the defensive.

"Niggers, by George!" exclaimed Dick.

"Where?" asked the professor.

"To the right, sir. Fire away, and chance it, or we shall all be killed."

There was an instant discharge of fire-arms, and a scuffling was heard behind some cactus and mimosa bushes.

A dozen savages, nearly naked, armed with spears and bows and arrows, were seen in a state of hesitation, whether to fly or stand their ground.

Three of their number had fallen from the discharge, and one who was mortally wounded, was crawling in a slow, laboured manner into the bush to die.

"At 'em again, boys; let them have it," said the professor.

"Hot and strong this time, sir," said Ted, advancing a step to take better aim.

Again the bullets flew, and three more savages bit the dust.

The others turned to fly to the shelter of the neighbouring forests.

"Hurrah! they're bolting," said Dick.

"But they've collared what was left of our bread, and the remains of the roast pork," said Ted, angrily. "Oh, the varmints! I'll just give them something."

He advanced a little more in front to fire better.

An aged chief, however, turned at this moment and discharged a parting shot, which took effect in the calf of Ted's leg.

"Oh, Lord! I'm hit," he cried. "A great wooden skewer's stuck right in my leg, sir."

Dick could not help laughing.

"Perhaps it's poisoned, sir. Oh, Lord! I know I'm only an odd boy; but I wish it hadn't been me. There's the professor now; he could have borne it better than me."

"Thank you, my young friend," said the professor, "the calf of my leg is as susceptible of pain as yours; let us get away, as arrow heads are sharp, and in certain parts of the body mortal."

"Where shall we go?" asked Dick.

"We are not safe here. The savages will return in larger numbers directly, and we shall probably lose our lives, so I propose we seek our boat."

"And go back to the 'Enigma?'" asked Messiter.

"Yes."

"Never. I for one will not go," cried Messiter.

"And I can't crawl. I'm as lame as a dog," said Ted, half crying.

"Roll, if you can't walk," said the professor, jokingly.

"Pull it out, sir. Give me a hand with it," cried Ted. "It hurts awful."

Dick advanced to Ted, and seized the arrow head, which he tugged at until with a torrent it came out of the wound.

The boy bled a good deal, and was evidently in great pain.

It was with difficulty he managed to limp on one leg, and seemed very grateful when his young master told him to lean on his shoulder.

"My dear boy," said the professor, "discretion is the better part of valour. I am averse to the taking of human life, for I am a man of science, and not a fighter. My advice is to check the advance of those bloodthirsty savages, and when your ammunition is spent, to run. As I am old, and not quick of foot, I will start at once."

So saying, he began to run with all his speed to the boat.

"Coward!" said Dick, angrily.

"What are we to do?" asked Messiter, blankly.

"Follow him, I suppose," replied Dick. "Bring up the rear, Harry, while I help Ted along, and if the beasts show again, call us, and we will turn and fire."

They began to beat a retreat in this

order, and, fortunately, the natives did not again make an appearance.

The half-mile was traversed quickly, Ted groaning dreadfully as he was forced along.

When within a few paces of the boat, the most awful yells were heard behind them.

Turning to see from whence they proceeded, Dick saw a horde of savages in pursuit.

The sands seemed to be alive with them.

Evidently the defeated party had returned to obtain reinforcements, and apprise their companions of the slaughter which had taken place, urging them to avenge it.

An army of at least three hundred wild-looking fiends was at their heels.

Not a moment was to be lost.

"Quick, for Heaven's sake," said Professor Crab; "the savages are upon us. Quick, boys, or we are lost."

The boys sprang into the boat, placing Ted in the bows, and pushed off.

Messiter and Dick plied the oars vigorously.

Fortunately, when the savages reached the beach, they were some distance out.

A flight of arrows fell close to them, without doing them any harm.

At least a hundred of the natives plunged into the sea up to the waist, but they did not attempt to swim after the boat, which soon reached the "Enigma."

Dick expected to see someone on the platform.

It was, however, deserted.

Not a soul was to be seen.

Dick at once went to the captain, being alarmed at the hostile attitude of the savages, whom he did not doubt were possessed of cannon and would make an attack upon the ship.

He was annoyed at being obliged to take shelter so soon, but what could he do?

All his hopes of liberty in flight were nipped in the bud.

He began to see now, that Captain Nemo knew the character of the coast, and had calculated well on their return to their captivity.

Imprisonment with him was better than death or slavery among the natives of Vanikova.

The captain was sitting in front of the organ playing an exquisite air of Beethoven.

Full of excitement, Dick had no time to listen.

He touched him on the shoulder.

Captain Nemo seemed unconscious of his presence.

He was absorbed in the music.

"Captain," said Dick.

The strange being shivered and turned round.

"Ah!" he cried, "'tis you, Mr. Lightheart. Have you had good sport? You have returned sooner than I expected. Pardon me for not noticing your entry. I was playing something which was a great favourite with one who was very dear to me."

He had not then forgotten the world, though he had broken with and separated himself from it.

"The sport was not bad," replied Dick, "but unfortunately, we met with a troop of savages, who spoilt our fun."

The captain smiled ironically.

"Savages!" he repeated. "Were you surprised at meeting with them? Have you so little geographical knowledge that you do not know they swarm hereabouts?"

"All I know is," replied Dick, "that if you don't want them on board the 'Enigma,' you had better look out."

"My dear fellow," said the captain, "I am not likely to trouble my head about such wretches."

"But there are lots of them."

"How many?"

"Over three hundred, I should think, as well as I could count."

"We have nothing to fear from them, nothing at all," said the captain. "Don't be alarmed."

Without another word, he turned again to the organ, and played a Scotch air, which had an indescribable charm about it.

He was plunged again in a reverie that Dick did not think it prudent to interrupt.

Dick could do more with him than any one else, but there were times when it was advisable to let him alone.

He remounted to the platform, without seeing a single negro.

The most absolute want of precaution

reigned on board the "Enigma," and it looked as if no one knew that hundreds of howling savages were within five minutes' row of them.

In the growing darkness, which came on while Dick was alone, he could see the forms of the natives running backwards and forwards on the beach.

They were evidently planning an attack upon a large scale.

What could account for the captain's strange apathy?

After a time he forgot the natives in admiring the lovely night of the tropics.

The zodiacal stars appeared, and the moon shone brightly amidst innumerable constellations of the zenith.

He wished that she would light the "Enigma" to the coral bed, and that they would sink to the bottom, where they would be safe from their enemies.

Proceeding at last, he sought his friends

The door giving access to the interior of the "Enigma" remained open, and he remarked a slave standing at the bottom of the staircase as if on watch.

Teddy had his leg bound up, and, though in pain, was much better.

Strange to say, all were pleased to return to the "Enigma," and to escape a fearful death of life-long slavery amongst the savages, who are known to travellers as the Papouans.

Still Dick slept badly.

He anticipated a night attack.

It is not pleasant to think that, as the Irishman said, you may wake the next morning with your throat cut.

CHAPTER XII.

THE ATTACK OF THE SAVAGES.

GOING to his hammock, Dick slept soundly, and woke in the morning much refreshed.

It was about six o'clock when he ascended to the platform.

The morning mist had lifted, and he could see the land distinctly.

The savages were very busy, and more numerous than they had been the night before.

As well as he could calculate, he counted six or seven hundred of them.

They were tall, handsome men, with an erect bearing, their features well chiselled.

Among them were some women scantily dressed, clothed with a garment made of leaves.

The men were almost naked.

In their ears they wore rings of bone.

Their arms were arrows and bows, spears and shields, made of the skins of fish, stretched over a wooden frame or the back of the turtle.

A chief rowed in a canoe towards the "Enigma," keeping at a safe distance.

He was adorned with a fantastic headdress of feathers and leaves, and seemed to be the king of the country.

Having nothing better to do, Dick got a fishing line from the negro who usually attended upon him, and amused himself with catching some of the fish that swam round the ship.

No one made any preparation to repel an attack of the Papouans, which alarmed Dick very much.

He had, however, so much confidence in the sagacity of Captain Nemo that he believed he would not be caught asleep.

For two hours he continued his sport with tolerable success, and was so wrapt up in it that he forgot the natives for the time.

While he was engaged in pulling up a good bite, an arrow whizzed past him.

Dick dropped his fish and very nearly his line too.

" Bother the brutes !" he exclaimed ; " can't they let a fellow fish in peace? Why doesn't the captain make a start and get away from them ?"

He was as eager now to leave the land as he had been the day before to reach it.

It was clear that the Papouans were puzzled.

They had seen European ships before, but what could they make of a long cylinder of iron, without masts, almost flush with the surface of the water, and no chimney like a steamer?

But they gained confidence as they saw no attempt made to drive them away.

They had seen some of their number killed by the air-guns, yet they had heard no noise.

All at once a flotilla, consisting of a score of canoes, full of savages, put off from the shore, and approached the "Enigma."

A flight of arrows flew around Dick, who had been looking for a fresh bait for his line.

"Deuce take them!" he said. "It rains arrows. This won't do."

He sought refuge in the interior of the ship, and ran to apprise the captain of the formidable state affairs were assuming.

Clearly no orders had been given to repel boarders.

Knocking at the captain's door, he was told to enter.

Captain Nemo was reading.

"Do I disturb you?" asked Dick, politely.

"A little," replied the captain; "but I suppose you have good reason for seeking me?"

"Rather," answered Dick. "We are surrounded by savages, and in a few minutes we shall have them on board."

"Ah," said the captain, "they have got their canoes, I suppose?"

"Heaps of them."

"Then we must do something."

"Shut up the shop," said Dick.

"That is easily done," replied the captain, touching a bell, and adding, "in half a minute the trap-door will be closed. You need not be afraid that they will break in."

"No, but to-morrow we shall want air, and you must open the door again for your pumps to work."

"Yes; our ship is like a great whale, and cannot live without air."

"In a moment the Papouans will be on the top of us, and I don't suppose they will go away in a hurry," replied Dick.

"You suppose they will take possession of the outside and keep it?"

"Exactly."

"Well, then," answered the captain, calmly, "I don't see why they shouldn't. Why should I kill the poor creatures if I can help it? I know many savages in the civilized world whom I would cut off with more pleasure. Leave them to me.

If it is necessary, I will make a terrible example of them."

"You have no cannon."

"I shall not fire a shot, and I shall not wound them in any way, and yet they will fall like leaves in autumn. Go to your friends, and rest perfectly easy," said the captain.

This was a dismissal, and wondering much, Dick went away.

As he sought his cabin he heard the fierce cries of the savages, who swarmed on the back of the iron ship like flies in summer.

The night passed without any incident.

Plenty of oxygen still passed through the ship, but it was time to renew the air, which was becoming impure.

Breakfast was served in the morning as usual.

Mid-day came, and the captain showed no signs of moving.

This apathy appeared incomprehensible to Dick.

Without any difficulty the vessel could have gone out to sea, risen in mid ocean, and taken in fresh air.

"It is very odd we don't move," he remarked.

"I can't understand it," said the professor. "But everything is so remarkable on board this ship that I have ceased to wonder at anything."

"I've had a taste of niggers, and don't want another," said Ted, who was lying on a mattress with his leg bound up.

"Hark at the reptiles! What a thundering row they're kicking up," remarked Dick.

"I never heard such a shine," answered Messiter; "our skipper must be off his nut not to start the vipers."

The captain appeared in the doorway.

There was a pleasant smile on his face, and he did not seem at all alarmed at the menacing aspect of affairs.

"Gentlemen," he said, "we resume our voyage at twelve o'clock exactly."

"It is now a quarter to," said the professor, regarding his chronometer.

"Precisely. I shall open the flap, and take in air directly."

"And the niggers?" said Dick.

"The Papouans?" replied the captain shrugging his shoulders.

"Won't they get in?"

"How?"

" Easily enough, by walking down the ladder. They can do that when the flap is up, and can kill us all without any trouble."

" Gentlemen," said Captain Nemo, " the Papouans will not descend the staircase, although the flap is open."

They regarded this singular man in amazement.

" You do not understand me," he continued. " Come to the bottom of the ladder, and you shall see."

" Shall we take our guns?" asked the professor.

" Not the slightest necessity."

" At least your slaves are armed?"

" They are all at their work; follow me," said the captain.

They obeyed his order, and walked to the foot of the metal ladder.

The captain folded his arms, and stood by the side of the professor.

Dick and Messiter were together.

Even Ted had crawled along the passage to see what would happen.

Captain Nemo made a sign to a slave, who, touching a spring, caused a trapdoor in the back of the " Enigma " to fly open.

The sunshine descended in a flood.

Terrible cries of rage and triumph were heard, and a swarm of natives appeared on all sides.

At least twenty made a rush at the ladder, brandishing their tomahawks and spears, while they uttered fierce yells and scraps of war songs.

The first who grasped the railing, and placed his foot on the ladder, gave a bound back, and the most fearful shrieks burst from his quivering lips.

A second, a third, and a fourth did the same.

What invisible force was at work Dick did not know.

He thought the days of magic and sorcery had returned.

A score of Papouans tried to descend: but they had no sooner made the attempt than they instantly retreated, yelling dismally, and threw themselves into the sea.

" Stunning," said Dick. " It's fine, but I don't know how you do it."

The captain smiled.

To get a better view, Dick put one foot on the staircase, and one hand on the railing.

He immediately withdrew them, uttering a cry which was loud enough to wake the dead.

" Oh, oh!" he cried.

" What's up?" exclaimed Messiter, who could not help laughing.

" I twig the dodge now," said Dick; " it's a galvanic battery applied to the metal of the staircase, and whoever touches it has a shock. I've had it before at the Crystal Palace, and at fairs. You pay a penny and get electrified."

" Ah!" ejaculated the professor, upon whom a light began to dawn.

" You are right," said the captain, calmly.

" I have connected the brass staircase with a powerful galvanic battery, and the ignorant savages are frightened at they know not what. If they had persisted in their attempt to enter the ship, I should have applied all my electric force, and they would have fallen as dead as flies on a fly paper; but I did not wish to harm them. They are enemies unworthy of my hatred."

The news of the dreadful and mysterious pains which they felt were spread by the shocked natives to their friends.

Alarmed and horrified, they beat a precipitate retreat, swimming and rowing back to the shore.

In half an hour the beach was deserted, and all flew away from the sea-fiend, whose nature they could not understand.

" They take us for the devil," said Dick.

" Twelve o'clock," exclaimed the captain, who was always as punctual as fate; " I said we should sail at twelve."

At this moment the engines began to revolve, and the " Enigma " skimmed over the surface of the sea like a bird.

The air was soon taken into the reservoirs, the flap or panel was closed, and sinking into the bosom of the waves, she glided along, moved by her powerful screw, like a big fish; only the helmsman, sitting in his solitary place of look-out, being responsible for her management.

CHAPTER XIII.

THE EVIL HOUR.

SOME days passed without any occurrence of interest, and the lives of the captives passed as uneventfully as the most timid could wish.

They were ashamed of their ineffectual attempt to escape, and did not talk much about it, though the desire burned as strongly in their breasts as ever.

Professor Crab took their reckoning every day.

Perfect liberty was accorded to them, and when the "Enigma" sought the surface of the sea, lying like a blackened log upon the waves, her engines still, and her crew silent, they could ascend to the platform, inhale the fresh air, and look about them.

Dick never neglected this opportunity.

It was the pleasantest thing that occurred to break the monotony of his captivity.

Towards the end of January, the professor calculated that they were in 105 degrees longitude, and 15 degrees south latitude.

The weather was threatening, the sea rough and stormy, the wind blew half a gale, and the barometer, which had been falling for some days, announced a war of the elements.

Captain Nemo appeared to have his evil hour upon him, for he did not allow himself to be seen, and the black slaves walked about with hushed voices, attending to their several duties like animated machines.

What dreadful thoughts were passing through this strange man's mind while he kept himself secluded from everyone?

Who could tell?

Dick found that the "Enigma" was stationary on the surface, and he ascended to the platform.

The captain and his second in command—a tall, wiry, intelligent negro—were both there.

They conversed in that mysterious language, to which we have before alluded, and which was incomprehensible even to the professor.

Captain Nemo was anxiously scanning the horizon with a glass.

For some minutes he rested motionless, the telescope fixed upon one particular point.

Then he lowered his glass and exchanged a few words with his subordinate.

The latter was a prey to violent emotion, which he did not take any pains to conceal.

The captain, more master of himself, remained calm and impassible.

He appeared to be raising objections, which the second attempted to put straight, but Dick could only fathom the meaning of their conversation from their gestures.

Dick looked in the direction in which the glass had been pointed, but could perceive nothing.

The sky and the water, meeting on the horizontal line, seemed to be perfectly clear.

Nevertheless, the captain walked impatiently from one extremity of the platform to the other without addressing a word to Dick, and, indeed, without appearing to see him.

His step was not so firm as usual, and he stopped several times, his arms crossed and his eyes observing the sea.

What was he looking for on this vast expanse?

The "Enigma" was certainly some hundreds of miles away from any shore.

Suddenly the captain gave an order to the engineer through his second officer, and the engineer at once went to work, impelling the ship swiftly through the waves.

Seeing that the glass was lying at the captain's feet, Dick ventured to take it up.

"I may as well have a spy," he muttered, "and see what it is."

He had not time to raise the telescope to his eye before it was rudely snatched from his hand by the captain.

Dick looked at, but scarcely recognised him.

He appeared to be strangely altered.

His eyes were burning like live coals, his forehead was bent and wrinkled, his lips, half open, revealed his clenched teeth, his head was shrunk between his shoulders, his fists closed, and a violent hatred seemed to be agitating him.

Dick was frightened.

Had he provoked this anger? No.

In a moment Captain Nemo mastered himself, and turning to Dick, said in an imperious voice—

"Go downstairs, boy, and keep yourself and your companions in your cabin until you have my orders to leave it."

"You are master here," exclaimed Dick, "and I will go, but may I ask you a question?"

"Not one. Go at once."

Seeing that further discussion was useless, Dick sought his friends.

Four slaves followed immediately on his footsteps, and when he had regained the cabin, he heard a key turned on the outside.

They were prisoners.

Dick related what had passed, and they were as much astonished as himself.

"Another confounded mystery," said Messiter. "Well, let's amuse ourselves. Who will play at dominoes? Will you, Dick?"

"No, thanks; I want to think and be quiet," was the reply.

He sat down in a corner trying to read a book, but the lines ran into one another.

Messiter and the professor played at chess.

Dick was thinking of the captain.

In half an hour he heard the panel of the deck shut.

The engines ceased working.

The pumps emptied the water reservoirs of air, and forced in a quantity of water, sufficient to cause the "Enigma" to sink, which she began to do rapidly.

Dick fancied that he heard a stifled cry before the ship lowered herself, as if some one was being dragged on board against his will.

It seemed to him as if the captain had come in contact with some vessel in mid ocean, and that an unhappy being had been the victim of his imprudence in trying to board the "Enigma."

The cries continued for some moments.

Then he heard a piteous cry for help.

"Spare me!" cried an English voice, agonised with terror. "Are you men or demons?"

Dick's companions listened in mute terror.

"I will not die, then," exclaimed the voice in a frantic tone. "By Heaven, I will struggle for my life. Beware, I am armed. Guard yourself."

"It is you who provoked this strife."

A noise, as of a fearful contest, ensued.

Men seemed to be rushing wildly about.

Fierce cries and wild oaths were heard faintly through the closed portal.

As for Dick, he threw himself against the locked door, and with strong efforts tried to open it, but without avail.

It resisted all his efforts, violent as they were.

At last a dreadful sound, as of some heavy instrument crashing through a human skull, was audible.

A deep groan followed, and all was still.

"Oh!" exclaimed Dick; "these people are murderers. Something horrible has happened."

An hour passed, and the captives conversed in whispers.

Then the door was unlocked, and Captain Nemo appeared.

His face was stern and sad.

Dick felt a repugnance towards him which he had never before noticed.

"Professor Crab," exclaimed the captain.

"Sir," answered the professor shuddering, he scarcely knew why.

"I think, in the course of conversation, you have told me that you were originally intended for a doctor."

"I walked Guy's Hospital for two years, but my thoughts were turned into another channel, and I gave up medicine as a profession."

"Still you have a knowledge of surgery?"

"Undoubtedly."

"Follow me, if you please," said the captain.

They quitted the cabin together, leaving Dick, Messiter, and Ted plunged in a new wonder.

"THE PROFESSOR SAW AT A GLANCE HE WAS BADLY WOUNDED."

CHAPTER XIV.

BURIED BENEATH THE WAVES.

IN a cabin, lying upon a mattrass, was a white man, whose head was enveloped in bandages stained with blood.

The professor saw at a glance that he was badly wounded.

He undid the bandages, which the man permitted without uttering any complaint, only fixing his expressive eyes upon him inquiringly.

The wound was a horrible one.

His skull was literally smashed in, and the brain protruded from the fissure; a quantity of coagulated blood had accumulated, and in his neck was a wound made by a knife.

He breathed slowly, and with apparent difficulty, and spasmodic movements of the muscles agitated his face.

The injury had produced a sort of paralysis, which deprived him of feeling and movement.

Professor Crab felt the pulse of the wounded person, which was intermittent.

The extremities of the body were already growing cold, and it was clear that death was coming on without any possibility of stopping it.

After dressing the wounds and readjusting the bandages, the professor rose.

"How did the wound happen?" asked he.

"What matters it?" replied the captain. "He brought it on himself. What do you think of his state?"

"It's very critical."

"What am I to understand by that?"

"He will be dead in two hours," replied the professor, solemnly.

"Can nothing save him?"

"Nothing!"

The wounded man's face grew paler under the electric light which bathed his bed, and he seemed to hear the words and accept his fate.

Perhaps he would be able to speak before he died; the professor lingered in the hope of hearing his last words.

But the secret of his death was to die with him as far as Mr. Crab was concerned.

"You can retire," said the captain to him.

"May I ask you to tell me how you intend to bury this unfortunate?" asked Mr. Crab.

"Certainly. In my cemetery."

"Where is that?"

"You shall see to-morrow. I invite you to the funeral and your companions also, if they choose to come. Prepare for a journey to-morrow at ten o'clock," replied the captain.

The professor joined his friends, telling them what had passed.

Dick was horrified, and said—

"I knew they were killing somebody. Poor fellow! What a place to die in!"

"Captain Nemo recognises no law but his own," answered the professor. "He is not answerable to any earthly tribunal, and it is not for us to say anything."

The next morning they were summoned to the dressing room, when to their astonishment they were supplied with helmets and knapsacks of compressed air, and with electric lamps.

It was evident that the funeral was to be under the sea.

When all was ready, the party assembled in the outer chamber, the water was pumped in, the door opened, and the procession was marshalled in the following order:—

Two negroes armed with guns went first.

Four followed, bearing the corpse, which was tied up in a white sheet, only the outline of the form being visible.

Next came the captain.

After him the four captives, and the rear was brought up by two more slaves also armed.

A slight declivity led to a level bottom, about fifteen fathoms from the surface.

This bottom differed altogether from that which they had explored before in the Pacific Ocean; there was no fine sand, no submarine prairies, no sea-weed forest.

It was a world of coral.

Everyone knows how the hard-working little insects build up the singular mounds which, in course of ages, rise to the surface and make islands.

The vast domain of coral arose on all

sides, branching out in fantastic forms, and in magnificent arcades, charming the eye with its colours and multitudinous groves.

They followed a bank in course of formation.

The vivid light of the lamps produced a thousand beautiful effects of colour, and the want of design in the singular architecture increased the effect.

As they proceeded the coral grew larger, and immense trees of this lovely substance seemed to stretch for yards over their heads.

The captain halted in a long gallery, and the sad procession stopped also.

On all sides the darkness was intense, except where the lamps made a brilliant light.

In front of them was a cross of coral, the upper branches having been torn off by the hand of man.

Below that was a grave, which had evidently been dug out during the night.

A sign given by the captain caused the corpse to be laid in this hole, and the soil was reverently put in and trodden down upon this inaccessible tomb in the middle of the ocean.

All were profoundly impressed.

The boys especially, and they felt the tears come to their eyes.

Extending his hand as a sign of a last adieu, Captain Nemo rested immovable for the space of a minute.

No service could be read.

Whatever prayers were said were uttered silently, under cover of their masks, and the funeral was over.

Sadly the procession wended its way back again.

In half an hour it regained the ship.

The submarine garments were removed, and the ship mounted to the surface.

No restraint being placed on his actions, Dick ascended to the platform.

The captain was there.

"You have assisted at a mournful ceremony, my lad," he exclaimed.

"Yes," said Dick, drily.

"Do you think any the worse of me for it?"

"I should not like to tell you what I think," replied Dick.

"Tell me. I shall not be angry. Did I not place the body in a peaceful spot, safe from sharks and men?"

"You did that; but you are no less a murderer. I heard the poor fellow begging for mercy, and——"

"You are wrong," interrupted the captain. "I only struck him in self-defence. You cannot be a judge of my actions. Say no more. If it were my pleasure to lay you by his side, rest assured it would be done."

So saying, he turned angrily away, and left Dick alone on the platform.

Even Dick, bold as he was, felt afraid of this terrible man, who reigned like a King of the Sea by his wonderful inventions and advanced scientific knowledge.

Whatever his secret might be, there was a chance that some day it would be revealed.

He had hinted that he had suffered wrongs, and lived to revenge them.

The link that bound him to the world was not entirely snapped.

None of the captives had given up the hope of recovering their liberty, and Ted especially declared that he was only waiting for the first chance that offered itself.

The professor scarcely knew whether he ought to hate or admire the remarkable man who had showed him the secrets of the "Enigma."

Was he a victim or an executioner?

Had he committed some awful crime, which compelled him to fly from human justice, or was he simply one whom cruel oppression had driven from his native land?

Though ardently longing for liberty, the professor had seen so many marvels of the deep already that he wanted to see more.

Not so the boys.

They had had enough of confinement, and panted for action once more.

CHAPTER XV.

A PEARL WORTH A FORTUNE.

A SIGN from one of the negroes warned Dick that the " Enigma " was about to continue her voyage.

He re-entered the ship, which soon afterwards sank.

The hatch was closed, and the professor, regarding his instruments, said they were going to the west.

They traversed the Indian Ocean at a depth of about a hundred yards from the surface.

The health of the captives continued good.

Ted was the only grumbler; the others read and talked, resigning themselves to their fate, and awaiting the next adventure which would befall them in their singular voyage.

" I tell you what it is, sir," exclaimed Ted, one day; " I wish I could get my bunch of fives near that there captain. If I wouldn't give him a domino, I'd let a whale come and eat me."

" What have you to grumble at, my friend?" inquired Professor Crab. " You are comfortably housed, well fed, and have a constant source of excitement in the movements of this remarkable ship."

" Bother the ship. Why didn't she strike on a rock, and bust up?" said Ted.

" Bide your time, my lad," continued the professor; " something will happen some day."

" Very prob'ble, sir, but it's waiting for it to turn up as I don't like. Just shove me alongside of that blessed captain, and if I don't give him toko for yam, and all his niggers, I'll——"

" Ted," interrupted Dick, " you shut up."

" Certainly, sir. I don't have much chance of talking. I shall forget my own language soon; but no matter, I am only an odd boy, I know, and, of course, shouldn't have no feelings."

Dick took the trouble to pacify him, explaining that to provoke a quarrel with the captain would not in any way improve their position.

On the contrary, it might deprive them of the little liberties and the comforts they now enjoyed, and make their miserable condition much worse.

Ted saw this and promised to be quiet

He was a strong lad for his age, as hard as iron, and brave as a young lion.

" Just promise me this, sir," he said.

" What ?"

" If I see a good chance of stepping it, you'll be on ?"

" Like a shot. But we mustn't do anything rash, you know, Ted," replied Dick. " Captain Nemo is not to be trifled with. A man who can build a ship like this, make electricity take the place of steam, and so store the air as to make it sufficient for use for twenty-four hours, is one of those great spirits who think of everything, and with whom we cannot hope to cope on equal terms."

" Don't know so much about that, sir," said Ted. " I once caught a fox asleep and gave him what for on his nut, before he could say Jack Robinson."

Dick laughed and the conversation dropped.

The voyage continued, and was not remarkable for anything more exciting than the capture of several turtles in nets, and the shooting of various sea-birds, which supplied an agreeable addition to the comforts of the table.

In the Indian Sea they encountered hundreds of the nautilus tribe floating gracefully on the surface of the water, their tiny sails spread, catching the wind, and looking like little ships.

Towards the end of February, the " Enigma," at mid-day, came to the top of the sea, in 9 deg. 4 min. North latitude.

About eight miles eastward, land was perceptible, of a mountainous character.

" Where are we now, Mr. Crab?" asked Dick.

The professor was busy looking over a map, making observations with certain instruments, of which he was allowed the use, and calculating the position to a nicety.

" This is the island of Ceylon," he replied; " one of the most fertile of the globe. It is between 5 deg. 55 min. and

9 deg. 49 min. North latitude, and 79 deg. 42 min. and 82 deg. 4 min. East longitude, taking the Greenwich meridian. Its length is 275 miles. Its——"

"Thank you, sir," interrupted Dick, who knew what the professor was when he began to talk; "that will do."

The professor was about to make some angry exclamation at being interrupted in the midst of his lecture, when Captain Nemo entered.

His eye glanced at the open map.

"Has the professor been giving you some interesting particulars about Ceylon, my lads?" he asked.

"Yes, sir," replied Messiter.

"Did he tell you that it was principally famous for its pearl fisheries?"

"No, sir."

"The fact is, Captain Nemo, that I was interrupted," said Mr. Crab. "But I am well aware that our pearls come from Ceylon, and could give you all some curious particulars respecting this remarkable fishery."

"Would you like to see the banks upon which grow the oysters which contain the pearls?" asked the captain.

"Under the sea!" said Dick.

"An excursion, submarine?" said the professor.

"Precisely so. Are you inclined to go?"

"Very much indeed," replied all in chorus, with the exception of Ted.

"This is not the time of year for the pearl divers to be at work," said the captain, "though we may see one or two. I will bring the ship nearer land, and show you some of the treasures of the deep. They fish for pearls in the Gulf of Bengal, in the Indian seas, as well as those of China and Japan, off the coast of South America, and in the Gulf of Panama, and that of California, but it is at Ceylon that they find the richest harvest."

"That is a fact," said the professor; "the richest pearls, as you say, are found here."

"Right," said the captain. "We, however, shall see more than any diver ever dreams of. I shall be at your service, gentlemen, in a few hours."

When the captain had departed the professor was very grave.

Messiter and Dick were delighted at the prospect of finding pearls, but Ted bit his nails in silence.

"I'll take home a pearl or two for Henrietta," exclaimed Dick.

"If you ever get home, sir," remarked Ted, half aloud.

"You'll go with us, Ted, won't you?" asked Dick.

"I'll go wherever you go, Master Dick," replied Ted, "because it's my duty to watch over you. But I ain't going to have no sort of truck with that captain cove."

"He's all right, Ted, when you know him."

"Is he? Then I don't want to know him," answered Ted.

Turning to the professor, Dick exclaimed—

"Shall we have good sport, sir?"

"Most likely," answered Mr. Crab. "I have heard of a huge oyster which contained fifty sharks."

"Fifty sharks!" ejaculated Messiter.

"Did I say sharks? I meant pearls," said Mr. Crab, confusedly.

"Are there so many sharks about?"

"It is no use disguising the fact. The sea hereabouts swarms with them. I should not like to meet one under the waves," answered Mr. Crab. "A pearl has been called by poets a tear of the sea, and anything more lovely round a maiden's neck cannot be conceived. I have a strong wish to hunt for those tears of the sea, and behold them growing in their shells, but Heaven protect us from the sharks."

Ted disappeared for a brief space, and returned with a long harpoon.

"What have you got there?" asked Dick.

"It's a reg'lar pig-sticker, isn't it, sir?" remarked Ted, regarding it admiringly.

"It does look as if it could give an ugly prod," remarked Messiter.

"They call it a harpoon; thing for sticking of whales," continued Ted. "Me and Number One, that's the nigger as waits on us, is pals, sir, and he's given me this to fight the darned sharkses with."

"Bravo, Ted!" exclaimed Messiter.

"It would be 'Bravo, Ted,' if I could rip up an inch or two of that captain, and seize the blessed ship," rejoined Ted, with a scowl.

Dick said nothing in reply, but waited patiently for the signal, which would summon him and his companions to the captain's side.

It came an hour or two before daybreak.

A negro summoned them to the platform, near which the boat attached to the ship was riding.

It was manned by four men, and when all the party were on board, the negroes began to row towards the island.

At six o'clock, the day broke suddenly.

They were a few miles from the land, which was distinctly visible, with a few trees scattered here and there.

The captain stood up in the boat, and narrowly regarded the sea.

He gave a sign and the anchor was lowered.

"Here we are," said the captain. "Put on your divers' caps, gentlemen, and follow me."

The heavy sea garments were quickly put on.

The electric lamps were not needed, because the depth was not great.

Besides, the electric light would attract the sharks, who were creatures they could not afford to despise.

The only arm given to each of the party was a long sharp knife.

Captain Nemo set the example of springing into the sea, the others following him as soon as they were thoroughly equipped.

The negroes remained in the boat, awaiting their return.

A depth of about three yards and a half did not give them a very great submersion.

To be supplied with condensed air, to be armed, and well lighted by the sun, they walked along the bottom of the sea, easily seeing the smallest object on all sides of them.

After some little walking, they came to some oyster banks, from which the shells containing the valuable pearls were dragged by the hands of the divers.

There were millions of them, and the mine seemed inexhaustible.

They could not stop to examine everything, for it was necessary to follow the captain everywhere.

The road was uneven; sometimes Dick could raise his arm and put his hand out of the water; at others, he was descending a slope, and the sun's rays were not so vivid.

Everything became more obscure, and great shells were seen sticking to curiously-shaped rocks.

After a time, a large grotto appeared before them, dimly lighted.

The captain entered, followed by the rest of the party, the professor eagerly taking note of everything.

Ted carrying his harpoon, which was a good deal longer than himself, and the two boys eagerly looking for pearls, as if they expected to find them lying at their feet.

Descending an inclined plane, Captain Nemo stopped and pointed out an object which they had not hitherto perceived.

It was an oyster of gigantic size.

Lying alone upon the granite rock, it took up a large space, and never had the professor even heard of such a huge bivalve.

The shells were open a little, as if the oyster was feeding, which enabled the captain to introduce his knife.

Keeping the two shells open by both ends of his knife, he pushed back the flesh of the oyster, and revealed a pearl as big as a small cocoa-nut.

It was a jewel of inestimable price.

Evidently the captain had been to this grotto before, and knew of the existence of the wonderful oyster.

Why had he not taken the pearl?

Probably because to a man in his position wealth was of no moment; having separated himself from the world, he did not care for riches, as it is only in the world that one can spend money.

Dick advanced to the oyster, and stretched out his hand, as if he would have seized the pearl, but he was disappointed.

By a sudden movement the captain withdrew his knife, and the two shells came together with a sharp snap.

Satisfied with showing them this treasure of the deep, he turned round, and retraced his steps, leaving the pearl, which was worth at least fifty thousand pounds, behind them.

Incomprehensible man, he was now more than ever a mystery to Dick.

Again they wandered along the bottom of the sea, beholding many things worthy of observation.

Sometimes the bank was so shallow that their heads came above the water; at others they sank several yards below.

Suddenly the captain stopped, and by a movement of his hand ordered the party to conceal themselves behind a projecting rock.

He pointed to the liquid mass in front of them, and all followed with their eyes the direction indicated.

CHAPTER XVI.

THE SEA BUTCHER.

ABOUT five yards off a shadow came between the party and the rays of the sun.

Dick thought of the "Sea Butcher," as the divers of Ceylon call the shark, and trembled a little at the idea.

But he deceived himself, for this time he had nothing to fear from the monster of the ocean.

A living man, an Indian, black as ink, shot through the water, doubtless an early fisher for pearls.

The bottom of his canoe could be seen up above, a few feet beyond his head.

Arriving at the bottom, which was about five yards deep, he fell on his knees, let go the stone he had held between his feet to sink with more rapidity, and began to rake up the oysters from the bank with both hands.

A cord was round his waist, the other end being attached to his boat, and this he pulled at when he wanted to rise.

To his loins was attached a little bag, into which he put the oysters as fast as he could gather them.

Little do ladies think how difficult and dangerous it is to obtain the pretty pearls which they wear round their white necks.

The Indian did not see anyone, and if he had, he would have been so alarmed at the strange spectacle of curious-looking beings walking at ease at the bottom of the sea, that he would quickly have retired.

Several times he remounted and plunged again, not getting more than a dozen oysters at each dip.

It appeared as if he risked his life for very little return, as in a score of oysters he might not find a pearl worth having.

All at once, while on his knees, he made a gesture of terror, and seized his rope to ascend to the surface.

A gigantic mass appeared close to the wretched diver.

It was a huge shark which advanced diagonally towards him, his terrible jaws open wide.

The Indian threw himself on one side and avoided the bite of the shark, but not the action of his tail.

Dick thought he heard the jaws snap, but he had not much time to think, as he saw the diver thrown down by a blow of the animal's tail, and stretched upon the ground.

All this was done in a few seconds.

The shark returned, lying upon his back, in order the better to bite and divide the Indian in halves.

Dick was about to rush forward to attempt to save the miserable wretch's life, when he was pushed rudely back by Captain Nemo.

In his hand he held a knife, and was evidently prepared to battle for his life against the shark.

The latter, just about to seize the Indian and snap him up, perceived his new adversary, and, replacing himself upon his belly, directed himself rapidly towards him.

Dick watched the captain with intense interest.

He waited coolly the attack of the shark, which was one of the largest of its species, and when it charged him, he stepped quickly aside, plunging his knife into its belly up to the hilt.

Then commenced a dreadful combat.

The shark began to bleed dreadfully, tinging the sea in such a manner as to hide the two in a sea of blood.

As the water cleared a little, Dick saw the captain, caught by one of the creature's fins, stabbing at it as fast as he could, but not being able to give it its death blow. The shark lashed the sea with fury, and almost prevented the professor and his friends from keeping their footing, though they were some distance off.

Neither the professor, Dick, nor Messiter dared to go to the help of the captain, for it seemed as if the shark would bite them in two, and they lost their presence of mind for a time.

By degrees the struggle was less fierce.

Captain Nemo was exhausted by his efforts; the shark, holding him tight in his fins, forced him to the ground.

His mouth opened like a pair of shears, and the death of the captain seemed but the work of a second.

Dick turned to Ted, who held the harpoon.

He knew Ted's dislike to the captain, but it seemed to him cowardly to let him die like this, while trying to save another's life, if anything could be done to save his.

It was impossible to speak, because of the helmet he wore, but he looked at Ted and pointed to the captain.

Their eyes met.

Dick's movements were an order to Ted; he couldn't disobey his young master, though the command was not expressed in words.

In an instant Ted precipitated himself towards the shark and struck it a terrible blow in the flank.

Again the sea was saturated with blood.

The shark agitated the water with indescribable fury, for Ted had not missed his aim.

It was the death agony of the monster.

Stricken to the heart, he struggled gallantly, but was powerless for further evil.

As the immense creature was dying, Ted pulled the captain from under him, and at the same moment the Indian, coming to himself, detached the stone from his feet, and shot upwards.

Following the example of the pearl diver, the captain struck the ground with his heels, as did the others, and all were soon at the surface.

The Indian had regained his canoe, but he was lying at the bottom in a half fainting condition.

Satisfying himself that the poor fellow would live, and was not seriously injured, the captain signalled to his companions to descend, leaving the Indian gazing at them with haggard eyes, thinking he had seen some supernatural beings.

Walking as fast as they could along the bottom of the sea, they came in time to the anchor of their boat, reascended to the surface, and taking their seats, removed their head-cases, with a feeling of relief.

The negroes immediately began to row back to the "Enigma."

Captain Nemo was the first to speak.

"Thank you, my lad," he said, extending his hand to Ted.

"It's nothing," rejoined Ted bluntly; "you saved my life when we were wrecked, and I have now saved yours with my harpoon. We are equal now, and I owe you nothing."

A sickly smile sat on the captain's lips for a second, and that was all.

"Lay to it!" he cried to his men "Pull to the 'Enigma.'"

At half-past eight in the morning, they were again on board the ship, having been absent a little more than three hours.

To Dick the captain was more difficult to understand than ever.

He had risked his own life to save that of a poor Indian whom he had never seen before, and was never likely to see again.

This showed he couldn't have a bad heart.

His heart was not entirely dead, whatever his faults might be.

As if the captain guessed Dick's thoughts, he observed to him at the bottom of the staircase, on board the "Enigma"—

"That Indian belonged to an oppressed race. I also am one of the oppressed, and to my last breath, I shall continue to be so. You recognise now the bond of union between us."

CHAPTER XVII.

THE TUNNEL THROUGH THE EARTH.

THE ship again continued her way, travelling towards the Persian Gulf.

If Captain Nemo wanted to visit Europe, it was clear that he would have to go round the Cape of Good Hope, but that did not appear to be his design.

He went direct to the Red Sea, and as the Isthmus of Suez was not then pierced by a canal, there was no outlet to the Mediterranean.

This puzzled the professor very much.

They had been imprisoned three months on board the "Enigma," and at present there were no signs of their deliverance.

What was to be the end of it?

Mr. Crab listened to Ted's grumblings, and said—

"If you will show me a chance of escaping, I will talk to you; at present all discussion is useless."

"It's very well for you, sir," replied Ted, "because you take an interest in all sorts of funny things, but I'm jolly miserable. I know I'm an odd boy, but——"

"Yes, yes," said the professor quickly, "we know that, and of course you have your feelings."

Dick and Messiter laughed, without saying anything.

On the sixth of February they passed Aden, which the English have made an impregnable place like Gibraltar.

On the seventh they went through the straits of Babel Mandif, which in the Arab language means the "Gate of Tears," and so entered the Red Sea.

The "Enigma" avoided the many steamers which throng this route, by travelling under the sea.

The Red Sea is famous in Bible history, for it was in its depths that Pharaoh and his host were lost, but every year it sinks lower by a yard and a half, owing to evaporation.

Through this cause, the part where the Egyptian king crossed, is already covered with sand, and the voyagers saw nothing of the chariot wheels or the armour which the men of war were clad in.

The vegetation under the sea was magnificent, and the party passed many hours in looking out of the window of the saloon, which was illuminated by the electric light.

Caring nothing for its currents or its fearful tempests, the "Enigma" ploughed her way through the celebrated Red Sea.

One morning the captain sought his prisoners, and said to the professor—

"To-morrow we shall be in the Mediterranean."

Mr. Crab looked at him with astonishment.

"Does that surprise you?" he continued with a smile.

"Certainly it does, though I thought I had given up being astonished since I have been on board your ship."

"You are a man of science; why should you be astonished?"

"Because you must travel with the speed of lightning almost to East Africa and round the Cape of Good Hope."

"I did not say I was going to do so," replied the captain.

"You can't go overland, since there is no canal through the Isthmus of Suez——"

"But one can go under land," interrupted the captain.

"Under land," answered the professor, holding up his hand.

"Undoubtedly," said Captain Nemo, calmly. "For a long while nature has made underneath this tongue of land what men are trying to do now on the surface."

"Does there exist a passage?"

"Yes, a passage or tunnel, which at fifty feet depth touches the solid rock."

"How did you discover it—by chance?"

"No," said the captain. "I guessed that such a tunnel existed, and I have been through it several times."

"May I inquire how you found it out?" asked Dick.

"Certainly. I need not have any secrets from people who are never likely to leave me. I had remarked in the Red Sea and the Mediterranean several fish of the same species. It was curious. I caught a few hundreds of those fish in the Red Sea, and put iron rings through their tails. Shortly afterwards I fished in the Mediterranean, and caught some of the ringed fish; then I knew that they must go under land, through a passage unknown to man, as it was impossible they could round the Cape."

"You are a most remarkable man," said the professor, using his favourite phrase.

"To-night you shall go with me through my tunnel," said the captain.

"Well," said the professor, "we live to learn. Our fathers never dreamed of gas, of railways, of telegraphs, and I did not suspect the existence of your wonderful ship."

"Shortly, my dear sir," said the captain, "your children, that is to say, the next generation. will travel through the air in flying machines; your railway engines will own electricity as their motive power. There is no end to scientific discovery; the world is in its infancy. We are just emerging from barbarism. Wait and watch, that's my motto. You must not be surprised at anything in these days."

"You are right—we are on the march," said the professor.

The day passed, and at half-past nine the "Enigma" rose to the surface to receive her supply of air.

Nothing disturbed the silence but the cry of the pelican and other birds of the night, with the occasional sound of the escaping steam of a steamer travelling towards the far East.

Dick could not rest below, and at once ascended to the platform to breathe the fresh air. In the darkness he saw a pale light, discoloured by the fog, which burned about a mile off.

"A lighthouse," he said.

The captain was by his side, and quietly replied—

"It is the floating light ship of Suez."

"We are near the mouth of the tunnel, I suppose? Is the entrance easy?"

"No," said Captain Nemo, "it is difficult. I always steer the ship myself, and if you like to come into the wheelhouse with me, I will show you the way. In a moment the "Enigma" will sink, and we shall not rise till we are in the Mediterranean."

Dick followed the captain into the pilot's cabin, which was at the bow of the vessel, the wheel working the rudder by long chains carried aft.

The cabin measured six feet square, four round windows of thick plate glass enabled the helmsman to see on all sides and the electric light, thrown well forward, made everything as clear as day.

A strong negro, with an eye like a hawk, was at the wheel, but he gave the spokes to the captain, and fell back.

"Now," exclaimed Captain Nemo, "let us search for our passage."

Electric wires communicated with the engine room, so it was easy to communicate directly with the engineers, by pressing a knob of metal.

Touching this knob, the speed of the screw lessened considerably.

For about an hour, the ship passed by a bank of sand, which was varied by rocks, on which Dick saw all kinds of seaweeds, coral formations, and curious fish agitating their fins in alarm at the apparition of the "Enigma."

At a quarter past ten, a long and large gallery appeared in front, black, and apparently deep.

The "Enigma" entered this gloomy tunnel boldly, and an unaccustomed rushing sound made itself heard against the sides, which arose from the waters of the Red Sea rushing into the Mediterranean.

Following the current with the speed of an arrow, the ship made its way, though the engines were reversed and the screw went backwards, to abate the velocity of its progress.

A single false turn of the wheel, and the "Enigma" would have been dashed to atoms against the iron-like rocks on each side, above and below.

Dick held his breath.

He could see nothing but the foaming waters made transparent by the electric light.

At thirty-five minutes past ten, the captain gave up the helm to the negro, and turning to Dick, exclaimed—

"We are in the Mediterranean."

In less than twenty minutes, the ship, carried by the current, had traversed the Isthmus of Suez.

The next morning, they came to the surface, and were able to breathe the fresh air again.

Ted was in high spirits when he found

that they were in Europe again, because he thought they had a chance of escaping, and this idea was always uppermost in his mind.

He spoke to his companions about it, and they all agreed to follow him, if a good opportunity offered.

The arrangement of the attempt was left to Messiter and Ted.

As for Dick, he did not think they would be successful, and the professor was too much occupied with putting down in a book all the wonderful things he saw, to bother his mind about anything else.

Being a studious man, and fond of science in all its branches, he was resigned to his lot, and if he could only have sent his notes in the shape of a yearly volume to his publisher in London, he would have been content to pass the remainder of his life on board the "Enigma."

Ted was very busy for a day or two, and Dick saw him talking confidentially to the negro who waited upon them.

Evidently there was something in the wind.

The ship travelled leisurely along the Mediterranean, often rising in sight of land, and laying like a log upon the water.

In the evening, it was the custom of the prisoners to play at cards, or some game they liked, and after the fourth day in the Mediterranean, Ted, instead of putting the pack on the table, shut the door, and in a mysterious way, exclaimed—

"I've squared the nigger!"

"Which?" asked Dick.

"Number one. He as waits upon us. His real name's Smunko. I've found that out. Me and he's pals. I've told him I want to bolt, and he says he shan't let on to the skipper, or any of them, though they are all a lot of spies."

"Perhaps he's one, too," observed the professor, smiling.

"Not he, sir," answered Ted; "Smunko's right enough. He's going to keep all the other coves quiet, some dark night when we're near land. Then we are to go on the platform and swim for our lives."

"A very good arrangement if it can be carried out," remarked the professor. "But I fear your friend Smunko is not to be depended upon."

Ted was indignant.

"You're Crabs by name and crabs by nature," he answered, angrily.

"Ted," cried Dick, warningly.

"Beg pardon, sir," said Ted. "I didn' mean nothing. The professor is always down on me; I'm only an odd boy, but I've got my feelings, Master Dick, and I'd rather be on the beach at Brighton than——"

"We've heard all that before," interrupted Dick; "you must take your chance with the rest of us. I did not think, when I left my school, to have a sail in the Channel, that I should in a few weeks be on board a mysterious vessel like this."

"Nor I either," observed Messiter.

"The fact is," said the professor, "I don't want to discourage the lad, but I have no wish that he should do anything rash, and involve us in a mess. The captain might doom us to solitary confinement. At present we are treated liberally, if we are prisoners."

"All right, sir," replied Ted; "I'll turn it up as far as you are concerned. If Master Dick likes to come with me, all well and good; if not, he can let it alone. I know my game, and I mean to step it."

"Don't show your nasty temper, Ted," said Dick.

"Ain't being cooped up here like a turkey in a pen, fatting for Christmas, enough to rile a bishop?" asked Ted. "But I shan't say no more. When all's ready, I'll give you one more chance, and if you ain't with me, I'm off alone."

It was impossible to check Ted's will. The only one who had any influence over him was Dick.

He was a boy rudely brought up, unaccustomed to control his passions, and having a decided character, but to Dick he was deeply attached.

The next day the "Enigma" floated near an island which the professor declared to be the Isle of Cyprus.

In the evening Ted whispered to Dick—

"Now, sir, all's ready. Smunko is piping off the other blacks; we're not a quarter of a mile from the land."

Dick's heart beat high.

"Tell the others," he said.

"No; let you and I go together."

"I can't leave Messiter, and the professor is one of us."

"Very well," replied Ted. "I spoke sharply the other night, but I'd do anything for you, and you know it, Master Dick. I'm an odd boy, but I'm all there."

Messiter and Professor Crab were apprised of Ted's preparations.

The latter, always distrustful, said—

"Is this Smunko, as you call him, to be depended upon?"

'Come on, sir, and don't fear," said Ted; "we shall lose our chance."

Without further remark all followed Ted to the staircase.

Scarcely had they set foot upon it, when the panel was rudely shut, and the ship began to sink rapidly.

Mocking laughter seemed to ring in their ears.

"Sold again," said Dick philosophically.

"Our skipper is a weasel who can't be caught asleep," remarked Messiter.

Ted was furious.

"I thought it was a mistake," observed the professor. "No matter; I'll go on with the fifteenth chapter of my book entitled 'The Submarine Kingdom, by one who has been there.'"

Turning up the corridor, Ted said, "I'll have it out of that Smunko."

Before he had gone a dozen paces, a hand was raised to stop his progress, and his eyes fell as they encountered those of Captain Nemo.

"Boy," exclaimed the latter, "when you again plan an escape, remember that you have me to deal with. Do not try to unsettle the minds of your companions, and recollect that I have the power to punish those who offend me."

"I never said I would not try it on," replied Ted, abashed.

"You are forgiven this time. Beware now you trifle with me again. Go."

Ted, with his eyes flashing, and his head hanging down in a bulldog sort of fashion, returned to his companions.

His only remark was—

"That captain cove's Old Nick himself; but I'll be one with him some of these days."

He made no reply to the jests of his companions, and bore their chaff with silent ill-humour.

The voyage continued, and when they neared the Straits of Gibraltar, they observed innumerable wrecks which had gone down in this narrow passage.

There they lay, strewed about in magnificent confusion, the home of strange fishes and stranger insects.

The "Enigma" entered the Atlantic, and did not stop till she was at the bottom of the Bay of Vigo, off the Spanish coast.

In 1702, a fleet of gold vessels from the Spanish possessions in South America was surprised by the English in this bay.

To avoid their falling into the enemy's hands, the admiral in command caused the galleons to sink with all their vast treasure on board.

Captain Nemo knew that, and opening the sliding shutter which concealed the window of the prisoners' cabin, he revealed to their view the sunken vessels.

Half-a-dozen negroes, furnished with the divers' helmets, had left the "Enigma," and were at work raising the chests of gold, and carrying the precious metal to the "Enigma."

From the barrels and cases, the ingots, the piastres, and the precious stones escaped in a perfect cascade of wealth.

For hours the men worked at their gold fishery, and it was clear that the captain did not altogether despise wealth, as he was collecting so much from the bottom of the deep.

It was strange that this gold, wrung by the followers of Cortez and Pizarro from the natives of Peru, and lost to the Spaniards, should be rescued from the bottom of the sea by Captain Nemo.

"What can he want with all this money?" asked the professor, aloud.

"He can't spend it," said Dick.

The captain's step was heard behind them.

For a moment, he watched his men at their work, collecting the precious metal, the jewels, the richly-chased cups, and all the sunken treasures.

Then he said—

"I cannot forget that there are people who suffer on earth; that there are persecuted races who stand in need of help. It is not for myself that I amass wealth; it is for those who deserve it. The sea is my bank. I am the banker of the poor and the oppressed; they draw upon me at sight, and I pay."

So saying, he withdrew as silently as he entered.

"A most remarkable man!" ejaculated the professor, as usual.

"A jolly old humbug, that's what he **is**," said Ted, in **a** tone which made everyone laugh.

The ship began to move again, and the professor did not like the look of the compass.

"South-south-west," he said; "we are turning our backs on Europe."

When she next rose to the surface to fill her reservoirs with air, Dick mounted the staircase, and went on the platform.

No land was in view.

Nothing but the immense and illimitable sea.

Bad weather was brewing, and the few sails in sight ran before the wind close-reefed.

CHAPTER XVIII.

A STRANGE SCENE.

AT two o'clock of the same day the professor calculated the position of the "Enigma" thus—

She was in 16 deg. 17 min. longitude, and 33 deg. 22 min. latitude, and 150 leagues from the nearest land.

Flight was out of the question, and the party resigned themselves to whatever fate their strange captain might have in store for them.

Dick felt rather oppressed.

He thought of his friends at home, of Henrietta, whom he loved, and wondered if he should ever see her again.

While he was thinking, the captain came up to him, and, touching him on the shoulder, said—

"I don't know why, my lad, but I have taken a fancy to you."

"Thank you," replied Dick, a little coolly.

"I must keep you and your friends prisoners here, but I can offer you occasionally a little diversion in the shape of an excursion."

"What is it?" asked Dick.

"You have only visited the depths of the sea near the surface. To-day I will take you to a wonderful place at the bottom of the Atlantic."

Any excitement was to Dick a relief under the existing circumstances, and he willingly closed with the offer.

"Our walk will be fatiguing, as we have to climb a mountain, though what you will see will well reward you for your trouble."

"You rouse my curiosity," said Dick; "what am I to see?"

"A city of the dead. Come with me. We will put on our sea dress while the ship sinks to the bottom," answered the captain.

By the time they were dressed the ship had gained the desired position.

Dick noticed that they were not provided with lamps, which seemed singular to him at such a depth, as the sun's rays could not possibly penetrate very far.

After the usual manœuvre, they set foot upon the bottom of the Atlantic, at a depth of three hundred yards.

The water was very dense, but the captain pointed out a large red spot at some distance — probably two miles — off.

It looked like fire.

But how it could exist under a mass of water Dick was unable to guess.

Its light was vague, still it was sufficient for their purpose, and they advanced slowly towards it.

Captain Nemo and Dick walked side by side, gradually ascending a steep incline.

The captain had two sticks, one of which he handed to his companion and this was very useful, as the path was slippery with seaweed and loose stones.

As they proceeded, Dick heard a hissing noise, mingled with a pattering sound, and varied with a crackling like a discharge of musketry.

It was like rain falling on the top of one's hat in summer

He slipped now and then over heaps of stones covered with zoophytes, and without the aid of his stick he would have fallen.

The light increased as they approached, and set the horizon in a flame, and Dick did not know what to think of it.

Captain Nemo advanced fearlessly, for he evidently knew the road.

At the base of the mountain the path was comparatively easy, but as they ascended, they had to traverse a forest of dead trees without leaves, black and funereal, mineralized by the action of the waves; it resembled a forest of pine trees in winter.

With difficulty they passed through this awful group of dead trees, and continued the ascent, and at last reached the top of the mountain.

The fish rose before them like birds surprised in a wood.

Gigantic crabs crawled slowly out of their way, and Titanic lobsters moved lazily on one side, and hundreds of polypi twisted their ugly limbs like writhing serpents.

Stopping on a ledge of rock, the captain signed to Dick to look down into the valley below them.

He saw a mass of picturesque ruins, heaps of stones, and magnificent columns, amongst which were splendid temples and beautiful villas, clothed with sea flowers, which served them as a winding-sheet.

The mountain did not rise above eight hundred feet beyond the plain, but they had not yet reached the top.

Captain Nemo urged him on, and when he got to the summit, a grand sight met his view.

The mountain was a volcano.

Fifty feet below them, a huge crater discharged a mass of flame and stones, accompanied with torrents of lava, all of which fell back into the bosom of the sea.

The lava, red hot as it was, caused the brilliant light before the water cooled it.

Dick saw before him a splendid city destroyed by volcanic agency.

The architecture was of the Tuscan order.

He saw an acropolis, an aqueduct, the remains of a quay where mighty ships might have lain, deserted streets, in fact, a Pompeii under the sea.

For an hour they remained watching the submerged city under the action of the volcanic flames.

Then they slowly retraced their way to the ship.

Having arrived and taken off his helmet, Dick seized the captain's hand, and asked—

"What have I seen?"

"The remains of one of the greatest cities of olden times," replied Captain Nemo.

"Tell me something about it."

"Tell your friend, Professor Crab, that you have been to the ruins of Meropis, the Meropis of Pliny and Tertullian; he will explain it to you," replied the captain.

Dick was obliged to be satisfied with the answer, and he sought the professor, to whom he related the wonders he had seen.

"My dear boy," said the professor, "I am ready to admit that the whole of this region, now covered with water, was one day land, and not so very long ago. Meropis stood on this continent, as we have evidence to prove. It was the oldest and grandest of the Greek cities. The people were great and powerful, but suddenly it disappeared, and the sea flowed over this large and great country—a day and night were sufficient for its destruction; and now, the islands of Madeira, the Azores, and the Canaries, with the Cape de Verd, are its highest peaks above the sea."

"The world is more wonderful than I imagined," replied Dick, thoughtfully.

"Perhaps our little England will be swallowed up some day," said Messiter.

Suddenly there was a noise in the passage outside the cabin.

Dick rushed out, and saw Ted beating a negro.

It was Smunko.

"You sold me," cried Ted, angrily; "what do you mean by it, you black beast? I'll give you something."

"No, Massa Ted, me not sell," replied the black, struggling gallantly with the bear-like hug in which he was held.

"I'll have your wool," continued Ted, twining his fingers in his short, crisp hair, and kicking his shins, which are the most tender part of a negro.

"Oh, him kick um legs; help, Massa Nemo! help!" cried Smunko.

The captain appeared on the scene, and struck Ted on the side of the head.

Letting the negro go, Ted, blinded with passion, drew a knife, and rushed upon the captain.

So sudden and unexpected was the assault, that the latter was unable to avoid it.

He was stabbed in two places before his cries brought his men to his assistance.

Dick saw with horror and dismay that blood was trickling down upon the iron floor of the passage.

Ted was held in a vice-like grip by four men, and glared savagely around him.

"Disarm him," said the captain, in a faint voice, "and confine him and his companions to their cabin."

Instantly all four were hustled into the cabin, and the iron door closed upon them, without their being able to ascertain the nature or gravity of the captain's wounds.

The professor was greatly agitated.

Messiter and Dick looked blankly at one another.

"Good Heaven! what have you done, wretched boy?" said Professor Crab.

"I couldn't help it," replied Ted. "The negro, instead of helping me to escape, went and told the captain, and I meant to have it out of him the first chance."

"You might have expected it; why should he prove false to his employer?"

"If the captain had not interfered, I should not have hit him."

"You have all the making of a murderer in you, my lad," continued the professor, "and I fear that you will get us into some serious trouble."

"I wish I had killed him; we might have got away then. What right has he to keep us here?"

"The right of the strong to oppress the weak, which we cannot dispute," replied Professor Crab, "and as by saving our lives in the first instance, we surprised his secret, he has some sort of right to keep us here."

"Are you all against me?" asked Ted, looking appealingly to Dick.

"I can't defend the use of the knife. It is cowardly," said Dick.

"He struck me first, and a thundering hard prop it was."

"No matter; you were wrong."

"I expect," said Messiter, "we shall all get it for this; the captain's a hot member when his back's up."

"I don't care what becomes of me," answered Ted sullenly. "I'd as soon croak and turn up my toes at once as be kept here. You think, all of you, because I'm an odd boy, I ain't got no feelings."

"We think nothing of the sort," replied Dick; "but we hold that it is cowardly to stab."

"And more than that, it is an abuse of hospitality to attack with a knife one who, like Captain Nemo, has treated us with as much kindness and consideration as lay in his power while we have been on board his ship."

"All right," answered Ted, "pitch in. I'm here to be shot at."

The remainder of the evening passed very gloomily.

Smunko brought them their meals, but did not speak a word, and would not even answer when appealed to as to the condition of the captain, about whom all were anxious except Ted.

CHAPTER XIX.

THE SENTENCE.

A WEEK elapsed and the prisoners were closely confined.

The freedom that had hitherto been accorded them, was wholly withdrawn, and one and all ascribed the harshness with which they were treated to the rashness with which Ted had acted.

Ted himself seemed sorry for what he had done.

Privately, he owned as much to Dick, saying that it was the impulse of the moment, and he did not think that the others would suffer for his deed.

"I have done it," he said, in a tone of contrition, "and I suppose I must suffer for it."

"You should have restrained your passions," replied Dick; "everything on

"TED DREW A KNIFE AND RUSHED UPON THE CAPTAIN."—(See page 64.)

board this ship should be done on the extreme Q. T. We are watched."

"You mean quiet, I suppose, sir, by Q. T.," answered Ted. "I'll be quiet enough in future, though this life is enough to drive an average chap like me silly."

The professor was able to continue his calculations by the aid of compasses and maps, with other scientific instruments.

He discovered to his surprise that the vessel was travelling with great swiftness to the south, following the fiftieth meridian.

On the 14th of March he perceived floating masses of ice on the surface of the ocean, when the "Enigma" stopped, and by means of the window in the cabin, he was able to peer into the sea.

Could it be the captain's intention to go to the Pole itself?

Was he dead, owing to the wounds given him by Ted, and were the men he left behind him unable to navigate the ship?

These and other questions received a prompt answer one morning.

Smunko came into the cabin and ordered the prisoners to follow him.

He was respectful in his manner, but there was not that freedom which they had hitherto remarked.

They were conducted into Captain Nemo's drawing-room, as his splendidly-furnished cabin may aptly be termed.

He was lying on a sofa, and a bandage could be seen round his right arm and another round his left breast.

His face was pale, and wore a more than usually severe expression.

On each side of him was a double row of slaves, each armed with a ship's cutlass.

The whole force of the ship, with one exception, was present.

"Gentlemen," said Captain Nemo, with his accustomed good breeding, "I have sent for you to inform you that you have been tried by me during my week of suffering."

"I hope, sir," said the professor, anxiously, "that you do not think we ordered this unfortunate lad to act as he did."

"No," exclaimed the captain, "I do not. I acquit you of any complicity in his design, but at the same time I have found you all guilty."

"Of what?"

"Of an attempt to murder.

"But, my dear sir——"

"Listen to me," cried Captain Nemo, waving his hand as he interrupted the professor; "you are each in my eyes responsible for the acts of one another. I have received two wounds from one of your number, either of which might have been fatal. Thank Heaven I have escaped from the knife of a cowardly assassin!"

"Think of his youth, sir," urged the professor.

"I have thought of everything," exclaimed Captain Nemo, "and it only remains for me to pass sentence upon all of you."

"What have I done?" asked Dick, flushing.

"I can make no distinction between you. I condemn you all four to death."

At these words all turned pale.

The professor trembled violently.

Messiter sought Dick's hand and grasped it warmly, as if he thought all was over and wished to take a long farewell.

Ted, however, was the most agitated of all.

He knelt before the captain, and said, with tears in his eyes—

"I don't beg for mercy for myself, sir, but for my young master and the other two. They are perfectly innocent. It was all my doing."

"You should have thought of the peril in which you involved your associates before you acted with such transparent folly and such great wickedness," answered the captain.

"Let them off and do what you like with me," pleaded Ted. "For the love of Heaven, sir, don't be hard on Master Dick."

"Silence!" cried the captain. "Remove him."

Two stalwart negroes seized Ted and dragged him back to the place where the others were standing.

"The sentence of death which I have passed upon you," continued Captain Nemo, "will not be executed for twelve months."

At this declaration the hearts of the condemned beat again.

While there is life there is hope.

"On the 1st of March, next year, you will die, but the manner of your death I shall keep a profound secret. It will be painful, as befits your crime. For twelve months you may brood over your doom, which I trust will increase the punishment."

"I hope you will reconsider your sentence, sir," said the professor.

"When my mind is fixed, I never alter; do not delude yourself with the expectation that I shall pardon you," exclaimed the captain. "You have twelve months to·live—that is all. During the remainder of your lives I shall accord you the liberty you have hitherto enjoyed, with the exception of the assassin, who must not venture on the platform without special permission."

The professor bowed, and leading the way, he and his companions withdrew.

Captain Nemo's utterances were those of fate!

It was useless to struggle against them.

There was no hope, except in flight, and that they would be more jealously guarded than ever, they did not doubt.

Owing to Ted's rashness, their condition was gloomy in the extreme, though they were thankful that they were not immediately put to death.

So many things might happen in twelve months.

But if nothing happened, what then?

It was DEATH!

CHAPTER XX.

IN THE CLAWS OF DEATH.

CAPTAIN NEMO did not seek the society of the captives as he had formerly done.

Keeping himself aloof from them, he led a solitary life, but when he met either of them in the passages of the ship, or on the platform, he spoke with civility, though not with friendship.

They, on their part, regarded him with awe, as their future executioner.

Ted was very sad.

He would have given worlds to have recalled the past, but it was too late, and though those he had condemned to death fully forgave him, he could not hide his misery.

Frequently, while talking to himself, Dick heard him say—

"I'm only an odd boy, but I'll get them all out of it yet, somehow."

This was a difficult task, however, and Dick scarcely dared to hope.

The captain's wounds were not dangerous, and he was soon able to walk about, and take the control of the ship as usual.

Its course was towards the Pole, and it continually met icebergs.

A dazzling white light was seen, which whalers call the "ice-blink," which announced the presence of a bank of ice.

The bergs resembled floating islands, and were used as resting places by hundreds of birds, such as petrels and puffins, some of whom perched on the "Enigma" when she rose to the surface.

Gradually the temperature lowered and the thermometer exposed to the outer air, marked three degrees below zero.

But the inmates of the ship did not suffer.

They were supplied with seal and other skins, while the ship was heated by the electric apparatus in such a manner as to defy the most extreme cold.

In these regions round the Pole, there is six months day, and the same period of night.

The dark time was coming on.

About the sixteenth of March they crossed the Antarctic Polar circle, and found themselves surrounded with ice.

Nevertheless the captain kept straight on, as if he did not fear being locked in the ice for the awful winter of the Polar Seas.

"If he goes on like this," remarked Dick, "he will save himself the trouble of killing us, as we shall all be frozen to death or starved."

"He can't go much further," exclaimed Messiter.

"Why not?" asked the professor.

" Because the ice will block us in."

" You forget that the ' Enigma' can go under the ice," observed Professor Crab, adjusting his spectacles to look better at a map he was studying.

The icebergs grew more numerous, and it was difficult to steer between them.

They frequently met with an awful crash, agitating the sea for a great distance, and the water appeared to be slowly freezing all round.

On the seventeenth, a field of ice absolutely barred the way, but the captain sent his ship forward with all its force, and split a way through like a battering ram.

The cold was intense.

With five degrees below the zero, the " Enigma " was coated with ice, and the snow fell in heavy masses, while the wind blew from every point of the compass in turn with a wild, melancholy howling.

Nothing but a sailless, mastless ship, warmed and worked by electric power, like the " Enigma," could possibly have lived in such latitudes and such weather.

At last, even the great strength of the " Enigma " was unable to force a way for them.

It was not a bank, a field, or a berg of ice which barred her path, but a succession of mountains in front of her, glistening like frosted glass.

" Longitude, 51 deg. 30 min. south ; latitude, 67 deg. 39 min.," said the professor, looking up from his books as the vessel became motionless.

" It's a case now," observed Dick.

Ascending to the platform with Messiter, he beheld a vast plain of ice twisted into all sorts of fantastic shapes.

Here were confused blocks, piled one on another.

There was a mass of waves tormented by the wind, frozen into small hillocks ; and, beyond, strange bergs, looking like mountains ; and all around reigned a sullen silence, which struck a chill to the soul itself.

For the first time since Ted's unfortunate attempt at assassination, the captain came up to Dick and spoke to him.

" What do you think of the situation, my boy ?" he asked.

" It looks as if we were fixed," replied Dick.

" How ? Did you ever see the 'Enigma' in a mess she could not get out of ?"

" But at present we can neither advance nor retreat; we are stuck fast."

An ironical smile sat on Captain Nemo's thin, aristocratic lips.

" You think we must stay here and hunt the seal, the bear, and the walrus till the ice breaks and lets us out ?" he said.

" The season is so advanced that we have no chance," replied Dick.

" I am of a different opinion; and I have the honour to inform you that we are going a great deal further yet."

" Further south ?"

" Yes ; to the Pole itself."

At this audacious announcement, Dick thought that the captain was mad, though it gave him an indescribable sensation of pleasure to think that he would have a hand in accomplishing what Frobisher, Franklin, and other Arctic explorers had failed to attain.

" To the Antarctic Pole," continued the captain, calmly. " You know that I can make the ' Enigma' do what I like. This is my first voyage in these seas, and we will discover the Pole together ; being the first to tread on that land which has never, since the creation of the world, been sullied by a human foot."

" How do you mean to do it ?" asked Dick, incredulously.

" By going underneath this bank of ice. My ship will swim through the water, as the ice only extends to a certain depth. If a continent arises at the Pole we shall be stopped and have to turn back ; but if, as I, and other men who have studied the question believe, an open sea, full of life and vegetation, is to be found, we shall succeed."

" It is a dangerous enterprise," said Dick.

" At all events, we are going to make the attempt," replied the captain.

No time was lost in making preparations.

The powerful pumps of the " Enigma " filled the reservoirs with compressed air.

At four o'clock the platform was deserted, and the panels closed.

The weather was clear, but very cold, being twelve degrees below zero.

An hour later, a dozen men, armed with picks and axes, went outside the ship to cut away the ice, and release the vessel from its embrace.

This being accomplished, she rapidly sank, attaining a depth of eight hundred yards, which prevented the possibility of her striking against the base of an iceberg.

The professor was enchanted with the new trip, which was the most daring Captain Nemo had yet taken.

Sitting before his maps and instruments, he said —

"We have to go from 67 deg. 30 min. to 90 deg., which makes twenty-two degrees and a half of latitude."

"How many miles is that, sir?" asked Messiter.

"Over fifteen hundred miles; but we are travelling now at a speed of twenty-six miles an hour, the engines working at high pressure. Therefore, in forty hours, we shall reach the Pole."

"It is a grand idea," said Dick.

"Perhaps," said Ted, "we shall get bunged up in the ice, and then, with no air, what will become of us?"

"Always grumbling, Ted," said Dick; "you're like the boy who would spell Constantinople with a 'k,' and was never satisfied because he got licked in consequence."

"I'm licked now, sir. This ship, Master Dick, is the greatest lick I ever had. Who'd have thought I should have come to hate the sea?" rejoined Ted.

Dick began to whistle "There's a good time coming, boys," and went into the library to read a book, in order to while away an hour or two.

Several times while thus engaged he heard the "Enigma" strike the roof of ice over his head with her sharp bows, as if trying to force a passage upwards.

In this attempt she continually failed.

The ice was too thick, and she had to continue her way.

At length he fell asleep on a divan in a dark corner of the cabin.

How long he slept he did not know. It might have been some hours. When he awoke he heard voices.

Evidently his presence was not suspected.

The captain was sitting down talking to a tall, well-made negro, who was the second in command.

Scarcely daring to breathe, Dick listened.

Perhaps the merest chance would enable him to hear the secret of the captain's mysterious life.

CHAPTER XXI.

THE CAPTAIN'S SECRET.

AS Captain Nemo spoke, it was observable that a soft melancholy had usurped the harshness which was usually perceived in his voice.

"How many years, Pedro, have we now been afloat?" he asked.

"Five, massa," said the negro.

"Five years ago. One year we were building this ship. That makes six. It is then six years since I last saw my loved Adele."

"Do you still think of Missy Adele, massa?" asked Pedro.

"Can a man, who has once loved as I have loved, ever forget?" said the captain. "I remember when I was the richest and most powerful planter of the Southern States of America."

Dick listened intently.

The captain, by his own confession, was an American, and had been a planter in the States.

"Then came the civil war. I fought with Jackson and Hood until his capitulation after the fall of Richmond. I returned to a ruined home to find that my wife, my darling Adele, was gone."

"But you were rich, massa."

"What was wealth to me? My money, fortunately, was invested in English securities, and Harold Dugard could defy the world. Who would recognise Harold in the eccentric Captain Nemo?"

"We were faithful to you," said Pedro.

"Yes; out of three thousand slaves but twelve remained faithful," returned the captain.

"I heard that my wife, while I was fighting against the Yankees, had oped with my friend, Crawley Vipond, ho had purchased a vessel of war, in hich he intended to sail about the world or the rest of his life."

" He 'fraid you, massa."

" Ha, ha!" laughed Captain Nemo, itterly. " He's afraid of me, because he new me but too well. As he had done me the greatest wrong one man can do nother, he felt that his life would not be afe on earth."

" We shall find him yet," said Pedro.

" Five years have I scoured the seas or his ship, which is called the 'Belle f New Orleans' as if to mock me, for ny wife was the most beautiful girl in hat city. I built this vessel to make ure of my revenge. Some day we shall neet, and then——"

He clenched his fists, and his teeth grated together fiercely.

All that there was demoniac in him came to his face at that moment.

His evil hour was on him.

Dick shuddered.

He had bared the secret of the captain's life.

Before the American civil war he had been a rich and prosperous planter in the Southern States.

As Harold Dugard, he was the happy husband of the fair Adele.

While he was fighting the battles of his country, his false friend, Crawley Vipond, had seduced the affections of his wife and taken her away.

Afraid of the vengeance of the outraged husband, the guilty pair found no rest for their feet on the earth.

They were not safe anywhere, for Harold Dugard was a man who could never forgive an injury.

So they bought a war vessel, and manning it, sailed from sea to sea, thinking themselves safe.

They heard that Harold Dugard had disappeared, no one knew whither.

Perhaps he was dead.

That they could not believe, for knowing his vindictive and determined character as they did, they guessed that he was hiding himself to inflict some terrible blow upon them.

Little did they think, though, that the wonderful " Enigma " was gliding after them like a sea snake above and below the surface of the sea.

Only waiting to find the " Belle of New Orleans," in order that she might strike her amidships, and send all on board to the bottom, as speedily as if she had struck upon a sunken reef.

Woe to Crawley Vipond when he met Harold Dugard in mid ocean!

Vainly would he shriek for mercy and pray for help!

A cruel and sudden death would be the portion of all on board.

Dick now clearly understood the design of Captain Nemo in quitting the world, and shutting himself up in the " Enigma " with his twelve faithful negroes.

" Our task must come to an end soon," continued the captain.

" Find the ' Belle of New Orleans ' before long, massa," answered Pedro, hopefully.

" And then you shall have your freedom and the land I have promised all of you," said the captain.

" Massa very good. Massa come and live, too, with Pedro?"

" No, my lad," answered Captain Nemo; " I shall be a wanderer on the face of the earth. When I have accomplished my vengeance I shall go from one city to another, staying nowhere long. Life lost its charm for me when my false friend robbed me of my wife Adele."

Dick felt for this strange man.

His lot was a hard one.

The war had ruined his home, and the treachery of his friend had broken up his domestic happiness.

Dick was afraid to move.

He had learnt the terrible secret of the captain, and he dreaded if he was seen that he might be put to death at once.

So he remained as quiet as a mouse.

Suddenly the melting mood of the chivalrous Harold Dugard, *alias* Captain Nemo, changed.

" The air is getting close," he said. " It is time we reached this open Polar Sea."

" If it exists, massa," replied Pedro.

" I am sure it exists. Are the engines worked at their highest pressure?"

" Yes, massa."

The captain looked uneasily at his watch.

" We are four hours already behind my calculations. Let some air out of the reservoirs, and try again if you can break the ice. Stay, I will come with you, my faithful Pedro."

To Dick's inexpressible relief, they both quitted the library together.

He crept silently away, and rejoined his companions, to whom he did not say a word of what had taken place.

It would be dangerous, he thought, to give utterance to such a secret as he had discovered.

The captives snatched a little sleep.

But the professor was unable to rest, and at three o'clock he rose to consult his instruments.

He calculated that only a hundred and fifty feet separated them from the surface of the water.

The "Enigma" continued to rise in a sliding oblique manner, which showed that the thickness of the huge bank of ice overhead was lessening.

Messiter woke next, and looked at Dick, who was tossing restlessly in his bed.

"Woe to Crawley Vipond," he muttered, "woe, woe, if Harold Dugard in his 'Enigma' meets the 'Belle of New Orleans!'"

"What's he talking about, I wonder?" said Messiter.

"Ah! Adele, how could you leave such a manly heart and such great love?" continued Dick, in his feverish sleep. "You are beautiful, but you deserve to die with your paramour, and you will die, or I am mistaken in Captain Nemo."

He awoke with a start.

"Hilloa, Harry," he exclaimed, rubbing his eyes.

"You've had a bad dream, haven't you?" inquired Messiter.

"Beastly. Did I say anything?"

"Yes. You've been talking to yourself like old boots."

"About what?"

"Crawley something, and Belles of New Orleans, and Dugards, and death, and I don't know what all."

"Ah, yes," said Dick, collecting himself, "I'm going to write a novel, to pass away the time here, and they are some of my characters."

"Bosh!" replied Messiter; "over the left."

"I am, really."

"What's the caper? There is something up, I know. Won't it tell its own Harry?" asked Messiter, coaxingly.

Dick was doubtful how to reply.

Suddenly the door opened.

It was six o'clock in the morning of that memorable nineteenth of March.

Captain Nemo appeared, looking radiant.

"I have the honour to announce, gentlemen," he exclaimed, "that we have reached the open sea."

Everyone ran to the platform with the utmost eagerness.

Even Ted, who had been kept a close prisoner, was allowed to go on the deck of the "Enigma," which was lying peacefully on the water of a sea free from ice.

Thousands of birds were flying in the air, while myriads of fish swam in the waves.

Towards the north the mountainous masses of ice could be faintly discovered.

The thermometer marked only three degrees centigrade below zero.

They had left winter behind them, and found an early spring.

CHAPTER XXII.

DYING FOR AIR.

A SHORT distance off, land was to be seen which appeared to be of large extent, and to form an important continent.

The boat was put together, and the captain invited the professor, Dick, and Messiter, to accompany him to this territory, which they were the first to explore.

A few vigorous strokes of the oars brought them to the shore.

Dick was the bow oar, and with a light jump he sprang upon the sand.

In his pocket he had a handkerchief of the Union Jack pattern.

An idea struck him.

Quickly tying two corners to the end of the oar, he raised it up, and the British flag was fluttering in the breeze.

"Here I plant the standard of old England," he cried, excitedly; " and defy anyone to displace it."

" Bravo, Dick !" exclaimed Messiter.

" I christen it South Poleland," continued Dick. " Hurrah for old England ! Hip, hip, hip, hurrah ! Go it, Harry. Give us a join in, sir," he added to the professor.

" Hurrah, hurrah !" replied both the professor and Messiter.

Captain Nemo seemed annoyed.

" You don't cheer, sir," said Dick, to him.

" No, my lad. You have been too quick for me," answered Captain Nemo; " I intended to land first, and raise the flag ; it is one of my own choosing. See, here it is !"

Unbuttoning his coat, he showed a star-spangled banner.

" It shall be a joint affair," he cried, placing his flag by the side of Dick's.

" Bravo, sir," said Dick, " we represent the two greatest nations of the earth."

" Some day," Captain Nemo went on, " when Arctic discoveries make greater strides, this land will become well known. It is one of the grand secrets of the future."

Professor Crab at once pronounced the land to be of volcanic origin, though no crater in activity could be seen.

Vegetation was very sparse.

A few lichens grew upon the black rocks, there were no trees, or shrubs, and the prospect was not inviting.

But if the land was barren, the air and the sea swarmed with life ; the former was filled with birds, who flew in eddying circles over the heads of the party, and the sea was the home of innumerable whales, seal, and walrus.

To the great delight of the captain and the professor, the sun rose a little before midday, for without its appearance they could have made no observations.

In a day or two's time, that is to say, on the twenty-first of March, the day of the equinox, the sun would have disappeared for six months; these regions having half a year of day and the same quantity of night.

Employing his chronometer, the captain found that at midday the sun's disc was evenly cut by the horizon of the north.

" I am satisfied," he said, calmly ; " we are really at the South Pole."

The professor was profoundly agitated at this brilliant scientific discovery, and remained silent for some minutes.

The sun slowly sank and the atmosphere became overclouded.

" Adieu," said the captain, extending his hand to the dying sun; " sleep in the bosom of this open sea and leave a night of six months to extend its shadows over our new land."

Soon the snow began to fall heavily, and the wind whirled the graceful flakes in every direction.

The party regained the ship and were glad to get below, where an excellent dinner of various kinds of wild fowl, recently killed, awaited them.

Winter had commenced.

On the following day the cold became intense, and the thermometer fell twelve degrees.

A thin ice began to form, the birds and the whales sought a warmer climate, only the seals and the walrus remained to brave the long period of coming cold.

The " Enigma " replenished her supply of air and sank slowly to a depth of a thousand feet, when her screw beat the waves and she advanced straight to the north at the utmost speed of which she was capable.

Towards evening she was making her way under the immense mass of ice which lay directly over her.

The professor was lost in admiration of the captain's daring.

Dick thought of the many wonders he had seen.

Ted and Messiter played at draughts ; it did not matter much where they went to, and they took everything as it came, like philosophers.

Towards eleven o'clock in the morning Dick was awakened by a violent shock.

The furniture in the cabin was overthrown.

It was clear that the " Enigma " had violently struck against something.

The professor was thrown out of his bed.

Ted and Messiter were quickly on their feet.

All looked anxiously at one another, and turned pale.

At this moment Captain Nemo entered the cabin, and for the first time since they had known him, they remarked that he was profoundly agitated.

"What has happened, sir?" inquired the professor.

"We have struck against an iceberg which has been travelling under the ice," replied the captain.

"Is our passage barred?"

"Unfortunately, yes. It is useless to attempt to return; our only chance lies in going on, but as our way lies through a comparatively small space, this iceberg prevents our doing so."

"We are hopelessly blocked, then?" said Professor Crab, with a voice of resignation.

"Yes."

Overhead was an impenetrable barrier of ice, and, unless the berg could be cut through in its thinnest part, their position was indeed deplorable.

"I knew how it would be," exclaimed Ted; "those mad tricks of going to Poles, where no one has ever been before, are sure to turn out wrong. Besides, what luck could we expect in a ship like this 'ere which is more like the devil's boat than——"

"Ted," said Dick, "will you hold your row?"

"Certainly, sir. I'm only an odd boy, I know that, but I have my feelings," replied Ted, using his favourite phrase.

The captain spoke again.

"Gentlemen," he said, in a more calm and collected tone, "there are two ways of dying in the condition in which we are."

He resembled at that moment a professor of mathematics who was explaining a problem to his pupils.

"The first," he continued, "is to die crushed to pieces by the ice which is floating this way; the second is to be suffocated. I do not speak of death by hunger, because our provisions will last longer than we; so we will occupy ourselves with the chances of crushing or stifling."

"As for suffocation for want of air," said the professor, "we have nothing to fear at present, as our reservoirs are full."

"You are right," answered Captain Nemo; "but they contain only two days' supply of air. We have been thirty-six hours already under the water, and even now the heavy atmosphere of the 'Enigma' requires renewing; in forty-eight hours more our reserve will be exhausted."

"Very well, sir," said Dick; "we must get out of it somehow in forty-eight hours."

"We will try, anyhow, to pierce the wall that stops us."

"Whereabouts?" asked the professor.

"I must make an observation, and will strike at the thinnest part; though we have not much choice. I will strike the berg near the top, and my men, in their divers' dresses, will cut away at the ice with picks and axes."

"You will not refuse our poor help?" said Dick.

"Certainly not," was the reply.

"As for me," exclaimed Ted, "I shan't work. If we've got to die in twelve months, we had better die at once. For my part, I'd as soon be dead as on board this ship."

The captain shot an angry glance at Ted.

"Gentlemen," he said, "I accept the services of you three, and in return for your prompt kindness I revoke the sentence of death I passed upon you; but as for this ill-conditioned fellow, I shall so far alter his doom, as to hasten it by six months, in which time I shall put him to death."

"Perhaps you won't have the chance, governor," said Ted, boldly.

The captain waved his hand impatiently.

"Ted," said Dick, "you are my servant. I order you to join in the work without another word."

"I'll do anything for you, Master Dick," replied Ted; "but this captain cove is always on to me like grub; and, though I'm only an odd boy, I have my feelings."

"Give us your orders, captain," said the professor, briskly. "We will do anything we can for our common safety."

Captain Nemo conducted them to the dressing room, and all, even himself, put on the divers' attire.

Each had his air knapsack; but the lamps were unnecessary, as the luminous masses of ice were saturated with electric rays.

A short while afterwards the party stepped into the outer room.

The water was let in, the door opened, and they emerged upon a bank of ice.

After a brief calculation, a spot was selected to commence operations upon; and it was thought that the thickness of the ice to be cut through did not exceed ten yards.

This was a formidable task.

A tunnel had to be made, sufficiently large for the "Enigma" to float through. When this was done, they would have a long distance to travel before they could reach the open sea, and take in a fresh supply of air.

At such a time moments were worth ages.

The work was commenced and carried on with wonderful energy.

All felt they were working for their lives except Ted.

Yet he did his utmost for Dick's sake.

Captain Nemo had pardoned the others, and this made them work harder than they otherwise would have done.

With his pick, the captain marked out the dimensions of the huge ditch which had to be made.

And as many men as could work at it at once set to.

Soon huge blocks were detached, and floated away in sullen majesty.

Dick and Messiter were in the first gang; and after working for two hours like Trojans, they retired exhausted.

Immediately their place was filled by others.

The water was singularly cold.

But the exercise kept the circulation of the blood in a proper state.

When the two friends re-entered the "Enigma" to take some refreshment, they found a striking difference between the air of the ship, already charged with carbonic acid gas, and that which they had been breathing in their helmets.

For forty-eight hours the air had not been renewed, and its vivifying qualities were considerably weakened.

Time went on; and in twelve hours the crew had only succeeded in cutting away about one yard of the ice wall.

If the work was to go on at that rate, it would require five nights and four days to get through.

"Five nights and four days," said the professor, as he joined the others, "and we have only two days' air in the reservoirs."

"Without counting," replied Dick, "that when we have cut through the berg, we have a long way to go before we can get up to the surface, for the ice-field over our head must extend a great distance."

Horrible reflection!

It seemed as if work was useless, and that nothing could save them from a death by suffocation.

Were they destined to perish in this ice tomb? It seemed like it.

But each bravely concealed his fears, and resolved to do his duty.

In the morning came a fresh danger.

The professor remarked that the cold was more intense.

The thermometer fell, and as the ditch extended, and the water flowed into it, it was seen to freeze, and it threatened to undo the work that had been accomplished.

The men ran the risk of being frozen in as they worked.

He re-entered the ship, and at once communicated his fears to the captain.

"I knew it hours ago," replied the captain, who was always calm, even in the most terrible situations.

"What can be done?" asked Professor Crab.

"Nothing, I fear; we must push on the work, and try to get out before the process of solidification is complete, that is all."

During the day everyone continued to work, though the herculean task seemed hopeless.

To Dick it was a relief to put on the helmet and breathe the fresh air supplied to the knapsack from the reservoir, as the condition of the ship became more and more insupportable.

Towards the evening another yard had been cut in the ice wall.

The captain opened the reservoirs and shot some fresh air through the ship.

Unless this precaution had been taken, those who slept would never have awakened more.

On the morning of the 27th of March Dick and his companions began at the fifth yard; but as the walls on each side were chipped away, they began to thicken as the water froze.

What was the use of excavating?

It seemed as if they were between the jaws of a monster, which was slowly closing upon them.

The most ingenious savage could not have invented a more awful death.

Professor Crab saw that the ice came nearer and nearer to the "Enigma," as the water froze.

He touched the captain on the arm, and pointed this out to him.

Captain Nemo made him a sign to follow him, and they re-entered the ship together.

When their helmets were removed, the latter said—

"We must do something heroic, Mr. Crab, or we shall be sealed up in the ice which creeps upon us hour by hour."

"I can think of nothing," said the professor.

"I fear the ship is not strong enough to bear the pressure when the ice closes all around us."

"If it were strong enough, what then?"

"My dear sir," returned the captain, "don't you see, that if we hold out, we might be saved, and the only means that occurs to me is to stop the solidification."

"How?"

"We must heat the water, and by lessening the temperature, we shall keep the passage we are cutting open, and also prevent ourselves from being crushed up like a match-box."

"How long have we to breathe?" asked the professor.

"To-morrow night the air reservoirs will be empty."

This was an utterance of fate.

The professor trembled in every limb, and a cold sweat broke out all over his body.

CHAPTER XXIII.

A NARROW ESCAPE.

THE professor was unable to continue the conversation for a brief space.

The precious supply of air was failing them.

Those who were at work were obliged to consume a large quantity, and all would be exhausted shortly.

"Yes," said the captain, breaking the oppressive silence; "nothing but boiling water can help us in this extremity."

"I am of your opinion," replied the professor. "The pumps of the ' Enigma' can send out a constant supply of hot water; this will check the freezing process."

"I will try it," said Captain Nemo.

The thermometer outside marked seven degrees below the freezing point, and the cold increased as the vast berg naturally cooled the water around it.

In the kitchen of the ship there was a vast apparatus for creating water by evaporation and making it fit to drink.

These were filled with water, and all the electric heat of the galvanic piles was put in action to heat the liquid, which in a few minutes attained a warmth of a hundred degrees.

As fast as the water became hot it was pumped into the sea, and a fresh supply taken in, so that a constant stream of boiling water was sent out.

In three hours after this work commenced the thermometer marked six degrees, and two hours later it was only four.

"We are saved from the chance of being crushed," said the captain, calmly.

"Yes," replied the professor. "But we may yet be stifled."

During that night the water was only one degree below zero, and as sea-water can only freeze at two degrees, they had effected all they wanted.

On the morning of the 27th of March six yards had been cut through the wall of ice.

Four only remained to be pierced.

This involved forty-eight hours' work.

During this time it was impossible to replenish the air of the "Enigma," so that everything went from bad to worse.

An intolerable heaviness affected Dick, and towards the afternoon his head ached violently, he breathed with difficulty, and his teeth chattered.

He was seized with a mortal torpor, and had no energy left to work, while his companions were no better off than himself.

Ted bore himself better than the rest, and chafed his young master's hands, saying—

"I wish I could give you the air I take, Master Dick."

Tears came into Dick's eyes as he reflected that Ted's devotion to him had brought him into that condition.

It was a positive pleasure to find that their turn had come to work, and they felt new life come into them as they put on their diving apparatus and shouldered their pickaxes, for they could breathe better air supplied from the reservoirs, which were getting so low, that not a breath could be spared for the ship itself.

No one shirked his work.

As soon as anyone was tired he went into the dressing-room and gave his helmet to another, who gallantly took his place, returning to the vitiated and stifling air of the cabin without a murmur.

The work went on better than ever, for all were animated with the spirit of despair.

During that day two yards were removed, and only the same number remained.

Beyond this thickness, according to every calculation, lay the open sea.

But the reservoirs were nearly exhausted, and what little air was left was kept exclusively for the miners; not an atom could be spared for the "Enigma."

When Dick returned on board, he was almost suffocated.

An awful night followed.

It was difficult to breathe at all, and he feared that this sleep would be his last.

"It will be over soon," he said, in a gasping voice, as he shook Messiter's hand.

"God bless you, old boy," exclaimed Messiter, who was suffering quite as badly.

Towards the middle of the night a sort of vertigo seized them, and they felt like drunken men.

Some of the negroes who formed the crew fainted.

The captain alone preserved his coolness and his energy.

In the morning he found that including himself, only five men were fit for work.

The professor was unable to move, and lay on his back, like a fish out of water, gasping and coughing.

These five men were joined by Dick, who, ill as he was, put on his diver's dress and shouldered the pick.

"I won't be licked," he exclaimed, with that braveness which distinguishes all our British boys. "If I am to die, I will die in harness."

He staggered rather than walked to the ice.

The men worked in a listless manner, as if they had scarcely any strength left in their trembling bodies.

It appeared that the end was drawing near with fearful rapidity.

Captain Nemo watched the tottering forms at their work. He reflected, and while he thought he acted.

"Another night would set us free," he exclaimed, "but we have not the time. I must act boldly."

He called the men at work into the vessel by a sign, and at his order the "Enigma" was placed at the entrance of the narrow shaft which had been dug out of the berg.

About a yard of ice, or perhaps a little more, now separated her from the sea on the other side.

The water reservoirs were opened, and a hundred cubic yards of water taken in to increase the weight of the "Enigma," just as if she was about to sink a great depth.

This was done to make her as heavy as possible.

Dick, lying on the bed, listened intently to all the noises that struck his ears, and heard with astonishment the screw of the ship in motion.

First of all, she backed a little.

Then she was thrown with immense force against the remaining yard of ice which was at the end of the tunnel they had, with so much toil, cut through the impeding berg.

A terrible shock resulted.

The ice cracked like so much paper, making a singular noise, just as paper does when it is torn.

She began to sink down rapidly.

Ted was on his knees at Dick's side, and putting up his hand to his ear, whispered through his fevered lips—

"We are through. We are through the ice!"

Dick was unable to reply.

He seized Ted's hand and pressed it in a convulsive grasp.

Ted was right.

The vessel had forced her way through, and she fell through the water like a bullet dropped into the sea, owing to her unusual weight.

Her captain left the helmsman's cabin, when he saw that his manœuvre was carried through satisfactorily, and went to the engine-room.

The pumps were at once set to work to send out the water.

In a short time the descent was stopped and she ascended until the captain thought he had gained the proper position, when he put the screw to work again, and travelled through the water with all the speed he could put on her.

How long would this last was the question everyone asked himself.

When would the open sea be reached ?

In a few hours several would be dead.

Dick's face was violet, his lips blue, and his faculties suspended.

All he could do was to listen to the screw, which made pleasant music in his ringing ears, although he could scarcely see or hear.   •

His companions were in the same wretched state.

What was passing on board the ship none of them knew, and they were too weak and ill to go and see.

The notion of time disappeared.

They were more dead than alive.

This agony continued for some hours.

They thought they were going to die, and in reality it was only a question of time.

Near the professor's bed was an instrument which marked the speed of the vessel, and casting his eye in that direction, he saw faintly that the hand indicated the fearful speed of forty miles an hour.

They were travelling like an express on the broad gauge of the Great Western !

Certainly their gallant captain was making a grand struggle for life.

What a man he was !

Nothing could conquer him !

He persevered to the last, when none but one or two faithful slaves remained at their posts.

Again the sinking professor looked at instruments which the kindness of the captain had placed in his cabin.

This time he sought one which marked the rising or falling of the vessel.

A simple calculation showed him that they were only twenty-five feet from the surface of the sea.

This was no very great thickness of ice.

Could it not be broken ?

Perhaps.

At all events, the attempt should be made, and he felt the ship assume an oblique position as if it was intended she should strike upwards, which was easily done by the introduction of sufficient water into the chambers prepared for that purpose to disturb her equilibrium.

Then she dashed at the ice-field like a formidable ram.

Again and again the attempt was repeated, and at last, carried upwards by a supreme effort, she flew up to the slippery surface, which broke under her weight.

The panels were hastily broken open, and a flood of air rushed into every part of the vessel.

They were saved !

Ted was stouter and stronger than Dick Lightheart, and had been accustomed to a rough life.

He held out longer than his young master, and when he saw the latter sinking, he went into the room where the cases of air were kept, and taking one half used, applied it to Dick's lips.

This kept him alive, and when the panels were opened he, with Messiter's aid, helped him on the platform, which was crowded by the crew of the ship.

The captain and the professor alone did not appear.

Wonderfully refreshing was the air of heaven to the poor captives who had been so long without it, and in a very short time they recovered themselves.

" Ted, dear boy," said Dick, " you have a claim upon me now ; I shan't forget you."

" Your life was worth more than mine, sir," answered Ted, " and so I did all I could to preserve it ; though I never expected we should get out of that mess."

" We are out of it, thank goodness," exclaimed Dick.

" I expect that captain cove will get us into another before long," said Ted ; " it's my opinion, Master Dick, that he isn't quite right in his head."

" He's a rum one, anyhow," remarked Messiter.

"A born rum un, Master Harry," exclaimed Ted. "I've seen a few off their chumps at Brighton, along of drink and that, but they wouldn't live as he does. Not much. He's going to kill me—let him, if he can. My name's Walker, I tell you, as soon as I get half a chance, and it isn't long odds I don't jump into the sea and have a swim for it soon."

"Don't do anything rash, Ted," said Dick; "the captain has pardoned us, and perhaps I can induce him to let you off, though you deserve punishment for stabbing him."

" Well, sir," said Ted, "I'm only an odd boy, but I have my feelings, and it does knock me silly to hear you take the part of that captain cove, who is off his nut as sure as eggs is eggs."

Dick made no answer.

He inhaled the fresh air, breathing new life every moment, and stopped on the platform until the hatch was battened, and the ship again went on her marvellous way.

On, on, she went, round Cape Horn and to the mouth of the Amazon River; still on, on, as if the captain was burning with feverish impatience to overtake something of which he was in chase.

Dick knew very well what this fearful chase was.

But he didn't dare to say a word to anyone about the discovery that he had made

The captain wanted to find the " Belle of New Orleans," which contained the betrayer of his wife, the infamous Crawley Vipond, who had carried off his darling Adele.

The captain did not show himself at all to his captives.

He shut himself up, and was seldom encountered in the passages or on the platform.

All his orders were given to Pedro in his cabin.

About the end of the first week in April they crossed the line, and when near the mouth of the Amazon, the ship rested for two days on the water.

About ten days passed there.

Then on the 1st of May she briskly took the northern direction, floating with that extraordinary current which is called the Gulf Stream.

Messiter came to Dick in the morning and said gravely, " Something's going to happen, old boy."

" Why ?" asked Dick.

" Ted says so, but you shall hear what his reasons are. Come here, Ted."

The boy approached.

" What's up, Ted ?" inquired Dick, anxiously.

" We're going to leave the ship, sir," answered Ted.

" How do you know ?"

" You'll laugh at me," said Ted, " if I tell you, but I'll chance that, Master Dick. Look here. This is how it is. When mother died I had a dream. When father went down at sea in the storm I had the same dream. Before we were upset and picked up by the ship, it was the same thing the night before."

" You mean to say, if you dream of a certain thing, you will be sure to have a violent change in your position," said Messiter.

" Just so, sir; I'm only an odd boy, but this is gospel truth."

" What did you dream of ?"

" White snakes," replied Ted, in a half whisper. " Last night they came to me awful bad, just like a lot of those nasty polypusses things. They swarmed over me all night long, and I knew something would happen when I dreamt of white snakes."

" Well," said Dick, " I shan't be sorry for a change. Shall you, Harry ?"

" Not I," replied Messiter; " I only hope Ted's strange dream can be relied upon."

The ship was lying on the surface to renew her supply of air, and while the boys were talking the distant sound of a cannon was heard.

" What's that ?" cried Dick, springing up.

" Sounds like a shot," exclaimed Messiter.

" Come to the platform. Quick," cried Dick.

Ted slowly followed his young master, rubbing his hands with glee.

" I knew something was bound to happen," he muttered; " I never dream of white snakes for nothing. We shall have a barney on board soon, and I'm not sorry for it. That captain cove is too much for me. If I am only an odd boy, I've got my feelings."

With his favourite phrase on his lips, he made his way to the platform, whither Dick and Harry had already preceded him.

CHAPTER XXIV.

A STRANGE SAIL.

"WHAT is it, sir?" asked Ted, eagerly.

"A cannon shot," exclaimed Dick, "and there is another. Look at the puff of smoke coming from that big ship over there. Duck, my lads, it's getting hot."

The report was now heard, and a ball ploughed up the sea at some little distance.

A large ship was steaming down upon them, and discharging shots at intervals at her, though it was extremely doubtful whether the people on board knew what they were firing at.

"She may fire away and sink us, for what I care," said Ted.

"What nation is she?" asked Messiter.

"I fancy I can see the stars and stripes flying," answered Dick. "If so, she is a Yankee."

The strange sail continued to advance rapidly, and as she carried big guns, it was dangerous to allow the strange vessel to remain on the water to be shot at.

"Where's the captain?" asked Dick.

"Below in his cabin. Can't you hear his organ going? He always pretends not to care when anything is going to happen," replied Messiter.

"Do you think he knows?"

"What is there an old fox like that does not know?" said Messiter, laughing.

"Tell you what," exclaimed Ted, "we shall have a chance soon, sir; I don't dream of white snakes for nothing."

"How do you mean, Ted?" asked Dick.

"Why, if the ship comes nearer, we can throw ourselves into the sea, and swim to her."

"Not a bad idea," exclaimed Dick, thoughtfully.

There was nothing impossible in jumping into the sea and keeping afloat until picked up by the boats of the strange ship.

"Go below and bring up a glass," said Dick, after a pause.

Ted did so, and Dick turned the telescope towards the vessel, at whose peak a small flag was flying.

On it he read this name—

The " Belle of New Orleans."

After what he had learnt of the captain's history, this came like a revelation upon him.

The strange ship was the one which the captain had been looking for during five long years.

On board her was his enemy, Crawley Vipond, who had stolen from him his loved wife, Adele.

The guilty pair were far from thinking that in attacking what seemed to them a strange monster, they were drawing near to their relentless foe.

"Something terrible will happen in an hour or two," exclaimed Dick, lowering the glass.

"You think so, sir?" asked Ted.

"I can't tell what is written in the book of fate," answered Dick, "but I'll take odds you will see something presently."

After a time Dick descended with Messiter, who asked him a variety of questions, but Dick was not in the humour to talk.

"Another time, Harry," he answered, "I will tell you all."

He was strangely excited, for he felt a horrible tragedy was contemplated.

There could not be less than fifty souls on board the strange ship, and all were doomed.

The panel was shut, but the " Enigma" remained on the surface as if she had nothing to fear.

Night came.

A perfect silence reigned on board.

Dick heard the measured beat of the screw as it struck the waves with rapid regularity.

"'LET HIM DROP GENTLY. THAT'S IT. LOWER AWAY,' SAID TED."

He could not sleep, for he thought it was to be a night of horror.

The greater part of the night passed without any incident of importance, except that the " Belle of New Orleans" appeared to be flying from their vessel, which was pursuing her.

The " Belle of New Orleans " was not more than a mile off, but they did not appear to be gaining very quickly upon her.

Occasionally she fired a shot, which disturbed the calm quietude of the night, doing no damage, as it fell harmlessly into the sea.

Towards morning a thick mist arose, which shut out all sight of the large ship.

The captain ordered the vessel's progress to be stopped, as it was useless to continue the chase until the sun caused the fog to lift.

He directed his steps to his cabin, when all at once a loud explosion was heard in the engine-room.

Everyone rose, and rushed in that direction.

" Back, gentlemen," exclaimed the captain, in the corridor, " there may be danger."

The professor and his companions halted, and looked curiously in front of them.

Flashes of light were dancing about the machinery, which showed that the electricity had made its escape somehow.

A quarter of an hour elapsed, during which time the captain, with his usual courage, entered the room with Pedro.

When they emerged, a gang of men were given some orders and set to work at once.

" I hope nothing serious has happened," exclaimed the professor.

" No lives are lost, happily," was the reply, " though the first engine is hurt. The machinery has broken down badly, I am sorry to say."

" Broken down ?"

" Yes. It is annoying when I am in sight of my prey, for I shall not be able to get my vessel under way again for twelve hours."

The professor looked pleased with the intelligence.

As if he divined his thoughts, the captain continued—

" You rest assured, that ship shall not escape me. I will scour the seas in all directions for her."

Dick returned to the cabin.

" Where's Ted ?" he asked. " I can't sleep, and I should like one of the captain's cigars."

Ted was nowhere to be found.

But in half an hour's time the lad entered the cabin on tiptoe, having his finger on his nose, which was his way of enjoining silence.

" Where have you been slinking to ?" inquired Dick.

" It's all ready," exclaimed Ted, in a whisper.

" What is ?"

Ted beckoned to the professor and Messiter, who approached him.

" They're all in the engine-room, doing up the machinery," he continued.

" Well, what then ?" asked Dick.

" You know the iron boat they've got, which takes to pieces and puts together ?"

" Yes."

" I've been and sneaked it bit by bit," continued Ted, in a tone of triumph.

" You have ?" said Dick, admiringly.

" Yes; and I put it together stunning, I have."

" Bravo, Ted; you're a genius," exclaimed Messiter.

" I don't know what it is, sir; but if I am only an odd boy, I have my feelings, and can't stand that captain cove, not at any price, and not by any manner of means," answered Ted.

" If I understand rightly," said the professor, " you mean to tell us that you have a boat on the platform ready for us to escape in."

Ted nodded his head violently.

" All being occupied with the disaster which has befallen the machinery, you think we can mount to the platform and get away unobserved ?"

" Blessed if you don't talk like a book, sir," said Ted.

" How about grub ?" asked Messiter.

" That we must chance," said Ted.

" We're not near any land," said Dick.

" Some ship may pick us up," said Ted, " at any rate, I mean to risk it, and I'm off in five minutes by myself if none of you ain't got the pluck to join me."

" I'll come," said Dick, decidedly.

" And I," said Messiter.

" Well, if you are all bent on going,"

remarked the professor, "I suppose I must accompany you. Just let me put my scientific notes in my pocket, and I shall be ready. Who leads the way?"

"I'm first," replied Ted; "Master Dick and Master Messiter next, and you can come up last, sir, like the old owl asked out to the birds' party."

"What did he do, Ted?" asked the professor, with a smile.

"I haven't time to tell you the story, now, sir; but you are the born himage of that there howl," answered Ted, grinning.

"Suppose the captain or any of his men should twig the little game," suggested Dick.

Ted's countenance became grave at once.

Putting his hand inside his belt, he drew out his knife, and held it up, letting it flash dangerously in the electric light which burned in the cabin.

"It's sink or swim with me this time," he said in a half whisper, "and I don't mean to be licked if I can help it. See this."

"Put it away. Someone might come in," said Messiter, nervously.

Ted replaced the knife.

"I mean to stick someone if I get half a chance," said Ted, with a grin, "and if that captain cove interferes with me, I shall be on to him like grub, and no flies. I'm only an odd boy, but——"

"Don't talk so much," interrupted Dick "You go on like an eight-day clock when you're wound up."

"All right, sir, I'm off. Don't funk, Mr. Crab."

"What does he mean by funking?" asked the professor, in a puzzled manner. "Is it a nautical term?"

"No, sir," replied Dick, "he means don't get frightened."

"I am a little nervous, but you can rely upon me at a pinch," replied the professor.

"The coves are all in the engine-room," Ted went on. "I've been piping them off."

"What does he say?" asked the professor.

"I've been a-foxing of them, sir."

"What is that? I really am at a loss to understand your meaning. Your conversation is such a peculiar and perplex-

ing mixture of slang and English, regard less of grammar, that——"

"Never mind what he says. sir," interrupted Dick, impatiently. "If we are going to make this bolt, we mustn't waste time."

"I am silent. Lead on," answered the professor.

"I'd give something," said Messiter, "to be playing 'shell out,' at some billiard-room in Brighton."

"You're a rat," replied Dick; "I like excitement. This just suits me. I feel as if I could back the field—that's ourselves—against the favourite—that's the captain—though he's no favourite of mine."

"And take long odds, I should think," answered Messiter.

"Ted's off. Now for business," replied Dick.

Every face wore an anxious expression, and in spite of Dick's banter, his heart was beating more quickly than he cared to admit, even to himself.

The captain was not a man to be trifled with.

He was, moreover, as powerful and absolute on board his strange craft as a sultan in the East is over his despotically ruled subjects.

His deadliest enemy had been in sight of him only a short time before, and he had hoped to send him to the bottom with all his crew and with the false woman who had betrayed her husband.

At the very moment when revenge appeared within his grasp the cup was dashed from his lips.

A dense fog had arisen on the surface of the ocean, fading for a time every object from view.

To add to the calamity, the complicated machinery of the vessel had just broken down.

This necessitated a long delay.

No wonder the captain fumed and fretted, and that his whole mind was bent upon repairing the machinery as soon as possible.

When he had killed the man who had ruined his happiness for ever he would have attained the object of his life.

It was hard to be frustrated when his prey was within sight.

He bestowed no thought upon his captives.

If he was thus remiss, there was one who did not forget the prisoners.

This man was Pedro.

Pedro, the right hand of the captain, a man who, though a negro, was at once sagacious, faithful, and bold as a lion.

Hearing footsteps continually passing up and down the staircase in the centre of the vessel, his suspicions were aroused.

He went up to the platform, and looked about him.

The mist was so dense that for a moment he could see nothing.

Presently a spectral form passed him, and seemed to glide over the side of the ship, which was, as we know, from her peculiar construction, almost flush with the water.

Peering into the fog, he saw the outline of a boat.

In this boat was a human being.

Without any hesitation he let himself fall into it, and found himself by Ted's side.

"What is this?" he asked.

Ted gave one glance at the swarthy skin of the negro, and his determination was taken. It was his life or Pedro's.

Perhaps the lives of his companions would also this time pay for the rashness of his daring scheme.

His hand sought his belt, and without a word he drew his knife and plunged it up to the hilt in the negro's body.

The blow was so well aimed that Pedro's heart was pierced, and he expired without a groan.

His body fell across the thwarts and lay motionless as a log.

The next instant Dick and Messiter let themselves down into the boat.

A sickening smell, such as is always sent up from recently-spilt human blood, assailed their nostrils.

Dick's foot slipped in a pool of the ruby fluid.

"Are you hurt, Ted?" were his first words.

"No, sir," was the reply.

"What has happened?"

"Only a nigger dead, sir," answered Ted. "I'm very sorry, but I was obliged to do it. Give us a hand to clear the boat. Let him drop gently. That's it. So—h. Lower away."

Pedro's body was allowed to fall into the sea.

Dick asked no more questions.

He could easily guess now what had taken place.

Though he shuddered at the idea of taking life, he felt it was necessary, and with a sigh he awaited the coming of the professor.

Minutes elapsed, and he did not make his appearance.

"What's got old daddy long-legs?" said Ted, in the same low tone in which all their conversation was carried on.

"Can't imagine," replied Dick.

"Hadn't you best go and look after him, Ted?" said Messiter.

"Not if know it, sir," replied Ted, "none of us three must go on board that ship again, unless we want to enter our graves."

"Is it safe to stop here?"

"Not long; but I don't like to leave a pal."

The boys scarcely knew how to act.

To stay where they were was undoubtedly dangerous, for their absence might be at any moment discovered.

Professor Crab had for so long a period been their kind and instructive companion in captivity, that they were extremely reluctant to desert him.

Still they could not wait for him any great length of time.

To do so would have been madness.

He knew perfectly well what their intention was, and had agreed to join them in their bold attempt.

When Dick and Messiter quitted the cabin, he had said he would follow them almost directly.

Something must have happened.

Wearily passed the moments, which seemed ages.

Messiter sat in the stern, waiting to shove off.

Dick and Ted had each grasped an oar, and were prepared to pull vigorously through the water at the first signal of alarm.

So passed five minutes.

CHAPTER XXV.

PICKED UP.

THE boys could hear their hearts beat. No sound broke the stillness of the night, save the mournful plashing of the waves against the iron side of the ship.

At length their anxiety became so intense that they could bear it no longer.

"I must go and see what has become of the professor," muttered Dick.

"You shan't," replied Messiter.

"Why not?"

"If you do, you will get collared. We've got a good chance of escaping, and we must be flats if we lose it."

"But," said Dick, "it isn't manly to desert a companion."

"Under the circumstances," answered Messiter, "we are justified in looking after ourselves."

"I shan't be a minute," cried Dick; "let me go. I can take care of myself, Harry."

"I'm blowed if you shall go," replied Messiter.

As he spoke, he shoved off the boat with a vigorous push, but just at that moment the professor tumbled into the boat with a groan, lying still as if suffering pain.

"Pull away, Ted. It's all right; Mr. Crab is in," he continued.

"Gently, Master Harry, don't kick up no more row than you can help," replied Ted.

The boat glided swiftly into the mist, and the gloomy form of the iron ship began to fade away from their sight.

When they had gone some distance, Messiter, who had been speaking to the professor, said—

"Mr. Crab has hurt himself in falling, but he hopes it is not much."

They pulled on steadily for about a mile.

Then Dick stopped.

"Let me take a pull," said Messiter, "you must be pretty well blown."

"No, it isn't that. I'm good for a five mile spin now," answered Dick. "But I don't think it advisable to go any further at present."

"You're captain, now, Master Dick," said Ted. "Isn't that right, Master Harry?"

"Quite right; Dick's head is worth both ours put together."

"Thank you for the compliment," replied Dick, smiling, "though I think we must admit we owe our escape to Ted, and when we come across our grog again we'll drink his health with musical honours."

"That would puzzle us now, unless we did it in salt water," said Messiter.

"If I am to be captain you must listen to me, and obey orders," exclaimed Dick.

"Certainly," replied both in a breath.

"My plan is to stay here till the mist lifts, because the captain cannot follow us until his machinery is repaired. Do you see?"

"Yes. What next?"

"I think we stand a chance of being picked up by that big ship we have been pursuing. She can't be far off, and we were close to her when the fog came on."

"Lucky for her, wasn't it?" said Messiter.

"Rather. I think the captain meant to force the ship at full speed right through her, just as a conical shot would go through a wooden vessel."

"Why?"

"I can't tell you the whole story now," answered Dick, "but I know enough of our strange skipper's history to say that the man of all others he hates most is the captain of that ship."

"I see."

"Therefore, if we are picked up by her, we must not say we have ever seen Harold Dugard."

"Who?" asked Messiter, in surprise.

"Harold Dugard. That's the captain's real name."

"Do you know anything?" asked Messiter.

"If we do say anything about him, Crawley Vipond will probably kill us."

"Who is Crawley Vipond?"

"The captain of the big ship called the 'Belle of New Orleans,' and Harold Dugard's enemy."

"Why his enemy?"

"Because he stole his wife, Adele, and keeps her now on board that vessel," replied Dick.

"What shall we do and say?" inquired Messiter.

"Oh! cook up some lie or other, in self-defence. Let me see, we sailed from Honduras in the mahogany ship 'Emma of Hartlepool,' and all hands were lost except us three. Can you think of that?"

"I'll try," replied Messiter.

"It won't do to make a mull of it," said Dick. "Suppose you and Ted are deaf and dumb? Then you can leave it all to me and Mr. Crab."

"Hang it all," exclaimed Messiter, "that's a little too hard. I don't mind being dumb for a time, but I won't be deaf. What do you say, Ted?"

"Must obey orders, sir," replied Ted, with a grin.

"Very well," continued Dick, "I'll let you off the deafness, but directly we are taken on board, if we should be picked up by the 'Belle of New Orleans,' you two are dumb, and that is arranged."

"Yes," answered both.

"That will leave the lying to me," Dick went on, "and, although I'm not a good hand at that sort of thing——"

"Don't be modest, Dick," interrupted Messiter.

"I only leave the truth in the lurch," said Dick, "when it is a matter of life and death to do so. A man who would tell the truth in our circumstances would be an ass. Crawley Vipond would think we were spies of Harold Dugard; we should have a long rope and a short shrift."

Neither Ted nor Messiter liked the idea of being dumb, but they reflected that it would only be for a short time.

They intended to leave the ship that picked them up at the first port.

"We are not yet on board," said Dick, after a pause. "So we mustn't count our chickens before they are hatched."

"It's worth anything to be out of the 'Enigma,'" said Messiter.

"So it is, Master Harry," said Ted. "You're right for once in your life. I've got my liberty now."

"And like me, you are willing to chance the rest, I suppose."

"I'll chance it all the way if ever I meet that captain cove again. Remember, I'm on to him like grub. If I'm only an odd boy, I've got my feelings."

There was another pause, which was broken by Messiter, who said, "I feel so happy I should like to sing a song."

"Strike up 'I'm a bold sailor boy,'" said Ted, "and I'll join you in the coal-box."

"What's that?" asked Messiter.

"Why, the chorus. My father learnt me that song, and a song he said was nothing without the coal-box."

"If you fellows are going to be dumb," remarked Dick, "you'd best not begin to practise it."

"Not at all," answered Messiter. "I want to make the most of my tongue while I can."

"I don't think," said the professor, in a low voice, "that I shall be much trouble to you, for I feel very ill. The excitement I have gone through has been too much for me, added to the confinement on board that horrible ship. I have also injured my head when I fell into the boat, and I feel as if a serious attack of illness was coming on."

"Don't say that, sir," said Dick.

"Leave me alone, and I will try to bear up. I won't be any drag upon you if I can help it."

Dick did not know until then that the professor was much hurt, but he directed his attention to him and bound up his head, which he had struck against one of the thwarts.

Suddenly Ted exclaimed—

"The mist's lifting, sir."

"So it is, Ted," answered Dick, as the air was agitated by a slight breeze, and the eastern horizon was suffused with a pale yellow.

"Daybreak for a hundred," observed Messiter.

"Light ahead, sir," cried Ted.

"Where away?"

"On the larboard bow," answered Ted.

"Pull now, my lads," said Dick, joyfully. "It can't be the electric light of the 'Enigma,' because we know she is on our right. It must be the 'Belle of New Orleans.' Stick to it, Ted; put some strength into it; we have no time to lose, or the ' Belle of New Orleans' will be off again as soon as she can see her way to get her steam up."

The boys bent over their oars, and the little boat flew over the waves in the direction of a bright red light which appeared from its position to be hoisted half mast high.

In a short time the breeze, aided by the rising sun, dissipated the mist.

Dick looked around him.

About a mile and a half off lay the black carcase of the strange ship, more resembling a dead whale than anything else.

A mile off on the other side was the vessel that the captain had been pursuing so relentlessly.

The smoke was already rising from the funnels as the fires were lighted preparatory to making a start.

" Hoist your handkerchief on the end of an oar, Harry," exclaimed Dick.

" All right," replied Messiter, doing as he was told.

" Wave it, because I want to attract the attention of those on board the ship."

" There is someone on the platform of the ' Enigma,' " answered Messiter, whose eye was as sharp as a hawk's.

" That's the captain—I'll bet he's mad," said Ted.

" Never mind him. Our only chance of safety lies in getting on board the ' Belle of New Orleans.' Pull away," replied Dick.

They pulled in silence until they were within a short distance of the ship.

The beat of the engines now made itself heard.

She was in the act of starting.

" Give her a hail," said Messiter; " she'll be off."

" Ahoy there ! Ship ahoy, ahoy, ahoy !" cried Dick, as loud as he could.

" Ahoy, ahoy !" cried the others, joining in the chorus.

The beat of the engines stopped.

They had been heard.

Another ten minutes sufficed to bring the boat alongside, and the boys clambered up the chains and got on deck, while the professor was lifted up in a sling.

A tall, thin man, with a closely-shaven face, advanced to meet them.

" Who are you ?" he inquired.

" Castaways, sir," replied Dick, making a bow.

" What ship ?"

Dick told him they were apprentices on board a ship trading in mahogany from Honduras to Hartlepool, which had been wrecked in a storm, they only contriving to get into the boat ; that his companions were dumb, and that they had been two days and one night without food, and that the professor was a passenger, who had been taken ill.

" I will give you a passage to the first port," answered the gentleman, who was the captain ; " you will have to mess with the crew. Go forward. The passenger who is ill shall be placed in a berth and attended to."

Turning away, he spoke to his lieutenant, and immediately the measured beat of the engines was heard.

The ship began to forge ahead and was soon dashing through the foaming waves, now roughly agitated by the rising breeze.

CHAPTER XXVI.

A DUMB BOY.

DICK saw that the name of the ship which had picked him up was the " Belle of New Orleans."

This set all doubts in his mind at rest.

He was on board the vessel owned by Crawley Vipond, the treacherous and false friend of Harold Dugard, otherwise Captain Nemo, of the " Enigma."

A strange curiosity to see Adele, the wife of Harold Dugard, took possession of him.

He did not doubt that he should have the opportunity before long.

Dick's first care was to see the professor carefully placed in a berth.

He was really very ill.

Dick advised him not to say anything to anybody, and to leave the management of affairs to him.

This he promised to do.

The first mate had a knowledge of surgery, and he said that the professor required profound rest for a few days, as his nervous system had been over-taxed, and the wound in his head might bring on brain fever, but that, if kept quiet, he would soon be well.

Ted wandered about the ship, looking here and there with boyish curiosity.

She was a fine vessel of modern build, well-fitted, and fully manned.

Messiter leant against the main mast, glad to think he had gained his freedom, and wondering what new adventure awaited him.

A sailor came up to him, and ex-claimed—

" Now then, you lazy lubber, I guess you'll have to stir your stumps on board this craft."

" Eh ?" said Messiter, forgetting he was dumb.

" The captain didn't tell you you was to be waited on, did he ?" continued the sailor.

" He !" began Messiter, checking him-self immediately.

" Get out of that, or I'll help you," answered the sailor, seizing a rope's end.

" I——"

Before he could commit himself further the sailor struck him across the shoulder.

" Oh !" cried Messiter.

He rubbed his back, and shaking his fist, exclaimed—

" You——"

But recollecting he was dumb, he broke off abruptly.

" Well, I'm blowed," said the sailor. " They say you're dumb, but you know your vowels. You've said A E I O U. Can't you go through the alphabet ?"

Messiter laughed, and shook his head.

He had, without intending to do so, gone through the vowels.

Moving away he joined Dick, who was looking over the taffrail at the strange vessel which they were fast leaving be-hind.

He could imagine the rage of her cap-tain, first at finding his captives gone, secondly at beholding the ship he had been chasing showing him a clean pair of heels, which he was powerless to follow until the breakdown in his machinery was made good.

Messiter was about to say something in a low tone, when a youngster about sixteen approached, and exclaimed—

" Are you the castaways ?"

" Yes," replied Dick.

" Captain Vipond has changed his mind respecting you."

" Indeed ?"

" I am Cyren Banks, captain of the midshipmen's mess on board the ' Belle of New Orleans,' and as we are short-handed, two of our fellows having died of yellow fever, you are to pig in with us, and do duty in your turns. How does that suit your complaint ?"

" Thank you, Mr. Banks," answered Dick ; " we don't want to eat the bread of idleness; but I am afraid my two com-panions are scarcely good enough to associate with gentlemen."

" Why not ?"

" You see I am the son of an English clergyman, and I ran away to sea; my name is Lightheart."

" Glad to make your acquaintance, Lightheart," said the midshipman.

" Same to you, Banks ; hope we shall live to be better acquainted."

" What were you going to say about your companions ?" asked Banks.

" They are of dreadfully low extrac-tion," answered Dick.

Messiter darted a severe look at Dick.

" Not thieves, I hope ?" said Banks.

" That's just it. In London, you know, street boys are often sent to train-ing ships when they do anything wrong."

" It's the same at New York."

" Is it ? Well, you will understand me better if that's the case. This poor dumb boy Messiter was brought before the beak for stealing a pig, and sent to a training ship, from which he was drifted on to a merchant vessel."

" Ha ! ha !" laughed Banks, giving Messiter a poke in the ribs, adding, " Who stole the pig ?"

Messiter was furious, but he did not dare to speak.

He saw that Dick was having a lark with him, and indulging his love of fun at his expense.

" Messiter's mother is doing time now," continued Dick. " She got five years for illegally pawning a mangle she had hired."

A sound like a howl mingled with a groan broke from Messiter.

" Poor fellow," continued Dick, " he feels it very much. He used to be very fond of his mother, I believe, for she used to let him have all he could cadge, and never licked him with the strap if he brought home from the streets anything over a bob."

"What's his father?"

"Oh, he's a lifer."

"What's that?"

"Got penal servitude for life for kicking a man to death and then biting his nose off," replied Dick.

Messiter was red with passion, and glanced fiercely at Dick.

At this moment Ted came up.

"Here's the other," exclaimed Dick; "he never knew his parents, and has lived principally on doorsteps and in the workhouse, with an occasional stay in a gaol."

It was Ted's turn now to stare.

"We must look after our valuables," said Banks, with a laugh.

"You should lock up the spoons, I tell you," answered Dick; "that fellow Ted would rob a blind man."

"I'll watch him. Tell you what," said Banks, "we will make them do all the dirty work. They shall be our servants, and if they shirk we'll cob them, eh?"

"That's it," replied Dick; "lay it on thick. That Messiter is very idle and sulky."

"Will you come below? It's time the grog was served."

"I shan't be long. Go on first," answered Dick.

Banks nodded, and the three friends were left together.

There was no one near them, so they were not afraid of speaking.

"You're a nice fellow," cried Messiter. "What the deuce do you mean by it? I've a very good mind to punch your head."

"Don't do that, Harry," answered Dick, laughing. "We've been so dull lately I thought you'd enjoy a little fun."

"Not at my own expense. Fancy saying I was a thief and stole a pig."

"And that I had been in gaol. It's too bad, Master Dick," said Ted. "If I am only an odd boy, I've got my feelings."

"You'd better be civil, both of you, or I'll get you a cobbing," said Dick.

"If you do, I'll blow the gaff," replied Ted.

"Then you will be put in irons as an impostor."

"And you too."

"Oh, no, I shall get out of it. Don't get riled. Come below and have some grog," said Dick.

Very sullenly the two dumb boys followed Dick into the midshipmen's cabin, where Banks and two others were assembled.

CHAPTER XXVII.

HOW TO MAKE A DUMB BOY SPEAK.

"MR. LIGHTHEART," said Banks, "allow me to introduce you to Menzies and Stevens, the other officers of the midshipmen's mess. I guess we shall all knock in like old friends."

Dick bowed, so did Stevens and Menzies.

"We've got up a little bit of a spread in your honour," continued Banks. "It's not up to much, but as I hear you've been without food since the wreck, perhaps you won't mind falling to without further ceremony."

"Not a ha'porth," replied Dick.

"You two fellows," continued Banks, to Ted and Messiter, "will wait at table, and then, like savages, you can pick up the crumbs that are left."

With a bad grace Ted took his place behind Dick's chair.

Messiter, however, sat on a locker, and would not move.

"Is he deaf as well as dumb?" asked Banks.

"Not he," answered Dick; "the lazy beggar can hear well enough."

"All right; we'll cob him when we've fed. I'll teach him who stole the pig. Here, you Ted, hand round the pea soup."

Messiter felt hungry when he smelt the savoury soup, and was quite wild with Dick for the way in which he had treated him.

"It's too bad," he muttered; "a joke's a joke, but this is going too far."

"What sort of ship's this?" said Dick.

"Very tidy," answered Menzies.

"Where are you bound?"

"Nowhere in particular. Our captain is a gentleman of fortune, and prefers the sea to the land, so he sails about from place to place. We have good pay, good grub, and plenty of liberty when in port."

"So you've got nothing to grumble at."

"No, I guess our lines are cast in pleasant places, Mr. Lightheart," answered Menzies.

"Never been in any danger," said Dick.

"Well, I've had my share," returned Menzies.

"Have you now? I'm fond of stories of adventure, danger, and such things. Can't you tell us some, while I'm tucking in the grub?"

"On land or sea—which will you have?" asked Menzies.

"Oh, it don't much matter, but as we are at sea, pitch the yarn ashore."

"You are a strange card," said Menzies.

"Yes, I was born so. Heave ahead. I can't bear to be kept waiting," Dick said, eating as he spoke.

"Well, I have crossed the desert," began Menzies.

"Eh?" said Dick. "Have you been across the desert?"

"Yes."

"Oh, you know something, then. Fire away. I'm all attention."

"I have felt the burning sun streaming down upon my head, and the hot sands blister my feet, while my thirst was so great as to be almost intolerable."

"Why didn't you drink, then?" said Dick.

"Our supply of water had become exhausted, and we travelled on, hoping to reach a spot where we could obtain a fresh supply. Struggling, fainting, almost despairing, and then it was we came upon a scene that I shall never forget till my dying day."

"What was it?" asked Dick.

"A couple of victims to thirst. One was dead, half-buried in the sand, the other all but gone. By his side knelt the camel he had rode, like himself, unable to move in search of the life-giving fluid, whilst overhead, whirling around with wild, discordant cry, a vulture impatiently awaited the promised feast beneath him."

Dick looked up as the other paused.

"Well," he said, "did you let him get it?"

"What could we do? We had not a drop to moisten our own lips. To stay beside the dying man, or attempt to take him on with us was to play into the hands of death; so we passed on, deploring the fate we were powerless to avert."

"And so the vulture got his banquet?" said Dick.

"Yes," replied Menzies. "When we looked back, the dying camel's eyes were turned with a despairing glance upon his shrieking foe, now flying lower and lower. Then we saw the head droop and the bird swoop down upon its prey, while a flock were skimming across the desert, having scented the feast afar off."

"Then travelling in the desert is not always a good thing," said Dick.

"No," replied Menzies, "and I never wish to cross it again."

"Don't you? Well, I hope to have the pleasure of doing so. But I think I shall do now," said Dick, lolling back, and wiping his mouth.

When the eating was over, Ted and Messiter; were allowed to regale themselves on the scraps.

Had they not been hungry they would have refused.

Dick went on deck, but Banks and Menzies stayed below.

"Oh! there's that cobbing to come off," said Banks.

"I've got a rope's end," exclaimed Menzies, "will you hold him while I lay in; where is Stevens?"

"It's his watch."

"Never mind. I'll collar him."

Before he could offer any resistance, Messiter was seized from behind, dragged upon the table and laid upon his face.

In an instant a shower of blows with the thick heavy rope's end descended on his back and shoulders.

"Here, I say. Hallo! Hold hard," cried Messiter, forgetting he was dumb.

"Drop it," said Ted, at the same time, as he gave the cobber a blow in the eye.

The rope fell from Menzies' hand.

Banks released his victim, and stared round him in amazement.

"Well," he cried, "may I be jiggered

half mast high if this isn't a lick. We've made the dumb speak."

" I believe it's some plant," said Menzies.

' So do I. The age of miracles is past. I'll go and report to Captain Vipond."

"Cut on. I'll keep guard over these two coves," exclaimed Menzies.

Banks sprang up the ladder and was soon on deck.

"What's up?" asked Dick, who saw his haste.

" Perhaps you know as well as I do," answered Banks, rudely.

Dick was puzzled.

He descended to the cabin, and Menzies explained to him in a few words what had happened.

"So you can talk, can you?" said Dick. " You deceitful beggars. What do you mean by shamming?"

" It's your fault," answered Messiter. " I shouldn't have hollared if you had not begun chaffing, and got me a cobbing."

"Oh, Harry, Harry," exclaimed Dick, with mock seriousness ; " you ought to have been flayed alive before you let on. But no matter, leave it all to me."

" What are we to say?"

" Say nothing. Refer everybody to me, that's all you have got to do."

At this juncture, the first lieutenant entered the cabin and exclaimed in a gruff voice—

" You three lads have to come to the captain's cabin at once."

" Lead the way," answered Dick, waving his hand with a tragic air ; " we are prepared to die ; but I warn you, Mr. Yankee, that we are English, and the British lion is not one of those animals with whose tail you can trifle with impunity."

Dick was in his element now a new danger had arisen.

He liked to get into rows and difficulties just for the excitement and fun of getting out of them.

Once, when in London for a holiday, he got into an omnibus without a farthing in his pocket to pay his fare, just for the amusement of having a row with the conductor at the end of the journey.

He said it made boys sharp to try experiments of that kind.

But on that occasion the conductor of the 'bus took it out of him by a good kick in the rear, which made him hobble home rather lame, sadder if not wiser.

Dick said it was all in the day's work, and his motto was, you must give and take in this world.

The lieutenant led the way to Captain Vipond's cabin, which was sumptuously furnished.

Every article had been purchased regardless of expense.

" You sent for us, I think ?" exclaimed Dick, who resolved upon taking the high hand.

Captain Vipond's face darkened.

" How dare you speak to me in that insolent manner ?" he asked.

" Because in the first place, I am a gentleman by birth and education, and therefore your equal," replied Dick.

" And secondly ?" demanded the captain, biting his lips.

Dick advanced to the captain, who cried—

" Stand back !"

" Pardon me. I only want to say something privately to you."

" I refuse to hear it. You come on board my ship as a castaway, representing that your companions are dumb, whereas they can speak as well as you."

" I thought possibly they might say too much," exclaimed Dick.

" About what ?"

" That which I want to talk upon privately to you."

The captain paced the carpet.

" You can speak before my lieutenant," he said at length. " I have no secrets from him."

" Does he know your history during the American civil war ?" asked Dick.

" No," exclaimed the captain, promptly.

" There you are !" exclaimed Dick, triumphantly. " Send everybody out of the cabin but myself, and we will have a chat."

" Lieutenant Jackson, will you oblige me by retiring?" said Captain Vipond.

" Certainly, sir," answered the lieutenant, with a respectful salute.

His face, however, expressed the astonishment he felt.

Captain Vipond was a tyrant.

The lieutenant could not understand his yielding to the caprice of a mere lad.

" Boys," he exclaimed, " you can go

and play. If there is any more cobbing, come and tell me. I'll promise the first one who touches you four dozen, in a brace of shakes."

Messiter and Ted followed the lieutenant out of the room.

Dick and Captain Vipond were alone together.

CHAPTER XXVIII.

DICK TALKS LIKE "A DUTCH UNCLE."

"I'M going to talk like a Dutch uncle, Captain Crawley Vipond," exclaimed Dick.

"I am here to listen," answered the captain.

"Perhaps you are not aware how a Dutch uncle does talk?"

"Frankly, I am not."

"Well, I'll tell you. He comes straight to the point. There is no humbug about him, and he generally knocks the man he talks to into a cocked hat."

"Does he?" exclaimed the captain, laconically.

"Perhaps you don't know what being knocked into a cocked hat is like?" continued Dick.

"No; I must plead ignorance."

"Suppose I were to make myself more master of this vessel than you are yourself, and do just as I chose on board—how would you feel?"

"Words would be unable to paint my surprise," replied the captain.

"Exactly. Well, that is being knocked into a cocked hat," said Dick, sitting down and crossing his knees complacently.

"You're a very curious boy," exclaimed the captain. "Who and what are you?"

"I have already told you I am the son of a gentleman," replied Dick. "I have never done anything seedy, and am not ashamed of the name of Lightheart."

"Well?"

"Can you say as much?"

Captain Vipond was silent.

"Some people," continued Dick, "would be uncharitable enough to call a man a scoundrel if he betrayed the confidence of a friend and ran away with his wife."

"From whom did you hear that scandal?" asked the captain, his livid lips quivering.

"From——" and Dick whispered in his ear.

Crawley Vipond staggered as if a snake had stung him.

"Have you ever been in America?" he asked.

"Never."

"Then you must have met him?"

"Yes."

"Where?"

"On board his ship," replied Dick. "Other men besides yourself can buy ships, you know, and when he found you had not courage enough to face him on land, he determined to hunt you down on the sea."

"He lives! he lives!" cried Vipond in an agonised voice. "Oh, God! my presentiments did not deceive me. He lives!"

"For vengeance," put in Dick, solemnly.

The wretched man sank upon a divan and covered his face with his hands.

"Now," said Dick, coolly, "that's what I call talking like a Dutch uncle. You are knocked into a cocked hat without any trouble."

"Boy," said the captain, raising his head, "beware how you madden me."

"Oh, I shouldn't be afraid of you," exclaimed Dick. "I've met a mad bull in a country lane before to-day. Shall I tell you how I manage a mad bull when I come across him?"

There was no reply.

"I dodge his horns and lay hold of his tail," continued Dick, "and then I leather into his flank with a big stick. It's a lovely plan. Try it."

"When did you meet him?" asked Vipond, his eyes almost starting from his head.

"On board his boat, or whatever you like to call it," answered Dick. "Didn't I tell you so before?"

" Where ?"

" I haven't left him more than half-a-dozen hours."

" Why did you tell me a lie, then ?"

" Because I did not know exactly how to treat you. My companions might have talked too much, so I said they were dumb. To avoid your asking unpleasant questions, I cooked up a story of a wreck."

" Then you were not wrecked ?"

" No more than you are," answered Dick.

" Why did you leave that vessel ?"

" I didn't like the captain, and took the first opportunity of breaking the connection which existed between us."

" You talk in riddles," said Crawley Vipond.

" Let me ask you one or two questions," observed Dick.

" If you like."

" How is Adele ?"

" You know that name ?" cried Vipond, starting again.

" Of course I do. I make it my business always to know everything. How is the lady ?"

" She is suffering. Her health is not good."

" Serve her right too," said Dick ; " she had no business to leave a good husband, who was gallantly fighting for the South, while you were skulking at home."

Crawley Vipond rose angrily.

He did not think it dignified to bear Dick's taunts any longer.

" Have you forgotten," he asked, " that I am captain of this ship, and have the power of life and death ?"

" You won't have it long, if you don't look out," answered Dick.

" Why shall I not ?"

" Simply because a certain person is after you."

" After me ?"

" Decidedly. If you had not had the luck of Old Nick, and your own too, you would all have gone to the bottom last night."

" How is that ?" asked Vipond, trembling like a leaf.

" If I tell you all, will you treat me and my friends as passengers on board this ship, and give us a hundred pounds each when we land at the first port, if ever we do land ?"

" Yes, I will ; but why should we not land ?"

" It all depends upon the captain ; had not his machinery broken down, you must have perished in the night."

" Impossible," said Vipond. " Look at my vessel ; do you see how she is armed and manned ?"

" I admit all that ; but suppose," said Dick, " that a thing like a conical shot darts right through your ship in the dead of night, and makes two big holes, one on each side, what would you do then ?"

" Sink," replied Vipond.

" Of course you would."

" I wish you would not mystify me any more. What it is I have to dread ? If I know what evil threatens me, I am better able to look it in the face !" exclaimed Vipond, impatiently.

" I will put you on your guard," replied Dick.

As briefly as he could, he told Captain Vipond how he had left his school for a sail, been run down, picked up, wrecked by the strange vessel, and taken inside.

And he concluded with the manner in which he had overheard the secret of the captain, and his escape during the night with Ted and Messiter.

Vipond was much agitated.

" I thank you," he said, " for your confidence. Your story comes upon me like a revelation. Not having heard of him for so long, I fancied him dead."

" You will always be in danger from him," said Dick.

" I know it, but I do not deserve his vengeance so much as you may think. He was always a morose and gloomy man ; I was his wife's sweetheart before she married him. I am willing to admit that I wronged him in taking her away from him, and I suppose sin always brings its penalty with it in this world."

A fragile form had entered the room without being perceived.

It was that of a slim, dark-haired, girl-like beauty, whose lovely countenance was very sad, but sweet even in its sadness.

Its expression was that of melancholy resignation.

" So," continued Vipond, " my enemy will be satisfied with nothing less than my death ?"

" And his wife's also," answered Dick.

A faint cry came from the fragile form.

Both turned round.

"Adele," exclaimed Vipond, "why are you here, and what have you heard?"

"The door of my cabin was open, and I have heard all this young gentleman has said," she replied.

Captain Vipond struck his forehead in despair.

As for Dick, he could not take his eyes off the saint-like countenance of Adele.

He thought it impossible that so beautiful a body could hide a sinful soul.

"Go to your cabin again," said Vipond, imperiously.

"No, I will not," she replied, gently but firmly. "I must speak to——"

"Lightheart," said Dick.

"To Mr. Lightheart," she continued. "You have been with my husband for some time. Perhaps you think I wronged him, but I give you my word of honour as a lady that I fancied—nay, I believed—that he died on the field of battle at Gettesberg."

"Who told you so, madam?" asked Dick.

"He did," she answered, pointing to Vipond.

The man writhed under this denunciation, and showed himself to be the treacherous coward he was.

"I deserve my husband's hatred, and do not dread his vengeance," she went on; "indeed, I honour and admire him for retiring from the world, and giving up all to work it out. If you should see him again, sir——"

"I hope not," interrupted Dick.

"You *may* meet. This is a world of surprises. Tell him, if you do see him again, that I only married Mr. Vipond when I was assured of his death."

So saying, she walked slowly away, treading so lightly, and seeming so fairy-like, that her visit was more like that of a ghost than that of a human being.

Crawley Vipond wiped the perspiration from his forehead.

"I would rather have given a thousand pounds than that lady should have heard what you said," he exclaimed.

"Was it my fault?" asked Dick.

"No; but you are like a stormy petrel—you forebode misfortune."

"You have brought it on yourself," replied Dick, boldly.

"Do not argue with me," said Vipond. "Mine is an irritable temperament. Talk to me about my foe."

Dick told him how the vessel was constructed, as well as he was able.

"He was always a wonderful engineer," observed Vipond. "I am not surprised at his building such a ship. At what speed can it go?"

"Under light pressure it could attain a speed of thirty miles an hour, but the heat would be so intense it could not keep it up long," answered Dick.

"You say that his machinery has broken down?"

"Yes. It was owing to the confusion that the breakdown made we were able to escape."

"Well, Mr. Lightheart," said Vipond, "we have a start, and I shall make for some port."

"That's the best thing you can do, sir."

"Now I know where my enemy is, and what his means and intentions are, I fancy I shall be safer on the earth than on the sea."

"He would follow you to the centre of the earth," answered Dick.

"I believe you. He is a terrible man, but I will do what I can to save myself and Adele, though I fear she is not long for this world," exclaimed Vipond, in a gloomy voice.

"One word, sir, before I go," said Dick.

"What is it?"

"My companions and myself are passengers."

"Certainly."

"We have the run of the ship."

"Yes. You shall have a mess to yourselves if you like."

"No, thanks. I like your middies, and if you will speak to them, and send us the usual rations, with any little luxuries in the shape of tinned things when you have the time to spare, I shall be obliged."

"It shall be done. To-morrow, Mr. Lightheart, I shall esteem it a favour if you will dine with me and Adele."

"With pleasure, sir, and many thanks for your invitation," replied Dick.

He walked away, but, turning suddenly, exclaimed—

" How many knots can you make an hour, sir ?"

" Fourteen," replied Captain Vipond.

" Is that your highest speed ?"

" Well, no. We went quicker when we were flying from the strange vessel, which we took to be some strange monster or sea serpent."

" Are you afraid to put any higher pressure on your engines ?"

" I am rather, because they are three years old and will not bear a high pressure," replied Vipond.

" Then you are doomed," said Dick.

" What do you mean ?" asked Vipond, aghast.

" I mean that your enemy will run you down as a sparrow is caught by a hawk, or its prey transfixed by a sword-fish."

" What would you advise me to do ?" asked Vipond, trembling like a leaf.

" Shall I tell you ?" demanded Dick.

" Yes."

" You have boats ?"

" Four."

" Very well. Where are we ?" asked Dick.

" In the Atlantic Ocean," replied Captain Vipond.

" If you will take my advice," said Dick, " you will get out your largest boat at once, put yourself, Adele, myself and my companions, and anyone else you care about in it, and take to the sea."

" But we are many miles from any port."

" No matter. Better trust to the waves than to your enemy. You can tell your first lieutenant to go to some harbour and await your orders."

" I must have time to think over it."

" The man who hesitates is lost," replied Dick.

" I will think," was Crawley Vipond's only answer.

Dick went away to join Messiter and Ted.

" At all events," he muttered, " we have a good start of the ship, and I will hope for the best."

CHAPTER XXIX.

DICK MAKES HIMSELF AT HOME.

GOING into the midshipmen's berth, Dick found his companions awaiting his return.

Banks and Menzies were also there.

" I say," said Banks, " your pals have become dumb again, for they won't say a word in answer to my polite inquiries after their health."

" May I talk, Master Dick ?" asked Ted.

" Now you may. Fire away."

" I will. I'll fire away a good un," replied Ted. " It's been hard lines for me to hold my tongue all this time, I can tell you, and since I may speak, I'm on to that cove like grub."

" What have I done ?" said Banks.

" You're the darndest specimen of a Yankee skunk I've seen this long time, and if you don't like that, I'm game for a dust up with fists or anything else."

" Turn it up, Ted," said Dick.

" Well, sir, if I am only an odd boy, I've got my feelings."

" Keep them to yourself. We are going to be jolly. I want Mr. Banks and his friends to join me in a little spread I am going to give."

" I'm on," replied Banks.

" What do you say to a little salmon, ducks and peas, lamb and mint sauce, etc., all potted, of course ?"

" Very good," said Banks. " But where will you get them ?"

" From the captain's servant."

" Next week," said Banks, derisively. " You won't get much out of him, I tell you."

" Why not ?"

" He's a hot member, he is, and not fond of parting."

" Ted," said Dick.

" Yes, sir," replied Ted.

" Go to the captain's servant, and present my compliments to his master, and tell him I want the best fare he can supply me with."

"'I'LL HAVE MY REVENGE FOR THIS,' CRIED MENZIES."

Ted went away.

"Well, you are a cool fish, I don't think," said Banks.

"Always was so considered," replied Dick.

In a short time Ted came back, loaded with a variety of potted and tinned delicacies, which, when spread out on the table, made a feast that had never been seen in the midshipmen's berth before.

"How do you do it?" asked Banks, with his mouth full.

"It's a way I've got," answered Dick.

"Did you know the captain before?"

"Of course I did; I know everybody."

"Don't chaff," said Banks, looking puzzled.

"I'm not chaffing; I never chaff; I leave that to Yankees."

"Don't you insult me because I'm an American," cried Banks. "My blood's soon up, my lad."

"So is mine," answered Dick.

"Will you fight?" asked Banks, getting up and clenching his fists.

"No," replied Dick. "For the short time we shall be together it is not worth while. I want to be jolly, but if you want a hiding badly, I don't mind coming on deck and giving you one."

"You shall have a try," said Banks, who was losing his temper.

"Just stop a bit," exclaimed Dick. "What's your father?"

"An apothecary at Salem, Mass."

"What's Mass.?"

"Why, short for Massachusetts, a state in America."

"Oh, I couldn't think of fighting with an apothecary's son," replied Dick; "I'm too much of a swell for that. Oh, no, too much the gentleman."

"How do you like that, then?" inquired Banks, as he threw a tin of salmon half empty at him.

Dick ducked his head, and the missile missed him.

"Thank you," he replied, "that's a bad shot. I prefer my salmon in small quantities; I am not a Yankee hog."

Banks got up and walked towards him.

"Ted," said Dick.

"Sir," answered Ted.

"Slog that fellow for me. I mean the chemist's assistant, apothecary's son, or whatever he calls himself."

"Yes, sir," said Ted.

"And when you have polished him off, put him in his bunk, for I know he won't be able to move for a day or two."

"Won't you fight me, you cur?" asked Banks, trembling with passion.

"No, you see I won't," answered Dick.

"Why not?"

"I only fight with gentlemen."

"What do you call me?"

"I think I said a chemist's assistant —a man who makes up pills and things of that sort, so I hand you over to my servant. Wire in, Ted," said Dick.

Ted did not require any further orders.

He quickly slipped into the midshipman of the "Belle of New Orleans," and in less than half a minute they were at it hammer and tongs.

Ted was as tough as a porpoise, and as wiry as a badger, having been knocked about all his life, and his knowledge of the art of fighting was pretty good.

In five minutes' time Banks was lying on his back, half stunned, and gasping for breath.

"Water," he murmured, faintly.

"Give him a drink, and put him to bed," said Dick.

Ted did as he was told, and about this time Stephens came down and joined Menzies, who told him what had happened.

"Gentlemen," said Dick, "if you are not satisfied, Ted, my servant, is at your service, and lives upon fighting. The more he has, the more he wants. If, on the other hand, you are satisfied, I shall be glad to receive you as guests at my festive board."

"Go on and feed," exclaimed Banks, from his bunk. "It was my fault. I guess I shall be all right soon. Lightheart isn't half a bad fellow, though I wish he had fought me himself."

"Too much the gentleman. You weren't good enough for me," answered Dick. "If you hadn't let on about the apothecary, I might have obliged you."

Banks could not help laughing, though he was badly knocked about.

"You make yourself at home," he remarked.

"Bound to do it," answered Dick; "it's my way."

The two midshipmen, Menzies and Stephens, did not hesitate any longer.

They set to work with knife and fork, and made an excellent dinner, of a sort they had not been accustomed to.

In the evening Dick went to dine with the captain.

He passed the afternoon in wondering what his decision would be, hoping that he would decide upon leaving the "Belle of New Orleans" to her fate.

While his enemy lived no one on board Crawley Vipond's vessel could reckon on living from one day to the other.

CHAPTER XXX.

A FATAL FALL.

THE "Belle of New Orleans" steamed night and day from the neighbourhood of her dreaded foe.

None of the crew could understand the captain's haste, but Dick smiled to himself, for he knew that Crawley Vipond dreaded the well-deserved vengeance of Harold Dugard.

The professor progressed slowly towards recovery, and the captain of the vessel behaved very kindly to him and his companions.

Dick dined continually with the captain and Adele, becoming on friendly terms with them, and recounting the singular life he had led on board the strange vessel.

Vipond and Adele were never tired of listening to him.

He discovered that Adele's life was not a happy one.

Since she had seen Dick and learnt that her husband lived, she could not forgive the man who had basely betrayed her into marrying him by saying that Dugard was dead.

Dick was the unwilling witness of se eral quarrels between them.

More than once Vipond had threatened her with personal violence, though he had not as yet resorted to extremes.

The ship's course was directed towards the African coast, but they only touched at ports to obtain coals, which were necessary for the working of the vessel.

Captain Vipond would not take Dick's advice, which was, to abandon the ship, lest the enemy should find and sink her.

He was an obstinate man and would have his own way.

Banks, the midshipman, freely forgave Dick for the thrashing which he had caused him to receive at the hands of Ted.

He was not a lad who would bear malice, but Menzies, the second midshipman, was of a very different disposition, and he had taken a full dislike to Dick.

It was an instinctive sort of hatred, for Dick had never done him any harm.

Perhaps he was jealous of his frank and generous nature, which did not contrast at all favourably with his own mean and malicious character.

However that might be, he never lost an opportunity of showing his dislike, though Dick treated him with the silent contempt that a noble mastiff displays towards a snarling cur.

Captain Vipond often used to take long walks with Dick by his side on the quarter deck, and invite him into his cabin.

This favouritism displeased Menzies very much.

"What does our skipper want to make a friend of a fellow like that Lightheart for?" he remarked to Banks.

"Because he chooses, I suppose," answered Banks. "I guess the captain isn't going to ask your permission."

"There is Lightheart," replied Menzies, his little eyes sparkling maliciously; "wait a bit, I'll show him something."

There was a pail, with a mop in it, close by.

It had been used for swabbing the decks, and taking up the mop, Menzies began to trundle it.

A shower of not over choice water sprinkled Dick in the face, much to his disgust.

"Now then, clumsy," he said, "what's your game?"

"Eh?" asked Menzies.

"Are you aware that my figure-head don't want swabbing."

"No. I thought, as you are dirty enough, a little water wouldn't hurt you," replied Menzies, instantly.

THE SCAPEGRACE AT SEA.

101

"What's sauce for the goose is sauce for the gander, my lad," answered Dick. "You look as if soap and water and you weren't very good friends."

"I always have a bath once a year, whether I want it or not," said Menzies, who was not noted among his companions for his cleanliness.

Dick laughed at this reply, though it was spoken seriously enough.

"I'll see what I can do for you," he said.

Quickly snatching up the pail, he rushed upon Menzies before the latter could escape, and emptied the contents over his head, upon which he let the pail fall.

Half smothered and blinded, Menzies was for a moment bewildered.

At last, urged by a kick from behind, he removed the pail and glanced fiercely at Dick.

Drawing a knife, he ran at Dick, who seized a spike which was lying near.

"No, you don't, my boy, not this time. Mother says you mustn't," he exclaimed, as he brought the spike down on his wrist, which he nearly dislocated, sending the knife flying along the deck.

Menzies uttered a howl of rage.

"I'll have my revenge for this," he cried.

"As soon as you like, my innocent," replied Dick; "only take a fool's advice, and don't try to knife me again, or I shan't let you off so easy. I hate such dirty Spanish ways. Be off."

Menzies slunk away without saying anything more openly, though his muttered threats were heard as he went towards the hatch.

"You've made an enemy there," observed Banks.

"I don't care; it wasn't my fault," replied Dick, "was it?"

"No, I can't say it was."

"I should be a blooming idiot if I were to stand any cheek fellows like that choose to favour me with."

"Still, I shouldn't like to offend Menzies. His father was Spanish, and he will cherish up a grudge for months and years."

"Let him; he won't get the better of me," replied Dick.

"Well, look out, that's all. You're so pretty I shouldn't like to lose you."

"Thank you. Do you want to borrow half-a-crown?"

"Not this time."

"Oh, I thought you did," said Dick, laughing; "it's generally that way when butter's plentiful."

Banks laughed too.

"There is the captain beckoning you," he said, all at once; "what do you find to talk about?"

"I'm teaching him navigation," replied Dick.

"Dickens," said Banks.

"I am really."

"You've made the skipper talk more since you've been on board than he ever did before. Cut along. His arm's going like a pump handle."

"Stroll on. See you at mess," said Dick, as he walked away, and joined Captain Vipond on the poop.

The latter seemed deeply agitated.

"Lightheart," he said, "will you do me a favour?"

"Yes, sir, willingly," answered Dick.

"Go into my cabin. I had an unfortunate quarrel with—with my wife. In the heat of my passion I struck her, and she fell against a chair. I saw the blood spurting from her head and I rushed away."

Dick recoiled in horror.

"You struck a woman," he said, "and one in feeble health?"

"I know it was the act of a coward, say of a madman if you will, for I have not been myself since you arrived on board, and told me that my enemy, Harold Dugard, was thirsting for my life."

"What do you want me to do?"

"See if Adele is much injured. Do what you can for her, and come to me again."

"Your place is by her side," said Dick.

"I have not the courage to bear the silent reproach that her eyes will give me, though I am certain her lips will not utter one word of censure. Go, my lad. I shall not forget you, and try to think as kindly of me as you can."

It was with a feeling of repulsion that Dick left the captain and made his way to the cabin.

He was profoundly sorry for the beautiful but unhappy Adele.

On entering the cabin, he saw the

ship's steward supporting the form of a woman.

He was bathing her head with a sponge, and the water in the basin was stained a deep red colour with blood.

It was Adele, who breathed heavily, and whose eyelids were closed.

" Is she much hurt?" asked Dick.

" It's what I call a crying shame," replied the steward.

" What do you know about it?" Dick said, wishing to screen the captain if he could.

" Why, sir, I was pottering about below, and I heard words, so I peeped in through the half open door and I saw Captain Vipond strike the lady; down she fell against a chair, and he rushed upon deck. She has not opened her eyes or spoken since. It's a shame, I say, and she in such weak health, too."

" Hush!" replied Dick, " there may be causes of quarrel between the captain and his wife which you know nothing about."

At this moment Adele opened her eyes.

" I am dying," she said, feebly.

" Do not say that," replied Dick; " It is only a slight shock; you will be better presently."

" Never in this world. You know Harold, Mr. Lightheart. Dying people speak with prophetic voices. You will meet him again."

" And if I do?"

" Tell him that the last word upon his once-loved Adele's lips was his name."

The tears sprang to Dick's eyes.

" Tell him," she continued, in a voice which grew fainter and yet more faint, " that in my last moments I prayed for him. Will you do this?"

" I give you my word I will," replied Dick.

" Do not let him know the manner of my death. Say that my spirit drooped day by day. His account with Crawley Vipond is bitter enough as it is, and when they meet one must die."

" I know which of the two I like best," said Dick.

" Everyone loved Harold. He was always noble. Let him hear from you that I only quitted his house when I was assured of his death, and that I did not

dream that he lived until you came to this ship."

Dick fell on his knees by her side, and took one of her hands in his.

" You will not die," he said.

" It is best that I should," she answered. " I thank Heaven for calling my spirit away from earth."

" There may yet be happy days in store for you."

" Never; my race is run. What happiness can I expect? Harold would only curse me; and with Crawley Vipond, since the discovery I have made of his villany, my life would be very—very bitter."

" You were not to blame," said Dick.

" Oh, yes; I should have cherished Harold's memory. I had no right to listen to Vipond. I am not the chaste, pure being that Harold loved to picture me in his silent tent upon the war-field. I loathe myself."

She fell back, and appeared to be greatly exhausted.

" Is she dying?" asked Dick, wildly.

" The lady's heart just beats, and that's all, sir," answered the steward.

" I will fetch Captain Vipond," exclaimed Dick.

He ran up the companion, and, clutching the skipper's arm, said—

" Come!"

" Is her condition dangerous?" asked Vipond, hoarsely.

" Lose no time, or you will be too late!"

The captain walked with long strides across the deck, followed by Dick.

" Anything up, sir?" asked a sailor of Dick, as he passed.

Dick's indignation was very great.

Without thinking what the effect of his words might be upon the crew, he answered—

" The captain's killed his wife by a foul and cowardly blow; that is all."

" And enough, too—douse my lights!" said the man.

He went forward to communicate the news to his shipmates.

Dick descended the companion after Captain Vipond, and once more entered the cabin where the dreadful tragedy had been enacted.

CHAPTER XXXI.

THE MUTINY AMONG THE CREW.

IN justice to the captain of the " Belle of New Orleans," we must say that he seemed deeply shocked at the result of his violent haste.

Evidently he had not contemplated such an accident as had occurred.

" Adele !" he cried, " Adele, speak to me, my pet, my best beloved one."

Only a feeble movement of the lips answered him.

" She will never speak more on earth," said the steward.

There was a moment's pause.

Everyone in the cabin suffered the most intense agony.

The steward was wrong.

She did speak once more, but it was her last utterance.

" Heaven forgive me !" she murmured, while a sweet, seraphic expression stole over her pale but lovely countenance.

" She speaks," said the captain, bending down.

" I sinned innocently," she continued ; " Jesus, Saviour, I come, I come."

Great beads of perspiration rolled down the captain's face.

Dick's tears flowed unrestrainedly.

The dying girl's lips moved once again.

Her utterance was scarcely audible, but Dick caught it.

" Harold, darling Harold, mine no more, oh ! the dreary, dreary moorland, oh, the barren, barren shore. Harold, dar—ling Har——"

That was all.

Her mind was wandering, and she was quoting Tennyson, mixing Harold Dugard's name in her confused speech.

She had said that his would be the last name on her lips.

It was her dying request to Dick that he should tell him so, if ever he again met the mysterious captain.

She had kept her word.

It remained for Dick to keep his, if he ever had the chance of obeying her.

Adele's head fell back, and the steward let her lay upon the carpet of the saloon.

" It is all over, sir," he said, under his breath.

Captain Vipond choked back a great sob that came up in his throat.

The steward and Dick were about to withdraw and leave him to his grief.

Suddenly he looked up, and glaring fiercely at Dick, exclaimed—

" This is your doing, boy !"

" Mine ?" said Dick.

" Yes ; had you not crept like a serpent into our Paradise, this would not have happened."

" I cannot have a row with you here, Captain Vipond," answered Dick.

" But you shall hear what I say !" thundered the captain, whose eyes rolled wildly.

" We are in the presence of the dead, and I will not answer you. Come on deck and I am at your service," said Dick.

He walked calmly out of the cabin, leaving Captain Vipond alone with the dead body of Adele.

Evidently at that moment the captain was not master of himself.

He saw snatched from him, and by his own wicked, cowardly act, the woman for whom he had sinned and dared so much.

She was gone.

Harold Dugard, however, lived, and he had to dread his vengeance.

When Dick reached the deck, he saw the crew all together in a group.

The man who had spoken to him before detached himself from the group, and advanced towards him.

" Well, my man, what is it you want with me ?" asked Dick.

" You're a gentleman, sir," was the reply.

" I hope so."

" I'm only a common seaman, but I've got a heart for all that, and I calculate I knows what's right, as well as any man

" Seamen are generally blunt, honest, straightforward fellows, and I see no reason why you should be different to the rest," said Dick.

" They call me Soft Tommy, sir, cos I was always a fool with women "

" Well, Tom, my old sea horse, what's your grievance ?"

"Is the lady dead, sir?"

"She is, I am sorry to say."

"And the captain struck her down?" asked the sailor.

"He did."

"Then we've made up our minds," continued Soft Tommy, "that we won't sail under him no more. I guess we mean it, boys."

He turned to the crew as he spoke, from whom came a unanimous shout of approval.

"Wait a bit," said Dick; "I'll go and talk to the captain about that. If I can make any arrangement for you, I will."

In an instant he had returned to the cabin, on the threshold of which he met Crawley Vipond.

"Back for your life!" he cried.

"Do you dare threaten me?" asked Vipond.

"No. I speak for your good."

"How?"

"The crew are in open mutiny," replied Dick.

"What for?" asked Vipond, aghast.

"They have heard that you have killed your wife, and refuse to sail under you any more. The mutiny has not assumed large proportions yet, and I do not see the officers with the men. There may yet be time to quell it."

"I will pistol the dogs," replied the captain, fiercely.

"Leave that to me. In the temper they are in now your life would not be safe on deck. Give me a brace of revolvers."

Vipond pointed to a case which lay upon a table. It contained two handsome pistols.

"Six-shooters," said Vipond.

"Are they loaded?"

"Yes."

"I will take them," replied Dick, "and see what I can do for you. It will be bad for us if we allow this mob to have their own way."

"I am nearly distracted," said Vipond; "forget what I said just now. You are my friend, Lightheart."

"Scarcely that," answered Dick, "but I feel sorry for you, and have been long enough on board ship to understand the value of discipline."

With a pistol in each hand, Dick regained the deck.

The crew were talking excitedly amongst themselves.

"My men," said Dick, "listen to me."

They all turned round, and no sound was heard but the beat of the engines, which rose and fell with a measured cadence peculiar to machinery.

"I am no friend to mutineers," continued Dick, "and it is my object to get to Zanzibar with my companions. When you arrive there, you can all be paid off."

"What's the use of paying us off in a place like that?" answered Soft Tommy, who constituted himself the spokesman.

"What do you want?"

"I guess our game is to make New York, but we are not going to sail about any longer under a murderer, who does no trade, and does not know where he is going to."

"You will do as I please, not as you like," replied Dick.

Soft Tommy laughed defiantly, and his merriment was echoed by all his companions.

"I calc'late," he continued, sneeringly, "that we ain't going to be put down by a strip of a lad."

"Go forward, my man, and all you fellows go about your duty," cried Dick, "or by Heaven, I'll shoot the first man who disobeys me!"

The men hesitated as they saw the gleaming barrels of the revolvers, one held in each hand, and flashing in the sunlight.

"I've got twelve lives here," exclaimed Dick, seeing the advantage he had gained, "and I shall not be particular as to what I do. You are mutineers, mind you, and the law will not take any particular notice if you are wiped out."

Soft Tommy did not move.

"I'll tell you what it is, youngster," he exclaimed, "you're in the swim with the captain, and have made your book to cast anchor with him."

"Yes, I have," answered Dick.

"Down you go, then," continued Tommy, making a rush at him.

Dick stepped on one side and put his back against the main-mast.

"I warn you, Tom," he said, "that if you don't obey orders, I shall shoot."

"Whose orders?"

"Mine. I don't want to hurt you,

but I am not going to be bullied by you or any man. Stand back!"

Soft Tommy laughed derisively.

"You daren't shoot," he said. "You're too much of a cub to hit if you did."

Tommy advanced again armed with an iron bar. Again Dick warned him.

No notice was taken of the admonition, and Dick fired one barrel.

Soft Tommy put his hand to his heart, and fell back, shot through the leg.

The men were appalled at this sudden act, and ran helter-skelter forward, not wishing to share the fate of their unfortunate companion.

At this juncture the captain, who had heard the shot, appeared upon the deck.

The sight of him was the signal for a howl of execration from the men.

Dick saw Menzies amongst the men, talking to first one and then another.

He was evidently inciting them to further acts of insubordination.

"What shall I do?" asked the captain, who, at this crisis, showed himself devoid of that courage which he ought to have displayed.

"Go below, Captain Vipond, and leave me to manage them," answered Dick.

It was clear that the men had been discontented for some time, and were only waiting for an opportunity to break out.

The captain did not like to retreat, but moved away towards the cabin without actually going below.

Dick advanced fearlessly towards the men.

"Look here, my fine fellows!" he exclaimed, "I will be your captain if you like, but we must have no mutiny. You wouldn't mind a boy captain, would you?"

"No, sir," replied half a dozen of them.

"Come and talk to me, then. Don't listen to that little abortion who is telling you a pack of nonsense and lies. He looks more like a dried-up olive than anything else!"

Dick succeeded in attracting the attention of the men.

"Your friend, Soft Tommy, isn't much hurt. I only sent a ball through his leg to keep him quiet. Pick him up and see to him. He won't say it's my fault when he gets better."

The crew seemed to be divided in opinion.

Some, led by Menzies, were against yielding to Dick, while others inclined to give in.

While affairs were in this desperate state, in a terrible shock ran through the ship.

She shook from stem to stern, and her mainmast went by the board.

Consternation seized everybody.

All thoughts of mutiny faded away from the minds of the dissatisfied.

"She has struck on a rock. She is sinking. Man the boats—rig the pumps," was heard on all sides.

Dick had his own opinion.

He fancied that the strange vessel had found them out, but nothing was to be seen, and it was difficult in the hurry of the moment to come to any settled conclusion.

During the time he was parleying with the mutineers, Ted and Messiter had come to his side.

The professor, who had improved in health, had also been attracted to the deck by the loud voices, and the sound of a shot.

"Stand by this boat," said Dick, pointing to one on the starboard side.

They obeyed him.

"Lower away when I give the word," he cried.

The captain came to his side, and seizing him by the arm, exclaimed—

"What new misfortune is this?"

"I leave you to guess," answered Dick.

"Do you mean——"

"I mean that it's good enough to get out of it at once, for you won't be afloat in ten minutes."

Captain Vipond pressed his hands to his forehead as if he was not master of himself at this terrible crisis.

The death of Adele had in reality unnerved him.

Taking the professor by the arm, Dick helped him into the boat, saying—

"Now, sir, age before honesty."

Mr. Crab obeyed like a child.

When he was in, Dick gave the signal, and the boat was lowered.

"Go on, Harry, and you, Ted," he said. "I'll come last."

"Hadn't we better get a bag of biscuits or something?" inquired Messiter.

"That be hanged; there isn't time. Go down the chains, quick," answered Dick

Both Ted and Messiter did so.

There were three in the boat.

"Don't leave me, Lightheart," exclaimed the captain. "I am rich; the loss of this ship is nothing to me. I can draw bills at any port, on New York, and get what money I like."

"All right; down you go. You're the man for me; I hate paupers," replied Dick.

The captain descended, and Dick followed him.

He was just about to shove off, when Banks rolled down the side, followed by Menzies, with whom he had been having a struggle as to who should go first.

"Bless you," replied Dick, "this is a nice way of getting downstairs. I don't mind you, Banks, but Menzies I didn't bargain for."

"I guess it's taken this child's wind," replied Banks. "However, we can pull for you."

The crew seemed to be alive to their danger, and had partially recovered from their panic.

They saw the boat safely launched on a quiet sea, and made towards the side of the ship as if they would crowd into her.

"Not if I know it," muttered Dick, between his clenched teeth.

"Hold on, captain," said one of the seamen. "We're a-coming."

"No, you're not," answered Dick, displaying a revolver; "this boat is for the women and children. Stand back, or I shoot!"

The warning was disregarded, for several crowded into the chains.

Dick fired three shots, and as many corpses fell into the sea.

The others retreated, muttering threats and curses.

"Pull away, lads," replied Dick; "I'm not going to have any mutineers on board my ship."

Messiter, Ted, Menzies, and Banks laid to with a will, and soon shot ahead.

The professor and the captain sat side by side in the stern sheets.

In five miuutes they were well clear of the wreck.

No one spoke, but each had his own opinion about what had happened.

CHAPTER XXXII.

DRAWING LOTS.

THE boat left the ill-fated "Belle of New Orleans" far behind in the distance.

Dick stood by the rudder, and guided her course.

Those on board did not seem to understand the danger they were in, for no other boat was lowered while the fugitives were in sight.

There was very little doubt in Dick's mind as to what her fate would be.

He imagined that the iron ship had struck her under the water line, and that, springing a leak, she must go down sooner or later.

Night fell, and tired out with rowing, the boys lay down to rest.

Already the pangs of hunger and thirst began to attack them.

Their only hope was that they might be picked up by some passing ship in the morning.

The illimitable sea was on all sides of them, and according to Captain Vipond's calculation, they were hundreds of miles from land.

The west coast of Africa was on the left, but there was little or no hope of reaching it.

Vipond, though very sad, seemed to recover himself slightly now that he had left the "Belle of New Orleans."

He took command of the boat, and declared that rowing was a useless waste of strength.

With Dick's help, he stepped a mast, and set a small sail.

The wind was favourable, and as they were in the track of ships, they reasonably expected to be picked up.

When the moon rose, and all but Dick and the captain were asleep, the latter said—

"If we should reach land, what are your intentions, my lad?"

"I mean to try and reach Zanzibar,"

replied Dick; "it has long been my wish to explore the interior of Africa, and join Dr. Livingstone if I can."

"You do not intend to follow the sea as a profession?"

"No. I like the sea well enough," replied Dick, "but not sufficiently to devote my life to it."

"Nothing would please me more," said Vipond, "than to bury myself in the African forests. Harold Dugard will scarcely find me there, and if he did we should meet on equal terms."

"Do not be too sure of his not finding you; Dugard is a wonderful man, and he only lives for revenge on you."

"If I find money for your expedition into Africa, will you allow me to join you?" asked Vipond.

"Gladly; the want of money is all that stands in my way," replied Dick. "I have heard that it is impossible for a caravan to travel in Africa without a vast store of cloth and beads to satisfy the natives."

"That is settled, then; in future, we shall be companions, and you shall take the command."

"We must get out of our present position before we can talk safely about the future," replied Dick, evasively.

Waking up Ted to watch and mind the sail, he and the captain lay down in their turn, and were soon asleep.

What the fate of "Belle of New Orleans" was they could only guess.

Both fancied that the strange ship had struck her, and she had gone down with all hands unless the crew took to the boats.

If so, Adele would find an eternal grave in the bosom of the ocean.

Morning broke serene and calm, but not a sail appeared upon the surface of the horizon.

The heat was very great, and towards evening the sufferings of the castaways became intense.

They looked hungrily at one another.

Dick remembered how he had heard of shipwrecked men devouring one another, and relishing the repulsive meal as famished dogs eat offal.

When the third day came, they sat staring at one another's parched and blackened lips, their faces haggard and pinched, their eyes sunk and lustreless.

It was evident that one thought filled each mind.

But no one liked to speak first.

Captain Vipond at last said, in a hollow voice—

"We are companions in misfortune, and life is sweet. The question is—Shall we sacrifice the life of one of our number to preserve the lives of the rest?"

There was a murmur of assent.

Hunger and thirst had transformed them into savages.

"It is a horrible thing to do," remarked the professor, "but if anything can justify cannibalism, it is our present condition."

"Let us draw lots," said Dick. "I will tear up the sleeve of my jacket in unequal strips, and the one who draws the shortest strip shall be killed with a knife for the benefit of the others."

Menzies drew his knife, which he always carried in his belt.

"This will do the trick, I guess," he observed.

Messiter and Ted trembled in silent horror, while Banks, who was thoroughly exhausted, lay at the bottom of the boat, as if he did not understand what was going on.

Finding that there was no opposition to the dreadful scheme, Dick tore off an arm from his jacket.

He then made seven strips, one being shorter than all the rest.

Tearing out the pocket from his trousers, he put the strips into the bag.

"Who'll go first?" he exclaimed, holding it up.

"Hand it over," answered Messiter.

He was the first to draw.

Ted followed, the captain going third, and the professor fourth.

No one had the courage to look at his strip, but held it firmly grasped in his hand, waiting until all were drawn, when they would be measured side by side.

Though staggering with weakness himself, and dizzy with thirst and hunger, Dick went through his work manfully.

He crawled over the thwarts and held out the bag to Banks, who extended his hand.

"What am I to do?" he said, faintly.

"Draw," said Dick, huskily.

"What for?"

"To see who is to be killed."

"I guess I'm on if there is any fresh

meat to be had," said Banks, his eyes sparkling. "It don't matter much whether it's cattle or human."

Menzies came next, and it was Dick's turn to dip his hand in last.

The fierce rays of the tropical sun darted **down upon their** unprotected heads.

The **sparkling sea,** shimmering in the sunshine, **lay temptingly** on all sides of them.

But they knew that to drink the salt water would produce madness.

The last act in the feast of blood was drawing near.

Soon the sickening tragedy would be accomplished.

As yet none of them realised the full horror of their fearful position.

There was a chance for each of them, and it was with tremulous anxiety that they watched Dick draw his lot.

"Put them all down on that thwart," exclaimed Captain Vipond.

Banks struggled to his knees, and each one bent over and displayed his strip of cloth.

Suddenly there was a murmur.

"Lightheart's got it," said Menzies, in a tone of triumph.

Even in such an hour he could not rise above his paltry hatred.

It was indeed true.

Dick had drawn the fatal lot.

CHAPTER XXXIII.

OLD FRIENDS.

WITH a sigh of resignation Dick sank upon a seat.

His heart was too full for words.

Death stared him in the face, but like a brave English boy, he did not shrink from it.

Menzies began to sharpen his knife upon the side of the boat.

He was like a butcher preparing to kill a sheep.

Suddenly Ted started up, saying, "Can't I die for Mr. Lightheart? My life ain't worth much. I'm only an odd boy, you know."

"That wouldn't be fair," replied Dick, trying to smile, but failing lamentably.

"Kill me, I say; I don't mind dying for my young master," answered Ted, earnestly.

"No," exclaimed Dick, firmly. "The lot has fallen upon me. I am ready."

"Look sharp," said Menzies; "I'm going to be butcher."

Everyone was horror-stricken at his indecent haste.

"Give the lad time to make his peace with Heaven," exclaimed the professor, who had hitherto been prevented from speaking owing to the impression made upon him by the heartrending scene.

"Good-bye, Mr. Crab," said Dick, shaking his hand.

"God bless you, my boy, and forgive us if we are committing a sin," replied the professor.

Ted and Messiter had each caught hold of one of Dick's hands, and their dry, bleared eyes moistened, though the tears could not flow.

"If ever you get home, Harry," said Dick, "tell them I died like a man, and didn't show the white feather."

"Why did you draw it?" exclaimed Messiter. "Why was it not somebody else?"

"Now then, stand up and look sharp," exclaimed Menzies, becoming impatient.

The savage instinct flashed from his eyes, and he longed to be drinking the warm ruby stream which would soon flow under the edge of his murderous knife.

"Farewell," said Captain Vipond; "I would rather it had been me."

"Never mind," replied Dick, bravely. "What is there to be downhearted about? One must die some day. We all owe Heaven a life. Good-bye, my friends."

He stood up like a hero as he was.

Unbuttoning his shirt, he bared his breast, and putting his hand on his heart, said—

"Strike home."

Menzies faced him.

His arm was upraised.

The murderous steel flashed in the sweltering sun, and yet Dick did not flinch.

His lips were moving as if in prayer, and his eyes were raised to heaven, as if he had already divorced his mind from thoughts of earth.

His life hung in the balance.

Just as Menzies' cruel arm was in the act of descending, Messiter dashed forward and stopped it half way.

Turning angrily upon him, Menzies exclaimed, with an oath—

" What did you do that for ?"

Scarcely able to speak, Messiter pointed frantically to leeward.

" A sail ! a sail !" he cried.

Every eye was turned in the direction indicated.

He was right.

A large merchant vessel, with all sail set, was bearing down upon them.

The knife fell from Menzies' hand, and a look of deep disappointment stole over his villainous young face.

" Saved ! saved !" muttered Dick, as he sank down upon a thwart, and covered his face with his hands.

The reaction was too much for him.

When about to die he could be brave, but now that salvation had come unexpectedly at the last moment, he was as weak as any girl, and trembled in every limb, whilst deep sobs burst from him.

Signals of distress were made, but it was doubtful for some time whether they were seen.

They sailed directly towards the ship, which at last perceived them and stopped her course.

The castaways were wildly excited now.

The revulsion from despair to the certainty of hope affected each differently.

Some wept, others laughed, and others again observed a stony apathy.

Banks was very ill; he seemed to have suffered more than the others, but even he roused a little at the good news.

When he was sure that they were saved, his mind became affected, and, jumping up, he sprang into the sea.

Too weak to swim, he sank like a stone, and all attempts to save him were ineffectual.

The suddeness of the act damped the spirits of the others.

They were taken on board the ship, and at once sent below, when a little broth and bread were given them, it being dangerous to allow them to indulge their appetites after such long privation from food.

Four-and-twenty hours' rest and a careful dieting restored the boys to something like their former condition, though the professor and Captain Vipond were not strong enough to go on deck for some days.

Dick could not look at Menzies without a shudder, for he had so nearly been his executioner.

Going on deck, Dick looked around him.

A group consisting of three people stood near the saloon hatchway.

A hale, middle-aged man, a pretty little woman—who had not yet lost her girlish appearance—and a thin, gaunt, wiry person.

Surely Dick knew the faces !

But he was not sure.

So he rubbed his eyes and looked again.

Advancing, he exclaimed—

" Am I mistaken, or do I address Mr. Snarley ?"

" That was my name in days gone by," answered the person spoken to; " but I am now known to an admiring public as Signor Snarlini, the champion comic artist of the world. And now, sir, who may you be ?"

" Have you forgotten your old friend and pupil, Dick Lightheart ? If so, I am sure Polly—that is to say, Miss Agatha Mountserrat, or Mrs. Snarlini, will recollect me."

Mr. Snarley gave a bound in the air, and danced a breakdown on the deck in most approved comic fashion.

" Well, I never did !" said Polly. " This is a surprise; but how thin you are, Mr. Lightheart, and browned by the sun !"

" I was one of the castaways you picked up a day or two ago," answered Dick.

" I shouldn't have known you," replied old Hopkins, who was the third member of the group.

" I am proud and happy to meet an old pupil," said Mr. Snarley. " Give me your hand, Lightheart. Whoever would have thought that we should see one another on the bosom of the briny ocean ?"

" What are you doing here ?" asked Dick.

" We are going to Zanzibar, having been specially engaged by agents in England of the Sultan of that far-off clime. My fame has travelled far and wide, Lightheart, and our show is hired for six months, expenses paid out and home."

" What do you call the entertainment ?" inquired Dick.

" ' Mirth and Mystery ; or, the Clown, the Clairvoyante, and the Crocodile.' You see, Polly's gone in for mesmerism and all that," replied Snarley.

" And she's very clever at it, too," put in Hopkins, " though I say it who shouldn't."

" What about the untamed savage ? Have you got that in the bill ?"

" No ; we struck it out because we are going among semi-savages, and it wouldn't do. The educated crocodile's sure to draw, though ; and what with the clown business, and the mesmerism, we are sure to be a success."

" We think of doing the East all round after fulfilling our engagement with the Sultan of Zanzibar," said Hopkins.

" I wish you success," replied Dick, " and am delighted to have met you all. It's like old times to see you."

When Messiter came up, he was as astonished as Dick had been to see the strollers.

A variety of questions were asked and answered, and old schooldays discussed.

The ship was the " Fanny Lorton," from Southampton, and had only Mr. Snarley and his little troupe on board as passengers.

Captain Vipond informed the captain of the ship that he would be answerable for all expenses incurred by his companions and himself.

Consequently they had the run of the saloon, and were well treated, travelling as first-class passengers.

Mr. Snarley and Polly were very happy together, and though there was occasionally something of the schoolmaster about the former, he seemed to have thoroughly entered into his new business as a showman.

Forgetting all their misfortunes, as boys will, they looked forward with hope to the future, and formed quite a merry little party in the saloon.

Captain Vipond joined them, and though reserved and somewhat sad, he listened with pleasure to Polly's songs, played at cards, and otherwise made himself agreeable.

The only exception to the rule was Professor Crab.

He hated professionals, and boasted that he had never been in a theatre in his life.

Mr. Snarley noticed that he always kept aloof from him, being always writing or reading.

One night, Snarley had brewed a glorious bowl of punch, and everybody was full of mirth and jollity.

" Crab," said Snarley, with that familiarity which distinguished him when a little elevated, " fill up your glass, old son."

The professor slightly lifted his spectacles, and stared at him.

" Did you address your remarks to me, sir ?" he asked.

" Of course I did. Come on, old flick. Here we are again. We don't kill a pig every day. Who says punch ?" replied Snarley.

" Really, my good sir," answered Mr. Crab, " I must request that you will be a little more choice in your language when you have occasion to speak to me, which I hope will not be often."

" Hullo !" said Snarley, " who's trodden on your corns, Old Beans ?"

The professor rose angrily.

" I protest," he said, " against being spoken to as Old Beans by a person of that fellow's calling."

" What do you mean ?" asked Snarley.

" You belong to a degraded class, sir. You are a strolling player, sir, and it is a disgrace to associate with you, sir," cried the professor.

" Here's a lark," exclaimed Snarley ; " somebody's combed the old boy's wool the wrong way. Now, Crab, be jolly, or Heaven won't love you. If I'm only a player, I can't help it. I didn't mean to turn your hair."

" Keep yourself to yourself, sir," exclaimed the professor.

" Look here, Crab," continued Snarley, " you go outside the door, and put yourself in any eccentric position you like, standing on one leg, or with one arm over your head, and I'll tell you how you're standing without looking at you. That's clever, isn't it?"

"You can't do it, sir," said the professor.

"Will you try?"

"If you turn your face to the wall."

Mr. Snarley immediately turned round, and the professor went outside the door, saying—

"I'll prove this fellow to be an impostor and a humbug. He can't have eyes in the back of his head."

Everybody crowded round Mr. Crab, who stood on one leg, and held his right arm fantastically up in the air.

"You are none of you near him?" he asked; "that's right. Now we will expose the mountebank."

"Are you ready?" asked Snarley.

"Yes," replied the professor. "How am I standing?"

There was a moment's pause.

Then Mr. Snarley exclaimed—

"Like a jolly old fool."

A roar of laughter burst out, and the professor got as red as a turkey cock.

"This is childish," he remarked.

He saw that the joke had gone against him, and he became furious, and when Snarley approached him, he shook his fist in his face.

"I have come to something to be jeered at by a clown," he exclaimed.

"It is my vocation," replied Snarley, "and Falstaff says it is no sin for a man to labour in his vocation."

"You quote Shakespeare," remarked the professor, astonished.

"Calm those transports. *Via brevis furor est*," continued Mr. Snarley.

"He speaks Latin," muttered the professor, in amazement.

"And Greek too," said Dick.

"Is it possible a man of education can have sunk so low?" cried the professor, clasping his hands.

"Come and join us over the friendly bowl—I forgive you, Crab," said Snarley, patting him on the back.

"Don't touch me, sir," said the professor, "or I may be tempted to dirty my hands with you."

"Go and play," answered Snarley, smiling benignantly. "It was a little stupid old man, and they won't get his shirt out any more."

The professor, boiling over with rage, retired to his corner, readjusted his spectacles, and went on writing.

In time his head fell back, and the spectacles fell from his nose.

He had gone to sleep.

The others had been playing at cards, but left off, as they were tired.

"Crab's gone to sleep," remarked Messiter.

"Let's have a lark with him," said Dick.

"What can we do?" asked Mr. Snarley. "He is a savage sort of scientific monster; but I have an idea some fun can be got out of him."

"Leave it to me," answered Dick; "I'll show you a spree."

Mr. Snarley grinned a ghastly grin, for he knew of old Dick's powers of getting fun out of people when he had made his mind up.

"Ted," said Dick.

"Yes, sir," was the reply.

"I shall want an old newspaper, some string, a little oil, a pailful of water, two plates, and some lampblack."

"What for, sir?"

"What's that to do with you?"

"No, sir; I only asked," replied Ted, apologetically.

"Then mind your own business in future. I am going to set booby traps," said Dick.

CHAPTER XXXIV.

BOOBY TRAPS.

"DID you say booby traps, Lightheart?" remarked Mr. Snarley, when Ted had gone to execute his errand.

"Yes," replied Dick.

"I define the word 'booby' thus: He is——"

"A clown," answered Dick; "so you're shut up."

"No; excuse me. He is more of a pantaloon. The clown plays the tricks; the pantaloon is the unhappy victim."

"That's what Crab will be; only don't talk so loud, or you'll wake him," said Dick.

When Ted returned, he half opened the door of the cabin and steadied the pail of water on its top so that anyone rushing from the cabin in a hurry would be sure to bring it down upon his head.

He rubbed the lampblack carefully on the back of one plate and handed it to Polly.

"That's for you," he said.

Then he went to the professor, and having rubbed the paper over with oil, tied it carefully round his boots.

Striking a match, he lighted the paper, and returning to the table, exclaimed—

"Now, gentlemen, get on with the game!"

"I can't," answered Snarley; "I'm dying to see what will happen."

"Make believe, then. If he sees us all watching him when he wakes up, there will be a row, and you'll be in it."

The cards were dealt, but nobody paid the slightest attention to them.

Seeing this, Ted quietly appropriated the stakes, which were in the centre of the table.

"What are you doing?" asked Messiter.

"It's only a shilling a head," answered Ted, "but it's worth having. Don't holloa, Master Harry. I'll put you on a bit. We shall want some coin when we get to Zanzibar."

Messiter laughed, and said no more.

Ted's sharp practice passed unnoticed, as everyone was engaged in watching the professor.

As the oiled paper began to burn, he moved first one foot uneasily and then the other.

The boots grew uncomfortably warm.

After writhing in a most laughable manner for some minutes, he jumped up.

The heat had become intolerable, and he was suffering intense pain.

"God bless me!" he exclaimed; "what is this?"

"Fire! fire!" cried Dick.

The startled professor ran helter-skelter to the door, which he pushed open.

This caused the suspended pail of water to fall on his head.

He was drenched through and through, and the water put out the fire.

Still the heat in the boots continued, though the oiled paper had ceased to burn.

Falling on the floor, he began to tear at his boots, which laced up.

It was no easy task to get them undone.

"Oh, good Lord!" he exclaimed; "I am burning. What's the meaning of this? My boots are like an oven, and my feet will be baked like bread."

Roars of laughter resounded on all sides.

At length he got his boots off, and sat rubbing his feet, which were aching dreadfully.

"Who did this?" he asked, angrily.

"I beg your pardon, Mr. Crab," said Dick.

"Someone has been playing a trick, I think. Perhaps it is that showman fellow."

"We have been playing cards. You must be mistaken."

"I really beg, Mr. Crab, you will not use such language to an old friend like Mr. Snarley, of long standing."

"I shall say what I think, Lightheart."

"That's a great mistake, sir. Now say what you think. That's the way people get their heads punched," said Dick, solemnly.

"Look at me. I am aching with pain and wet through. Who did it, I ask? I will know," vociferated the professor.

"Consult the medium," replied Dick.

"What?"

"Be mesmerised by Mrs. Snarlini, and you will soon find out."

"How?" asked the professor, in a bewildered manner. Dick then put a few words to Polly, who advanced to Professor Crab, and said, "I will gladly mesmerise you, and then you will know all. Take this plate, hold the front towards you, and do as I do."

Mr. Crab jumped to his feet, and fell a prey to Polly's beauty and apparent simplicity.

She was a good actress.

He took the plate in his hand, and watched her carefully.

"Do as I do," she said.

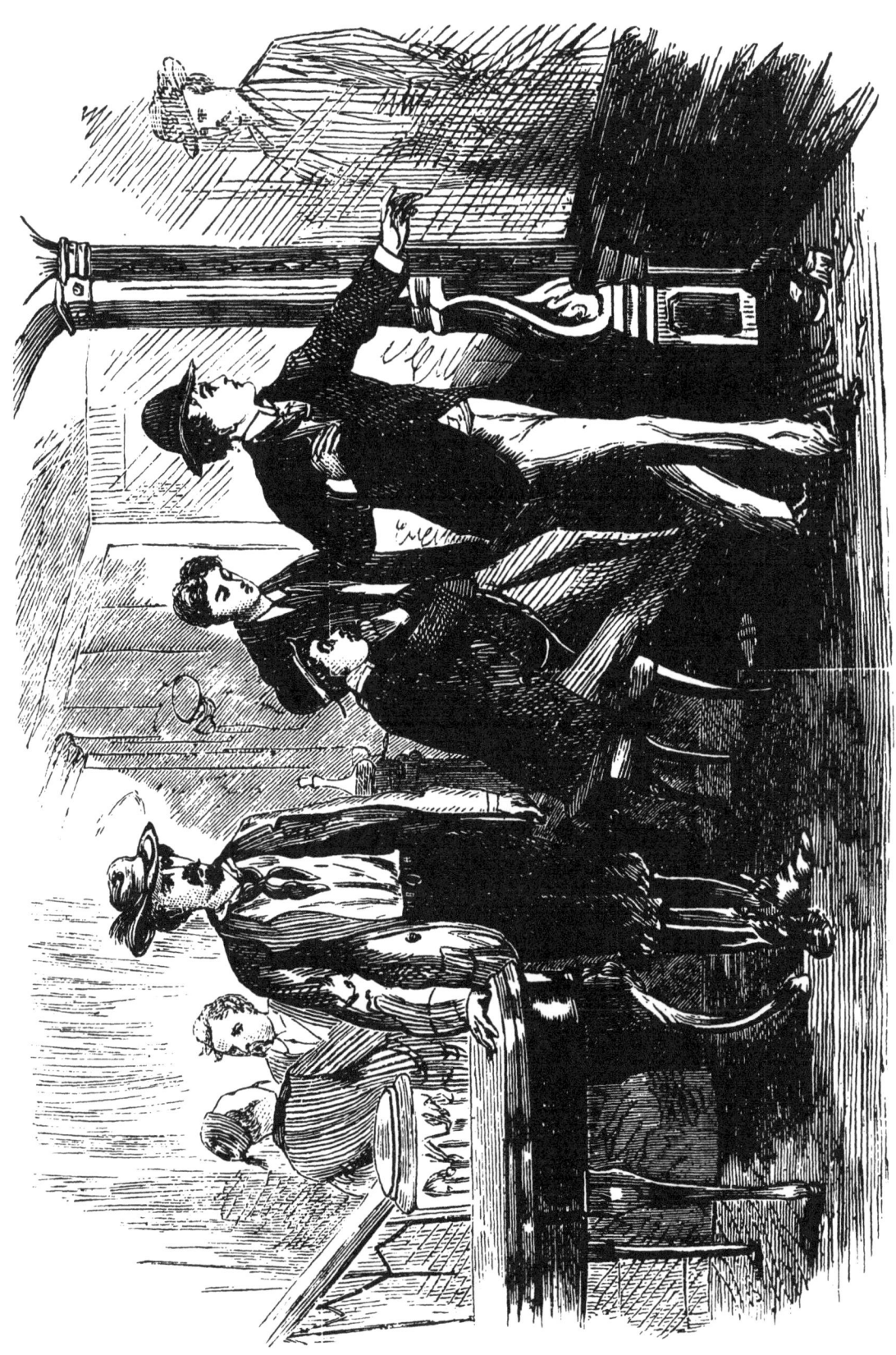

"DICK STARTED SO SUDDENLY THAT THE GLASS FELL FROM HIS HANDS."

No. 8.

"Begin," he replied.

Polly had a plate which was perfectly clean, and she drew her finger across the back and then down one cheek.

The professor followed her example.

But his plate was covered with lamp-black, and he made a dark streak along one side of his face. Polly continued to draw all over her countenance, forehead, nose, mouth, chin, and even her ears were touched.

The professor was soon painted like an Indian on the war path.

"The charm is finished," said Polly at last.

"But," said the professor, "I am no wiser than I was before."

"Go," replied Dick, "to the glass, and you will see the face of your tormentor."

There was a handsome mirror in the saloon, and the professor went to it like a lamb.

He started back in horror.

"More tricks!" he exclaimed, fiercely. "When will this end?"

"Not till we get to Zanzibar," answered Mr. Snarley, mildly, "unless you get rid of your high-flown ideas that a man who is a strolling player is not so good as you are. I have had to teach you a lesson, Mr. Crab, and I hope you won't forget it."

"But my feet are burnt, I am wet through, my face is as black as a negro's, and I am made a laughing stock"

"What else could you expect.?"

"Sir," said Mr. Crab, vehemently, "you're a disgrace to civilization."

"And you, sir, are no ornament to it," answered Mr. Snarley.

Trembling with rage, the professor left the saloon and went to his private cabin.

Captain Vipond laughed till the tears ran down his cheeks.

"I didn't think anything would have made me laugh, Lightheart," he said, "but you have succeeded."

"Glad of it, sir," answered Dick; "a merry heart will go miles further than a sad one."

CHAPTER XXXV.

IN the first week of May the "Fanny Lorton" rounded the Cape of Good Hope, and some days later passed through the Mozambique Channel on her way to Zanzibar, which is a low-lying island, but extremely fertile, having the coast of Africa on its left at no great distance.

Professor Crab and Mr. Snarley had continued at war with each other during the passage.

The boys enjoyed themselves, as boys will under any circumstances.

Captain Vipond seemed to labour under a depression which he could not shake off.

He thought continually of Adele's untimely death, and dreaded above all things meeting with his deadly enemy, Harold Dugard.

His great wish was to fly into the interior of Africa, where the foot of man had never yet trod.

Here he fancied he would be safe.

But he had miscalculated the strength of his enemy's hatred, his powerful will and his resources.

They were destined to meet again—how soon will be seen as we progress.

Dick and his companions, including Mr. Snarley and his troupe, found lodgings at a house known as "Charley's," a place where foreigners who had no friends generally resided.

Zanzibar, being a great trading place, had its harbour full of ships, including same British men-of-war.

The flags of the various consulates floated gaily in the breeze, while the banner of the Sultan was of a deep red colour, and overtopped all others.

Mr. Snarley reported himself at the palace, and had an interview with the Sultan's Grand Vizier, or prime minister, the manager of all his affairs.

This gentleman was an Arab, of short stature and a crafty face, named Selim-el-Mandeb.

Selim received him graciously, and commanded him to appear with his entertainment at the Sultan's palace next evening.

The theatre was a large room, which had been fitted up for the purpose.

It was intended to hold the Sultan and his suite, any strangers and resident

Arabs and Banians he chose to invite, and the ladies of the harem, as well as the servants of the household.

The Banians are the commercial class in Zanzibar, and when we say that in trading they can outwit a few, we give a very good idea of their buying and selling capacities.

The entertainment was a great success.

None of the outside public were admitted, and Dick waited impatiently to hear the result.

He played at billiards all the evening in "Charley's" with Messiter, while Ted marked.

Professor Crab was engaged in writing a learned book about the wonders he had seen under the sea.

The clock stood at eleven o'clock, and it was very hot, although all the windows were open.

"Snarley's late," remarked Dick, as he wiped his perspiring forehead with a new Bandana handkerchief he had bought at a Banian's bazaar or shop.

"Three more to spot," said Messiter. "It was a pocket off the red. Bother Snarley. Don't talk to a fellow on the stroke."

"Thirty-five, forty," said Ted, marking the game; "you'll have to pull up your boot if you mean to win, Master Dick."

"You dry up," answered Dick. "I can't play against flukes, and Harry hasn't got above twenty by legitimate strokes.

"What's this?" said Messiter, making a losing hazard.

"Go on. Give me as much Whitechapel play as you like. Pot your adversary. That's the proper play, of course. It's better to have two balls on the table than three," answered Dick, shrugging his shoulders.

"Never mind. It's two to me," said Messiter, trying for an all-round cannon, and missing it.

"Well tried for, but no luck, Harry," said Dick, poising his cue.

In a few more strokes, Messiter won the game, and they all adjoined to the bar to have a cooling drink.

"What will you have, sir?" asked Charley, the proprietor of the house. "I guess the Yankees like a gin sling, or an eye opener, or a corpse reviver, and I

calculate the Britishers will do well to follow their lead."

"Then you guess wrong," answered Dick.

"Please yourselves, gents; it's no business of mine; you've got to pay, and I've got to serve," said Charley, who was an American born and bred.

"Give me some seltzer and brandy," said Dick.

While he was drinking the cool and refreshing beverage, he chanced to look up at a large mirror which was in front of him.

He started so suddenly that the glass he was holding fell from his hand and broke in pieces on the floor.

Behind him, as it appeared, was a face he could not mistake.

It was sad but handsome, and over it was spread a look of terrible determination.

Turning sharply round, Dick in vain searched for the countenance which had so disturbed him.

It was nowhere to be seen.

But he remarked a dark figure gliding out of the doorway.

Messiter noticed that Dick was agitated in a peculiar manner, and he said, "How pale you are."

"Yes, so would you be, if——" began Dick, shuddering again and breaking off abruptly.

"What's upset you? Has one of those red-turbaned beggars threatened you with a knife because you looked at his girl?"

"I've seen the captain of the strange ship," said Dick.

"Go and put your boots on," replied Messiter, laughing incredulously.

"I have indeed."

"Harold Dugard, as you call him, is at the bottom of the sea, in his floating coffin, as Ted christened his confounded ship."

"No fear," answered Dick; "I can't be mistaken; I was looking in the glass, and I saw the reflection of his face over my shoulder."

"Did you, by Jove!" said Messiter, becoming serious.

"Don't say a word to Captain Vipond it will make him so nervous and miserable that he'll commit suicide."

"He's bad enough as it is; talk of wet

blankets! why, he's half-a-dozen, and gives me the horrors," said Messiter.

"He's got good cause to be sad. I wouldn't have on my mind what that man has, for a million."

"Nothing like a clear conscience, is there, Dick?"

"I always try to sail fair," said Dick. "But, I say, keep this dark."

"Of course I will, since you ask me. What do you think Mr. Dugard's game is now?"

"He means to kill Vipond. There is no doubt about that. Perhaps he visited the wreck of the 'Belle of New Orleans,' and found only the body of the dead Adele; anyhow, he has discovered that Vipond is in Zanzibar."

"And us also."

"Clearly. We have a great cause to fear him," continued Dick, "because we know his secret, and he may try to kill us altogether. He knows Professor Crab is writing a book about him, and he would not like to have it published."

"But he can't kill us all here. Zanzibar is not his ship, and there is law to protect us."

"I know that, and have no funk just at present. He is watching us and making his plans up. You know what a wonderful cove he is, up to all sorts of dodges."

"Yes; every move on the board," said Messiter.

"I am sorry he is on land. We had enough of him on board his vessel," replied Dick.

Menzies approached Dick, and asked him if he would have anything to drink.

"No, thanks," answered Dick. "I don't want to get swipey."

"Will you come and mark for me?" continued Menzies. "I am going to play one of those Arab swells at billiards, and I guess he isn't in it with me. Just forget to score for him now and then, and shove me half-a-dozen forward when no one's looking. If I win I'll put you on a dollar."

"You dirty little humbug! If you dare to speak to me like that, I'll wring your neck," answered Dick, indignantly.

"What's the harm?"

"I'm not a cheat, if you are."

"I suppose you're not better than the rest of us, if the truth were known," sneered Menzies. "I never think much of fellows who pretend to be so awfully righteous."

"Get out of my sight, or I shall be tempted to kick you," replied Dick.

Menzies walked away grumbling to himself.

"That shows you what a little rascal he is," observed Messiter to Dick.

"Yes, he'd rob a church," answered Dick. "Fancy his cheek in talking to me. Hullo! here's Snarley."

Snarley at this moment entered the room with Polly on his arm.

Hopkins had remained behind.

"How did you get on?" inquired Dick.

"We were an unqualified success," answered Mr. Snarley, who strutted about like a stage king. "We secured the unanimous approbation of a delighted and crowded audience. The Sultan sent Polly a ring, and we are to appear again to-morrow."

"Bravo!" said Dick, adding, "Let's look at your ring, Polly."

Mr. Snarley went to the bar to refresh himself, and talked to Messiter and Ted.

He told them that the Sultan's Vizier had expressed his master's great delight with their performance, which was to be repeated three times a week in the palace, with variations and new songs.

Polly took a handsome diamond ring off her finger, and handed it to Dick.

"That's awfully spiff," he said; "but you look rather sad, dear."

"I am a little, though I scarcely know why."

He replaced the ring on her finger, and, stooping down, kissed it, saying—

"Pretty little hand."

"Is it?" she asked, smiling.

"I always liked you, Polly," continued Dick. "By Jove! Snarley's a lucky fellow; but tell me, dear, what makes you look so dismal?"

"The Sultan never took his eyes off me. Such eyes he has; they go right through you."

"Well, what of that?"

"I am afraid of that man. The Sultan has a lot of wives, hasn't he?"

"The old gent has more than a hundred," replied Dick, "and they live in a place set apart for them in the palace, which is called the harem."

Polly lowered her voice, and looking down timidly, said, " Could they steal an English girl ?"

" What for ?"

" To put her in the harem."

" They could, but it isn't likely," said Dick ; " what put that in your head ?"

" I don't know," she answered, with the same worn, startled, anxious look ; " I've got it in my head, though, that the Sultan has taken a fancy to me, and that makes me miserable."

" If he is spooney on you, why not feel flattered ?"

" I wish I had never come, only father said it would be a good thing, and we should make a lot of money, and then go on to India, and make a tour of the world, finishing with America, and coming back to England to live happily all the rest of our lives."

" Like the good children in the story-books, eh, Polly ? But don't worry yourself. You have plenty of friends about you. Come and have some champagne. Snarley shall stand it. I'll tell him he is the first comic actor in the world, and then he'd give me his head if it was loose."

Polly smiled faintly as Dick squeezed her hand.

The champagne was soon ordered, and Professor Crab, who descended from his room, where he had been writing, was asked by Snarley to take some.

" Thank you, no," replied the professor, curtly.

" Come, be jolly," said Snarley, who was getting excited.

" I am always contented and happy, though perhaps I do not find contentment where such men as you would look for it," was the answer.

" Get a wife, old cock; her sweetness would take some of the sourness out of you, my learned and scientific crab-apple," said Snarley.

" Do I look like a fool ?" asked the professor.

" I never judge by appearances," answered Snarley.

" Don't be insolent, because I condescend to talk to you," said Mr. Crab, " or you may find that I'm not so peaceable as I seem."

" Well, tell us your idea of marriage," exclaimed Dick.

" I will define it thus. Marriage is an insane desire on the part of a man to provide some woman with board and lodging for life."

" Oh, Mr. Crab," exclaimed Polly, " what ought to be done to you for saying such dreadful things ?"

" I speak from the head, madam," he answered.

" Not from the heart, I'm sure."

" Madam," continued the professor, " matrimony is also to be compared to a bag full of snakes, into which a man puts his hand, thinking to find an eel. I have the honour to wish you good-night, as I am about to inhale the fresh evening air without doors."

" What an old bear," remarked Polly, when he was gone.

" He ought to be ashamed of himself," said Dick, " to insult the first of living comic actors."

" Lightheart," said Mr. Snarley, shaking his hand, " you are a boy after my own heart, because you appreciate my talent. Let us have another bottle of champagne."

" I shall get squiffy," answered Dick.

" Never mind. You must celebrate my success. I appear again before the Sultan the day after to-morrow. I wish you could come to see me."

" I'll be there," rejoined Dick.

" Impossible !"

" No, it isn't. You ought to know me well enough by this time, sir, to be sure that when I say I will do anything, it will be done."

" How ?"

" I've got an idea. Wait a bit," answered Dick, smiling complacently.

It was very late when they retired to bed.

Soon after they were up in the morning, it was announced that the Grand Vizier Selim-el-Mandeb had come to see Mr. Snarley.

The latter hurried downstairs to receive his distinguished visitor, wondering very much what he could want.

" Perhaps he's brought some present from the Sultan for me," he observed to himself.

The Vizier's visit was of a peculiar character.

This Mr. Snarley soon found out.

CHAPTER XXXVI.

POLLY DISAPPEARS.

SELIM-EL-MANDEB had not come in state.

He was attended only by two slaves, who waited outside the house while he entered.

The Vizier spoke English, which he had learnt early in life from the traders who come to Zanzibar.

He had been an ivory merchant before he entered the Sultan's service, and rose to his high office.

His turban was of blue and silver algerine materials, and his flowing robes were of rich cashmere.

Beckoning Snarley on one side, he said—

"Salaam Snarlini Basha, the Sultan sends you greeting."

"Much obliged to his highness, I'm sure," replied Snarley, overpowered by the compliment.

"The power of my royal master is boundless as the limits of the universe," continued the Vizier.

Snarley nodded his head.

"His wealth would take many scribes all their lives to tell, and his jewels are as numerous as the stars that stud the firmament of Heaven."

"Glad to hear it, governor," said Snarley, not exactly knowing what to say.

"In the name of the prophet, the Sultan sends you his good-will, and trusts that Allah will prosper his undertakings."

"May his shadow never grow less," said Snarley.

"His highness," said the Vizier, "has cast the eye of favour upon your damsel whom you call Pollina."

"The d——I mean, has he really?" said Snarley, with a start.

"Yes. She's highly honoured, and destined to a higher estate. It is for you to name her price."

"To do what?" cried Snarley, excitedly.

"Snarlini Basha," said the Vizier, "we shall not quarrel about the amount, for when his highness covets a female slave to adorn his harem, he don't care what he pays for her."

"So I understand you that he wants to buy Polly?"

"Exactly. Allah be praised! I have a man of intelligence to deal with. Shall we say ten thousand doti of fine cloth, five hundred elephants' tusks, a thousand dollars and fifty female African slaves?"

Snarley shook his head.

"You are hard to please, Snarlini Basha," said the Vizier. "Suppose I throw in a white elephant?"

"Blow your elephant," said Snarley.

"Allah protect us!" gasped the astonished Vizier, as Snarley began to dance wildly in front of him.

"You be bothered," said Snarley.

"There is but one God, and Mahomet is his prophet," said the Vizier. "What's this, Snarlini Basha? Think of the ten thousand doti of fine cloth."

"I don't want any cloth."

"I will add a hundred strings of coloured beads."

"She ain't for sale," screamed Snarley.

"Come. You are as hard to drive a bargain with as a Banian. Just reflect upon the fifty African female slaves."

"She is my wife," replied Snarley.

"That won't matter. Allah be good to her. Cannot I tell a lie for your sake? Is there no friendship in this world? The Sultan shall not know."

"Look here, my friend," said Snarley, "Englishmen don't sell their wives, and your master cannot have Polly."

"Not have her?"

"No; he ought to be ashamed of himself to think of such a thing. If I hear any more of it, I'll give the old gent a bit of my mind."

The Vizier looked confounded.

"By Allah!" he exclaimed, "the rage of the Sultan will fall heavily upon the head of his slave; he will be like a raging lion."

"I can't help that; take your hook," replied Snarley, who was furious.

Sadly and slowly the Vizier wended his way to the door, and walked back to the palace, followed by his trembling slaves, who saw the frown upon his brow.

When their master was angry, it was no uncommon thing for them to be punished, just to relieve his mind.

Nor were they mistaken in the anticipations they had formed.

No sooner had they arrived at the palace than the Vizier ordered them to receive fifty blows each with a stick, and looked on with a grim smile at their howls and contortions under the punishment.

Mr. Snarley rejoined his party, and everyone saw at a glance that something had occurred to disturb his usual serenity.

"What has ruffled your feathers, sir?" asked Dick.

"The most unaccountable thing that ever you heard of. The Sultan has sent here to buy Polly," answered Snarley.

Polly, on hearing this announcement, uttered a shriek.

"I would rather die than be sold!" she exclaimed.

"I very soon put a stop to the business," continued Snarley, "and if the Vizier had not drawn in his horns, I should have kicked him out."

Polly put her arm round Dick's neck as if clinging to him for protection, and he slipped his hand round her slender waist.

Snarley was too much preoccupied to notice this bye-play.

The insolent proposition of the Sultan was canvassed in every possible way.

Even the professor descended from the pedestal of his reserve, and was pleased to express his greatest sympathy with the players.

He advised them to call upon the British consul and state their case, because there was no telling what an Arab might do when he had taken a fancy to a girl.

In the afternoon Polly grew feverish and restless, and when the cool of the evening came, expressed her intention of going for a stroll.

"Take Ted with you," said Dick; "Snarley will be jealous if I come."

"I am only going to the Cocoa Tree. That is the proper place to walk; all the English go there, and I shall meet plenty of people," answered Polly.

"Never mind. Take Ted, I say!" exclaimed Dick.

Ted had his broad-brimmed straw hat on in a moment, and placed himself by her side.

"I'm only an odd boy, miss," he remarked, "but you may find me useful at a pinch."

"Thank you, Ted," she answered. "You shall come if you like."

They started together for the walk to the Cocoa Tree, while Dick and Messiter lounged about among the shipping in the harbour.

Captain Vipond had been very busy all day arranging matters for his caravan.

He had bought donkeys and engaged carriers and guards for the expedition.

In the interior of Africa money is of no use.

Everything must be paid for in clothes or beads.

There are many chiefs and sultans in different parts, and as they all have numbers of armed men in their service, they can and do stop travellers and traders, and make them give up so many yards of cloth and strings of beads as tribute, without which they will turn them back, and not let them pass through their dominions.

Some tribes will only take English cloth.

Others will only receive American or Yankee goods.

This makes it necessary to engage about seventy men as pagazi or carriers, to bear the cloth and beads, as well as the flour and tinned provisions requisite to feed such a little army.

Then, again, there are powder and shot and rifles to be conveyed, all of which make the fitting out of a caravan, as it is called, a work of time and labour.

Captain Vipond had not spared money, and he found gold as powerful at Zanzibar as it is elsewhere.

Consequently he made good progress, and announced to Dick that all would be ready to start in a couple of days.

"I have got a good supply of Lancaster rifles and those bone-crushers known as Frazer shells, which will bring down anything, from a giraffe to a nigger," said Vipond.

"How do we go?" asked Dick.

"From Zanzibar we cross over to Bagamoyo, on the coast of Africa, and then plunge into the interior."

"To what part?"

"Towards Ujiji, on Lake Tanjanyika, where Livingstone was last heard of. I care not so long as I get into the wilds of Africa," said Vipond.

"I shall be ready," said Dick; "the fact is, I long to penetrate this mysterious land, so nearly a blank upon the map."

"You shall be the overseer and leader of the expedition, Lightheart."

"And you, sir?"

"Oh! I will not interfere, except in case anything goes wrong. Our native servants will fear me more if I am reserved and do not mix much with them."

It was growing dark while they were talking about their future prospects.

Suddenly Snarley entered.

"Where is Polly?" was his first question.

"Gone out for a walk with Ted to Nazi-Moya, or the One Cocoa-tree, as they call it. She felt dull."

"It is time for her to be back. I don't like her to be out after dark," said Snarley, shaking his head.

"How did you get on with the consul?"

"With him? I did all I expected to do," replied Snarley; "he promised me all the assistance in his power, if anything happened to Polly, but advised me to take the first ship on to India, or back to England, as those Arabs are as artful as they are daring."

"What are you afraid of?" asked Captain Vipond.

"Simply that my little wife Polly will be carried off to adorn the Sultan's harem, and that would be a pretty kettle of fish, wouldn't it?" replied Snarley.

He paced the room uneasily, peering now and again out of the window into the hazy foreground of lengthening shadows, spectral and misty.

His mind was ill at ease.

Two hours passed thus, and he could bear the suspense no longer.

"Lightheart," he said.

"Sir to you," replied Dick.

"Something must have happened."

"I hope not, most sincerely."

"So do I. But I can't stop idle here. Will you come with me to Nazi-Moya? Polly has evidently disappeared."

"But where is Ted?" asked Dick, puzzled.

"Dead, perhaps. Who can tell?" answered Snarley.

His agitation showed that he fondly loved his young wife, and Dick gladly prepared to accompany him, for he was as much interested in Polly's fate as if she had been his own sister.

CHAPTER XXXVII

DICK'S PLUCK.

BOTH Dick and Mr. Snarley armed themselves with six-chamber revolvers, and walked quickly to the fashionable promenade known as the One Cocoa-tree, where the *élite* of Zanzibar congregated in the cool of the evenings.

Here the refreshing breeze blew from the sea over the low-lying island, and fanned the pale cheeks of the residents.

Neither spoke during the journey.

It was late.

The throng had long since departed to their homes, to drink coffee and talk scandal—that never-failing resource of a little European community when abroad.

They found the promenade entirely deserted.

"No one here," said Dick, as they halted to look around them.

"Too late!" cried Snarley, with a groan.

"I wish I had stopped Polly from going, but she seemed so faint and ill I thought the air would do her good."

"It wasn't your fault," answered Snarley, generously.

"I can't help blaming myself, though. But where is Ted?"

He took a few steps forward.

Suddenly his foot struck against something.

Bending down, in the uncertain light, he discovered the body of a boy.

"By Jove!" he cried, "it is—no, it can't be—yes, it is Ted!"

Snarley shivered from head to foot, as if attacked by the ague.

A brief inspection of the body showed that Ted still breathed, though he was perfectly still and motionless.

Dick's foot slipped in a pool of blood.

"There has been some foul play here," he remarked.

Feeling the lad's head, he found a long incised wound, which had evidently been made with some sharp instrument.

"Lend a hand, sir," he continued; "we must carry him back, and get surgical assistance."

"All right, Lightheart," answered Snarley; "you take his legs, and I'll carry his head and shoulders."

Taking up the body, they slowly retraced their steps, feeling that it was useless to look further for Polly just then.

From Ted alone, when he came to himself, could they hope to gain information as to what had happened.

After going some little distance, the motion revived the lad, who opened his eyes.

"Is that you, Master Dick?" he asked, in a faint voice.

"Yes. I am with Mr. Snarley," answered Dick.

"Where am I? Oh! I remember. Have you found her?"

"No."

"Set me down now. I think I can walk with a little help, though I got an ugly knock on the head, and bled a good deal, I suppose."

They put him down, each supporting him under the arm.

"Tell us all about it, if you are strong enough," said Dick.

Snarley was too much upset to speak, and he continued to shiver like an aspen.

"You see, sir," began Ted, as he staggered along the dry, sandy road; "me and Miss Polly stopped a bit behind the rest, because she said it was so calm and peaceful-like, and all at once it came on dark.

"'We'd better be getting on towards home, miss,' I says.

"'Yes, Ted, I think so too,' she replies; 'Mr. Snarley will be anxious about me. But I have enjoyed my walk more than anyone would think.'

"'That's lucky,' says I.

"'Ted,' says she, all of a sudden, 'did you hear anything?'

"'No, miss.'

"'There's a sound of footsteps,' says she.

"And so there was; for just then about a dozen Arabs came up to us, and one, who seemed to be the head of them, collars hold of Miss Polly.

"Now, I know I'm only an odd boy, sir, but I has my feelings, and couldn't stand by and see it done.

"So I lets him have it hot and strong, just between the eyes, and he rolls over just for all the world as if he'd been shot.

"You should have heard the beggars growl; they did holler and cuss a good un.

"'Come on,' says I; 'one down, and I'm game for the next. Old England for ever!'"

"What did they do?" asked Dick.

"They don't fight fair, sir. A second Arab catches hold of Miss Polly, who was a-screaming awful, and claps his ugly black hand over her pretty little pink and white face, and jaws away a lot of jabber that I couldn't make head or tail of.

"It wasn't good enough for me, so I hits out, and he goes down and gets a mouthful of sand, like the first chap.

"'Number two,' says I; 'come on, gentlemen; you're kind, and I'm grateful.'

"But the beggars were like a rusty old gun—they hung fire.

"'Cut,' says I to Miss Polly; 'get out of it as quick as lightning when it's been well greased.'

"She started for to fly, when another cove put out his ugly leg, and tripped her up. I went for that heathen Chinee, sir, but a swell with a turban, with ends streaming down his back like a woman's false hair, ups with something and catches me a prop on the nut that knocks me silly.

"I fell down flat, and never saw or heard no more till I seemed to wake up, and found myself with you."

"She's gone!" cried Snarley, with a deeper and more prolonged groan.

"We'll soon have her back," said Dick; "don't be a coward, man alive. We can guess where she is."

"In the Sultan's palace," returned Snarley; "that's just where the mischief is. I'm poor, and I can't fight a man like the Sultan."

" I'll do it for you."

" You! what are you against so many?" said Snarley, almost contemptuously; " if I trust to you, I shall never see my darling again."

" I tell you you shall."

Snarley broke down.

Covering his face with one hand, the tears glided down his cheeks, and his sobs were audible.

" Come, I say!" exclaimed Dick, " remember you're a man, and men don't cry."

" I can't help it."

" You must; I'd be ashamed to give way like that. I would indeed. You're not the Snarley you used to be."

" I don't care for myself. It's for her, Lightheart. You don't know what a good wife she's been to me."

" Of course she has. If I hadn't been engaged to Henrietta, you should never have had her," said Dick.

" It has been her love which has reconciled me to my new profession, at which your friend Professor Crab sneers. I'm broken-hearted to think she is taken from me."

" We'll have her back. Come on, old fellow, you mustn't be selfish in your grief. Think of Ted. He did all he could for Polly."

" And I thank him for it," replied Snarley.

" You ought to do more than that," said Dick; " his head is badly broken, he wants a doctor, and you keep jawing away here, instead of taking him home."

" I'm very sorry. I didn't think of him," answered Snarley.

" Don't mind me," said Ted; " I am only an odd boy, and ain't got no pertickler feeling except about the heart. That's all right, but my head's a bit wooden, or else that blow I got must have let the daylight in considerable."

With some difficulty they got Ted back to Charley's, where he was seen by a surgeon, who said that, thanks to a rather thick skull, no great harm had been done.

He prescribed some medicine, bound up the wound, and ordered him to keep in bed for a couple of days.

" I ain't going to die, Mister Doctor," said Ted.

" Not this time, my lad," was the reply.

" What saved me?"

" Well, your head's something like a cocoa-nut."

" That's what they said when I went to school. My chump will stand punching," said Ted, philosophically.

There was great excitement at Charley's about the disappearance of Polly, who had made herself a general favourite.

Mr. Snarley went to the British consul again.

He was promised all the assistance that the consul could give him.

This, however, was slight consolation.

He could not say who had carried her off, and it was impossible for him to go to the Sultan's palace and swear that she was there.

His decided opinion was that she was in the power of the Sultan.

This was not evidence, though, being mere conjecture.

Snarley returned to Charley's cast down and dejected.

Dick was waiting up for him, and Professor Crab condescended to sympathise with him, though he did it in a disagreeable manner.

" My good sir," he said, " I am sorry for your loss, deeply sorry; for your wife seemed to me to be a most deserving person."

" Cut it short," said Snarley.

" I haven't much to say," said the professor, drawing himself up with dignity. " A woman is a high type of mammalia, and as such I respect her. She is classified, and I regard her as I would a highly developed species of any kind."

" Lightheart," said Mr. Snarley, " take this man away, will you. I'm not up to kicking him to-night."

" Sir," said the professor, " hear me out. Kick if you like and can, but hear me. People who follow your degraded profession must expect to be regarded with suspicion, and actresses are not remarkable for their virtue."

" By George," said Snarley, clenching his fists, " I can't stand much more of this!"

" Still you have given her your name, such as it is, and she is, I presume, legally married to you," the professor went on.

" I'll show you the certificate."

The professor waved his hand.

"The point is of no great importance; married or not married, she was a source of gain to you, because she was clever."

Snarley turned to Dick.

"Isn't he an insulting beast?" he asked.

"Yes, don't take any notice of him," said Dick.

"I will make a note of the fact that you appear to have loved her, in my essay upon 'morals and manners in various professions, callings, and countries,'" continued the professor.

"Put that down also," said Snarley.

He sprang up and hit Mr. Crab a violent blow in the face.

The professor rolled against the wall, and his spectacles were shattered to atoms.

"Dear me, this is an assault," he remarked.

"Yes, and you'll have another directly, if you don't shut up," said Snarley.

"Is this right, Lightheart?" asked the professor. "Will you stand by and see me smitten in the eye?"

"It served you right, sir," said Dick.

"May I venture to inquire why?"

"You chaffed Mr. Snarley, when you knew he was already excited."

"Is that any reason why I should have my nose bruised and my spectacles ruined; they were pebbles, and I doubt if I can match them in Zanzibar."

"Stop it, or I'll do it again," said Snarley; "I can't stand it."

"Quite right too," said old Hopkins, who had been remarkably quiet hitherto.

"What have you to do with it, my friend?" asked Mr. Crab.

"Polly is my daughter, and you've been a bullyragging of her. She's as honest as ever your mother was, though she do play on the stage for her living."

"My friend, pray calm yourself," said the professor.

"I is calm, but Snarley shan't be put upon and nagged at by the likes of you."

"Do you know who I am?"

"A jolly, insulting old fool, that's what I call you."

"Lightheart," said the professor, "I shall wish you good night and return to my studies. I cannot put up with the ungrammatical passions of these people."

"Good night, sir," rejoined Dick.

The professor had almost gained the door when an idea struck Hopkins.

"Blessed if I can't help him on his way," he cried.

Rushing after him, he raised his foot, and the unlucky professor, springing high in the air, missed the first step and rolled down to the bottom of the staircase.

Old Hopkins returned, rubbing his hands.

"That's done me as much good as an encore," he said. "The nasty, crabbed old wretch. He never opens his mouth unless it is to talk skientific or say something nasty."

"Never mind him," said Snarley. "What's to be done about Polly?"

"God knows, poor girl! I'd give my right hand to have her back again. Shall we return to the palace?" said Hopkins.

"That's all rot," said Dick.

"Ah! my boy, you don't know the feelings of a father."

"Nor those of a husband," said Snarley.

"I had an idea of getting into the palace to hear your next performance," said Dick.

They both looked up hopefully at him.

It was strange to see two men so much older than he was pinning their faith to a mere boy.

"What's the dodge?" asked Hopkins.

"The wheeze is this," answered Dick. "You dress me up in Polly's clothes. Twig?"

"Not yet."

"You go and sell me to Selim-el-Mandeb, the Vizier, as a slave for the Sultan."

"Well?"

"That will get me into the palace, won't it? I've got good features, and no hair on my face yet. My hair has grown pretty long—I can stick on a chignon, and there we are."

"But," said Hopkins, "they'd murder you when they found you out."

"First of all they'd have to spell 'able.' I'm not so easily disposed of as you think, and I'll back myself to get Polly out of this scrape."

Hopkins reflected a moment.

"Upon my word," he exclaimed, at length, "there is a good deal of sense in what Master Lightheart says."

"Of course there is, old son," answered Dick. "I know what I'm about. The consul can't do anything. He will only promise to help you."

" Save her, Lightheart, and you will save my life," exclaimed Snarley.

" All right. Leave it to me. Have a drink, and go quietly to bed. To-morrow we'll dress up, and I'll chance the rest."

" You are risking your life, though," remarked Snarley.

" That's of no consequence. A man can but die once, and I think I proved I was not afraid of death when I was in the boat, just before you picked me up, and we drew lots who should die."

" I admire your spirit," exclaimed Mr. Snarley.

" And I like your pluck, my boy," said old Hopkins, " but you were always a oner."

" A British boy," replied Dick, " should always be like Nelson and not know fear. I don't say I shall succeed in saving Polly, but I say I will try."

" I shall not forget your kindness," said Snarley.

" We haven't much in the treasury, Master Dick; only a matter of a hundred quid, or so, but it is all at your service," added Hopkins.

" My dear fellow," answered Dick, " what I do is without hope or expectation of reward. Polly and I are old friends; you are an old pal; Mr. Snarley was my tutor at school; and if my daring and dodginess will put you all right, you're welcome."

" You're a brave boy," said Snarley; " you don't want flattery or thanks, do you ?"

" Not I."

" My heart's too full for talking. I accept your offer with pleasure, and God speed you."

" Amen!" exclaimed old Hopkins, solemnly.

" If I get killed and find a nameless grave, you'll tell the people at home all about it, won't you ?" asked Dick.

" We'll do more than that—we'll avenge you," said Snarley, theatrically.

" That's settled. Let's have another bottle of fiz, and go to bye-bye."

" I could drink a gallon to-night, and it wouldn't hurt me," said Snarley.

They passed an hour very pleasantly, and went to bed, Dick dreaming that he was the favourite sultana of the harem, and that all the other ladies were trying to poison him.

Such is the strength of the imagination when the body is at rest and the mind perturbed.

CHAPTER XXXVIII.

THE WHITE SLAVE.

IT would have been impossible for any one of mature years to successfully undertake the task Dick had set himself.

The palace of an Eastern sultan is jealously guarded.

Potentates in the East are permitted by their religion to have as many wives as they can buy.

Solomon in the Bible is said to have had six hundred concubines.

In our prosaic England a man sometimes finds one wife to be one too many.

Few who are married would like to have two.

But the harem, in the East, is the place where the ladies who enjoy their royal master's favour live, and it is guarded, as we have said, most carefully.

The Kislar Agha, or chief eunuch, has the command of the seraglio.

He answers with his head for the integrity of its seclusion; and to venture into such a place, on the part of a man or boy, is the height of imprudence.

Dick, however, had determined to risk it.

He had a dare-devil spirit.

The day after the disappearance of Polly, the Sultan was reclining upon a pile of soft cushions, lazily smoking scented tobacco in the richly-carved bowl of a narghily or Eastern pipe.

The hubble-bubble of the smoke as it passed through the rose water in the bowl was the only sound that disturbed the stillness of the room.

The apartment opened on to a court or yard, open to the sky; the floor was of marble, the walls inlaid with mosaic and gold in the Moorish fashion.

Beds of sweet-smelling flowers and orange and lemon trees in tubs were scattered about.

While in the centre of the court a fountain rose, melodiously falling in a rich and sparkling cascade into a marble basin, in which gold and silver fish sported gaily.

Birds with gorgeous plumage hopped from tree to tree and chirped their sweet notes.

It was a scene at once melodious and enchanting.

The Sultan suddenly clapped his hands, and a tall slave, pushing aside the heavy velvet hangings which supplied the place of paper on the walls, made his appearance.

"The sovereign lord of the universe called his slave," said the negro, making a profound obeisance, which nearly prostrated him full-length on the floor.

"Let the Vizier attend me," exclaimed the Sultan.

A few minutes elapsed, and Selim-el-Mandeb entered the room with a smile of satisfaction on his face.

He, too, made a low bow and waited for the Sultan to speak.

"Selim," said the latter, "has the sun risen on the refreshing slumber of the fair Feringhee?"

"My lord, her maidens have informed me that after passing the night in tears she sleeps."

"It is well. When she has partaken of food let me be summoned, for I will repair to her chamber and endeavour to melt the ice of modesty with the sun of love."

"The British consul has been to the palace to see your highness," continued Selim.

"Ha! Is the disappearance of the girl set down at our door? This is too much," ejaculated the Sultan.

"It is said, my lord, that as I offered to buy the maiden and she was refused to me, I have stolen her for your highness's seraglio."

"But you have stifled the voice of suspicion with the cloak of a lie. You have sent the consul away satisfied she is not here?"

"I am the meanest of my lord's slaves, and I trust I have not failed in my duty. The consul went away in contentment;

you will hear no more from him. Allah is my witness, I have said it," answered Selim.

"Bismillah, Allah be praised; these English have ships that sail all seas, and guns that make the earth tremble. It is not well to offend them. Allah, resoul, Allah!" said the Sultan, with pious gratitude.

"My lord need not fear the Feringhees; he also has guns," said Selim. "Is not my lord the governor of the world and the mightiest among men? What are the English? They are as dirt compared with your highness."

"It is well said, Selim," answered the Sultan, smiling at the flattery.

"May thy slave speak to your highness concerning another matter?"

"Say on, Selim. Thy words are as sweet music in my ears."

"A merchant has sought admission to the palace; he brings with him a child of the west, fair, young, well-favoured, and plump as a young quail."

"What is the price of the white slave? Give him what he asks and bring her before me," said the Sultan, eagerly.

"Her price is one thousand dollars," replied Selim, adding mentally, "and to pay that will nearly empty the treasury."

"Pay it. How call you the maiden, O Selim?"

"Aida. She is from the cold clime of Frankestan. She speaks no word of Arabic, but her form is well-moulded and pleasant to the eyes."

"Go, Selim, son of my heart," exclaimed the Sultan, "fetch me the slave. Thrice blessed is the master who is served quickly."

The Vizier shuffled away to bring the white slave to the Sultan.

In a room near the principal entrance to the palace stood old Hopkins, who was dressed as an English sailor, lest the Vizier should recognise him in his ordinary attire as one of the players.

By his side sat a tall girl, dressed in white muslin and closely veiled.

Her manner was modest and somewhat sad.

Casting down her eyes, the white slave sat with her hands folded meekly on her lap.

"Here he comes," whispered Hopkins. "He's been to speak to the Sultan,

I expect. Keep up your spirits, my lad, and God be with you."

" I'm all there," said the girl.

" Hush !" said Hopkins. " Now for the deal."

Selim approached the pretended sailor, and began to haggle about the price of the slave.

Eventually Hopkins agreed to take eight hundred dollars, by which Selim was a gainer of two hundred, as he could charge his royal master a thousand dollars.

" Come, my child, thou art bought and sold," said Selim ; " and thy good fortune has guided thee to the palace of the Light of the Universe. Walk by my side."

Casting a farewell look at Hopkins, Dick, for it was he disguised as a girl, put himself by the side of the Vizier and traversed a lengthy corridor.

His heart beat wildly at the thought of the desperate adventure he had embarked in.

If he were unlucky and his plans failed, he could not hope to come out of the palace alive.

But the reflection that he was there for a good purpose, and that Polly's honour and liberty depended upon his coolness and nerve, gave him courage.

A few hours at most would determine his fate.

CHAPTER XXXIX.

WHAT HAPPENED IN THE SULTAN'S PALACE.

WHEN Selim-el-Mandeb had advanced halfway along the corridor, he stopped and pinched Dick's arm.

" The English maiden is fair to see," remarked the Vizier, with a leer.

He encircled his waist with a long, twining arm, and attempted to kiss him.

Dick immediately gave him a slap in the face with his open hand.

The Vizier rolled up against the wall, crying—

" Allah protect us ! How hard she hits for a woman !"

" Turn it up," exclaimed Dick ; " I'll tell the Sultan !"

" He don't understand English, my child," replied the Vizier ; " I have to interpret for him ; and you must know that in time the Sultan will tire of your charms, and then I can get you put in a sack and thrown into the sea."

" That would be getting the sack and no mistake," said Dick, laughing.

" More than you think depends upon me. It is not wise to throw dirt on my beard. Come, sweet Aida, smile upon me, and no longer refuse me a pretty kiss."

" You mustn't do it," answered Dick, remembering that he was playing the part of a girl.

" Why not, sweet Aida ? No one will know."

" Mother says I mustn't," replied Dick.

" You are far away from home, and it is the destiny of girls to be kissed," urged the Vizier.

" Well, kiss my hand ; won't that do ?" said Dick.

He extended his hand, and the Vizier raised it passionately to his lips.

" Come along, do," said Dick ; " I want to see the Sultan."

He ran on first, and the Vizier, amorous though he was, desisted from his efforts to obtain a kiss and followed him.

After going some distance, Dick stopped, and Selim overtook him out of breath.

" Go it, old fellow ; I'll lead you a dance," said Dick to himself.

" How you run," said the Vizier ; " fleet as a deer are you."

A slave met them at this juncture, and, addressing the Vizier, said in Arabic—

" The fair Feringhee is awake. Her maidens attend her, but she will not eat or drink. Her tears fall like the rain in spring. Who shall comfort her ?"

This slave was the Kislar Agha, or chief of the eunuchs, who had the entire charge of the harem.

" Seyd himself shall comfort her," said Selim, in English, calling the Sultan by his name. " Yes, Seyd himself shall see this Western pearl and kiss away the tears. Ah ! son of Eblis that I am," he added, "I am talking in the foreign tongue, which the Kislar Agha cannot interpret."

He repeated his reply in Arabic.

Dick concluded that the lady they were talking about must be Polly.

He said nothing, however, it being his plan to seem as simple and innocent as possible.

"Hassein," cried the Vizier, addressing the Kislar Agha, "take this white slave to the harem, and have her scented and painted for his highness's inspection."

"Is she a new purchase?"

"Yes, our master wishes something always new; take him with you; I will hasten to Seyd," said the Vizier, shrugging his shoulders.

The Kislar Agha pushed Dick rudely along the passage, and made signs that he was to walk before him.

A short walk brought them to the harem, which was a distinct block of building from the rest of the palace.

Here resided all the ladies of the Sultan's household and their attendants.

They were never allowed to appear in public.

All the exercise they obtained was in a large, high-walled garden, where they played like children when they were not quarrelling, which was often enough.

At other times they indulged in the pleasures of the bath, ate sweetmeats, smoked cigarettes, and lounged upon piles of cushions, listening to the ripple of numerous fountains, the songs of birds, and the plaintive music of the little Arab boys who played on various instruments.

A more lazy, unnatural, useless life for a woman cannot be imagined.

Crossing a yard Dick was ushered into the seraglio or harem, and handed over to an old woman, who could not speak a word of English.

She conducted him to a large room, elegantly furnished, where upwards of sixty women of all ages were lounging about.

They stared insolently at him as he entered.

Some ran up to him and talked in Arabic.

He shook his head as a sign that he did not understand them.

The old woman called in a loud voice for Anna.

A woman, with a very ladylike appearance, but old, haggard, and worn, came up.

A few words passed between them, and the one named Anna said, in excellent English, to Dick—

"I hear you are a countrywoman of mine."

"Are you English?" asked Dick.

"Unfortunately, I am."

"How long have you been here?"

"Seventeen years, now. This place is a grave. When I first came, I was young and handsome, like yourself. My father was a shipowner. He took me for a voyage, we came here, and I was stolen."

"Is there no escape?"

"None. When once within these walls, you are dead for ever to the world. I was the Sultan's first wife for a time," continued Anna. "But he got another, and I was thrown into the background. I have not spoken to him for years, and my life glides away without anything to interest me. I am a prisoner. They clothe and feed me, that is all."

"Sorry for you," said Dick. "I should bolt."

"You can't. The Kislar Agha would kill you if he caught you."

"I'd try it on."

"Ah, you do not know. You are young and inexperienced. Where do you come from, and what brought you here?"

"That's a secret, my little dear," replied Dick. "When we know one another better, I may tell you."

"I am willing to be your friend," she answered, "because I feel for a countrywoman. One's beauty soon fades here, and then you are thought nothing of."

"Perhaps I may want a friend, Anna," replied Dick, seriously.

"I feel sure of it."

"Where can I find you if I want you?"

"Here. I am always in this room or at the bath. Would you like to come and bathe with me now? There are always several ladies in the bath."

"Not at present," answered Dick, smiling. "I'll just walk about; you sit here, Anna, and go on with your cigarette. I'll come back directly."

"Where are you going?" she asked.

"'NOW FOR YOU, MY BOY!' CRIED DICK."

"Only to have a look round"

"Do not be too proud and confident," said Anna. "I hear that a new and lovely bird has just been caged."

"Indeed?"

"An English girl who came over with some actors. She is in the palace, and has been stolen or decoyed from her friends."

"How do you know this?"

"Oh, we know everything. This is the most gossiping little place in the world. But you cannot blame us, we have nothing else to do but gossip."

Dick laughed.

"I'll give you something to talk about," he thought to himself. "Wait a bit."

The ladies favoured him with an insolent stare as he walked about. They wore the eastern dress, having tunics and yellow or blue drawers, puffed out at the sides, while he had on an ordinary muslin skirt.

A pretty Georgian slave was reclining on a divan, and he sat down close by her side.

He gave her a pinch to attract her attention, and said—

"Ain't you a little duck, eh?"

The lovely Georgian did not understand him.

"Give us a kiss for luck," continued Dick.

He bent over her and kissed her, squeezing her hand at the same time, and the Georgian, thinking that the new slave was lonely and miserable, and wishing to make a friend of someone, had saluted her, returned the caress.

"This is nice," thought Dick; "I like this."

The Georgian talked to him in her own language, which he could not understand, but her tone was encouraging, and she seemed to be saying that he need not fear anything.

Dick thought of that Georgian for a long time afterwards.

She gave him a cigarette and a glass of iced water, and as often as he kissed her, she kissed him, believing him all the time to be a woman, like herself.

An hour glided by, and Dick was roused from his happiness by a loud shriek.

Two of the inmates of the harem had quarrelled, and were fighting, scratching, and even biting.

Instantly they were surrounded by a crowd, and all the ladies chattered away like a lot of monkeys.

The harem, before so quiet, was all alive with excitement.

Nothing roused the ladies so much as a set-to between two or more of their number.

Everyone was gesticulating and shouting except Anna, who put herself by Dick's side, and said—

"That sort of thing is common enough here. It is not worth looking at. Talk to me."

"It's fine to see a mill between you women," answered Dick.

"If the Kislar Agha hears them, he will come in with his whip, and soon quiet them."

"What! whip a woman?" exclaimed Dick, indignantly.

"Yes, and serve them right too. He lashes at them as does the huntsman in a kennel full of hounds. What a Babel there is! But it is always thus. The women have no minds. They are only taught to cultivate the body."

"That's a staggerer," said Dick, as one of the fair combatants knocked the other into a small fountain which was in a marble basin.

"Here comes the Agha," exclaimed Anna, "and I'm not sorry."

The Kislar Agha had heard the noise, and he stalked into the room, holding in his hand a sort of dog whip with a long lash.

A score of women instantly surrounded him, all talking at once, and giving a different version of the quarrel.

He pushed them all on one side, and proceeded towards the originators of the discord.

"If he touches either of them," exclaimed Dick, pressing his teeth together, "I'll give him something."

"Do not be rash," said Anna.

"But I can't stand by and see it done."

"They do not deserve your sympathy. If they were not all treated like children, and punished when they are naughty, there would never be any order in the harem."

"Shut them up in a room by themselves on bread and water, or something of that sort," said Dick.

" When you have been here some time, you will not interest yourself in anybody's business. One effect of the life we lead is to make everyone hate everyone else like poison. There is no friendship in the harem."

" My little Georgian was kind to me."

" Because you are a new comer, and will have some power for a time, and she wishes to send a message to the Sultan through you. Silly fool, her day is past, like mine," answered Anna, bitterly.

The sharp crack of the whip was heard, followed by cries of pain.

" He's at it," exclaimed Dick, trembling with excitement.

Anna laid her hand upon his arm.

" Are you mad ?" she asked.

" I can't stand it," replied Dick.

" You will be bastinadoed if you touch the Kislar Agha."

" What's that ?"

" Beaten with a stick on the soles of your feet."

" We'll see about that," answered Dick, struggling to get away from the embrace in which she held him.

The next moment he was free.

Pushing his way through the crowd of ladies, he got to the front, and saw the chief of the eunuchs chastising one of the women who had been fighting.

She cowered at his feet, and only uttered short, sharp, whining cries, as each stroke of the whip fell upon her defenceless shoulders.

" You cowardly brute !" cried Dick.

At the same time he struck him a violent blow under the ear.

The Kislar Agha fell like a log.

" Down you go like a bullock. That was a good floorer," said Dick.

The noisy crowd was hushed in an instant.

A great and solemn fear seemed to fall upon all in the spacious apartment.

Such a thing had never before been witnessed in the harem.

The Kislar Agha, stunned, lay still and motionless, as if he were dead.

Even Dick was astonished at the success of his blow.

If he had not struck him just under the ear, which is a tender spot, the result would not have been so serious.

What was he to do now ?

When the Agha came to himself, he would certainly deal out a heavy punishment to Dick.

Perhaps his feet would be beaten into a jelly under the process of the bastinado.

Suddenly Anna touched him on the elbow.

" This way, quick. You must hide," she cried, hurriedly.

" What can he do ?" replied Dick.

" I know not ; but you had best avoid him if you can at present."

The Kislar Agha moved uneasily.

" What force you have in your arms," she said. " Who would have thought you could hit so hard ?"

" It's gymnastics ; I used to be a good hand at that sort of thing," replied Dick.

" You will find it an unlucky blow, I fear, for you have made an enemy of the Agha for life," continued Anna. " But come this way."

She led the way towards a door which conducted to the garden.

A black slave, who was one of the Agha's attendants, stood there and waved them back.

They went to the principal entrance, which was similarly guarded.

" Flight is impossible ; I thought as much," said Anna, despairingly. " The Kislar Agha seldom comes unattended."

Dick sat down upon an ottoman, feeling puzzled.

He had come into the harem to rescue Polly, and all he had done was to make love to a Georgian and get himself into serious trouble with the Agha.

Blaming himself for his folly in losing his temper and acting as he had done, he waited impatiently for the Agha to come to his senses.

" I suppose I shall be beaten or locked up in a vault, or something of that sort," he muttered. " What a fool I was, to be sure !"

It too late to think of that now.

He should have checked himself before.

Suddenly the buzz of conversation began again. The Kislar Agha was recovering himself.

He staggered to his feet, and glared savagely around him.

" Now for it," said Dick, who felt anything but comfortable.

The crisis was approaching.

CHAPTER XL.

THE BASTINADO,

SEVERAL ladies of the harem who wished to curry favour with the Agha pointed out Dick as the one who struck him.

The Agha spoke a few words in Arabic to some slaves, and Dick was seized by the arm.

They half led, half dragged him into the passage, and conducted him into a small room at the end.

He was suddenly thrown on his back, and his feet were held up in the air, while his slippers were taken from his feet.

The Agha provided himself with a long cane.

Raising it in the air, he brought it down with all his strength upon the soles of the unprotected feet.

A stinging sensation, which numbed his legs up to the knees, was felt by the sufferer.

Blow followed blow until Dick could bear it no longer.

Exerting all his strength, he threw off the two negroes who were holding him.

"I've had enough of this," he said.

A chair stood near him.

Seizing it in his powerful grasp, he tore off one of the legs, and, as one of the slaves approached him, he hit him on the forehead.

The wretched eunuch fell down with his skull broken.

Another blow prostrated the second slave, who was prostrated by the side of his companion.

"Now for you, my boy," exclaimed Dick, rushing upon the Kislar Agha.

The chief of the eunuchs extended his arm to save his head, but a blow from Dick's formidable weapon broke it.

Retiring with a howl to a corner, the Agha sank upon the floor.

Dick looked around him.

His enemies were defeated, and flight was easy; but what puzzled him was where to fly to.

He did not understand the intricacies of the Sultan's palace.

"Better give this cove a crack on the head, too," he thought, approaching the Kislar Agha for this purpose.

The latter pointed to his broken arm, which caused him great pain, in token that he was defenceless.

"Well," said Dick, "I won't hit a wounded man; that would be cowardly; but when I think of my poor feet, which are smarting and aching most infernally, I've a jolly good mind to give you a topper."

However, he did not do so.

Going to the door, he saw that the key was outside, and he contented himself with locking it.

Perhaps he might have escaped from the harem, but this he did not want to do.

His object was to rescue Polly.

He had pledged himself to Mr. Snarley and old Hopkins, and if he did not keep his promise, what would they think of him?

While he was hesitating what to do, and which way to go, he saw his friend of the harem, Anna, who glided up to him with the utmost care.

"How did you escape?" she asked. "I heard your cries while you were being bastinadoed."

"That I'll bet a sovereign you didn't," replied Dick.

"But——"

"I didn't halloo at all. I've too much pluck for that. You might have heard the Agha when I broke his arm, or the slaves when I cracked their skulls with this leg of a chair."

He pointed to his weapon, which he still carried in his hand.

"Oh, I see now," she cried. "How strong you are for a woman."

"I am not a woman," said Dick.

Anna uttered a little scream.

"What?" she exclaimed.

"No; I'm a young man," said Dick, "disguised as a woman."

"But it is death for a man to enter this place unless he is in the service of the Kislar Agha."

" I know that."

" What, then, induced you to be so rash ?"

" Humanity and friendship. I wished to save a friend of mine from the fate which you deplore so much."

" Whom do you mean ?"

" The lady of whom you spoke to me. She who was stolen for the Sultan's pleasure. The last bird who has been caged in this den of infamy."

" Ah! it is very grand of you to entertain such an idea; but I fear you will not be able to accomplish it, yet I honour and admire you for your courage," said Anna.

" Do you know where she is ?"

" Alas! I do not."

" By Jove! how my feet sting," exclaimed Dick ; " that bastinado is no joke ; I shouldn't like a couple of dozen cuts on each foot."

" It would cripple you for a week."

" How do you know ?"

" Because I have been subjected to it myself; it is nothing here," answered Anna.

" The brutes, I should like to set fire to the place.

" But tell me, what can I do ? Where can I go ?" said Dick.

" You see that staircase ?" replied Anna.

" Yes."

" It leads to the roof, which is flat. Go up there. I will spread a report that you have escaped through the garden, a door of which you found open."

" And what then ?" asked Dick.

" Wait till nightfall, and I will seek you, and conduct you out of the palace."

" I cannot, will not go without Polly," said Dick, in determination.

" Are you so resolved to save the last victim of the amorous Sultan ?" asked Anna.

" Or die in the attempt."

" How you must love her !"

" As a sister I do, but in no other way. She is the wife of a friend of mine. As for me, I have a sweetheart in England."

" Why risk your life, in what I fear will be a vain attempt ?"

" Because I cannot leave the poor girl to her fate. It would be cowardly, and whatever else I may be, I hope I am not a coward," answered Dick.

" I forgot for a moment that I was speaking to an Englishman. You are like the rest of them. You know not fear, and are ever ready to do a generous action. So different to the soulless Turks and Arabs, among whom my lot has been cast for so many years."

A loud noise was heard at the extremity of the corridor.

The Kislar Agha was kicking against the door and calling loudly for help.

" Haste, haste," said Anna; " we are wasting the precious minutes. In a short time the whole of the seraglio will be aroused. Expect me at midnight."

Dick pressed her hand in token of gratitude.

Then he rushed up the staircase, his ears being filled with the wild cries of the Agha.

His progress was stopped by a trapdoor, which he pushed open, stepping upon a flat roof, such as is common in the East.

Its level character was only broken here and there by chimneys, which rise at various points without any design or regularity.

Ensconcing himself under the shelter of a chimney, he sat down in the shadow to avoid the heat of the sun.

His feet began to swell from the effects of the bastinado, but he did not dare to take his shoes off, which he had hastily put on before he locked the Agha in the room, because he did not know if he should be able to get them on again.

The heat was tremendous.

A fierce thirst attacked him, which he was unable to quench, though he would have given anything for a draught of iced lemonade.

" Lucky dog, Snarley," he thought ; " he's at Charley's, and can swim in lush if he likes."

He heard the mew of a cat.

Looking up, he saw a fine Persian, arching its back, and indulging in those melodious cries which make the night lively in any country.

" Blow the brute; why can't he keep quiet," he exclaimed.

He was in a bad temper, which is not to be wondered at, considering the various occurrences of that eventful day.

Chipping off some pieces of cement from the chimney, he began to take shots at the cat.

The animal annoyed him.

One or two pieces hit the cat, which ran to the parapet, casting frightened glances around to see where his enemy was hidden.

It was not thus that his favourites attacked him generally.

" That's a sort of Sultan cat, a regular vicious old Tom, calling his harem around him. I'll spoil his game," said Dick.

He took up half a brick, which he dislodged with some difficulty, and threw it with all his skill at the cat.

The brick struck it on the side, and brick and cat rolled over the parapet into the garden.

Creeping up to the edge, Dick looked over.

The garden swarmed with black slaves, who were hunting the trees and bushes thoroughly.

It was evidently thought that Dick was concealed somewhere about there.

" What a lark," said Dick to himself.

The Kislar Agha was swearing in choice Arabic at the slaves, and as he stood nearly under Dick, the latter could not resist the temptation of having a shot at him.

Creeping back, he dislodged another half brick. This he took to the parapet, and let it fall on the Agha.

There was a cry, a fall, and an immense hubbub.

The unfortunate Agha received the brick on his head, and as it fell from a considerable distance, it hurt him.

His turban, which consisted of many folds, and would have made a decent-sized shawl for a lady, protected him from the full force of the blow.

Nevertheless he fell on his hands and knees, bellowing like a bull.

The slaves looked up and saw Dick.

They raised a shout and pointed to the roof.

Instantly half-a-dozen launched themselves towards the nearest door, evidently with the intention of coming up to the roof.

" It's a case of pickles," groaned Dick. " I've done a nice thing. Why couldn't I let the old fool alone?"

It was too late to indulge in regrets now.

In a few minutes the roof would be alive with the attendants of the harem.

The thoughts of more bastinado nearly maddened Dick.

But how could he escape it?

This time he would be bound, well-guarded, held down, until his soles were beaten into a pulp, to gratify the malice of the Kislar Agha.

Suddenly the chimneys struck him as a means of safety.

He might descend one, or hide in the shaft till the hue and cry was over.

Precipitating himself towards the nearest, from which no smoke issued, he let himself down, clinging to the irregularly placed bricks of which it was composed.

The soot nearly stifled him.

He coughed and spluttered, but continued to descend.

Fierce cries and exclamations reached his ears in a confused murmur.

" They're sold," he thought. " But what if they twig my little game, and light all the fires. Scissors !"

A cold sweat broke out all over him at the bare idea.

He went down gradually, placing his foot on every projecting ledge, holding on by his hands, which were scratched and torn by the sharp edges of the bricks.

At length he felt something which seemed to be flat and solid.

" Land at last," he murmured. " I thought this beastly old chimney was like the shaft of a coal-pit."

Lowering his body, he emerged from the chimney, and proceeded to rub the soot out of his eyes.

It was impossible for him to say where he was.

The room was scantily furnished, and appeared to be what is called an ante-room, leading into some grander apartment.

Dick looked down at his skirts as soon as he had got the soot out of his eyes.

" I ought to arrange my dress," he remarked, with a smile, as he smoothed down the blackened garment.

A door stood half open on his right.

He heard a voice, which spoke in Arabic, issue from it.

" I'll go and listen," he said to himself. " Perhaps I shall hit upon Polly after all."

His conjecture was nearer the mark than he believed at the moment. The unfortunate girl was in need of help.

Her position was as desperate as his own.

Perhaps more so.

Stealing along on tiptoe, Dick approached the half-open door.

His heart beat high with expectation.

The least sound would betray him, and he had a wholesome dread of the Kislar Agha.

Those four strokes of the bastinado had made a salutary impression upon Dick.

"Never no more," he muttered, rather ungrammatically; "at least, not if I know it."

CHAPTER XLI.

THE ESCAPE.

PEEPING carefully in through the door, he beheld an elegantly furnished apartment, everything in which was in the Oriental style; but the effect was at once voluptuous and entrancing. In it were three people.

The first he easily recognised as Selim-el-Mandeb, the Grand Vizier.

The second, from the gorgeousness of his attire and the quantity of jewels which sparkled all over his dress, he imagined to be the Sultan, while a glance sufficed to show him that the third was Polly.

Her hair hung in dishevelled masses all over her shoulders.

Her eyes were red with weeping, and she sat with her hands clasped as if in an agony of doubt and despair.

Selim acted as interpreter for the Sultan, who spoke to him at intervals.

"Why not be resigned to your fate?" Dick heard Selim-el-Mandeb say.

"Never! never!" answered Polly. "Death would be preferable to a life within these walls."

"But his highness will make you his favourite Sultana."

"I have only one wish, and that is to return to my husband and my friends."

"When the sun shines upon the drooping petals of the flower after the rain in spring-time, it raises its bowed head and looks up smilingly to the skies," said Selim.

"Tell your master," replied Polly, "that he will never warm my affection into life for him. I will defend my honour at any price. He can kill me, and that is all."

"Maiden, beware," said Selim, changing his tone.

"Of what?" she asked.

"The sovereign displeasure of his highness. Kneel before him, kiss the hem of his robes, and beg his forgiveness."

Polly laughed scornfully.

"That may be the custom among slaves, but you will never get me to do it," she answered.

"Reflect that there are dungeons black as night under this palace, where you will spend your weary days, with loathsome snakes and crawling insects."

"I care not."

"There are whips which hurt the tender skin."

"Better solitary confinement and daily punishment than the love of that monster," replied Polly, boldly.

"What does she say?" asked the Sultan, in Arabic.

"She is like the timid fawn, your highness, and is overpowered by the sun of your favour. Her virgin modesty embarrasses her."

"Tell her that my love for her is like the mighty waters of the Red Sea in a storm, and that she has nothing to fear."

"Girl," continued the Vizier, sternly, "will you renounce luxury, and all that wealth can buy and love bestow?"

"I will," said Polly.

"You cannot get away. The dungeon and the chastisements which fall upon the unruly await you."

"Oh!" groaned Polly, "if Dick Lightheart were only here, he would make short work of all of you. Oh, Dick, Dick, if you could only hear me and come here. I wish some kind fairy would transport you into this den of iniquity."

Dick sprang forward with a bound.

"I am here, Polly, dear," he cried.

The amazement of the Sultan at this

sudden apparition was ludicrous to witness.

He turned as pale as his dusky skin would allow him, and his complexion assumed the hue of chocolate and cream.

Jumping quite a foot high in the air, he sank upon a divan and went into a fit.

Foaming at the mouth, his feet kicking up and down, his turban having fallen off, revealed his ugly little bullet-shaped, bald head, and piteous whines issued from his lips.

A handsome scimitar hung by his side.

Dick made a dash at this, secured it, and was just in time to catch Selim at the door.

The Vizier was going to call assistance.

Hitting him over the head with the scabbard, Dick had the satisfaction of seeing him fall senseless at his feet.

Polly was in a state of nervous apprehension.

With his blackened face, his torn and dirty women's clothes, and his altered appearance generally, she could not bring herself to believe that it really was Dick Lightheart.

"Don't you know me, Polly?" exclaimed he.

"Can it be you?" she asked, timidly.

"It's the Bank of England to a China orange, or Wall Street, New York, to a pawnshop, that it's nobody else."

"But this disguise?"

"Is easily explained. I determined to rescue you, and dressed up as a girl, was sold as a slave this morning, introduced to the harem, and after a series of surprising adventures, which would make your hair curl to listen to, I got down a chimney, and fluked it so well that I tumbled upon you at a most critical moment."

"Thank goodness you have come," she answered.

"'I guess,' as the Yankees say, 'we're in a fix, though; regularly fixed up,'" remarked Dick.

All at once Polly burst out laughing.

"What is the joke?" he asked.

"Oh, I didn't think I could laugh. It's horrible to be taken away by a man who can have as many wives as he likes."

"But where is the fun? Hanged if I see it."

"You look so funny in that dress," said Polly, laughing again.

"Don't the togs fit me? I flattered myself the get-up was quite O. K.," said Dick, arranging his skirts.

"You are as black as a sweep."

"That is the chimney. It will wash off."

At this moment the Sultan began to recover from his fit, and getting up, looked about him.

"Hallo, old man, how do you find yourself by this time?" inquired Dick.

There was no answer.

The Sultan felt for his scimitar.

It was gone.

He made a movement towards the door, but Dick stopped him.

"I can't talk your language," he remarked, "so it's no use parley-vousing. Take that, old son."

He struck the Sultan as he had done Selim.

"Down you go like a bullock in a slaughter-house," he said.

"Oh, don't kill him," said Polly, nervously.

"Not I," said Dick, "I'm sorry for spoiling his little game, but if he holloas we're lost. It isn't nice to be baulked and have your head cracked in the bargain. Come along, Polly; we'll see if we can't get out of this somehow."

"Stop a moment," said Polly.

"What is it?"

"I have heard in the East, you can do what you like in the palace of the great men, provided you have one thing."

"Money?" asked Dick.

"No; the Sultan's ring."

"Not a bad idea," said Dick; "but I'll improve upon it."

"How?"

"I'll dress up in his clothes; I'll not only have his ring, but his togs, and all his jewels, and everything. My face is black; isn't it?"

"Yes."

"If you see any white part, wet your finger in your mouth, and rub the soot in."

Polly did so, and Dick began to strip the insensible Sultan.

"You go into the next room, Polly. I shall leave him as naked as a robin," said Dick.

Polly blushed, and retired while Dick dressed himself in the Sultan's garments.

He was about the same height and build, though younger-looking; but when he had the turban on, he did not look very unlike his majesty.

"Now, then," he said, rejoining Polly, "we'll try our luck."

Walking together, they traversed numerous corridors and galleries, until at length they came to a small courtyard, in which were three negro slaves.

Espying a small postern, Dick waved his hand as if he wished it opened.

The slaves prostrated themselves to the earth, and the door swung back on its hinges.

It happened that the gate was a private one, by which the Sultan often went out, accompanied by his Vizier.

Therefore there was nothing extraordinary in his majesty wishing to pass out that way.

It seemed strange, however, that he should desire to take a girl dressed in the English fashion with him.

However, it wasn't the duty of the slaves to make inquiries of their sovereign lord and master.

All that they understood was to obey.

The door led into a small lane, flanked on each side by a low stone wall.

This went into the interior of the island, and was little frequented, the palace being on the outskirts of the city.

Walking hastily along without speaking, they got away from the palace.

They had not gone more than half a mile when they heard the great bell of the palace sounding the alarm.

"Hark!" cried Dick.

"Oh! what does it mean?" asked Polly, shivering with fright.

"Our escape is discovered; we shall be pursued. Let us turn on one side."

"I will do anything you tell me," she answered. "You are so clever, and I am only a poor, weak, foolish girl."

"You're a trump, Polly, that's what you are," replied Dick. "I wish I knew where we are; I was afraid to skirt the palace and get into the town, thinking I should arrive at Charley's by some roundabout way."

"They will kill us if they catch us, will they not?" she demanded, nervously.

"Not you. They would take jolly good care I didn't make old bones. As Ted says, they'd be on to me like grub; but you would not be hurt."

"Oh, if we were only amongst our friends again! They couldn't take us away then, could they?"

"Not much. We would put ourselves under the protection of the British consul. We have two English men-of-war in the harbour now, and they would soon blow the town about the ears of the Arabs."

"But you have half killed the Vizier and hurt the Sultan."

"Serve them right. What did they carry you off for? They were in the wrong to start with. I have jolly well mauled the old Agha, too, which is worth a fiver to me."

The wall on each side of the road now came to an abrupt termination, and on each side they saw a large, sandy plain, covered here and there with scanty shrubs.

In the distance lay the city of Zanzibar.

"That's better," exclaimed Dick. "Let's walk round to the left."

Polly took his arm, and could not help smiling as she exclaimed—

"It seems like being on the stage."

"Why?"

"Walking with a Sultan, you know, who is not really a Sultan, but only dressed up."

"Oh, I see. But I'm not a bad imitation, am I?"

"You are capital. If ever you go on the stage, you ought to play Sultans' parts."

"And you shall be my Sultana, eh, Polly?" he said.

She answered him with a smile.

Stooping down, he said—

"Give me a kiss, Poll. Snarley won't know."

"Only a stage kiss," she replied.

"What's that?"

"Why, business. You know. Stage business."

He kissed her, and she kissed him, and then they both laughed.

"It's a sort of business I like," he exclaimed.

They pressed on hurriedly after this, getting nearer the city.

The great bell continued to clang and boom as if the palace was on fire, and there was no water to be had to put it out with.

Occasionally they passed tunnels or mounds, which seemed to be old, forgotten, disused tombs.

The setting sun glared in their eyes, and the hot sand reflected the heat, till their feet felt scorched.

Now and then a gliding snake got out of their way with a hiss.

Afar off they could hear the howl of a sneaking jackal.

Clang! clang! went the great bell.

Boom! boom! came the echo.

Looking towards the lane they had just quitted, Dick saw the tips of spears glistening in the sunshine.

Evidently a body of horsemen had been sent out to scour the country for them.

"By Jove!" exclaimed Dick, "they're after us."

"Oh! run, and let us hurry," exclaimed Polly, clinging close to him. "I am so frightened."

"You silly little puss, we are all right," he exclaimed, trying to reassure her.

Quickening their pace, they drew nearer the city, whose white walls gleamed like polished marble, square and massive before them.

Another half-hour, and they would reach Zanzibar.

But would they be safe there?

In their present costumes it was doubtful whether they would.

How they were to procure a disguise it was impossible to say.

A frown gathered on Dick's brow.

He saw the danger of their situation, and was far too sensible to underrate its magnitude.

CHAPTER XLII.

IN THE TOMB.

TURNING round again with an anxious face, Dick perceived that the horsemen had quitted the lane as he had done himself, and were careering over the plain.

They hunted in couples, each two taking a different direction.

"It's getting hot," he muttered, through his clenched teeth.

Suddenly he heard a slight scream behind him.

It was Polly's voice.

He looked in the spot where he had left her, and could not perceive her anywhere.

She had vanished as completely as if the earth had opened and swallowed her up.

Rubbing his eyes to see if he was not the sport of some delusion, he became convinced that she was really gone.

What could have become of her?

Was the place enchanted?

All the singular and mystical tales of the East he had ever read crowded into his memory.

Did the spot abound in djins, or evil spirits?

Was it the favoured haunt of the genii?

In vain he asked his troubled mind these questions, but without receiving any satisfactory answer.

He was standing amidst what appeared to be the ruins of some old temple, for large blocks of stone and broken columns were on all sides of him.

Casting his eyes on the ground he saw a hole.

It was not more than two feet square, but quite large enough to admit of the passage of a human body.

Could she have fallen through this trap into the mysterious recesses of some vault, hidden from the eyes of man for untold centuries?

It was possible.

In no other way could he account for her absence from his side.

If so, what had become of her?

Would she be killed by the fall, or smothered with the dust of mummies buried for ages in this hollow tomb?

Half distracted by doubts and fears, he fell upon his knees and peered into the murky depths below.

All was black as night.

No sound could he distinguish, no form could he behold.

He called the missing girl by her name in a voice that trembled with apprehension.

" Polly ! Polly !"

There was no answer at first.

" Polly !" he said again.

And a sullen echo seemed to answer him from the bowels of the earth.

" Polly," he said, " " are you there ?"

He held his breath for the answer.

" Yes," came the reply faintly.

" Are you hurt ?"

" No. I have not fallen far—only a little shaken."

" Hold on," said Dick ; " I'll come down too. Those beastly horsemen are all over the plain, and I may as well hide with you as anywhere else."

Before he let himself down, he proceeded to widen the aperture so that a stream of light might illumine the cavern.

" Stand from under," he said.

Polly removed some little distance, and with the utmost care Dick began to kick away the thin crust which covered the tomb.

All at once, the earth gave way with a crash.

Dick fell down amidst a blinding cloud of dust.

The fall was not more than eight or nine feet, and disengaging himself from the rubbish, he picked himself up laughing.

" That's a pretty getting down stairs, as an old aunt of mine says," he exclaimed. " How awfully rotten the ground must be."

" Where are we, Dick, and how shall we get out ?" asked Polly.

" Not knowing, can't say," he replied.

" We shall perish of thirst and hunger if we cannot get out."

" It's got to be done somehow; let me put on my thinking cap," said Dick.

A very clear stream of light came into the cave through the big hole he had made, and when his eyes became accustomed to the shadows, he was able to explore the interior.

It was evidently a tomb, belonging to a family of rank, for the sides were garnished with mummies, or embalmed bodies, upon whom still hung fragments of rich attire.

This crumbled into dust at the slightest touch.

There were fifteen mummies on each side of the cave, standing on pedestals of hewn stone.

These were held in position by wires going into the sides of the cavern.

How long it had been disused and closed up he could not guess.

The mummies seemed to gibe and jeer at him with their shrunken, blackened faces.

It was awful to be shut up with those ghastly relics of the past, who represented a forgotten age, and a civilization that had passed away.

" Sit down, Polly," said Dick.

He gave one of the mummies a push, and it fell headlong to the ground, tumbling into fragments.

A wild and sullen echo rolled through the tomb.

" I'll try and move this stone pedestal," he said.

To his surprise, he was able to push it along with ease.

Looking at it, he found it was hollow; he plunged his hand into the hole, and uttering a cry of surprise, withdrew it, filled with pieces of gold, bearing Egyptian characters, and having the solid feel of an English sovereign or an American eagle.

" Money," he said; " gold. Here's a find. We'll go halves, Polly. I wonder if they are all alike."

He began to kick and push the mummies over as if they had been nine-pins.

" Oh, don't, Dick," said Polly ; " something dreadful will happen. You ought to respect the dead."

" What's the good of the old heathens ?' replied Dick.

An examination showed him that each pedestal contained over two hundred pieces of gold, though with what object they had been put there was a difficult question to answer.

Perhaps it was a part of the religion of these ancient inhabitants of this island to propitiate their gods by burying presents of gold with their deceased relatives.

At all events it was a haul which Dick thought himself lucky to have made.

Emptying all the gold out on the ground, it formed a glittering heap in the centre of the cave.

He gazed rapturously at it.

"What is the use of money if we are to die here?" asked Polly, in a tone of despair.

"We are not going to die, silly goose," said Dick.

"You cannot tell."

"Can't I?" said Dick. "I'll bet you a new hat I restore you to the arms of your loving Snarley before night."

"Oh, don't joke. Snarley is very kind to me; he loves me."

"Do you love him? But I ought not to ask you; of course a wife loves her husband, and I am sure you seem very happy."

"You know you were engaged to Henrietta," said Polly, with an arch look.

"Yes, you little rascal," said Dick, squeezing her hand, "or you mean to say you might have been Mrs. Lightheart."

"Perhaps."

"Well," said Dick, philosophically, "we have both got our berths in life, Polly, haven't we?—and as the old saying goes, 'We must lie on our beds as we make them.' Are you strong enough to lend a hand with those pedestals?"

"I will do all I can."

"Help me to place them one on the top of the other, and then if we can climb up we may be able to get out of this hole."

Polly began to assist Dick in moving the blocks, which was a work of time and labour.

There were twenty-six of them, and when they had placed four, one on the top of the other, they put one at the foot, pyramid fashion, and then another on the summit of the first heap, and so on.

"Hot work, isn't it?" said Dick, wiping the sweat from his brow. "I'd give something for a pot of beer, if it was only Sussex swipes."

While they were moving the thirteenth block, Polly sprang back with a shriek.

"What is it?" asked Dick.

"A snake, a dreadful, horrid serpent. Oh, mind, Dick, mind; he is coiling himself up to spring."

"Is he?" said Dick, coolly. "Keep out of his way; I'll give him something."

He drew his scimitar and looked before him.

A copper-coloured snake of a venomous tribe was standing on his tail, darting his forked tongue in and out.

He had his eye fixed in a fascinating manner upon Polly, who was riveted to the spot with terror.

"Off with his head," cried Dick, making a slashing cut at him.

The creature was severed in two.

The upper part fell to the ground and joined the other, the two writhing in hideous contortions liked a bruised worm for some moments.

Polly fell fainting upon the remains of half a dozen mummies and became insensible.

"Here's another go," exclaimed Dick; "I won't give in, though. Best let her lie still. I've no water or vinegar or salts to give her. Bother the snakes. I hate the plaguey varmints."

He went bravely on with his work.

In half-an-hour he had completed a very decent imitation of a staircase.

Polly had come to her senses, but she was very weak and ill, which could be accounted for easily by the worry and annoyance she had gone through.

"How are you, dear?" he asked.

"Better, thanks, Dick, but I don't think I can move without assistance," she answered.

"I'll carry you up," he exclaimed, gallantly.

Going to her, he took her up in his arms.

"Oh, my, aren't you a lump," he said.

"I am afraid I'm a very great worry to you," she exclaimed.

"Not the least bit in the world. Up you go, my little beauty," rejoined Dick.

He mounted his extemporised staircase gallantly with her in his arms.

In a few moments he hoped to see the bright sky and be free once more.

CHAPTER XLIII.

A DEALER IN NOTIONS.

THE time passed very heavily for Mr. Snarley and his friends.

Hopkins came back and told him that he had succeeded in selling Dick as a female slave, and that, his disguise not being guessed at even, he had seen him conveyed into the Sultan's palace.

In proof of his statement he displayed the dollars he had received.

"What a lark," said Messiter. "Dick deserves half the posh for his pluck."

"He shall have the whole if it will be any good to him," replied Hopkins.

"Did you ever know anyone to whom money was no good?" asked Messiter.

"Well, as a showman, I must say I never did," said Hopkins, with a grin.

"I should think not."

"As a matter of dry fact," continued Hopkins, still laughing, "it was always a sight to me to see the actors come up on treasury day to get their screws."

"Not very lively when you hadn't the coin to pay," remarked Messiter.

"In that case I did the dignified, and had a supreme disdain for filthy lucre, as the poet calls it, though I should have been glad enough to have laid my forks on it myself."

"Mr. Snarley, you don't talk," exclaimed Messiter.

"I can't, my boy," was the doleful reply.

"He's thinking of his poor Polly."

"So am I, Master Harry," said Hopkins. "She's my poor Polly as much as his, and I do feel dreadful funky about her now."

"You're a nice pair, both of you, not to think of Lightheart as well," said Messiter.

"I do," answered Snarley. "I honour that brave boy for his courage. But perhaps we shall never see them more."

"I'll bet Dick will pull through. He's like an eel, he'll wriggle out of anything," replied Messiter.

A bell rang downstairs.

"Dinner," said Messiter. "Come and grub."

"I can't eat," said Snarley.

"Can't I! I should like to see what would put me off my feed."

"I'll drink something," continued Snarley.

"Come on, then. What's your lotion? Put a name to it, and I'll stand a corpse-reviver," added Messiter.

The two men followed him to the dining-room, where about half-a-dozen others were assembled.

An American had taken the chair, with the usual enterprise of his race.

"Now, my gay and gallant citizens," he exclaimed, "who says soup?—cos I'm hungry, and want to pitch in; though I guess, as I'm boss, I haven't got the first start."

Everybody answered in the affirmative except Mr. Snarley, who sat absorbed in thought at the extremity of the table.

"You, sir," cried the Yankee, "for the third time, do you vote for soup, or is fish your platform?"

There was no answer.

"I calculate the critter's either deaf o. dumb," said the Yankee.

"He's lost his wife," remarked Messiter.

"Has he? I guess that would make me tarnation glad. I've got one; but she's to home, in Boston, Mass., and if they cabled me that she had gone under, I shouldn't cave in, no how."

Raising his voice, the American added—

"You, sir, will you take soup? It's the last time of asking."

Still absorbed in his own thoughts, Mr. Snarley made no reply.

"Will somebody chuck a brick at him? Who's got the salt-cellar handy?" said the Yankee, in despair. "Well, may I be eternally, and everlastingly, and cata-wampously chawed up," continued the Yankee, with a scream; adding—"I say, stranger, are you agwine for soup or not?"

"Eh?—What?— Did you speak to me?" asked Snarley, awaking to the reality of the things of this world by a prod in the ribs from Messiter.

"That's a good joke. He asks if I spoke to him," said the chairman, "when I've been making myself as hot over him as if I'd been playing at base ball."

"Ah! thank you, no. I don't eat to-day; I'm rather thoughtful," answered Snarley.

"Pleasant companion on a long journey if you're like that always, I guess," said the Yankee.

"Sir, you have no right to insult me! Eat your soup and respect my silence."

"Chain up, old hoss, and put the drag on," answered the American. "I reckon I don't care a yard of Bunker's Hill for a Britisher who won't say soup!"

"Who is this man that he should insult me?" demanded Mr. Snarley, looking round him as fiercely as he could.

No one spoke.

"What is he? I know what I should call him—a—a humbug; a thorough-going humbug!" continued Snarley.

"I guess, stranger, I'm a traveller in notions," replied the Yankee, beginning to eat his soup.

There was a merry twinkle in his eye, as if he had selected Mr. Snarley as the victim for a joke.

"Notions, sir?" said Snarley; "what may that ambiguous phrase mean?"

"Am——I beg your pardon," said the Yankee, politely.

"Ambiguous."

"Ah! I guess I don't know him."

"Uneducated brute! But this is the penalty of mixing in promiscuous company."

"Pro——what did you say?" again asked the Yankee.

"Promiscuous, sir. That means mixed. Ambiguous is doubtful. Go to school again, sir," answered Snarley, severely.

"Wall, raise my hair," said the Yankee; "the gentleman's as good as a dictionary, and I am obliged to him. I shouldn't mind travelling with him as a learned show; he'd draw in the country district."

"Notions?" reflected Mr. Snarley. "What are notions?"

"That depends. I guess wooden nutmegs are notions, so are glass beads for the benighted savages of Africa. So are Amerikane cloth and diseased donkeys," replied the Yankee.

"What may be the nature of the pecu-liar notions in which you now travel?" asked Snarley.

"Noses," was the reply.

"What, cardboard noses, or masks, for carnivals and balls?"

"Not a bit. I guess I mean human noses."

"Go to Putney," exclaimed Mr. Snarley, snapping his fingers derisively. "I'm not going to believe that."

"Well, I tell you what I'll do with you, old hoss. I'll buy your nose."

"Mine?"

"Yes. It's not a very pretty or high-class nose, but I'll be game if you're on for a deal."

"I object to sell my nose, sir," exclaimed Mr. Snarley, with dignity.

"I don't want to cut it off until your death. You may do what you like with it, and take it where you like, during life, but at your death it belongs to me."

"Oh, that alters the case. What will you give for my nose on those terms?"

"That depends. I have a graduated scale. So much for a Roman nose, so much for a Grecian, a pug, and a squash."

"Mine isn't a squash," said Mr. Snarley.

"I didn't say it was, but if you ask me to classify it, I should call it a cross between low Roman and debased pug."

"You are not flattering."

"I am a dealer, sir," replied the Yankee, "and when I mean business, I guess I never cry an article up."

"What's your price?" asked Snarley.

The Yankee looked at him attentively for a moment.

"Fifty dollars," he exclaimed.

"I am on," answered Snarley. "It is a deal."

"Done with you, stranger. To-morrow morning I'll part with the cash. It's a bargain, though I am afraid I shall lose by you, as you are beginning to paint it already."

"Paint what?"

"The proboscis. Nose, I mean. Guess you alcohol it. Take a drop for a night-cap, and so on."

"That is my business," answered Mr. Snarley, pouring out some champagne. "I consider it very impertinent of you to make any remark of that nature."

"Well, we're on. Whoever breaks the bargain between this and to-morrow morning shall pay for two dozen of cham. for the company ”

“ I guess it won't be I,” said Mr. Snarley.

“ Nor this child.   I’m death on noses,”

replied the Yankee, adding, “ Gentlemen all, I take you to witness that I’ve fairly bought this stranger’s nose, and you all understand the deal.”

There was a chorus of assent.

CHAPTER XLIV.

SNARLEY AT WORK.

TURNING to Charley, the proprietor of the establishment, the Yankee whispered a few words in a low tone.

Charley disappeared.

“ Will you buy my nose?” asked Messiter.

“ Not much,” replied the Yankee; “ it’s too ugly.”

Messiter subsided.

Presently Charley returned with a pair of tongs, made red hot in the fire.

He handed the instrument to the Yankee, who got up and walked round to Mr. Snarley, presenting it to his face.

“ What are you about?” cried the latter. “ The tongs are red hot.”

“ I guess I know that,” said the American.

“ Are you mad, man?”

“ Sane as a ’possum.”

“ What are you going to do? I say, take those things away from my face,” said Snarley, leaning back in his chair.

“ I reckon, stranger,” answered the Yankee, “ it’s my custom, whenever I buy anything, to mark my merchandize, and it’s necessary that I should stamp your nose.”

“ What!”

Snarley recoiled in affright.

“ I’ve bought it, and I must stamp it. When it has my mark on it I shall know it is the nose I bought, otherwise you might alter it so that I couldn’t recognize it.   Sit still; I won’t hurt you much, but I must mark the nose!”

“ I’ll be hanged if you do,” shouted Snarley.

Turning to the company, the Yankee said, “ Gentlemen, you are witnesses that the stranger has shifted round, and consequently the bargain’s off.”

“ Certainly,” said everyone.

“ Then I guess he’s lost the cham.”

Again there was a unanimous chorus of approval.

“ Charley,” said the Yankee, “ bring in the mutton and let us have the champagne at the same time.   Thank you, stranger; and I say, Charley, mind it’s well iced, or I guess there’ll be a row in the house and you’ll be in it.”

Mr. Snarley sat the picture of despair.

He was the victim of Yankee cuteness.

Still he had fairly lost the champagne, and could not dispute the payment of the two dozen bottles.

Scarcely had he made a wry face over the first glass, and while the others were drinking his health, than the great bell of the Sultan’s palace was heard ringing.

“ Hallo!” said Charley; “ something’s up in the palace.”

Snarley and Hopkins looked at one another.   They could guess that Dick had done something.

“ You can talk Arabic, Charley,” said Mr. Snarley; “ go out like a good fellow and bring in the news.”

Charley put on his straw hat and departed.

He was gone nearly an hour, and the anxiety of those who were in the secret was almost uncontrollable.

They crowded round Charley when he returned with eager faces.

“ There is a dust-up,” said Charley.

“ What’s happened?” asked Snarley.

“ Well, you see, I have a friend who is one of the guards of the harem, and he told me all about it.”

“ Yes.”

“ Two of the ladies have escaped; one was only brought in last night, and the other was brought this morning.”

“ Bravo, Dick!” cried Messiter. “ I told you he’d do it.   Hurrah!”

“ Are they pursued?” asked Hopkins.

“ I should think so.   The slave who came in this morning seems to be Old Nick himself.”

"I WILL HAVE YOU BEATEN WITH A STICK, DOG THAT THOU ART!' CRIED SELIM."

"How is that?"

"She has broken the Kislar Agha's head with a brick, and nearly killed the Grand Vizier, and even the Sultan himself. They can't make it out," said Charley.

"What are they doing?"

"Why, it appears the white slave dressed herself in the Sultan's clothes, and passed out of the east gates with the other slaves. She had darkened her face, and the disguise was so perfect, the guards were deceived, and opened the gates for them to pass through."

"Where have they gone?"

"Along the road to what is called the Old Tombs."

"Where's that?"

"Why, a sandy tract, where some time ago they used to bury people in tombs. It's the home of the jackal and the pariah dog now, and all the tombs have fallen into decay."

"Do the Sultan's people know which way they have taken?" asked Snarley.

"Certainly they do."

"What's their game now, then?" inquired Messiter.

"A troop of horsemen have been sent after them, and everyone expects they will be brought back soon."

Snarley, Hopkins, Messiter, and Ted looked at one another.

It was clear that each had the same thought in his mind.

"We must have a cut-in," said Messiter.

He had rightly interpreted what was in everybody's mind.

"Charley, old man," said Hopkins, "I don't mind telling you the truth."

"What's that?"

"The two who have escaped are Mrs. Snarley and Dick Lightheart, your lodgers."

"Bless my soul, who'd have thought it?" said Charley.

"Now, you're a countryman, and you won't see them captured and brought back, will you?"

"I shouldn't like to."

"Of course you wouldn't."

"What can I do?" asked Charley.

"Guide us without delay to the Old Tombs, give us what arms you have in the house, and let us see if we cannot help them."

"Captain Vipond has just got some revolvers and ammunition sent in," answered Charley.

"Call him," said Snarley.

Vipond did not mix himself with the other boarders at Charley's; he kept himself very much secluded, had his meals in a private room, and indulged himself in that melancholy which was his chief characteristic.

He knew nothing about their affairs as a rule, though he had heard of Polly being carried off.

The expectation that Harold Dugard was on his track continually haunted him, and he could think of nothing else.

We must except one thing.

That was the melancholy death of Adele.

He had not even the poor privilege of weeping over her tomb, for she lay at the bottom of the deep blue sea.

When Charley called him, he came down at once.

"Did you send for me, Mr. Snarley?" he asked.

"I did," was the answer, "and I will explain what I want briefly. My wife has been carried off by the Vizier of the Sultan, Lightheart has gone in disguise to rescue her, they have both escaped from the harem, and the Sultan's soldiers are pursuing them. Will you kindly help us to look for the fugitives?"

"With pleasure," said Crawley Vipond; "that's to say, you are welcome to what arms I have, but I cannot go with you."

The man was a coward in his heart.

"Very well, we accept your offer as far as it goes," said Snarley, concealing his disgust.

"Good morning," said Vipond. "I am occupied with important business; help yourselves to my stores."

He walked away.

"Not much to be expected from him," said Messiter.

"Never mind. We are strong enough," answered Hopkins.

"D——I was just going to swear, but that wouldn't be right," said Charley. "But I'll come with you, and do my little worst."

"Bravo, Charley," said Messiter; "you're a cock."

"I never put a pal in the hole in my life, sir," cried Charley.

" Well, come along at once," said Hopkins, "and don't talk about it. I'm in a stink about my gal, and I want to see her safe home with Master Lightheart, who's done his duty, God bless him !"

The member of the little party provided themselves with six-shooters, or revolvers of American make, and sallied forth under Charley's guidance for the tombs.

They did not guess at that moment how much Dick Lightheart required their services.

But his adventures will be related in the next chapter.

CHAPTER XLV.

JUST IN TIME.

AS soon as Selim-el-Mandeb came to himself, he raised an alarm in the palace, and as the slaves crowded into the room in answer to his frantic cries, he caused his royal master to be put to bed.

His wounds were bound up, and so were the Vizier's.

The latter, though weak from loss of blood, could not allow himself to feel ill.

He organised a pursuit of the fugitives, and even set out after them himself.

When, with four soldiers and two slaves, he arrived at the sandy plain we have described, he selected a spot, where a small tent was pitched for him, and guarded by the soldiers, he resolved to stay there till night.

His object was to make the sultan believe he was the most indefatigable of his ministers.

Several hours passed.

The captain of the guard, who was in command of the troops, came to the Vizier, who was sitting cross-legged at the entrance to the tent.

" In the name of the prophet, what news ?" asked Selim.

" Bad," replied the captain. " I have been unable to find the runaways, O Selim—may thy shadow never grow less —and seeing that we waste our time, I have thought it good to send all my men back to their barracks."

" Now may Allah put a bridle on my tongue," said Selim.   " But, O Hafiz, is thy brain in a state of sanity ? The Sultan——"

" May Allah shower on him blessings and peace," put in Hafiz.

" I say that our master will call for our heads if we return without these women of the Franks, whom may the seven plagues overtake. Let us but catch them, and we shall be loaded with favours. I will promise thee a dozen of the shawls of Cashmere, woven in the looms of industry by the hand of science."

The captain of the guard shook his head.

" What can a man do more than his best ?" he answered.

" Are your men dogs that they should be laughed at by these girls ?"

" They say that one of them has the evil eye. Several horses have fallen and injured their riders. Two soldiers were stricken by the sun. They have fear in their hearts, O Selim. I am less than dust, but I have said the words of truth."

" O Hafiz," said Selim, " I am not one of those who keep the inside of my palm in darkness. Scour me the country again; take with you the four soldiers who are my guard. You shall have gold, for of a truth I do not like to return to my master without the Frankish women."

The captain of the guard again assured him that nothing could be done.

At this the Vizier lost his temper.

" Contemptible slave," he cried, " you shall be disgraced from your command ! I will have thee beaten with the stick, dog that thou art !"

" God is great ; may he take you in his holy keeping," said the captain, in alarm.

" Inshallah !" cried the Vizier, " I will strike you myself. I will teach you to play at hide and seek round my little finger. What, will you laugh at my beard ?"

The fact was, the Vizier had been drinking some strong wine, and his head was inflamed.

Losing all control over himself, he rushed upon the captain of the guard and struck him with the palm of his hand.

" Take that, dog !" he cried, " and that,

and that ! Am I dirt to sit behind you and be led by a string ?"

The captain drew his scimitar and kept the Vizier at arm's length.

He too was furious.

" Dog yourself," he said ; " I will tell our royal master how you sit in your tent, drinking the wine of the Franks."

Selim trembled with rage.

" There is no word in Arabic which is strong enough for me to express my contempt for thee, O Selim, but I will say to thee what I have heard the Franks say when they come over in ships and quarrel in the wine shops of Zanzibar, ' dam.' It is spoken. I have called thee ' dam,' O Selim."

The captain of the guard was quite satisfied with this.

He thought he had overwhelmed the Vizier.

The English sailors had used the word to one another once in his hearing, and a free fight was the result.

This made him think it was a contemptuous epithet.

The insult was doubled and intensified in Selim's opinion because he was sworn at in a foreign and hated language.

Jumping up and down, he in vain tried to get at Hafiz.

He " went for him," but was kept off at the point of the sword.

" ' Dam,' do you say ?" he cried, hoarse with rage. " Am I ' dam ?' If I am ' dam,' then you are the father of ' dam.' Why should I stay here to be called ' dam ?' After all I am somebody. I will defile the grave of ' dam's ' father, and all his ancestors. I haven't lived to my age to eat ' dam,' and to eat it from such hands."

" Mashallah !" cried Hafiz, " thine is the anger of the fool. Thou art bereft of reason. Shall I pluck thee by the beard ?"

A set-to would have taken place had not loud cries on their right arrested their attention.

The soldiers were shouting at the top of their voices.

Looking in their direction, the captain of the guard beheld two persons struggling with his men.

One wielded a scimitar.

A soldier fell.

" It is the Frankish women, O Selim," exclaimed Hafiz.

" Hurt them not. The whip shall score their fair skins, but they must not fall before the sword," answered the Vizier.

He entirely forgot his ill-temper in his delight.

" Allah el Allah !" he cried, grasping the hand of Hafiz. " Praise be to God! You are a man indeed."

The captain of the guard ran to the spot.

It happened that the soldiers had picketed their horses close to the mouth of the old tomb in which Dick had taken refuge.

As he emerged with Polly in his arms, he saw his mistake.

It was too late to retreat.

In fact, his retreat was cut off.

Encircling Polly with one arm, he fought fiercely with his right.

Two soldiers fell mortally wounded before his strokes.

The remaining two were incensed against him, and had not Hafiz come up, they would have taken advantage of his failing strength to cut him down.

Eventually he was overpowered and disarmed.

He and Polly were dragged roughly to the tent, where the Vizier was standing rubbing his hands, and calling upon the prophet to witness that he would be thankful for his star being in luck.

" Bismillah !" he exclaimed. " In the name of the prophet, this is good for the eyes. Let us start for the palace at once. The Sultan will order them the stick till every toe they have shall ache with pain."

Both Dick and Polly were too much dejected to speak.

The setting sun covered the sandy plain with a pale, yellowish flood of light.

It was a lovely evening.

How pleasant would it have been to sit at the open window at " Charley's," looking out upon the harbour, and sipping iced wine !

But alas ! that was impossible.

They had no such pleasant prospect before them.

Suddenly an idea occurred to Dick.

" Selim," he said, " you love gold. If I give you five thousand pieces, will you let us go ?"

" Yes, I will," he replied. " Five thousand pieces is a king's ransom; but where.

in the name of the prophet, are you to find this gold?"

"In a tomb close by; descend with your slaves, and you will find it heaped up on the floor."

"It is well," said the Vizier.

He repeated his promise that he would let them escape, and Dick showed them the entrance to the tomb.

The gold was discovered, and sacks for it were hastily made out of the tent cloth.

It filled thirteen bags.

"Now," said Dick, "good night. Give our love to the Sultan."

Selim made a sign to the soldiers.

They seized Polly and Dick, and binding their arms behind them, fastened the end to the stirrup irons of the two horses.

"March!" said Selim, "we have already lost too much time."

"You treacherous old villain," said Dick, "have you no respect for your word?"

The Vizier made no answer.

"You have got the gold; what more do you want?" continued Dick.

Neither Selim nor Hafiz spoke.

The soldiers mounted their horses, and the two chiefs walked in front, and the two slaves behind; thus the captives were in the middle.

In this division they took the road to the palace.

They were dragged along by the horses, and could make no resistance.

Dick was frantic with rage.

If he had not given the Vizier the money he would not have minded so much, though he had nothing but death to expect when he was found out.

Polly was a woman and her sex would save her life.

When his imposture was discovered, he did not doubt he would be cruelly tortured and killed.

Crossing the plain, they came to the road with high walls, which they had traversed in the morning flushed with hope.

"I've done my best," he muttered, with a downcast air.

All at once the horses stopped.

Two shots were heard.

At the same instant two saddles were emptied, and the dying soldiers bit the dust.

The horses reared up, and would have dashed away had not their heads been seized by strangers, whom for the moment Dick did not recognise.

Again two pistols were discharged.

This time the slaves, who with difficulty carried some of the gold, the rest being slung over the saddle, fell to the ground.

The Vizier took to his heels and ran as fast as he could.

Hafiz was a brave man, and drawing his scimitar, made a stand, which did not avail him much.

A shot broke his arm, and he fell by the side of his men.

"That's the lot, I think," exclaimed a voice, which Dick instantly knew to be Messiter's.

"Cut the captives loose, then, and let's get off home, or that old coward who ran away will send a troop of horse after us," said another voice, which was Charley's.

Polly, half fainting, was released from her uncomfortable position, and soon found herself in the arms of her husband, while old Hopkins pressed a bottle of brandy and water to her lips.

Ted and Messiter attended to Dick, whom they chaffed about his disguise.

"Don't chaff now," replied Dick. "I want to get home; we are not safe yet. Sling those bags of gold over one of the horses."

"Gold?"

"Yes; heaps of it. Look sharp."

Messiter and Ted obeyed his instructions.

Polly was placed on a horse, being too weak to walk any further, and the little party started for the city, Dick explaining all that had happened as he went along.

"By jingo!" exclaimed Mr. Snarley, dancing with delight; "we were only just in time."

Then he caught hold of Dick's hand, and wringing it warmly, added—

"I shall never forget you, my boy—never."

CHAPTER XLVI.

THE MYSTERIOUS CARAVAN.

FEARFUL lest the Sultan should take some steps to be revenged upon Lightheart, Captain Vipond, whose preparations were all made, resolved to leave Zanzibar the next morning at daybreak.

Dhows, as the boats there are called, were in readiness to take the party from the island to Bagamoyo.

Mr. Snarley, Polly, and old Hopkins determined to quit Zanzibar at once and return to England.

Dick and Messiter was very sorry to part with their old friends.

The former insisted upon Snarley accepting three of his bags of gold.

" Sure to find it useful, sir," said Dick.

" My dear boy, I thank you," replied Snarley, " for all you have done for me. We shall meet again, I hope."

Polly also thanked Dick, and old Hopkins' eye was guilty of a tear when he took leave of the gallant preserver of his daughter.

Just as day broke, the ship hoisted her anchor, set sail, and glided majestically from the harbour.

Half an hour afterwards Dick's party started for Bagamoyo.

Banks the midshipman was absent.

His non-appearance was explained by Menzies, who said that he had shipped in the " Hartlepool," not caring to face the perils of a long travel in East Central Africa.

The party then consisted of Captain Crawley Vipond, who wished to settle in some lonely spot, where the foot of a white man had never before rested.

On the sea he was not safe from his terrible enemy.

Would he be so in the vast recesses of the African continent ?

That was the question, which time alone could solve.

After him as captain, or head of the expedition, came Dick Lightheart, whose object was to trade in ivory and gold dust with the natives, and, if possible, discover the whereabouts of our illustrious countryman and African explorer, **Dr. Livingstone.**

Ted accompanied him as his servant.

Messiter went with him as a friend and companion.

Professor Crab's idea in joining the party was to collect materials for his great book, he being entirely devoted to science and nature.

The first point they intended to make for was Uuyanyembe, 360 miles from Bagamoyo, an important trading station of the Arabs.

To reach this place they had to pass through dense forests, swamps of black mud, to cross rivers, to face lions, hippopotami, and other wild and savage creatures.

To pass through the countries of petty chiefs, hostile to the whites, whose friendship could only be bought by paying tribute.

To encounter the dreaded Mukunguru, or intermittent African fever, which keeps attacking those unused to the climate.

The fever which made Livingstone a mere " ruckle of bones," as he himself expressed it, and which has been known to turn a young man's hair grey for ever.

But the boys cared little for those dangers.

They were full of the spirit of adventure, and longed for the march.

It was necessary to stay a week in Bagamoyo to collect Pagazi, or native carriers and donkeys.

Horses will not live in this part ot the country, and as the goods, consisting of cloths, beads, ammunition, arms, wire and provisions, were numerous, one hundred and fifty Pagazi at least were required.

The native leader of the Pagazi was a tall, thick-set man, named Sangaru.

He spoke broken English, and was a trustworthy fellow from all accounts.

A caravan, he said, had quitted Bagamoyo for the interior the day they arrived.

It had departed in a great hurry on hearing of their approach.

Its commander was a white man, and he had with him fifty Pagazi or carriers.

Dick inquired what the white man was

like, and the description he received exactly resembled that of Harold Dugard, the strange commander of the still stranger ship.

It was Dick's firm opinion that Dugard had left his ship and was following close upon the heels of his enemies.

He would not tell Crawley Vipond this, for fear he might give up the expedition, and think of hiding elsewhere.

It was arranged that the Pagazi should all have arms, so that they might fight as soldiers if necessary.

It was the middle of June when the caravan started, being preceded by the mysterious party about a week.

The masika, or rainy season, was over.

During the masika the rain comes down in sheets almost incessantly for weeks.

It swells the rivers and creates swamps of black mud, breeding fevers and diseases.

Dick and Sangaru started at the head of the caravan, Ted after them, carrying the British flag.

" Binderi kisungu," cried the natives, meaning the white man's flag.

" Hurrah! we're off," cried Dick.

" Sofari, sofari," exclaimed the carriers. " A journey, a journey."

Turning round, Sangaru cried—

" Pakia, set out, start."

Dick fired each barrel of his six-shooter, and Messiter, who brought up the rear to see there were no stragglers, answered him.

Away they went, full of life and hope, beneath the blazing sun of an African summer, into the wilds of Africa.

CHAPTER XLVII.

RIVER HORSES.

IT is not our purpose to describe the countries and names of all the places through which our travellers passed.

That would better become a writer of travels.

It is with incident and adventure that we have to deal.

Suffice it to say that after a fortnight's travel the tents were pitched on a small plateau.

A river ran by about a mile off, and game abounded in the neighbourhood.

The thorny acacia covered the ground, and the African flies buzzed around.

Most dangerous of these is the setse fly.

Its sting pricks like the point of a needle, and soon men and donkeys stream with blood.

Water melons grew on the ground.

Amidst the trees and long grass could be seen antelope and deer, with many strange birds among the ebony and calabash trees.

The journey so far had not been productive of any serious accidents.

A few Pagazis had deserted, stealing what they could lay hands on.

Some donkeys were dead, and others had rolled in the mud, doing no great damage to their packs.

It was a fine opportunity for a hunting expedition, and Dick, Messiter, and Menzies agreed to go out separately and see what sport they could meet with.

Captain Vipond kept in his tent, seldom speaking to anyone, and evidently occupied with his own bitter thoughts.

Menzies still hated Dick as much as ever, but he had not shown any signs of open hostility.

Perhaps he was biding his time, like a snake in the grass, as he was.

Dick strolled along with a couple of rifles.

One he intended for big game, such as hippopotamus, giraffe, lion, rhinoceros, should he be fortunate enough to meet with them.

The other was for deer and antelope, for which the Frazer shell, or bone crusher, was unnecessary.

At length he came to the river, the stream of which was not very swift in the summer months.

Here he saw several fine hippopotami, or river horses, at play.

Their huge heads and tremendous jaws were fearful to look upon.

He watched them for some time, and was just about to fire, when he saw a roughly-hewn canoe paddled along by one man.

Getting behind a tree, he bent his gaze upon it.

To his surprise, the man was young Menzies, who ran the little boat into some rushes, and jumped on land.

"What's his little game?" said Dick to himself.

He had always distrusted Menzies, and he determined to follow him, as he appeared to have some fixed purpose in view rather than to be in pursuit of game.

Menzies came very near the tree behind which Dick was hidden.

Raising his gun to his shoulder, he fired two shots, which, in the wilds of Africa, is a signal that travellers wish to trade with any natives living near.

Dick's curiosity was raised to the highest pitch.

In a few moments the shots were answered by a similar number, though they appeared to be distant.

Menzies at once started in their direction.

Dick followed him cautiously for about a quarter of a mile without being perceived.

Then he saw before him, on the skirts of a forest, a camp pitched in a hollow.

The dusky forms of the resting Pagazi were lying about in the shade.

A tall, handsome man quitted a large tent, and advanced to meet Menzies.

Again Dick sought the shelter of a friendly tree.

The stranger and Menzies halted within hearing distance of Dick.

Still more was the latter astonished, when, in the handsome form of the stranger he recognised Harold Dugard, the eccentric commander of the strange vessel.

This, then, was the owner of the mysterious caravan which had started so hurriedly from Bagamoyo as they entered.

His plans were not yet matured.

The time had not come.

That Menzies had been and was in communication with him there could be no doubt.

Menzies was a traitor.

The conversation that took place between them settled this question beyond the shadow of suspicion.

"Well," said Dugard, "what news do you bring me?"

"We are camped within a mile and a half of this place, on the same side of the river, which I have descended in a canoe to avoid observation and pursuit," replied Menzies.

"Is Vipond in camp?"

"He is."

A terrible shiver ran through Dugard at this reply.

"At length my enemy is within my grasp," he continued, "but I want him delivered into my hands alive."

"You shall have him within three hours, provided you do not forget your part of the contract. That must be stuck to, I guess," answered Menzies.

"What do you want?"

"Dick Lightheart must be given up alive to me. I've got one or two Red Indian tortures I want to try on him, I guess."

"How has he offended you?"

"Oh, in lots of ways. He's a most insulting brute, and too cocky by half for a down-easter like me, I reckon."

"It's a pity. I took a liking to that boy," replied Dugard.

"That's more than I ever did, so that's the straight tip," answered Menzies.

"Will nothing else than his life content you?"

"Nothing. What do you think I came into this humbugging Africa for?"

"Revenge," said Dugard.

"Exactly. You have the same motive. You heard of the death of your Adele through his violence, and——"

"Speak not of her," said Dugard, interrupting him, as he dug his nails into his flesh spasmodically; "I cannot bear it."

"Didn't mean to rile you," replied Menzies, "but I tell you, whatever you feel for Crawley Vipond, I feel for Lightheart. I'm death and snakes on that fellow, and I calculate I'll give him toko before long."

"You have come to the right place," answered Dugard, with a grim smile; "there is no law here. You may murder an enemy without the fear of a rope; but in my case it will not be murder."

"What then?"

"Justice."

As he uttered this word, Harold Dugard drew himselt up proudly, and folding his arms, looked up to heaven.

"It is settled, then, that if I betray Vipond to you, I shall have Lightheart and his money as my share and reward?" asked Menzies.

"It is."

"My watch is to-night," continued Menzies, "all will be asleep, and you will capture them as easily as lambs in a fold."

"Will you?" thought Dick.

"I think I shall bind Lightheart to a tree," continued Menzies, "and stick knives into him all over, and then burn him slowly over a fire."

"You're a precious scoundrel and a nice companion, I don't think," muttered Dick.

Harold Dugard exclaimed after a pause, in a sad and solemn tone—

"My life's work is nearly accomplished. When I found that Vipond had escaped from the 'Belle of New Orleans,' I followed him, and hearing that he was going to hide in the recesses of Africa, I came here to make sure of my prey."

"You won't have long to wait," remarked Menzies.

"No. It seems as if the sands of his life were running out."

"How shall you kill him?"

"I shall make him die a slow and lingering death, and watch him while he dies, taunting him with his fate, and reminding him of the wrongs he has done me,' replied Dugard.

"Hang him up to the branches of a tree by his hair, with his feet just touching the ground—his toes, I mean," said Menzies, exulting like a demon. "That will wake him up. He'll feel as if the roof of his head was coming off, and when he gets thirsty and hungry, you'll have the whip hand of him."

"Not a bad idea," replied Dugard. "Nothing is too bad for him, and what would to many appear cruelty of an inhuman kind is only simple justice to him."

"You won't forget the money you promised me at Zanzibar if I would betray my party?" said Menzies.

"No. You can have it now if you like."

"I can wait. Come at midnight for the attack."

"Very well. How far off are you, and in what direction?" said Dugard.

"North-east, about two miles. You can't make a mistake."

"Adieu," said Dugard. "Do your best."

"I guess I shall this time," answered Menzies.

They shook hands, and Menzies walked away whistling, while Harold Dugard returned moodily to his camp.

The conversation being ended, Dick started on the homeward track.

Nearing the place where Menzies had left his canoe, he thought it would be good fun to get in and have a shot at the river horses.

Accordingly he put his Lancaster rifle on the bottom, sprang in, pushed off, and was soon paddling lazily down with the stream.

All at once he found himself in the centre of a group of river horses, which sprang up on all sides of him.

Steering gently through the huge brutes, he got clear, and began to think himself lucky.

But one monster hippopotamus followed him, blowing the water out of her mouth in a long stream.

She seemed very angry, and he soon saw the cause.

Her young one was in the direct way of the canoe, which struck it on the head.

The mother made a strange noise, and her mate came swimming and diving from the herd to her assistance.

Seeing that he was menaced with danger, Dick took up his rifle and put a shell in the creature's head.

With a plaintive cry, she splashed about in all the agonies of death.

The male looked at her inquiringly for a moment, and rushing at the boat, the monster seized the side in its immense jaw.

His teeth made the wood crack like pasteboard, and before Dick could fire again, he was struggling in the water.

He began to swim towards the shore.

The hippopotamus, with a snorting noise, followed him.

Dick gave himself up for lost.

Happening to look to the bank, he saw Menzies, who was searching for his canoe, among the tall reefs which fringed the river.

"Help! help!" he cried.

"Is it you, Lightheart?" replied Menzies.

"Yes. Fire quickly, or the river horses will make a meal of me," answered Dick.

"What a nuisance," said Menzies. "I'm not loaded, and I've left my powder and ball in camp."

"You won't leave me to die like this?" exclaimed Dick, despairingly.

"What can I do?" asked Menzies, folding his arms and looking on contentedly.

The snorting of the hippopotamus grew nearer.

Dick turned round and faced him.

He was an enormous specimen of his kind, and his hideous head, just raised above the water, was within a few feet of its prey.

Suddenly throwing up his heels, Dick dived.

The monster passed over the spot where he had been but one moment before.

Collecting his senses as well as he could, Dick remembered that he had a bowie knife in his belt.

It was his only weapon.

Drawing it with his right hand, he opened it, treading water to keep himself afloat.

The river horse had turned, and espying him again, made another rush at him.

Menzies continued to look on as calmly as if he had been at a theatre witnessing a tragedy.

Dick throw himself a little on one side by a vigorous stroke of his left arm, and dexterously drove the knife into the beast's eye.

A howl of pain and rage broke from it.

Again Dick dived, coming up this time nearer the shore.

He dared not swim lest he should be overtaken and snapped in half.

So he remained still.

The hippopotamus found him out again, and dashed at him as before.

Dick awaited his onset, and repeated his manœuvre.

This time he was lucky enough to strike the remaining eye.

Completely blinded, and half choked with the blood which streamed down over his snout, and tinged the water with a crimson hue, the beast churned the stream into foam.

His piteous cries attracted the attention of the herd, who came up, as if to his assistance, from all parts.

"Now for it," thought Dick.

Casting away the knife, which had done him such good service, he struck out for the shore.

The nearest point was at least fifty yards off.

On all sides the hippopotami were nearing him.

CHAPTER XLVIII.

THE COURT MARTIAL.

BY dint of much exertion, Dick managed to reach the reefs, through which he pushed his way.

Several infuriated river horses were just behind him.

Another moment, and he would have been too late.

Menzies was standing close by, leaning upon his rifle, and he stretched out his hand with a smile.

"Lucky shave that, I guess," he cried.

"No thanks to you," said Dick, who knew what his words were worth, since he had overheard his treacherous conversation with Dugard.

A thought entered Dick's head as he spoke.

Without any warning he seized Menzies' rifle, and fired it at the nearest of the hippopotami.

The brute fell with a ball in his skull, the bone being regularly crushed by the massive leaden bullet.

"I thought you said it wasn't loaded," said Dick, with a look of contempt.

"Well, hang me, that's curious," said Menzies, turning pale.

"What is?"

"The shooter was loaded all the time, and I did't know it."

" You're a humbug," said Dick.

" May I drop this minute if I knew it," asserted Menzies.

" Rot," said Dick ; " you were never my friend, and you wanted to see me dead, didn't you ?"

" All right," said Menzies, changing his tone ; " if you will have it, I did, and it's a pity that old hoss you blinded didn't chaw you up. Guess I wish he had."

" It would have saved you the trouble of hanging me up off my toes by the hair of my head," said Dick, with a sneer.

Menzies' face became livid.

" And sticking knives into me," continued Dick, enjoying the effect of his words.

" How do you know that ?" gasped Menzies.

" I know more than you think for, my pippin," said Dick.

" By the living jingo," said Menzies, who was not deficient in courage, " you know too much, my bully boy. It's your life or mine."

Dick held the rifle firmly, but Menzies drew his knife, and running upon him, tried to stab him.

Stepping back and receiving the point in his sleeve, Dick clubbed the gun in a dangerous fashion.

" Put down that knife, or I'll brain you !" he exclaimed.

Menzies saw that it would be almost impossible to get within his range.

Sullenly he threw the knife on the ground.

" Curse you to all eternity !" he growled.

Dick drew a piece of rope from his pocket, and seizing his arms, bound them behind his back.

" What are you going to do with me ?" inquired Menzies, trembling.

" Try you by court-martial and give you the doom of a traitor."

" I've done nothing, so help me bob ; I'm innocent," cried Menzies.

" Are you ? Then I don't know what being guilty is."

" At least, let me hear what I'm accused of."

" You'll find out, time enough," said Dick.

" You could not have seen me with— with——"

" To cut it short," said Dick, " I not only saw you with Harold Dugard, but I heard you promise to betray the camp at midnight."

" Then I suppose it's all U P with me," exclaimed Menzies, shrugging his shoulders : " I'm not afraid to die, Lightheart, but I'm young, and I've friends at home in the States whom I should like to see again."

" So have I got friends," said Dick ; " you did not think of me."

" I was wrong, I own it ; you are brave, and the brave are always generous."

" You have heard us talking, and you know very well that Dugard is Captain Vipond's mortal enemy. You are with us, and you have sold us. We should all have been shot as we slept if I hadn't twigged your game."

" I'm very sorry. If I swear I won't do it again, will you say nothing about it ?"

" No."

" You won't ?" said Menzies, with a despairing glance.

" No, I tell you. What was your object in selling us ?"

Menzies was silent.

" My life," continued Dick, " and when I think that you have carried your hatred to that extent against a fellow who never did you any serious harm, you can't wonder that I look upon you as a snake to be trampled on."

" I don't deny that I'm a varmint that wants wiping out," said Menzies ; " all I ask is mercy."

" You won't get it," said Dick, who had steeled his heart.

" Think of my poor mother," said Menzies, while a tear came into his eye.

" Your mother will be well rid of a son like you."

" However bad I may be, she won't think so, poor old soul. Look here, Lightheart, will you do this ?"

" What ?"

" Turn me up in this wild region, without arms, food, or anything, and let me take my darned chance ?"

" Which would be to go and join Harold Dugard at once," replied Dick, with a harsh laugh.

" No, it wouldn't. I'd steer right away from him. On my soul I would."

" I am green. I know I am green, but I'm not so jolly green as all that," answered Dick, "so belay jawing, and march. You'll have to be tried, and that's flat. When it comes to trying to get a whole caravan surprised and murdered, it is time to do something."

Menzies saw it was no use to urge Dick further, and in his own mind he was forced to admit that he was acting as he had a right to do for the general safety.

His crafty mind became bent upon the best means of escaping, and he resolved not to lose the first chance that offered.

The tramp back to camp was performed in silence.

Dick held the end of the rope, and Menzies followed after him, utterly powerless to attack him.

A fierce hatred burned in his heart.

He thought his time might come again yet, for while there is life there is hope.

When the camp was reached, they found the Pagazi cutting up a fine deer and an antelope, which Messiter had shot.

The latter was proud of his success.

"What sport, Dick?" he asked. "Look at my deer."

"I've caught a traitor," said Dick.

"And got a ducking," said Messiter, who looked first at his wet garments and then at Menzies. "But what has happened?"

"Come to the captain's tent, and ask Professor Crab and Ted to follow," replied Dick.

"One moment," said the professor, who was close by; "I was just explaining to this boy Ted, whose ignorance would be amusing if it were not so dense and lamentable, the difference between a springbok and a deer. You see the spring——"

"It isn't spring now, sir; it's summer," interrupted Messiter.

"A bad pun," said the professor. "Recollect what Dr. Johnson said, namely, that a man who would make a pun would pick a pocket."

Dick led his captive to Captain Vipond's tent.

"May I come in, sir?" he asked.

"Certainly, Lightheart. What is it?" said Crawley Vipond.

Dick entered, leading Menzies, his captive.

Messiter, the professor, and Ted followed.

"I want this fellow," continued Dick, "to be tried by what I may call a court-martial, for if one of our own number, in a wild place like this, plots against us, we cannot appeal to the law, because there is none. We must be our own judges. Is that fair?"

"Quite," said the professor. "In the wilds of America the settlers have instituted Lynch law. That is a law made and carried out by themselves without judges or courts."

"Very well," said Dick; "you, sir, Captain Vipond and Messiter, and Ted, if you like, shall be the court or the judges."

"Exactly. State your case."

Menzies stood sulkily, with his eyes cast on the ground.

"We all know that Captain Vipond has an enemy who seeks his life," began Dick.

"Harold Dugard," said the professor.

"That is the man. Well, Dugard is encamped within a mile and a half of us, with about fifty Pagazi."

Vipond turned deadly pale.

His limbs trembled under him. He drew his breath with difficulty, and seemed in danger of fainting.

"Brandy, brandy," he murmured, in a hoarse voice.

Messiter ran to a case and poured out a dram, which he drank eagerly.

The spirit seemed to revive him somewhat.

"Go on," he said.

"This morning, as I was out shooting, I saw Menzies, and followed him."

"Call him the prisoner," observed the professor; "he is in custody, and it will sound more legal."

"Certainly. The prisoner fired two shots as a signal, and a man, whom I instantly recognised as Harold Dugard, came up. While they were talking, I hid behind a tree close to them."

"You are sure you are not mistaken," said Vipond; "it seems so odd that he should be here on the African continent."

"Not at all. I saw him once at Zanzibar, but I did not tell you for fear of alarming you."

"Proceed," said the professor, with a judicial air.

"It was arranged between them," continued Dick, "that to-night at twelve o'clock, it being Menzies' watch, an attack should be made upon our camp."

" What were the prisoner's motives ?"

" First of all revenge, secondly money."

" Revenge upon whom ?"

" Me," said Dick ; " he stipulated that I should be taken alive and given up to him to be tortured and killed."

" You swear that what you state is true, upon your honour," said the professor.

" Dick never told a deliberate lie in his life, and a question like that is an insult," observed Messiter.

" It is a form," answered the professor. " This is a matter of life and death, and we must not have anything on our consciences. I have known Lightheart for some time, and have every confidence in his honour, but the best men are always sworn in a court of justice."

" I understand you to say that the prisoner Menzies has sold us to the enemy," said Vipond, speaking with evident difficulty.

" Yes, sir. I had a narrow escape of my life with some river horses afterwards, and he left me to my fate, when he might have saved me, but I escaped by the skin of my teeth——"

" Pardon me, but that is not a fit expression for a witness in a court of justice such as this is," interrupted the professor.

" Well, I'll say I escaped simply—had a rough and tumble with him, and——"

" That I also object to. What is a rough and—what did you say ?" cried the professor.

" It is evident you don't tumble," replied Dick, with a smile. " But to please you, I will say we had a fight, in which I got the best of it. I captured the prisoner, taxed him with his crime, which he admitted, and binding him, brought him here to be tried."

" That is your case," said Vipond.

" It is, sir."

CHAPTER XLIX.

LYNCH LAW.

CAPTAIN VIPOND and the professor talked together in a low tone for some time, afterwards appealing to Messiter.

At length Captain Vipond said—

" Our thanks are due to you, Lightheart, for your watchfulness and courage."

Dick bowed.

" Under Providence it is to be hoped that you have been the means of saving our lives, for to be forewarned is to be doubly armed."

" Not so much fear now, sir," replied Dick.

Menzies looked up with his usual insolent air.

" Am I to have nothing to say ?" he asked.

" I was about to call upon you for your defence," answered Vipond.

" About time too," exclaimed Menzies ; " I thought you'd get tired of listening to a parcel of lies. Lightheart and I are enemies ; he hates me and I hate him, so he has cooked up this story about Mr.

Dugard, who, I'll take my solemn oath, I never saw in my life."

" Beware !" said the professor, solemnly.

" Of what ?"

" Beware how you go to your death with a lie on your lips."

" There is no lie about that. I speak the truth."

" You have no doubt been brought up in the sublime truths of the Christian religion, and said your prayers at your mother's knee."

" Don't talk about my mother. I don't like it," said Menzies, fidgetting restlessly.

It was clear he loved his mother, and any allusion to her in his desperate state irritated him.

The fact was, he had been a source of great trouble and worry to her before he ran away to sea, and his conscience smote him.

However bad a boy may be, he has got a soft point somewhere.

" You plead not guilty ?" said Captain Vipond.

"Of course I do, when I am innocent."

"Is that all you have to urge in your own behalf?"

"I am the victim of Lightheart's spite, and all I ask is to be allowed to go away—right away. I guess I shan't trouble you any more."

Again the judges conferred together.

The president, who was Captain Vipond, then said—

"Prisoner Menzies, the court has decided against you on Lightheart's evidence, and we condemn you to death."

At the word death, all Menzies' insolent manner vanished.

His colour went and came.

"You have no right to take my life," he cried. "Why should you make yourselves my judges? You will be my murderers if you use your power to kill me, and my blood will cry to Heaven for vengeance."

"Owing to your youth, we would willingly look over your fault, but it is impossible," said Vipond.

In his terror at being found out by Dugard, he would have condemned a dozen to death for betraying him.

"Is there no hope?" asked Menzies.

"None."

"You will plead for me, Lightheart," he cried.

Dick shook his head moodily.

"How am I to die?" asked Menzies.

"You will be hanged to a tree in an hour's time," answered Vipond.

"At least let me be shot; that is an honourable death, the other is the fate of a felon."

"Well," said Vipond, "I've no great objection to that; you shall be shot. Tell off a squad of Pagazi, Messiter, if you please, to be ready with rifles for the execution in an hour's time by your watch."

"Aye, aye, sir," said Messiter.

"Remove the prisoner, boy"—this to Ted; "you are answerable for his safety."

"Come along, governor," said Ted. "I must look after you. I'm only an odd boy, but I've got my feelings, and shouldn't like my promising career to be cut short."

He took hold of the rope's end, and dragging at it, continued—

"Gee up. Pull along, Smunko. I'll see you don't give me any leg."

While Ted conducted the wretched Menzies out of the tent, Messiter went to select six Pagazi for the execution of the sentence.

Dick remained with Vipond and the professor.

"It grieves me to the heart," said the latter, "to see a lad of that age cut suddenly off."

"There are plenty of boys, goodness knows," said the captain. "I'd as soon shoot as flog one. This Menzies deserves no pity. He would have betrayed me into the hands of Dugard. We might all have been killed."

"Very true. It is wrong, perhaps, of me to grieve, but I am averse to bloodshed if it can be avoided. However, he has richly deserved his fate, and I suppose self-preservation is the first law of nature."

Dick went out and met Sangaru, who had heard an explanation from Messiter of the crime and sentence.

"What this, Bana (which is the native word for master)?" he said. "Is it true that Miringu (the Almighty) is about to take the soul of white man?"

"Yes," replied Dick. "His life is to be taken in a short time. He would have got us all shot."

"This is news. How can a white man be so base?"

"There are bad whites as well as blacks."

"Alkema, Bana (no, master)," answered Sangaru, with the flattery peculiar to his race. "The Wasungu (white men) all good, have religion, law, educate; only poor savage black man who bad, because he not told, and can't know right."

"Get your men ready, and tell them to load with ball cartridge," answered Dick.

Sangaru departed to obey orders, much astonished at what he had heard.

So were all the Pagazi.

Neither Messiter nor Dick remarked that a short time afterwards Sangaru and Menzies were in close conversation together.

The native gave him a cup of water.

This Ted reported.

"It's not against orders, is it, sir?" he asked Messiter.

"No; let him have what he likes, poor beggar," replied Messiter.

"Can the nigger talk to him, sir? They're as thick as thieves."

"It doesn't matter."

Ted was satisfied, and did not interfere with the interview between Sangaru and Menzies, who were in the prisoner's tent together.

At length the stern figure of Captain Vipond emerged from the central tent.

Dick was on duty outside, one of the three boys being always on the watch, unless they delegated the task to Sangaru in the daytime.

"Time," ejaculated the captain.

Beckoning to Sangaru, Dick exclaimed—

"Is the firing party ready?"

"Yes, Bana," was the reply.

"Lead out the prisoner, and have a grave dug when the shots are fired. I will let this handkerchief fall from the top of my rifle as a signal."

Menzies was led out of the tent, where he had passed his few remaining moments on earth.

He passed Dick, who held out his hand and said—

"Good-bye; I am sorry for you."

"*You* sorry for me!" almost yelled Menzies; "why, it is you who have brought me to this."

"Your own evil disposition rather."

"*I* shake hands with you? Ten thousand curses on you! Wait a bit, my lad; you'll find some day what it is to have made an enemy of a thorough-bred Yankee."

Dick smiled sadly.

He thought this was the bombast of despair.

Conducted to the fatal spot, which was just outside the camp, Menzies stood upright and faced the six Pagazi who were to shoot him.

"All ready, Bana," said Sangaru.

Menzies did not flinch in the least, and although the hot sun poured down upon his unprotected head, he did not close his eyes.

"Fire!" exclaimed Dick.

He lowered his rifle as he spoke, and the handkerchief fell to the ground.

There was a discharge of fire-arms.

Menzies staggered backwards.

Dick turned away his head, for he did not wish to see his justly-punished companion rolling in the death agony.

All was over.

CHAPTER L.

ATTACKED BY NIGHT.

THE professor came out of the tent at the sound of the shots.

"Poor fellow!" said Dick to him. "He's gone where the good niggers go."

"Hey, lad!" answered the professor; "what's this?"

Dick turned hastily round, and beheld Menzies rise to his feet perfectly unharmed.

He took one glance in Dick's direction, shook his fist at him, and disappeared in a thicket of shrubs on the left.

"Treachery!" cried Dick.

"I thought he was shot," said the professor.

"So did I. He fell sure enough at the discharge. Where is Sangaru? Ted."

"Yes, sir."

"Call Sangaru."

The leader of the Pagazi was at the head of the firing party, and he reluctantly approached.

"What is the meaning of this, you rascal," said Dick.

"Me know nothing more nor you, Bana," replied Sangaru.

"No lies, you scoundrel," thundered Dick, raising a thick whip he held in his hand.

"Me tell **truth**, Bana. Me half Christian."

"You black villain! How was it your soldiers did not kill the prisoner?"

"Tell them to fire high, so as to make for head and heart. S'pose they fire too high."

There was a grin on the fellow's face as he said this, which he could not repress.

In an instant Dick seized him by the

"MENZIES STAGGERED BACKWARDS."—(*See page 160.*)

hair, and dealt him a couple of dozen blows on the back with all his might.

His yells might have been heard a mile off.

"No more beat, Bana; that do; leave off, Bana," he said, in a spasmodic voice.

"Get out, you wretch," replied Dick, casting him from him; "if I have any more of those tricks, I'll have you shot."

Sangaru slunk away, rubbing his back, which was pretty well welted.

"That accounts for the nigger being with Menzies in the tent so long," remarked Messiter.

"Why did you allow it," asked Dick, "if you knew it?"

"What was I to think? Ted told me."

"No doubt," said Dick, "Menzies bought him over in some way, but those niggers are so artful and such liars, it is hopeless to expect the truth from them. I'm sorry for it, because we have another enemy let loose."

"It was a dodge," observed Messiter.

"A cleverly-concocted plan, you should say," replied the professor; "the language of you young men is anything but pure Saxon."

"That be bothered; we talk as all other boys talk," answered Dick. "Don't rile me just now. I am put out enough."

The professor took a little book from his pocket, and turning over the leaves, looked carefully at them.

"This is Walker's dictionary," he said; "it is received as an authority everywhere, and I cannot find the word 'rile' there. It must be slang."

"Go and hunt beetles," exclaimed Dick, angrily.

"That's unkind—more, it is rude. I appeal to Messiter if I deserve it," replied the professor.

"Oh! cut along and write books; that's all you're good for," answered Messiter.

"I am insulted," cried the professor; "it will be some time before I shall forget it."

"Haven't you the sense to see that we must look out for fighting to-night?" said Dick.

"Fighting? Bless me! I hope not. I am not a fighting man. What is going to happen?" exclaimed the professor, in alarm.

"What did we condemn Menzies to death for?"

"Planning a night attack."

"Exactly, and now he has escaped he will carry it out with Dugard."

"Ah! ah! I did not think of that."

"But somebody must think, my dear sir. It strikes me that we must be very careful. That fellow Sangaru has sold us once over to Menzies, and he is capable of doing it again."

"Well, well. Pax," said the professor. "I will not be angry with you, who are only boys after all."

"Thank you," replied Dick, satirically.

"I mean what I say. Your rudeness is forgiven. Make all preparations for the defence of the camp. I am not a man of war, and shall not interfere."

"You'll shoulder a rifle, sir, won't you?"

"No, no. Excuse me. It is not in my line. I will get up a tree, and do you some good there. I have a chemical compound which you will find of use. Leave me to my science. You go to your battle."

The tall, gaunt form of the professor disappeared under the canvas of his tent.

"He's gone to stick some wretched butterfly on a pin," said Messiter.

"Or skin a toad," suggested Dick.

"Those men are not much good when it comes to fighting," continued Messiter.

"I don't know. He's got a chemical box, and lots of drugs and things. He may do something. Science is a wonderful thing," answered Dick.

"I can see how it is," observed Messiter, after a pause; "Menzies got over Sangaru, who made his Pagazi fire high. He pretended to fall down dead, and then bolted."

"He will give us some trouble," replied Dick. "We must put the camp in order. If we are not attacked to-night, we shall be soon."

"Go and see Captain Vipond."

"I will. He knows he is in danger, and will do his best for our defence."

"We are stronger than they are in numbers, and well armed. What have we to funk?"

"A stray bullet, that's all. You would not like to lose me any more than I should you, and every bullet has its billet, the soldiers say."

"I don't think my ounce of lead is moulded yet," said Messiter.

"Let us hope not," said Dick.

He went to Captain Vipond's tent and had a long conversation with him.

The setting sun flooded all around in a sea of golden splendour.

Innumerable birds and insects fluttered and hummed in the long grass and trees.

Occasionally the hiss of a snake was heard, as it glided away in the long grass.

In the distant forest the lion roared, and his loud voice found an echo in the far-off mountains.

It was arranged that the Pagazi should pretend to go to sleep as usual, but they should really keep awake with their arms by their side.

A strict watch was to be kept.

The professor was very busy in his tent, and had various things taken up into a tree and placed upon a fork, on which was put a board which served him as a table.

Then with some difficulty he climbed up, and declared that he was ready for the enemy.

The time passed slowly.

Dick and Messiter patrolled the camp, one on each side, with unceasing vigilance.

A little clock in Vipond's tent struck the hour of twelve.

"Look out," said Dick.

"No fear," returned Messiter.

"Rather a difference this from being at school in Brighton."

"Rather."

"It's a funny world," continued Dick, the solitude and peculiarity of his position making him thoughtful. "Who'd have thought we should have been here three months ago?"

"Not I, for one," said Messiter.

"Wonder if we shall ever get back again."

There was a noise on the right side of the camp.

"Hush!" said Dick, under his breath. "Did you hear that? Call Sangaru."

While he was speaking a shot whistled past his ear.

This awoke those of the Pagazi who were asleep in disobedience of orders.

All sprang to their feet and grasped their weapons.

The night attack had begun.

CHAPTER LI.

THE REPULSE.

OWING to the darkness of the night, and the skill with which the attack had been directed, it was impossible for the defenders of the camp to see their enemies.

All that could be done was to fire in the direction of the flashes of fire which came from guns discharged by the enemy.

Several Pagazi fell, and their companions became alarmed; for though they would have fought bravely by daylight under white leaders, they had not sufficient stamina to stand and be shot at in the dark.

Messiter and Dick ran about encouraging the men, and firing whenever an opportunity presented itself.

Many a shriek and death-cry in the long, reedy grass outside the camp told that the shots went home.

"If the moon would only rise, and we could see," said Dick, "we should soon make short work of them."

Suddenly the professor cast something from his tree into the thick of the enemy.

As it struck the ground a brilliant white light burst forth, leaving the camp in darkness, but making all without as light as day.

Another and another followed, causing the utmost consternation among the astonished Pagazi.

"Hurrah!" cried Dick. "The professor is worth his salt after all. Pepper away, my lads; give it them hot!"

The tall, manly form of Harold Dugard could be seen exhorting his men to stand firm.

By his side was Menzies.

Many bullets were directed at their persons, but they seemed to bear a charmed life.

The Pagazi, however, fell thickly.

It was in vain that their leaders tried to lead them to the attack.

They threw down their arms, and ran for their lives, seeing that further fighting was useless.

At first they had only been hit at random.

Now they were picked off like birds on the bough of a tree in winter.

Utterly confounded by the brilliant device of the professor, and deserted by his men, Dugard beckoned to Menzies, and together they disappeared in the darkness.

The attack was repulsed.

Captain Vipond breathed again, though he had hoped to see his enemy fall.

His loss amounted to seven men and two donkeys shot by accident, while that of the enemy was nineteen.

By daybreak the dead were buried in a narrow trench, and the camp being struck, a forced march was made to get away from the vicinity of Dugard.

The professor was very proud of his exploit, and never tired of talking about it.

After this fight, another hundred miles were traversed, when it was requisite to call a halt.

Captain Vipond and Ted were down with the mukunguru, while Messiter was suffering from dysentery.

Several of the Pagazi were ill, and the demands for dowa, or medicine, which were made upon the professor's chest were frequent.

No longer did the men shout, " Sofari, pakia—a journey, start."

They were tired out and exhausted.

Water had been scarce, and they had slaked their thirst from muddy pools.

It was only by Dick's good health and energy that the caravan was kept together.

The men had heard of Dick's fight with the river horse, which was a great achievement in their eyes.

And as the native name for a hippo is kiboko, they nicknamed Dick Kiboko Bana, or Hippopotamus Master.

Dick was a great favourite with all, and as he had halted on the banks of a stream of good water, and was able to shoot some fresh meat, the spirits of all revived.

The whites now knew the horrible discomforts of African travel.

They were accustomed to fever, dysentery, flies, muddy water, ague, swamps, fording rivers, attacks by night, want of food, wild beasts, insolence and laziness of the carriers, with other trials.

Nothing more had been seen of Dugard.

But both Vipond and Dick knew the man too well to doubt that he was not far off.

While encamped, a slave gang came by from Unyanyembi.

There were sixty slaves in all, captured in war, and sold to the Arabs, who loaded them with chains.

It was a horrible sight to see the poor creatures' despairing faces and lacklustre eyes.

But Dick was powerless to interfere, and contented himself with asking the leader the news.

This was an Arab named Abdallah, and he reported that there was a war going on between the Arabs of Unyanyembi, and the dreaded chief Mirambo.

" Who is this Mirambo ?" asked Dick.

" He was once a robber in the forests, who attacked caravans. Now, Mashallah ! he is a great warrior," replied Abdallah.

" Has he many men and arms ?"

" More than we could count, and it was only by paying a large tribute, which I could not afford—Allah be good to me in trade !—that I got through at all with my slaves."

" What did you give Mirambo ?"

" Three doti of merikani, three of kaniki cloth, and two fundo of sami-sami, red beads."

A doti is about four yards of cloth and worth about ten and sixpence, which was not much after all.

" They tell me that Mirambo is joined by two Wasungi and five and twenty Pagazis," continued Abdallah.

" Two white men ?" echoed Dick, in surprise.

" Yes, and he declares that no caravan shall pass through his land to Unyanyembi."

" That remains to be seen. What news from Ujiji ?"

" I heard that a great white man was there without stores and sick, his men having deserted."

" It must be Livingstone," thought Dick.

The Arab took his leave, and the weary slaves marched along, a monotonous chant issuing from their lips.

Dick went to Captain Vipond, who was getting better from the fever, which seldom lasts more than three days, and told him the news.

"Do you think that those Wasungi, or white men, can be Dugard and Menzies?" asked Vipond.

"Not at all impossible. However, we must push on and chance it. We cannot stay here, and to go back would be absurd."

The captain was of the same opinion.

Dick next went to Ted, to whom he gave some medicine.

"How do you find yourself now?" he asked.

"Gallows bad, sir," replied Ted.

"Do you think you could ride on a donkey to-morrow?"

"I'll try, sir. This 'ere Africa don't agree with me; I'm only an odd boy, but I've got my feelings, and bust me if I don't wish I was out of it!"

Dick laughed and sought Sangaru, telling him that they would make a sofari the next day, and ordering the men to have a double allowance of pemba, a spirit made by the natives, of which they had brought several gourds full.

When the men received the spirit they cried, "Hi, hi, hi! ha, ha, ha!" which are exclamations of joy.

Then they drank health to Kiboko Bana, the young hippopotamus master.

Dick smiled and busied himself with preparations for the morrow's march.

He felt that coming dangers were about to fall thick and fast upon them.

It was instinct.

If Dugard and Menzies were with the ferocious Mirambo, through whose country they were going to travel, perils were indeed ahead of them.

CHAPTER LII.

MIRAMBO.

ON the following day the caravan made another start.

The route lay through a splendid country, well watered and wooded; iron ore cropped up on the surface, and it was clear that if Europeans would settle there and make a railway from Bagamoyo to Unyanyembi, an immense trade might be done and a successful colony planted.

But this is a question of the future.

Perhaps the teeming population of Europe may yet find a vent and a resting place in East Central Africa.

On the third day's journey, as the caravan halted for refreshment at mid-day, a party of soldiers was descried.

Sangaru, who was alike guide and interpeter for the expedition, advanced.

After a short parley he returned to Dick.

"What do they want?" inquired the latter.

"They are the advanced guard of Mirambo's army," answered Sangaru.

"The deuce they are!"

"They say that we can proceed no further, and must give presents to Mirambo to be allowed to go back."

"Tell them they will have nothing from me," answered Dick, "and that I mean to push on."

"Pagazi won't fight, Bana," said Sangaru.

"Why not?"

"They much fear Mirambo, you see, Bana. I asked them."

Sangaru spoke to several of the Pagazi, who, with one accord, said, "Acuno, Kiboko Bana. Acuna, acuna (no, Hippopotamus Master. No, no)!"

Dick foamed with rage at the cowardly conduct of the carriers.

"Ask Mirambo's men what present will satisfy their master?" he said.

"They say leave that to you," answered Sangaru. "You great chief, very rich, able give much."

"Tell them they shall have fifty doti of merikani and sixty of kaniki, with twenty fundo of beads."

Sangaru went to the natives, and held another parley with them.

"They say that handsome present, Bana," he said, when he returned. "But they not able to make promise. Kiboko Bana must bring present of tribute himself, and make terms."

"Very well. How far off is Mirambo?"

"Six miles west."

"I'll go with them unarmed; or stay, I'll take Ted with me. He is better now, and he shall carry the flag. They will respect an envoy, I suppose," said Dick.

"I s'pose so, Bana. Not trust much, though. Better go back."

"I shan't," said Dick, obstinately. "We want to go on."

"Bana must have own way," said Sangaru, respectfully. "But Mirambo great rogue."

Dick's mind, however, was made up, and he resolved to go in person to Mirambo and negotiate.

Seeking Captain Vipond's tent, he told him how affairs stood.

"The Mirambo is the greatest and most warlike chief in the whole of this part of Africa," said Vipond, nervously.

"I know he is," replied Dick, calmly.

"He has a large army."

"Over ten thousand men, well armed."

"And we have reason to suppose that Dugard and Menzies have joined him," continued Vipond.

"That's as safe as houses," answered Dick.

"Why put yourself in their power? I am obliged to you for your courage. You know my sad history, and that Harold Dugard would do anything to obtain my body."

"He shan't have it."

"You think, then, that I am not so bad after all?"

"I don't say anything about that," replied Dick.

"But I should like to know."

"Well, if you will have it," said Dick, "I think you are as big a villain as there is in the world, but you saved my life when you took me on board the 'New Orleans,' and you are paying the expense of this expedition."

"You are blunt, young man," said Vipond, biting his lip.

"I can't tell lies. It isn't my fashion. Besides, it's too much trouble. The truth always comes out easier."

"At all events you will stick by me?"

"To the last."

"That is something. A large-hearted boy like you for a friend is worth a dozen hired men," said Vipond.

"I'm not your friend. Don't you run away with that idea."

"What then?"

"Simply your companion and the leader of this expedition, and as such it is my duty to do my best."

"Are you not afraid to put yourself in Dugard's and Mirambo's power?" asked Vipond.

"No. I want to make terms if I can."

"But if you can't."

"I shall gain time. If we were attacked here we should have no chance. You must break up the camp at once and retire to some hill, where you can throw up stockades, and dig rifle pits. Entrench yourself strongly, and send me a message by a Pagazi to-morrow, stating where you are and all about you."

"Shall you not return to-day?"

"No. I shall certainly stay with Mirambo until to-morrow, perhaps longer, if the beggar won't let me go."

"If Dugard is with him, he will regard you as an enemy."

"My great hope is that Captain Dugard may be with Mirambo, for, whatever your difficulties may be with him, I have always found him a chivalrous gentleman."

Vipond winced at this.

"You are bold, and your courage ought to be successful. Do you take anyone with you?" he asked.

"Ted, if he is well enough."

"I fear not. Messiter came for some medicine just now. He has got a relapse."

"Then I'll go alone. Good-bye."

"God bless you!" exclaimed Vipond. "You are doing your best for me, I know."

They shook hands, and Dick, going to his tent, made a few preparations, and then joined the messengers of the dreaded chief Mirambo.

Their way lay through a fertile and well-wooded region, very different from the marshes and bogs they had lately traversed.

Here they found the lion and the zebra, the antelope and the ostrich, instead of the boa and the scorpion, with all the tribe of slimy crawling reptiles.

The latter frequented the regions of black, putrefying mud, and revelled in the damp and steaming neighbourhoods of rivers.

It was a bold idea of Dick's to beard the lion in his den.

For Mirambo was reported to be as savage as he was clever.

He had traded with the merchants of Zanzibar, and made money.

English he could talk fluently.

But he found he could make himself richer and more famous by robbing caravans and levying war upon his neighbours than he could by honest trading.

It was said that he had killed his father in a fit of ungovernable passion.

And amongst other rumours respecting him was one that he had carried off a lovely English girl from the coast near Bagamoyo, whom he kept as his wife in his thickly-fenced city of Yamwezi.

CHAPTER LIII.

DICK IN YAMWEZI.

THE city of Yamwezi was one which contained about seven hundred inhabitants.

These lived in curiously-constructed huts, made of clay and stones, having round rather than conical bee-hived roofs.

They were surrounded by a high palisade made of thick timber, almost bullet-proof.

But two gates gave entrance to the fortified city of Yamwezi.

One on the east side, the other on the north.

The army of Mirambo was encamped outside the stockade, it being principally composed of the men of Yamwezi and the warriors from villages in the neighbourhood.

This great chief, who is even now robbing caravans and disturbing the interior of East Central Africa, had just repulsed the Arabs of Unyanyembi.

The Arabs were beaten with great slaughter, and this made his name more reputed than ever.

Amongst the peculiarities of Mirambo was his extreme superstition.

His constant companion was a Uganga, or medicine man, a fellow we should call a fortune teller, or one divining by the stars.

His name was Sagazi.

The influence of this quack over his royal master resembled that of Galeotti the astrologer over Louis XI.

Never did Mirambo undertake a war,

or even a hunting party, without consulting his medicine man, Sagazi, who gave him various charms.

One of these was a talisman, made of a plant and sewn up carefully in a leathern bag, which was worn round the neck, suspended by a bit of yellow cloth.

In another bag was the tongue of a large boar, the ear of a zebra, the claw of a lion, a bit of the hoof of a giraffe, a portion of buffalo hide, and a dried golden beetle.

Sagazi told him that with those things about him he might be wounded in battle, but never killed.

A belief in this prediction made Mirambo the bravest and most foolhardy fighter in Africa.

It gained him his reputation for courage, and his men would follow him anywhere, while the terrified enemy fell back at the sight of the war sword of the dreaded Mirambo.

The Uganga man could also predict the coming of rain, heal the sick, and was a very great man indeed.

In fact, he was a clever fellow, knowing the signs of the weather, having some knowledge of medicine, and a good collection of herbs to cure diseases with.

And last, but not least, his judgment was very shrewd and keen.

If the enemy were reported strong, he advised his royal master not to go to war.

If the clouds were thick and heavy, he said it would rain.

And so on.

In a word, he was a clever humbug and impostor.

Mirambo was standing outside his tent, talking to Sagazi, the Uganga, and expecting the return of his messengers to the white caravan.

Turning to the Uganga, he said—

"Shall I have a rich tribute from these whites?"

"Yes," replied Sagazi; "but in the end you will have all they have got."

"Why so?"

"Because they will offend you, and you will make war upon them."

Mirambo laughed.

"I do not make war upon a handful of men," he replied; "I send my chosen warriors to kill them. But who have we here?"

His keen eyes descried a party of the men of Yamwezi leading in a prisoner.

He was a tall, ungainly-looking man, wearing spectacles, and holding in his hands bundles of grasses and plants.

When he approached he looked angrily round him, and said, snappishly—

"Who's master here?"

"I," answered Mirambo, drawing up his tall form, and speaking in his usual brutal, overbearing tone.

"Oblige me by telling your men to let me alone, most noble savage," was the answer, "though, as you speak English, you must have some cultivation."

"I am Mirambo, and when I have said that, what is the use of further words?"

"Indeed! Well, I am Professor Crab, and while engaged in botanizing, your men seized me. I demand to be released at once, and I will tell you something of importance."

"What is that?" asked Mirambo, regarding the strange figure of the professor curiously.

"Your crops about here are dried up, but in an hour's time or thereabouts you will have a night's rain."

"Ha!" cried Mirambo, "can you make medicine like that? Are you a Uganga?"

"Look here," said the professor, exhibiting a barometer which he had under his arm; "this is a glass to tell the weather with."

Mirambo grasped it and showed it to Sagazi, who shook his head and smiled incredulously.

"When that white substance, which we call quicksilver, rises," continued Mr. Crab, "it will be fine; when it sinks it will rain or blow. You see how low it is now?"

"By my father Makololo," cried Mirambo, "this is indeed medicine. Take him away; we will put him to the proof. If it rains before sunset, let him go free; if not, strike off his head."

A dozen Yamwezi seized him, much to his indignation.

"Give me my glass," he shouted; "this is not fair. Hands off, you rascals. A plague take the savages! There go my rare specimens, my grasses and my plants."

He was forced into a tent, where four men kept guard over him, two with drawn swords and two with loaded guns.

Mirambo contemplated the glass with the pleasure a child looks upon a new toy.

"If this is true," he remarked, "it is better than your medicine, Sagazi, and you are worse than a fool."

"Words, words," said the Uganga, "though I think I see signs of rain in the clouds."

"Why didn't you see them before?"

"They have only just come. Yes, yes," continued Sagazi, holding up his hands, "praise be to Mungu, the Almighty, the wished-for rain is coming. I feel it. I see it. Thanks, mighty Mungu, our crops will be saved, and our warriors will not starve."

Though this was only a piece of acting on his part, it imposed upon Mirambo.

Sagazi believed in what he had heard and seen of white civilization, and put confidence in the weather-glass of the professor.

He was sharp enough to benefit by it.

Suddenly, a beating of native drums and a clashing of cymbals announced the return of the messengers of the caravan.

Dick, carrying the British flag, was brought before Mirambo.

"Who is this?" demanded the king.

"I am the leader of an expedition from which you demand tribute, if you are Mirambo," replied Dick, "but perhaps you do not understand me?"

"I speak English," was the answer. "What tribute do you propose to give?"

"How much do you want?"

"One hundred doti of merikani, a hundred of kaniki, and a hundred fundo of beads."

"It is too much," said Dick; "I cannot give half that."

"Ha!" screamed Mirambo. "You dare to refuse me?"

"Yes. I am not afraid of any insolent tyrant. You are a well-known robber, but our guns are a match for your army."

Mirambo foamed at the mouth with rage.

"Hang him up to the nearest tree," he cried, "and let my army prepare to march against his friends."

Dick did not understand this, because it was spoken in the native dialect.

But when a stout cord was placed round his neck by half-a-dozen grinning savages, he knew something was wrong.

"Take care what you are about," he said; "I am a British subject, and my Queen will revenge my death."

Mirambo snapped his fingers.

"That for your Queen," he said. "She will not waste her money and her men in sending after me here in Africa. What is your life to her? Pah! I have been to the coast. I know all about England and her Queen."

He made a sign to the soldiers, who rudely dragged Dick to a tree close by.

The rope was thrown round a branch, several hands seized the loose end, and Dick thought his last hour was come.

"I came here," he said, "as a messenger. Are you such a ruffian as not to respect an envoy?"

"What's that to me?" asked Mirambo. "Your words are insults—you must die!"

While Dick's life was hanging on the balance, a white man emerged from a tent, with a stately step.

He approached Mirambo.

"This must not be," he said; "keep him a captive in Yamwezi, if you will, but shed no blood."

"Why should you interfere, Bana?" asked Mirambo, surlily.

"He is my friend. Let that be enough. I leave you at once if my request is not complied with."

Mirambo hesitated, and bit his thumbnail.

"Nay," continued the speaker, "I will do more. See you this revolver? It holds twelve lives in its barrels. I will shoot you through the heart, and yonder curs also."

"It is not well that we should have differences," replied Mirambo, who was cowed by the resolute demeanour of the European. Turning to his men, he continued—"His life is saved; take him into our city of Yamwezi. Let him be guarded, but treated as becomes a prisoner of rank."

The soldier loosened the noose and removed the rope, motioning to Dick to march towards the city, which could be seen easily about a quarter of a mile off.

"A narrow squeak that," muttered Dick, rubbing his neck.

As he was being taken away, he saw the features of his preserver, who was Harold Dugard.

The latter seemed to wish to avoid any conversation with him, for he walked hastily back to his tent.

"He's done me a good turn, and I won't forget him," thought Dick, adding —"I was on the brink of eternity that time, and in another minute I should have been in kingdom come."

They led him into the stockaded city through the eastern gate, and placed him in a lower room of a hut, which was superior to most others in its having two floors, and an enclosure of ground or garden about it.

Boiled rice, a roast chicken, and water were set before him, and when the door closed he sat himself down on a rude stool to think and recover himself.

In half-an-hour the rain descended in torrents, and the professor was set at liberty to walk home through the drenching downpour.

"The brutes," he said to himself; "I told them it was going to rain, and they might as well have lent me an umbrella."

He regained his camp in safety, and related his adventure amidst some laughter, though he could give no account of Lightheart, not having heard of or seen him.

The rain lasted all night, but towards morning the sky cleared, the sun broke out, and a steaming mist arose from the damp, soddened ground.

Captain Vipond gave orders to march. The camp was struck, and he, with Messiter and the professor, went in front to select a good place for defensive purposes, as Dick suggested.

They found this on the summit of a hill, which had a river with a swift stream, but of small breadth, running at its base.

Here they made every preparation for an energetic resistance if attacked.

CHAPTER LIV.

THE HIDDEN QUEEN.

AFTER refreshing himself with the fare provided for him, Dick began to look round his prison.

A window opening to the ground gave him a view of the garden, which had a wall as high as that of the neighbouring huts, for they did not deserve the name of houses.

Trees and flowers grew in rich profusion, without any plan or arrangement.

From under one of the most leafy of the trees came a tinkling sound, as of a guitar.

A low, sweet voice sang a plaintive, sad song, which thrilled Dick to the heart, for the words were English, and he could not doubt that the songstress was a countrywoman, perhaps a captive like himself.

Pushing open the window, the door only being guarded, he stepped gently forth, and walked boldly to the spot from whence the music came.

At the sound of his footsteps the singing ceased, and as he came in sight, a tiny scream informed him that he had startled the fair musician.

Before him, upon a bed of grass and leaves, lay a lovely English girl, her beautiful eyes moist with tears recently shed.

Her long hair streaming over her shoulders, black and glossy as a raven's wing, allowed the zephyr to wanton through its tresses.

The silken eyelashes were raised in wonder at the sight of the manly, open-faced English boy.

A plain white muslin robe, girdled round her waist by a rich blue silk sash, served to set off the symmetry of her peerless form.

"Don't be alarmed." exclaimed Dick. "I am a friend, and beg pardon for coming upon you so suddenly."

"How did you get here?" asked the lady.

"I am a captive in the hands of Mirambo, and I suppose they have put me on the ground floor of what he is pleased to call his palace, while you occupy the attics. But allow me to ask what on earth a lovely creature like yourself is doing in the house of a savage thief?"

"You may well ask," she answered, sadly. "My name is Alice. I am the daughter of an English merchant at Zanzibar, whose name is Mr. John Smiles, but owing to his immense size and strength, and his success in hunting big game, everyone calls him Sampson Jack."

"And the wife of Mirambo?"

"No, thank Heaven. I have resisted all his efforts to make me *that*," she replied, with a shudder.

"How did you come here?" asked Dick.

"During one of my father's hunting parties, I accompanied him to Bagamoyo, and I was stolen from the house of a rich Banian where I was staying, and taken through the jungle to this walled city of Yamwezi."

"Have you been here long?"

"About six weeks, as well as I can reckon, though I have been unable to count properly."

"I have heard of you from the natives, as the Hidden Queen of Mirambo," said Dick.

"Rather would I die than be that wretch's wife," she continued; "my only hope is in Heaven and my father."

"Will he rescue you?"

"I know that he will never rest until he has made the attempt. Oh, Mirambo does not know my father. Well versed in African travel, and bold as a lion, he will hunt after me like a bloodhound after a runaway slave."

"Thank you for your confidence," said Dick. "I am a perfect stranger to you, but rest assured I will do what I can for you."

"Alas! you are a prisoner like myself," said the unfortunate Alice. "What can you do?"

"I'm a very peculiar sort of fellow," answered Dick, with a smile, "or else I should not now be in the wilds of Africa."

"What is your object?"

"Trading, principally, with some friends; and also a wish to discover Dr. Livingstone."

"Ah! the brave, good man," cried Alice. "I saw him four years since at Zanzibar. He is, indeed, a fine, large-hearted Christian gentleman."

"Perhaps we shall yet discover the sources of the Nile together and settle the question of the East African watershed, visit the dwellers underground, and do a few other trifles," replied Dick, with a quiet smile.

"I hope you may; but tell me, if I am not too inquisitive, how you came to fall into Mirambo's power."

"I went into his camp to settle a question of tribute, as our caravan wants to pass through his dominion to Unyanyembi, and so on to Ujiji, where Livingstone is reported to be."

"Well?"

"Well, I offended his savage highness, who threatened to hang me. I escaped by a fluke, and am a prisoner of state. By the way, are those water lemons growing over there in that bed?"

"Yes, I think so," answered Alice.

"And peaches on those trees?"

"Yes."

"I'll have a tuck-in, for I'm jolly thirsty. Will you do ditto?" asked Dick.

"I am too miserable to take any interest in anything, and only eat to keep body and soul together," replied Alice, mournfully.

"That's a mistake. Never say die. What would you say if you were shut up in a wonderful ship that went under the sea, and went out shark hunting, and got stuck in the ice near the Pole, and got accustomed to your hair standing on end with funk every ten minutes?"

"All that would be better than my condition," answered Alice, looking at him curiously.

"Don't you put your pretty self in a fluster," continued Dick. "You shan't be Mrs. Mirambo."

"Perhaps, Mr. —— you did not tell me your name."

"Lightheart. Rather more suggestive than elegant as a name; but still, it is what my father had before me, and not my choice."

"Perhaps, Mr. Lightheart," she went on, with a tinge of coquetry, "you would like me to be Mrs. Somebody-else?"

"Not the least bit in the world," replied Dick, with his hands full of peaches. "Have a peach. Catch. Well done! No, butterfingers! There, a clean, neat catch, like the man at slip when the cove at the wicket gives him half a chance."

"You are a funny boy, Mr. Lightheart," said Alice, amused in spite of herself.

"Funny is not the word," he answered. "Try a slice of melon."

"Well, you are peculiar."

"That's all right. Now listen to me, Miss Alice Smiles; I'm not ambitious of being your lord and master, because I have a little pet of my own at home, but I'll be like a brother to a sister to you."

"Thank you," added Alice, feeling disappointed that her beauty had made no greater impression upon the handsome lad, who was at one and the same time as cool as a cucumber and as daring as a lion.

"I have friends in the neighbourhood who won't leave me in the hole, if your governor, Sampson Jack, doesn't find you out, and I'll bet we warm Mirambo between us."

"I hope he will not find you talking to me. The wretch is wicked enough to kill us both."

Dick opened his shirt, and showed the butt of a small revolver.

"I'll make that speak to him," he said, "if he comes any nonsense over us; and as I'm the ground floor lodger and you've got the first pair front, sing out like steam if he tries his game on."

"I will," she added, profoundly thankful.

"I'll be there," said Dick, sucking his melon.

"Hush!" she exclaimed, "I hear some-one at the garden gate. It is Mirambo."

"Mirambo?" repeated Dick, in dismay.

"Yes, it is his custom to enter that way when he comes to make what he calls love to me. For Heaven's sake hide yourself."

Dick made a few antelope-like bounds to the house, darted through the window, shut it, and was soon once more in his prison.

It would have been folly to beard Mirambo.

Nor would it have done the Hidden Queen any good.

CHAPTER LV.

SAMPSON JACK.

PROFESSOR CRAB had imbibed a great contempt for the native Pagazi.

He said they were lazy, cowardly, and thieves.

They irritated him beyond endurance, and swearing not being one of his accomplishments, he had to invent a word to express his disgust.

This was "poof," and whenever he was annoyed he said, "Poof! I am a Saxon; these dog-faced rascals are worse than pigs."

The day after the camp was moved the professor and Messiter went out together.

It was the professor's purpose to collect specimens of flowers, shrubs, and herbs, with any rare animal life he might meet with, such as beetles, butterflies, etc.

Messiter meant to shoot large game if he could find it.

The Pagazi had reported giraffe, elephant, and rhinoceros in the neighbourhood.

While it was known that the boa constrictor lurked in the long grass fringing the river, and twined in the boughs which overhung the forest bordering the stream.

Ted accompanied them, bearing two guns, loaded, to hand to Messiter if he should miss his first shot.

They were Lancaster rifles, loaded with the Frazer shell, which could drop an elephant at ten or a dozen paces if the ball was planted in his skull.

Climbing up and down inclines, clambering over grass-grown ant-hills, and struggling through reedy grass which came up to their necks, they at last espied a herd of giraffes plucking the green branches of the trees with their long and graceful necks outstretched.

"Gently," said Messiter, knowing that the giraffe is as timid as a deer when aroused, and can dart out of sight like a flash of lightning almost.

"Poof!" said the professor; "I am a Saxon. Do you think I am afraid of a long-legged, long-necked nothing like that? Poof!"

Concealing himself behind an ant-hill, Messiter threw himself down and fired.

The giraffe had one of its legs broken, but he raced away.

It had not gone far before a second shot reached its heart, and it measured its length on the grassy plain.

"Poof!" said the professor, "two shots to kill a thing like that."

"You wouldn't have done it in a dozen," said Messiter proudly, as he walked up to the noble creature, feeling very much elated at having killed such kingly game.

"Poof!" said the professor; "I am a Saxon. Ted, give me some of that stuff the rascally natives distil as liquor."

It was becoming noticeable that since he had had an attack of fever, the professor drank very much more than he had ever done before.

"Pretty scenery," he said, as he put down the gourd. "I rather like life in Africa. Poof! what's that?"

In a tree over his head was something half dark, half yellowish, and glittering.

It kept moving about the branches rustling the leaves and shaking the tree.

Two bright, glistening eyes stared out at him, like an electric light at sea on a dark night.

"A snake, by Jove," said Messiter. "Look out, sir."

"Poof!" said the professor, "I didn't bargain for snakes, and I don't think I like Africa quite so well as I thought."

"It's a boa constrictor," cried Messiter, "by its size, by gum! Its body is as thick round as a man's thigh."

"Yes," said the professor. "It is the famous boa of Africa—not poisonous, but when it throws its folds around a stag, or even an elephant, it can crush their carcases into pulp."

"Get out of the way, sir," said Messiter.

"Poof! I am a Saxon!" exclaimed Mr. Crab, who was made bold by the palm spirit. "Who's afraid? Poof!"

He began a fantastic dance under the tree.

This seemed to irritate the huge snake, which detached a part of its body from the branches.

Quick as lightning, it swung its folds round the unlucky professor.

This was like the twining of the lash of a whip round a post.

Mr. Crab yelled desperately, and struggled fiercely to free himself.

But in vain.

"Help! help!" he cried. "Poof! I am being doubled up. Poof! poof! I can't breathe."

"Remember you're a Saxon, sir," said Messiter.

"Bother Saxons! Poof! He is trying to drag me up into the tree. Cut him down. Poof!"

Messiter drew his knife, and rushed upon the snake, whom he slashed at, drawing the dark, steaming blood, without doing much harm.

The snake, seeing another enemy, immediately let his head and the upper part of his body fall to the ground.

Before Messiter could escape, he was in the dreadful coils.

Professor Crab was held tightly by the tail part, and Messiter was surrounded by four coils of the head or upper part.

The boa's huge, flat head flung itself about in the air.

Its forked tongue darted in and out.

The eyes glowed like burning coals.

It was an awful moment, and Messiter gave himself up for lost, but, disengaging his right hand, he again used his knife.

Owing to the tightness with which the snake was coiled, and the constant squeezes he gave his prey, it was difficult to move or breathe.

Messiter felt his ribs crack.

The perspiration burst out from every pore in his body.

His eyes were starting from their sockets.

The professor kept on saying "Poof!" and cried dismally for help.

Messiter could only stab the reptile, whereas he ought to have cut him in half, but he could not get free play for his hand and arm.

The pricks of the knife only enraged the boa without disabling him.

In a few moments it seemed as if all would be over.

Messiter was gradually sinking.

A tightness round his chest warned him of approaching suffocation.

Suddenly there was a shout.

He looked up, while hope struggled with despair in his dim and bloodshot eyes.

"Hold on there!" cried an English voice; "I'm in this."

The next minute a tall, strapping man rushed upon the snake with a sharp knife.

One vigorous blow cut the loathsome thing in half.

The head and the tail relaxed their folds at the same time, and fell to the earth.

Here they twisted and writhed, while fearful hisses came from the dying boa.

The stranger fired a revolver into the head, and seizing the professor and Messiter one with each hand, carried them as if they had been children to a grassy knoll.

For a brief space they were too much exhausted to speak.

"Well," said the stranger, "as sure as my nickname is Sampson Jack, that's the biggest serpent I've seen since I've been vagabondising in these parts. He's a regular whopper, and no mistake."

When the professor and Messiter had recovered from their fright and the severe hugging they had endured, they thanked Sampson Jack for his timely rescue.

"Say no more," he said.

"But we shall never be able to return your kindness," said Messiter.

" Yes, you will. You are here with a caravan I suppose ?"

" We are. And you ?"

" I've come to fight Mirambo. He stole my daughter, the richest heiress in Zanzibar."

" Really," said Messiter; " perhaps we shall have a go-in at Mirambo on our own account."

" How's that ?"

" We have sent our best man to arrange the tribute, and if the messenger does not come back to-day, we shall think there is something wrong."

" Bravo! the more the merrier !" cried the giant Sampson Jack. " I've got a battery of six cannons, and English sailors to serve them, which will make us a match for the savage villain. Give me your hands. We are in the same swim, I can see."

They shook hands heartily.

Sampson Jack then led them to his party, who were encamped a little way off.

He had been attracted to their help by the cries of the professor.

English beer in bottle awaited them, and as he drank it, Mr. Crab said——

" Poof! I was not afraid of the snake. In two minutes I should have killed him. You came too quickly, sir. Poof! After all, an African boa is a contemptible worm in the hands of a Saxon."

" You're lucky, my man, not to be in the worm's belly by this time," replied Sampson Jack, " so give us no gas."

This rebuke silenced the professor.

After they had refreshed themselves, Sampson Jack accompanied them to Captain Vipond to organise an alliance against Mirambo.

CHAPTER LVI.

THROWN TO THE LION.

ON the day following Dick's interview with the pretty Alice, he again walked in the garden.

It was his hope that he might meet with her.

In this expectation he was disappointed.

She did not make her appearance.

While he was walking about, plucking the fruit, and wondering how long his captivity would last, he heard an English voice.

" Master Dick," it said.

Turning round he looked up and down, but could see no one.

" Who spoke ?" he cried.

" This way, sir," was the reply.

Casting his eyes to the palisade, he beheld the face and hands of a dark-coloured boy, who was hanging on the palings which ran round the garden.

" Who are you ?" he asked.

" Don't you know me, Master Dick ? I'm only an odd boy, but I've got——"

" Is it you, Ted ?" asked Dick, in surprise.

" Yes, sir."

" What have you done to your mug ?"

" I've altered it, sir, to get into this blessed town of Yamwezi, and I've had a job, I can tell you."

" How did you find me out ?"

" By listening to Menzies talking to that captain cove. They've got a tent outside."

" I know they have," said Dick.

" Menzies wants to have you killed, but captain cove won't have it by no means. Can I come down ?"

" Yes, jump over and chance it," said Dick.

In a moment Ted had drawn himself up and lightly descended on the other side.

" What's the news, Ted ?" said Dick, as he shook him warmly by the hand.

" We're going to make an attack on Mirambo," answered Ted.

" Nonsense. Are you strong enough ?"

Just at that moment the garden gate opened slowly.

The swarthy form of Mirambo appeared, but neither of the boys noticed him.

Seeing that there were two persons in his private garden, the savage king advanced angrily.

But when the words "attack Mirambo" fell upon his ears, he changed his mind.

With a craftiness peculiar to himself, he crept behind a tree.

Here he was safely concealed and within earshot.

It was his intention to listen.

"I'll tell you all about it, Master Dick," continued Ted, "but I must begin at the beginning."

"Cut along."

"Don't you hurry me, sir, or I shall forget something," said Ted, scratching his head.

"Take your time."

"You see, sir, it was Master Messiter that sent me to you."

"What for?"

"He got anxious when you didn't return, and we've had a reinforcement, I think he called it."

"All the better," remarked Dick.

"Have you seen a young lady here, named Alice?" asked Ted.

"The daughter of Sampson Jack, of Zanzibar?"

"That's her."

"Yes, I have."

"That old thief Mirambo carried her off," said Ted.

"He did."

If they could have seen Mirambo's face twitch convulsively with rage, they would not have conversed so much at their ease.

But this was lost upon them.

"Sampson Jack's joined us, with several men, a lot of English sailors, and six cannon," continued Ted.

"Hurrah for him!" cried Dick. "Cannon is just what we want to fight niggers with."

"He's after his daughter, and he's offered a hundred pounds reward for Mirambo's head."

"I'll have that money, if I get a chance," said Dick.

Mirambo, at hearing this, trembled violently, but not with fear.

His emotion was the anger of a wild beast.

"I shall have a try for it," replied Ted, adding—"Master Messiter wanted me to help you to escape, if I could, and if not, to tell you the attack would be made to-morrow night, so that you might, if possible, get out and help us a bit when you hear the guns firing."

"Thank you, Ted," said Dick; "I'll do my best, but I can't get away now. Tell our friends that my life is safe."

"Is it?" muttered Mirambo, between his teeth.

"I must get back then," said Ted. "I'm not at all comfortable, though I have stained my face and body and put on a nigger's dress, if you can call a bit of cotton a dress."

Dick laughed.

"Good-bye, Ted; God bless you," he exclaimed. "I hope you'll get away all right. Are you armed?"

"No; I haven't even a pocket to put a revolver in."

"Of course you haven't; I forgot that. Take care of yourself, and thank you for coming."

"I'm only an odd boy, sir, but I've got my feelings, and I shall never forget your kindness to me."

"Rot," said Dick; "I owe you quite as much as you do me."

"Ah! I don't know about that. You saved my life on the beach at Brighton, when I hadn't a friend or a crust of bread to eat."

"I've never been sorry for it, Ted."

"And you never shall, sir. It's my belief an act of kindness is never thrown away."

"I think not."

"Tell you a curious thing," continued Ted. "Yesterday, in the forest, I heard a beast yelping and going on. It was a lion, and at first I thought I'd pot it, but it seemed in pain, and I went up to it cautiously."

"To a lion?"

"Yes, sir. Well, it's a funny thing, but I've got my feelings, Master Dick."

"So you said before."

"The lion was a-limping, sir, on three legs, and I saw he'd got one of those acacia thorns in the ball of his foot."

"That wasn't your fault," said Dick.

"Perhaps it was his. However, he let me come up quite close, and I said, 'Poor lion! gently, lad,' to soothe him."

"It's a wonder he didn't eat you."

"Not he. He was too bad. What do you think he did?"

"Can't tell."

"He held up his paw," continued Ted, "and I wasn't at all funky. I pulled out the thorn, and he licked my hand for it. That's a fact."

"'HOLD ON THERE, I'M IN THIS!' CRIED AN ENGLISH VOICE."—(See page 174.)

"I won't say I don't believe it," answered Dick, "but it's one of the toughest yarns I've had to swallow for ever so long."

"Take my gospel oath of it," exclaimed Ted, indignantly.

"Never mind. Cut off. Remember me to all, and say I'll listen for the guns, and see what I can do. They've made me a prisoner, but I've got my wits about me."

Ted was about to run for the wall, when the tall, commanding form of Mirambo emerged from his place of concealment.

In his hand he held a sword, which he did not take any pains to hide.

"Mirambo!" exclaimed Dick.

"Yes," answered the king; "and, by the bones of my ancestors, I will make you repent what you have been saying."

"Ancestors?" exclaimed Dick, scornfully. "I shouldn't think you had any."

"My family is ancient," said Mirambo. "Beware how you irritate me."

"Shake hands, old cock," continued Dick. "I don't want to cut off your head, and shouldn't like to hurt you."

While he was chaffing the king, he made a sign to Ted to be off.

It was to enable the lad to escape that he tried to banter Mirambo.

But the latter was too clever for him.

He saw the sign, and made a spring upon Ted, threatening him with his sword.

Dick broke down a stout bough from a tree.

Armed with this, he ran up just in time to beat down the tyrant's sword.

"No, you don't," he exclaimed.

Strong as Mirambo was, he had no knowledge of fencing.

Dick, however, could fence pretty well, and when Mirambo turned upon him, trying to cut him down with his sword, he parried his cuts very skilfully.

Ted sank on his knees, and crawling towards Mirambo, put his head between his legs, seized his shins with each arm, and giving a jerk, caused him to fall backwards.

In an instant Dick was upon him.

He snatched the sword from his hand, and stood over him.

The powerful Mirambo was helpless before the two boys.

"Very neatly done, Ted," exclaimed Dick.

"It wasn't bad, sir, was it?" said Ted, complacently.

"The luck is against me," exclaimed Mirambo, with a grim smile.

"You can't expect to have it all your own way. Very annoying, though, isn't it?" said Dick, mockingly.

"What do you want as the price of my life?" asked Mirambo.

"Instant liberty for myself and Ted, as well as for a young English lady you have here, a prisoner."

"It is granted."

"On your honour?"

"On the faith of Mirambo."

Dick was satisfied.

He fancied he detected on his face a crafty look, but to this he attached no importance until afterwards.

At present he was too young in African warfare to have learnt to distrust the word of a great chief.

He did not know that Mirambo, though brave and daring, was at the same time a thorough liar, whose pledged word was not worth half a fundo of red beads.

Putting his sword across his knee, he broke it in half.

Mirambo ran to the house.

Clapping his hands, he shouted—

"Hi! hi! Sagazi. Hi! hi!"

In an instant a door opened, and Sagazi, the medicine man, at the head of a dozen native soldiers, rushed into the garden.

These formed the private or body guard of the king.

"Seize the Wasungu (white man)!" continued Mirambo.

Escape was impossible.

With a groan Dick saw that he was deceived, and had foolishly trusted to the good faith of a man who did not know what truth was.

The soldiers grasped him and Ted firmly.

"Take the youngest outside the city," continued Mirambo; "in an hour's time he shall be thrown to the lion we caught in the nets this morning."

At this speech, the soldiers' faces were lighted up with a fierce joy.

They were promised a spectacle which appealed strongly to their cruel natures.

It was to be a feast of blood.

As for Dick and Ted, they knew nothing, as they did not understand the dialect in which the king spoke.

" I cannot kill the big one," continued Mirambo, " as the Wasungu Bana, Captain Dugard, my ally, has bargained for his life."

" Let him see his friend torn limb from limb, that will be as bad," suggested the medicine man.

" Well said. Bind him, and take him with the other to the lion's pit."

" It shall be done, master," answered Sagazi.

" How many lions have we ?"

" Only the one caught this morning."

" True. The others were killed in the last fight with elephants we amused ourselves with."

" That was so," said Sagazi.

" Away with them. I am going to see the captive maiden. In an hour's time I shall be ready."

With these words, Mirambo, the cruel and bloodthirsty, strode away.

He turned and bent a vindictive look upon the boys.

Dick returned it with one of defiance.

CHAPTER LVII.

THE FEAST OF BLOOD.

THERE was a deep, well-like pit outside the fortified town of Yamwezi.

In this were placed the lions which the king's huntsmen caught alive in nets or traps.

The great amusement of the chief men of Yamwezi was to behold a combat between a lion and an elephant, or a lion and a tiger, or sometimes a lion and a crocodile.

This was to them what a bull-fight is to the Spaniards of the present day.

Or what a contest between gladiators was to the ancient Romans.

Sometimes great culprits were thrown to the lions, and the whole court would assemble to see them torn to pieces.

There was but one lion in the pit at present.

This had quite recently been caught.

Dick and Ted had their arms bound behind their backs.

They were marched, carefully guarded, out of the garden.

The people of Yamwezi looked curiously at them as they passed through the streets.

But those benighted savages were so accustomed to scenes of blood and deeds of violence that, though they guessed the boys were going to execution, they did not exhibit any sympathy.

" Master Dick," said Ted.

" What ?"

" Isn't that Mirambo a lying old thief ?"

" Rather. That name's too good for him," replied Dick.

" Weren't you a flat not to give him a good hyke up with the sword when you had the chance ?"

" I was worse than an idiot."

" You was so," said Ted, thoughtfully.

" Wait till I get another chance. But who was to think he'd behave like that ?" replied Dick, bitterly.

In a short time they quitted the city by one of the gates, and reached the plain on which the army was encamped.

Although the sun had passed the meridian, the heat was intense.

The rays of the sun poured down with a fury that is only to be met with in tropical regions.

The boys were halted within a few yards of the pit, in which the lion was kept.

Round this were erected two rows of wooden seats like benches.

Here were accommodated the chief officers of the army and the household.

Meaner persons were allowed to crowd round and look on as best they could.

To Dick's great satisfaction he saw a white man emerge from his tent.

A glance sufficed to show him that it was Captain Dugard.

He approached Dick.

" What is the cause of your being here ?" he inquired.

Dick explained in a few words.

" I have pledged my word that your life shall be held sacred," replied Dugard. " and I do not think Mirambo wishes to quarrel with me."

" Not he, sir," answered Dick.

" If it were not for my influence your life would not be worth a minute's purchase."

" You will protect Ted, sir ?" said Dick.

" No. I have nothing to do with him," said Dugard, coldly.

" Will you let Mirambo kill him ?"

" If he likes."

" But he is one of your own race and blood. He is in a foreign country. One word from you would save him."

" It shall not be spoken."

" Why not ?" exclaimed Dick, indignantly.

" Ted is a bad boy. He tried to take my life. Let him perish."

" I wish my hands were not tied; I'd have a good try to save him."

" What could you do against hundreds, foolish boy ?"

" Hiding among savages seems to have made you as bad as they are," said Dick.

" Be silent, or I may withdraw my protection from you," said Dugard.

The dark frown which Dick knew so well came over his face.

" I don't care if you do," cried Dick. " I hate cruelty, and you know Ted is my servant and friend. I would as soon die myself as see him killed."

" Don't worry about me, sir," said Ted; " that captain cove and I never were friends."

" Tell me one thing ?" asked Dick.

" Well ?"

" What are they going to do with the lad ?"

" Throw him to the lions, to make what they call a feast of blood."

" Horrible," said Dick. " Is it possible?"

" Daniel in the lions' den," said Ted, attempting a smile, though he was in reality very much alarmed.

Captain Dugard walked away.

Scarcely had he gone when Ted exclaimed, " Look out, Master Dick."

" What for ?"

" Here's Menzies."

Turning round, Dick saw his enemy walking up rapidly.

His little ferret eyes gleamed with a malignant satisfaction.

" Hullo, Lightheart," he exclaimed. In for it at last, are you ?"

" Fish and find out," said Dick.

" They say the lion is going to have a tuck-out."

" Perhaps."

" Won't I look on and laugh while you holler ! Won't I just, that's all," said Menzies.

" You're bad enough for anything," said Dick.

" That's what you say. Hullo, Ted are you in for it too ?"

" Ax," answered Ted, sullenly.

" Here's a lark," said Menzies, dancing about for joy; " we haven't had any excitement for a week, since Mirambo burnt six men to death for mutiny. It's a godsend."

" All right, my boy. Wait till my turn comes," said Dick, biting his lips.

Menzies, in his dance, came a little too near Dick, who raised his foot and kicked him as hard as he could.

Uttering a howl of pain and putting his hands behind him, Menzies said, " What did you do that for ?"

" Cheek," answered Dick. " If I can't hit I can kick."

Menzies was coward enough to have struck Dick in the face, bound as he was.

But fortunately the guards saw the king approaching, and removed the prisoners.

They were placed in the first row of seats, in a little box, which was a sort of condemned cell.

The lion could be seen in the pit, looking up, lashing his sides with his tail, and licking his mouth.

Occasionally he gave utterance to deep roars, which found an echo half a mile off.

Ted trembled.

" Keep up your pluck, old fellow," whispered Dick; " unfortunately I can't help you, but there is One above."

" I'm all right, Master Dick," replied Ted.

Mirambo speedily took his place on a rude throne which was erected for him.

The principal officers of the court and army placed themselves on the seats.

The soldiery and the inhabitants of Yamwezi crowded round as well as they could.

All were anxious to get a good view of the sanguinary spectacle.

Dick noticed that, though Menzies was in the second row of seats, Captain Dugard did not appear.

He had too much humanity in his composition to wish to see a fellow-creature torn to pieces and devoured by a wild beast.

At a sign from the king, two soldiers seized Ted, and unbound his arms.

Holding him over the side, they gently lowered him into the pit.

"God help him, poor fellow," sighed Dick.

It was an awful moment.

Even the savages held their breath.

CHAPTER LVIII.

A MIRACLE.

EVERY neck was craned and every head bent forward as the boy sank into the pit.

The lion advanced to his prey with a roar.

The majestic brute had been kept without food for the purpose of making him more savage.

All at once he stopped.

Instead of rending the lad limb from limb, he smelt his body, as a dog might that of his master.

Then he licked his hands affectionately, and sank passive at his feet.

Ted patted his neck without showing any fear.

A hoarse murmur arose from the crowd.

The king sprang to his feet.

Turning to his favourite Sagazi, he said, "This is medicine indeed."

The Uganga was stupefied.

"What manner of boy is this," he exclaimed, "who can tame a wild beast?"

"Mungu, the Almighty, protects him. Give him life and liberty," shouted the crowd.

At first Dick was at a loss to understand this extraordinary occurrence.

But a moment's reflection recalled to his mind the story that Ted had told him in the garden.

He did not doubt that the lion was the same animal whom Ted had found in the forest, and from whose foot Ted had extracted a spike of the thorny acacia.

It showed that, savage as was the nature of a lion, he could be capable of gratitude.

The superstitious character of the Yamwezians was profoundly affected.

"Give him life and let him go free," they cried.

Mirambo consulted with the Uganga.

"You must not anger the soldiers," said Sagazi.

"But this boy has seen our army and defences; he will go back and report to our enemies," replied Mirambo.

"My lord is strong enough to laugh at the beards of those white men."

"Not so; they have cannon."

"What of that? Is not our master brave in battle?"

"But I have overheard their plans. To-morrow night they attack us in force."

"All the more reason why the prisoner should be released," answered Sagazi. "Our soldiers regard this as a miracle."

"Curses on the lion," growled Mirambo.

"Hark at the crowd; they cry with one voice, 'It is the will of Mungu, the All-wise!'"

With a bad grace Mirambo gave orders that Ted should be taken up out of the pit.

Ropes were lowered, by means of which he was raised.

Mirambo addressed him—

"Go," he exclaimed; "you are free; your Mungu has protected you."

Lowering his voice, he added—

"Beware how you fall into my hands again!"

Directing one look of advice at Dick, the lad darted through the crowd and started off at a quick pace across the plain.

Menzies was much disappointed.

"That's what I call a sell," he exclaimed. "Bother that stupid old lion; I guess he's gorged."

Dick was ordered back to his former prison, only having been brought out to witness the cruel death of his friend.

The wicked mind of Mirambo thought that this would be almost as great a punishment to him as death itself.

A brave mind does not shrink from death, but it does from the contemplation of torture.

During the remainder of that day Dick in vain tried to see Alice.

Perhaps she was confined to her apartments.

The next day he beheld her in the garden.

She was playing upon an instrument resembling a guitar, and her song was of love.

Gently stepping forth, he joined her.

With an exclamation of pleasure she held out her hand to Dick.

"I am so pleased to see you," she exclaimed. "That terrible scene in the garden yesterday with Mirambo alarmed me dreadfully."

"My companion is safe," answered Dick, " and I am unhurt."

"That is good news."

"I have intelligence for you," he said.

"Indeed?"

"Your father is close by; he has joined my party with a force of English and six guns."

"Noble man!" she cried. "I knew he would not desert me."

"To-morrow night they make the attack. I wish I could fire a shot to help them."

"You are safe here," said Alice. "Think of the danger you are exposed to in warfare."

"I love danger," he answered.

"Perhaps you have some dear one at home who loves you. For her sake you should be prudent."

"I have. My darling Henrietta loves me, but she would not wish me to skulk when my friends are risking their lives."

A shade of disappointment seemed to steal over Alice's beautiful face.

Did she already love the handsome English boy?

"Ah! it is well to be loved!" she sighed.

"And have you no one to love you?" he asked.

"No. My father excepted, I am alone in the world."

"You are young and lovely. There is plenty of time yet," said Dick.

She shook her head with a sad smile.

Fearing the coming of Mirambo, they did not prolong the conversation.

Dick retired to his prison and anxiously awaited the fall of night.

Mirambo busied himself all day in making the camp as strong as possible.

The soldiers were informed that they might expect a night attack.

A double allowance of spirits, that is pombi, or palm wine, was served out to them.

They sang weird songs and brandished their weapons.

Mirambo had so often led them to victory that they did not dream of the possibility of defeat now.

Captain Dugard brought his experience as an engineer to bear upon the situation.

He had rifle pits dug and entrenchments thrown up.

It was with the calm confidence of hope that the savage army awaited the attack.

Dugard did not fear the result in a hand-to-hand combat, because Mirambo had an advantage in numbers of over twenty to one.

It was the cannon that he dreaded.

Mirambo's men had never seen a cannon fired, and did not know what a shell was.

At last the golden sun sank to its fleecy bed in the west.

A luminous haze overspread the sky.

Precisely at eight o'clock a puff of smoke was seen half a mile off.

This was followed by a loud report, and a heavy shell fell in the midst of the encampment.

The effect upon the natives was indescribable.

A dozen or more were killed and wounded by the explosion.

All stared blankly at one another.

What manner of warfare was this?

Did the Wasungu send thunderbolts from the skies?

The enemy was invisible, and yet they could kill with their wonderful engines of destruction.

Having got the range, Sampson Jack poured in shell after shell.

The Yamwezi could not stand this mode of warfare, and they demanded to be led against the enemy.

Dugard, frantic with rage, saw that the men would be routed without firing a shot.

Calling Mirambo on one side, he said—

"Withdraw one half of the army into the entrenchments, and let the other half charge the guns."

"Who will lead them?" asked the king.

"I will," answered Dugard, calmly.

The necessary orders were then given.

A thousand men, making a *détour* to avoid the fire of the guns, ran in a disorderly mob along the plain.

They did not understand marching.

It was in vain that Dugard tried to discipline them.

Keeping up with them, he hoped for the best, knowing they were brave at a charge, and meaning to try to capture the guns.

It was time that something was done.

Sampson Jack had elevated a mortar, which cast shells into the town.

Already the walled city of Yamwezi was on fire in different places.

The terror-stricken inhabitants were rushing frantically about with water, trying to extinguish the flames.

CHAPTER LIX.

THE BATTLE.

WHEN Sampson Jack and Vipond saw the natives approaching, they loaded four guns with grape shot.

Depressing the muzzles so as to sweep the field, they awaited their onset.

Behind the guns were two ranks of infantry, the first kneeling, the second standing.

These were armed with breechloaders of the most approved fashion.

The half-naked warriors of Mirambo were stoutly built, agile fellows, and got quickly over the ground.

Their arms were chiefly old-fashioned muzzle-loading ship's muskets.

These Mirambo had purchased from trading caravans, in exchange for slaves and ivory.

The natives were in high glee at finding their approach was not stopped.

When they were within twenty yards of the guns, Sampson Jack said to the artillery men—

"Now, my lads, give 'em pepper."

"Aye, aye, sir," was the ready response.

The next moment the match was applied, and the polished tubes belched forth their iron hail.

A terrible carnage ensued.

The savages halted in terror, and wavered.

"Forward," cried Dugard, waving his sword.

He bore a charmed life, for he came out of the deadly fire unscathed.

With the rapidity of practice the gunners loaded again, and ere the natives had recovered from their surprise, were ready to deliver a second murderous discharge.

"At them! Mungu is with you!" shouted Dugard, in the Yamwezi dialect.

The example of the white man inspired them. A second time they rushed to the charge with fierce yells.

Quickly and terribly the guns did their work.

Another report was heard, and the grape shot carried death to hundreds of the brave warriors of Mirambo.

Those who survived did not hesitate again.

They dashed forward, going up to the muzzles of the guns, discharging their pieces in the faces of the infantry.

The latter mowed them down with a calm and steady fire.

It was not a defeat; it was a butchery.

Dugard performed wonders.

His sword was ever at work, and his effort seemed to be to find Vipond.

But his reckless bravery led him too far.

Hemmed in on all sides, he was called upon to surrender, and faint with exertion, he delivered his sword to Sampson Jack.

The battle in this part of the field was over.

Nearly seven hundred dusky warriors lay upon the bloodstained plain.

The others scampered across the waste, in wild confusion, to carry the news of the awful disaster to their comrades.

Looking sternly at Dugard, Sampson Jack asked—

"How is it, sir, that I find a European fighting against his own race?"

"Ask your leader, Crawley Vipond," answered Dugard.

"For what purpose?"

"We have a feud, which can only end with the life of one of us, as he has done me the most deadly wrong one man can do another."

"That is a poor reason for me. I consider your life forfeited, as you have fought against us," answered Sampson Jack.

"You will act as you please," answered Dugard, with a calm majesty, "though by the laws of civilised warfare I am a prisoner."

"This is not civilised warfare."

"No matter. Fate has thrown me into your hands. Shoot me, if you like, at once."

He bared his breast as he spoke, as if he did not fear the coming of the messenger of death.

"No, no," cried the voice of Vipond, "shooting is too good for him. Hang him! Hang him!"

The scene in the semi-darkness was very striking.

Vipond had, with his characteristic cowardice, been hiding in his tent while the battle was going on.

Seeing that it had terminated favourably for his side, he came out, in time to find that his dreaded enemy was in his power.

His face lighted up with exultation.

He heard not the cries of the wounded and the groans of the dying.

He saw not the whites carrying their dead to the rear, and attending to their wounded.

What mattered it to him that fifteen of their small force had fallen in the wild charge of the Yamwezi?

Dugard regarded him with a smile of ineffable scorn.

"Hang him if you will," said Sampson Jack, in his bluff way, "but give him till sunrise. Bind him, some of you, and see that he is well guarded. I have work to do yet."

He went away to the guns, and speedily the bombardment commenced again.

The utmost confusion prevailed in Mirambo's camp.

Furious with rage, the tyrant ordered Sagazi, his favourite medicine man, to be executed immediately.

The wretched quack was tied to a stake, in spite of his protestations and piteous cries.

Everyone thought that he deserved to die, as his medicine or charm had worked badly for the army.

A dozen guns were levelled at him.

There was a report; his head fell on his shoulder. He was shot through the heart.

Shell after shell continued to fall in the camp.

Dugard was either killed or a prisoner, they did not know which.

The darkness increased the confusion.

Natives continued to run out of the burning city, wringing their hands, and calling upon Heaven to help them.

Women and children uttered piercing shrieks.

The lurid light of the flames from the city lit up the ghastly scene with a horrid glare.

Mirambo gave orders for an immediate retreat to the mountains.

While the soldiers were preparing for the march, Mirambo called an officer to him.

"Go to my palace," he said, "and bring the two white captives. The girl I will take with me. The other shall be an instant sacrifice to appease the anger of the mighty Mungu, who is displeased with us."

"You have killed that rascal Sagazi, my lord," replied the officer.

"True. He deserved to die. He was an impostor. Perhaps his death will do good. Quick. Be off. I await the coming of the prisoners."

The officer hastened away.

Fortunately for Dick, he had not waited to experience the tender mercies of Mirambo.

When the shot and shell began to fall into the devoted city, the palace guards quitted their posts, and hurried to the front.

This was enough for Dick.

He sought Alice, who, from excess of terror, had fainted.

Seizing her in his strong arms, as he would have done a child, he bore her through the burning streets.

The inhabitants were too much alarmed to try to stop him.

Proceeding with his inanimate burden, he made for the gate which was situated farthest from the camp.

There were no guards.

Passing through, he left behind him the dull roar of the cannon, the explosion of the shells, and the screams of the frantic women and helpless children.

Having gained a safe position, he rested awhile, in order that Alice might recover herself.

This she did at last.

"Where am I?" she asked, looking around her wildly.

"With me," answered Dick, "outside the city. The attack has been commenced, and we are safe."

"Oh, take me to my father," said Alice.

"Are you strong enough to walk?"

"I think so. Let me cling to you," she answered.

"Hold on. That's it," said Dick.

"Your Henrietta would not be jealous if she saw me now, would she?"

"I hope she would have more sense," replied Dick.

"I am such a poor, weak, foolish thing, and you are so strong," she continued. "Oh, how proud I should be if I were your Henrietta."

Dick, with his usual gallantry, thought there would be no great harm in giving the pretty Alice a kiss.

The touch of his lips thrilled through her like electricity.

"You must not do that," she said, gently; "your Henrietta would not like that."

"But I love you like a—a—sister," said Dick.

"Well, you shall be my brother, though that's rather a cold relationship," said Alice. "Come, let us go; I am strong again now."

Dick thought Alice was beginning to love him. Nor was he wrong.

She had conceived a strong liking for him, which was rapidly ripening into something warmer.

We must leave them to make their way to the camp, while we return to Harold Dugard and Crawley Vipond.

The latter did not dare order Dugard for immediate execution.

Sampson Jack wouldn't have allowed it.

But in a couple of hours' time, when the latter thought he had shelled the enemy's position sufficiently, he ordered two guns to be drawn along by donkeys, and as many men as he could spare for an attacking force were told off.

He was going to the walled city of Yamwezi to rescue his daughter.

His mind was in a whirl.

Perhaps the tyrant Mirambo had ordered her to be killed.

Or she might have lost her life by the explosion of some unlucky shell.

He could only hope that she was living.

When he approached the city he found none to oppose his victorious progress.

Mirambo had retreated to the mountains, with those of his men who were left.

Menzies accompanied him in the character of his lieutenant, and did effectual service in organising the retreat.

The city was a heap of smoking ruins.

Outside the walls was a weeping crowd of old men, helpless women, and houseless children.

It was a sad sight.

In the morning the dawn would reveal, in all its hideousness, the ghastly horrors of war.

No sooner had Sampson Jack departed than Vipond sent for Messiter and Ted.

They had both been fighting bravely, and were black with smoke and dust.

The stain of blood was on their hands and dress, as if they had taken life in the battle.

"Messiter," said Vipond, "bring the prisoner here."

In a few minutes Dugard was standing before his enemy.

He was calm, brave, defiant.

Vipond was in a state of nervous excitement. Although he had nothing to fear, he trembled in every limb.

His evil conscience smote him, and the man whom he had so deeply wronged was hateful in his eyes.

The moon had risen, and the two forms stood out in bold relief.

At this moment a wild-looking, gaunt figure, covered with blood and dirt, appeared.

It was the professor.

He had been drinking palm spirit all day to get himself ready for the battle.

He had been placed in the first rank of the infantry with a rifle.

When the charge was made, he shut his eyes and fired. Half a dozen natives fell dead, in a bloody heap, upon him.

Overcome by fear and palm spirit, the professor slept calmly for some hours.

At length he woke up, and made his way from under the stiffening corpses.

"Poof!" he exclaimed, "I have done my duty this day; I have slain the Philistines and the Amalekites, as did Joshua and other chiefs of old. Poof!"

"I thought you were dead, sir," said Messiter.

"Not much. Do I look like it? Poof! I am a Saxon."

His eyes fell upon the majestic form of Dugard.

"What!" he cried, "can it be? Whom have we here? Is it indeed our old friend the captain?"

"We meet under unfortunate circumstances, Mr. Crab," answered Dugard.

"Poof!" said the professor, "we have sailed together; come to my tent. I have cold pig and palm spirit wherewith to regale you. We are both Saxons. Poof!"

"Stay, Mr. Crab," said Vipond, "this cannot be."

"Cannot? Poof! who says that word to me?"

"I do. Mr. Dugard is a prisoner."

"Never mind. If he is, treat him well. Poof! let us be jolly. Have I not slain the Amalekites? Poof!" rejoined the professor.

CHAPTER LX.

DEATH BY THE CORD.

COMPREHENDING how affairs stood, the professor remained silent.

The pause was of brief duration.

Crawley Vipond exclaimed, in a voice which he made as strong and resolute as he could—

"Mr. Dugard is a prisoner of war."

"Is that any reason why he should be killed?" asked the professor.

"Mr Crab," answered Vipond, "he was captured in arms against us."

"What then?"

"Is it fair for a white man to league himself with half-savage people against his own countrymen?"

"Perhaps he had an object in it."

"He had," replied Vipond; "and that object was my death. We have a private quarrel. He would kill me whenever he had the chance."

"Why?" asked Dugard, in a deep, commanding voice.

"We need not go into that," answered Vipond.

"But we will," continued Dugard. "I will explain to these gentlemen, if they do not know already, why your death is an object to me—why, in fact, it has become the one object of my life."

"There is no necessity for it," screamed Vipond.

Disregarding the rage of his enemy, Dugard went on—

"This man," he said, "knew I was fighting for the South, for my country, my home, my property. He basely told my wife I was dead, and seduced her affection from me."

"It's a lie!" cried Vipond, stamping his foot on the ground.

"Silence!" exclaimed Dugard, raising his voice. "Not satisfied with that, I have learnt that he caused her death by a cowardly blow."

Vipond bit his lips.

"Mr. Crab, Messiter, you, Ted, boy as you are, can judge whether or not I have cause to hate and despise this scoundrel, who has blighted my life."

"It certainly seems to me," replied the professor, "that you have much to complain of."

"What matters it?" exclaimed Vipond. "You are in my power!"

"Perhaps not so much as you think," returned Dugard, with a quiet smile.

"We shall see. I must rid myself of a nightmare. Man, you are killing me by inches."

"Not I. It is your conscience which weighs you down."

"It seems to me," remarked the professor, "that Saxons should not kill Saxons. Poof!"

"Allow me to do as I like in this instance," answered Vipond, "I may never have such a chance again. Messiter and Ted."

"Well, sir," replied Messiter.

"Put a rope round this man's neck, and hang him up to the nearest tree."

Messiter shrugged his shoulders.

"What!" screamed Vipond, "do you disobey orders?"

"Yes," answered Messiter.

"I can have you shot."

"Can you? It will take you all your time, I can tell you."

"What is this fellow Dugard to you?"

"We have sailed together, and although I have no particular fancy for him, I think he is in the right in his quarrel with you."

"Ted," said Vipond, "will you obey orders?"

"No, sir," answered Ted; "I am only an odd boy, but I have my feelings, and ain't going in for Calcraft's berth."

"What do you mean?"

"I'm not an executioner, and don't want to turn hangman," answered Ted.

He put his hands in his pockets, and walked away.

"We shall see," said Vipond.

Raising his voice, he cried—

"Sangaru! Sangaru!"

The native guide ran up.

Whispering in his ear, Vipond said—

"You shall have fifty doti of fine cloth if you will take the prisoner away and hang him at once."

"That suit me, Bana," answered Sangaru, with a smile.

"Call your men about you. Keep back Mr. Crab and Messiter. Never mind what they say."

"Right, Bana," said Sangaru, nodding his head significantly.

He whistled in a peculiar manner, and a dozen Pagazi, well armed, came up.

Touching Dugard on the shoulder, he said, "March."

The latter having his arms bound behind, he could not help himself.

Messiter turned to Captain Vipond.

"What do you mean to do?" he asked.

"He must die!" answered Vipond.

"Die? How?"

"His will be death by the cord."

"You will not hang him. Let him die a soldier's death if he must die," urged Messiter.

"No," answered Vipond. "He is in my power now. It is useless to speak in his favour."

"At least wait till Sampson Jack returns."

There was a noise at the north side of the camp.

"Here he is," said Vipond. "It is Sampson Jack who has come back, and you will find that he will not interfere to save the prisoner."

"I am not so sure of that."

"Stay, boy," cried Vipond, laying his hand on Messiter's shoulder.

"Leave go!" cried Messiter.

"Why should you interest yourself in Dugard? Was he too kind to you on board his submarine ship?"

"I like him better than I do you," answered Messiter, adding loudly, "Here! I say, Captain Jack. Come here."

Sampson Jack, who had returned from the burning city of Yamwezi, approached.

He had been unable to find any trace of Dick or his daughter.

"Look here," continued Messiter; "will you let Captain Vipond hang a white man?"

"What white man?" asked Sampson Jack.

"The one who was fighting with Mirambo."

"Certainly I will, and serve him tarnation well right, too."

"More shame for you," said Messiter, fearing that nothing could save Dugard.

Already the Pagazi had dragged him away.

Death by the cord stared him in the face.

But like a brave man, he did not flinch from it.

Perhaps, if his heart could have been examined, there would have been found a sigh of regret that he could not avenge the death of his beloved Adele.

Most likely, hero as he was, he felt a pang, to reflect that a scoundrel like Vipond should escape the consequences of all his villany.

But the brave soldier who had fought upon a dozen fields with Jackson and with Lee had seen death too often to feel any fear for it.

Sangaru was engaged in making a ose in a rope.

The prisoner stood under a tree.

Not a spasm of fear contracted his atures.

He was as calm as he had been under ie fire of the Federals at Gettysburg, when blocked in the ice near the Pole.

" Has anyone seen Lightheart?" asked Iessiter, turning his thoughts to Dick.

Unexpectedly a voice answered in the arkness without the camp.

" There's someone coming, Master Iarry, leading a young lady, as well as I an make out."

It was Ted who spoke.

" By Jove!" cried Messiter, " that nust be Dick."

" I trust it is," remarked the professor, vho was close by, drinking palm spirit ut of a gourd. " I am a Saxon—poof! —and I have faith in Lightheart. He may stop this butchery. Poof!"

Captain Vipond ran towards Sangaru.

At the same moment Messiter rushed in the direction of Ted's voice.

The darkness of the night was only relieved by the occasional glimpses which ragged clouds gave of the moon and the light shed by a few straggling stars.

It was Messiter's wish to save Captain Dugard if possible.

He had not the power, but he knew Dick could do it if he liked.

In fact, Messiter's confidence and belief in Dick were unlimited.

When Vipond got up to Sangaru he found the rope slung over a branch.

" Make haste ; how slow you are," he exclaimed, nervously.

" Me turn him off quick, Bana," answered Sangaru.

The fellow put the rope round Dugard's neck.

Not a word did the brave man utter.

" Hoist away," cried Vipond, eagerly.

At this moment torches were seen approaching, and Lightheart appeared, out of breath, led by Messiter.

Sampson Jack followed, his daughter leaning on his arm.

" Stop," cried Dick. " What would you do?"

" Stand back, boy," exclaimed Vipond, furiously.

" By George !" continued Dick, " I'll shoot the first man who moves."

With his own hands he removed the rope from Dugard's neck.

" Life for life, sir," he said.

" Thank you, my lad," said Dugard.

He evinced no more emotion than if he had received a cup of water from him.

" Captain Jack," cried Vipond, " will you see me thwarted in this way?"

" I have nothing to say," answered Sampson Jack. " Mr. Lightheart has saved my daughter, and he may do what he likes."

" Fall back, you cattle. Back, you brutes," exclaimed Dick, pushing his torch in the faces of the Pagazi.

They slunk away.

" Crawley Vipond," said Dugard, " we part. My turn will come next time, and then beware !"

Vipond, foaming at the mouth, and speechless with rage and fear, walked back to his tent.

He saw that his vengeance was lost.

The professor had watched this scene with great interest.

" Poof !" he exclaimed, " I like this. Captain Dugard, I congratulate you. Poof! are we not all Saxons ?"

Dugard approached Sampson Jack.

" I am glad," he said, " your child is safe. I have had more to do in preserving her life than you may be aware of."

" She's all right," answered Sampson Jack ; " Mirambo can't harm her now."

" Is Mirambo beaten ?"

" Badly. He has retired to the mountains with less than half his army."

" And Yamwezi ?"

" Is in ruins, thanks to my guns."

" Farewell," said Dugard ; " I shall not forget my friends, but let my enemies tremble."

" Stop with us, sir, and make a night of it," said Dick.

" Yes," said the professor, " let me beg of you to stop. Poof ! We don't win a battle every day."

" I cannot stay," answered Dugard.

He seized Dick's hand, and shook it warmly. Then he stalked away in the darkness, being soon lost to sight.

" A remarkable man," said the professor. " Poof ! But we are all remarkable. Are we not Saxons ? Poof !"

Being tired with the day's work, all were glad to turn in. A watch was set, and soon the boys slept soundly.

CHAPTER LXI.

THE SLAVE GANG.

SO complete was the victory the white men gained over Mirambo that there was no fear of his renewing the contest.

Sampson Jack in the morning saw to the burying of the dead.

Then he collected his men together, and prepared to return with his daughter to the coast.

Alice was full of gratitude to Dick for his kindness to her, and seemed very sorry to part from him.

Her father gave him an invitation to visit him if he ever came to Bagamoyo or Zanzibar again.

Captain Vipond was surly and ill-tempered.

He would not speak to Dick, because he had thwarted him the night before.

The country being open now, there was nothing to prevent them from pressing on.

As Dugard was free, and Sampson Jack was going, it would not be prudent, he thought, to remain where they were.

So he sent Sangaru to inform Dick that the march would be resumed at noon.

An hour before the time Sampson Jack and his party were ready.

Alice and Dick were taking an affectionate adieu.

Sangaru came up to him, and said—

" Bana, a slave gang."

" Where ?" asked Dick.

" Outside the camp. They are from the coast, and have brought white slaves for Mirambo to exchange for ivory."

" White slaves?" said Dick. " How the deuce did they get them ?"

" The chief says there was a British ship wrecked on the coast, and they made many prisoners and took much spoil, though some men have died."

" The villains."

" Are there any women in the gang ?" asked Alice.

" One white girl," answered Sangaru.

" Poor thing; do not let her be sold to Mirambo, Mr. Lightheart."

" I'll be jolly well flabbergasted if she shall," said Dick, adding, " Sangaru."

" Bana," answered the guide.

" Let a score of armed Pagazi surround the slave caravan, and you shall answer with your life for the rascals moving."

Sangaru bowed and departed.

Dick went to Sampson Jack, and told him what the guide had reported.

" It's a crying shame," said Captain Jack. " The villains daren't sell white men on the coast, so they have brought them inland."

" Will you stand by me if it comes to a riot ?"

" Will I not ?" was the ready reply.

" We will liberate them then," said Dick, generously and confidently.

He went to the outskirts of the encampment, where the slave caravan had halted.

The leaders wished to obtain information about Mirambo, with whom they were going to trade.

On the ground, lying and sitting, were the white slaves.

Their number was reduced by death to half a dozen, one of whom was a woman.

The men were chained together by heavy iron links, which went round the neck of each of them.

But the woman was by herself, and had a donkey to ride upon.

Her life was deemed to be too valuable to be trifled with in such a climate.

The first glance Dick gave at her made him start.

" My stars !" he exclaimed. " It can't be——"

Going close up to the white girl, who was sitting disconsolately upon the donkey, and looking as if all hope had left her breast, he glanced again.

The glance became a stare, and he could no longer doubt.

" Polly," he ejaculated.

She turned her eyes towards him with an expression of deep joy.

But the once happy face was so sad, so worn and altered, that he scarcely knew it again.

" Oh !" she exclaimed, " Heaven must have sent you to my help !"

" How is it I find you here ?"

"We were wrecked in a storm in the Mozambique Channel, and those of us who were saved fell into the hands of the natives, who have taken us such a weary journey inland to be sold as slaves."

"Is Hopkins alive?"

"Alas! no," replied Polly. "He died at sea. When the storm rose the waves washed him overboard."

"Poor fellow," said Dick, feelingly.

"I am glad of it now," said Polly. "He has been spared so much suffering."

"And Snarley?"

"Better had he shared my father's fate, sad as it was."

"Why?"

"He has marched through swamps and forests, chained to the others, but this morning he was seized with the fever."

"Is he dead?"

"I cannot say," replied Polly. "They would not let me nurse him; but when they found he had what they call the mukunguru——"

"That's the intermittent fever," put in Dick.

"Yes; well, they unchained him, and left him on the road to die."

"Horrible!"

"It nearly broke my heart to leave him. But what could I do? They threatened to kill me if I moved, and tied my legs under the donkey's stomach," said Polly.

"Can I do anything?"

"Oh, do please try!"

"I will, like a shot."

"Can I come with you? I know the way we came," said Polly.

"Of course you can."

"Are you not afraid of those cruel, savage-looking men?"

"Not a ha'porth. It isn't a pound to a shilling I don't shoot the lot," replied Dick.

"Are you so strong, then?"

"We've been strong enough to lick Mirambo into fits and burn his town."

"Yamwezi?" said Polly.

"Yes."

"That's where I was to be taken to. And have you really beaten Mirambo? I thought he was the strongest king that ever lived, and the richest, from the way those slavers talked."

"All bosh," replied Dick; "we doubled him up like grass."

"If you can do anything for my poor husband I shall be so grateful, Dick," continued Polly.

He squeezed her hand, which, like her face, was tanned by the sun, and saying, "Wait here for me an instant," went to Messiter.

"What's up?" asked the latter.

He saw by the expression of his face that something unusual had happened.

"Polly's in the slave gang," answered Dick.

"Nonsense."

"She is, though, and Snarley has been left to die of fever in the bush."

"How did it happen?"

"They were all wrecked on the coast. Hopkins was drowned, and the survivors were made prisoners, and brought inland to be sold as slaves to Mirambo."

"What next?" said Messiter, astonished.

"Get some quinine, and come with me to help Snarley."

"All right; I shan't be a minute."

Dick next sought Sampson Jack.

"What is it now, my lad?" asked the latter.

"I want you to do me a favour, sir," replied Dick.

"You have only to name it."

"The slaves in that gang over there are British, and some of them are friends of mine; just have their chains knocked off and take possession of them, while you send the slave dealers about their business."

"Of course I will," answered Sampson Jack.

Dick was joined by Messiter, who carried with him some medicine, such as was generally used in cases of fever.

They caused Polly to dismount, which she did amidst the murmurs of the slaves.

But Dick showed them a revolver.

"Tell them to slope at once," said he to Sangaru, "or I'll shoot every mother's son of them."

The display of force was so great that the traders dared not interfere.

They were, however, very savage at seeing Dick take away their chief prize.

Grumbling was of no use, and they were forced to submit.

Polly acted as guide.

The little party proceeded in melancholy silence.

Tears fell from pretty Polly's eyes, and Dick and Messiter were much affected.

It seemed but yesterday that they were all together at Zanzibar.

And it was not so very long ago that they were at Harrow House Academy with Mr. Snarley as their tutor.

Now he was dying, if not dead, in the wilds of Africa. Perhaps the wild beasts were even then fighting over his remains.

Dick could not help thinking of the words of Scripture—

" In the midst of life we are in death."

This simple truth came home to him in the vast solitude in which for the time his lot was cast.

CHAPTER LXII.

THE DEATH OF SNARLEY.

THE distance they had to go was not great.

A path had been made by the slave caravan through the long grass.

For two miles, or a little more, Polly led them along, and at last she halted under a spreading tree.

At its foot lay the body of a man.

They recognised it instantly as that of Mr. Snarley, though it was strangely worn and altered.

In a few weeks he seemed to have aged twenty years, such was the effect of the hardship, captivity, and exposure upon him.

But he had led a free life.

It is only the young and temperate, who neither eat nor drink too much, who can successfully withstand the dangers of the African climate.

Polly threw herself on her knees beside him, and overwhelmed him with passionate exclamations and caresses.

He did not recognise her.

Though not dead, he was in an alarming state of delirium.

His feeble frame was almost exhausted, but the mind, for the present, triumphed over the body.

" Ha! ha!" he cried. " Here we are again! what jolly dogs are we!"

" He fancies himself on the boards," whispered Polly.

" I'm the boy for fun," he continued. " How many sausages go to a pound, when you never pay for them? Ha! ha! There was an old woman her living she got by selling hot codlings, hot, hot, hot."

He paused, and his eyes rolled fearfully, while his black and parched lips twitched nervously.

" This little old woman she thought it no sin," he went on, " to buy herself a penn'orth of——I didn't say gin, you swell in the gallery! What do you mean by it, sir? Come down here, and I'll give you a taste of the red hot poker. Ha! ha!"

Suddenly his mood changed.

A contraction came over his gaunt features, and he said—

" Chain me, will they? Sell me, will they? Make me a slave? They wouldn't do it if Lightheart was here."

" He's talking of you," said Polly.

The tears fell fast from Dick's eyes.

Beckoning to Messiter, he took some medicine in the half of a cocoanut shell and poured it down Snarley's throat.

There was a faint sob and a spasmodic movement of the limbs, and that was all.

Polly had sunk on her knees, and was crying bitterly.

" Too late!" said Messiter, under his breath.

" By Heaven! he shall not die!" cried Dick.

The recording angel caught the words and carried them up to Heaven's chancery.

But to use Sterne's beautiful words—

" As he wrote them down a tear fell from his eye and blotted them out for ever."

" Mr. Snarley," cried Dick, chafing his hands, " do you not know me, sir?"

The eyes of the dying man rolled fearfully.

" You?" replied Snarley. " Yes, I know you. You are the Sultan; you stole my Polly!"

" No, no; I am here," said Polly.

"THEY RECOGNISED MR. SNARLEY, THOUGH STRANGELY WORN AND ALTERED."—(See page 192.)

"You lie!" ejaculated poor Snarley. "Fiends, avaunt; you mock me. Polly is dead; we are all dead! Where am I? Is this hell? Oh! how my head throbs and my brain burns!"

"I am Lightheart. Surely, you know your old friend and pupil, sir?"

Snarley stared vacantly at him.

He shook his head mournfully.

"Why will these unreal shadows gibe at me?" he exclaimed.

"His mind is wandering," observed Messiter.

"It's the effect of the fever," replied Dick.

Suddenly Snarley's head fell back upon Polly's lap, and she tried to make him comfortable.

"It will soon be over," said Messiter.

"Poor fellow!" exclaimed Dick. "It is horrible for him to die like this out here. Those slavers ought to be shot for leaving him."

The fast-failing breath came slower and yet more slowly from the cracked lips.

A dull, heavy stare, the precursor of death, stole into the glazed eyes.

The hands clenched and unclenched themselves.

A convulsive action of the limbs took place, and an unearthly rattle sounded in the throat.

"God have mercy on him," said Dick.

He placed his hand upon his heart.

It had ceased to beat.

Mr. Snarley was dead.

Tearing up some long grass, Dick laid it very gently over the still, wan face.

Then he placed some flowers over all.

"Stay here, Harry," he said, "and keep the wild beasts off; I will bring some Pagazi to dig him a grave.

He turned away and wiped his eyes with the sleeve of his jacket.

"Come, Polly, my poor, stricken dear," he said.

"Oh, let me stay. May I not die with him?" she replied, appealingly.

"This is no place for you; come with me, my child," continued Dick.

He spoke in the manner of one much older than himself.

But a life of adventure had made a man of him before the time.

It had taught him self-reliance, and how to act in moments of danger and distress.

Polly suffered herself to be raised up, and clinging to his arm, she walked away from the mournful spot, weeping as if her heart would break.

Her husband had fallen a victim to the deadly African climate.

Her father had perished amidst the cruel waves, and she was now alone in the world.

Dick was the only person she could call a friend.

No wonder she was bowed down and afflicted.

Heaven had sorely tried and afflicted her in these latter days.

Thousands of miles away from home, in a foreign and savage land.

War fever, death raging around her.

What a situation for a young and delicate wife!

When they reached the camp, Dick led her up to Alice and put her hand in hers.

"Alice," he said, "you told me I had some slight claim on your gratitude."

"A very great claim, and one I can never repay," she replied.

"You can pay me in full."

"How?"

"Take Polly to your arms; make her your sister," he replied. "She has lost all her friends, and just closed the eyes of her husband."

"Come, dearest," said Alice, with that tenderness which the affliction of one of her own sex ought always to inspire in the breast of another.

She drew the weeping girl to her bosom, and Polly's head sank down, as if she wished to hide it for ever.

"You will take her to the coast with you," continued Dick, "will you not?"

"Oh, yes."

"Cherish and guard her till you can send her back to England."

"She shall be my sister," replied Alice, affectionately.

"You are a good girl," said Dick, "and God will reward you."

Having disposed of Polly, his first act was to dispatch the rascally slavers about their business.

The English sailors had been released, and were being regaled by Ted on such fare as the camp afforded.

At first the traders were disposed to be insolent.

But a display of force awed them, and muttering curses, they went away.

Dick next ordered a party of Pagazi to go, with picks and shovels, to the spot where he had left Messiter with the body.

Their task was to dig a grave.

In his baggage Dick had a prayer-book, and he put it in his pocket.

Calling Ted to his side, he told him what had happened, and together they sadly wended their way to the grave.

The Pagazi had worked with a will.

All was now ready for the interment, which in such a hot climate must always follow quickly upon death.

Tender and loving hands laid Mr. Snarley's body in its last home.

Very feelingly did Dick read the beautiful and affecting burial service of the church.

Seldom, if ever, had it been given under more simply touching circumstances.

" When he came to the words, " Ashes to ashes, dust to dust," he cast a few clods on the corpse.

Both Ted and Messiter were affected to tears. Even Dick's voice trembled with uncontrollable emotion.

In that wild country, which of them could tell that he would not share the same fate?

The death of a friend comes home terribly to the traveller in a savage and far-distant country.

Standing in an attitude of respectful attention, the Pagazi were grouped at the foot of the grave.

They watched with interest the strange ceremony of the Wasungu.

Closing the book of prayer, Dick made them a signal to fill up the grave.

This was quickly done.

Then they made a rude cross of stones to mark the resting place of the unfortunate Snarley.

" His troubles are over," remarked Messiter.

Dick said nothing, and the party returned to camp.

CHAPTER LXIII.

A GHASTLY SIGHT.

WHEN they reached the encampment they heard the Pagazi shouting and singing in celebration of their victory.

Vipond, to encourage them, had given each two days' pay in cloth, and an extra allowance of pembi.

" Hi! hi! hi! Lu! lu! lu!"

The many shouts were borne upon the breeze, affording a strange contrast to the melancholy scene the boys had just passed through.

Firearms were discharged, songs sung, and dances kept up till the sweat poured in streams from their nearly naked bodies.

The professor, half drunk, had joined in the merriment.

" Poof!" he said, " go it, you nigger fellows. Poof! I fought like a Saxon, and have a right to enjoy myself."

The natives sang a rude, wild song, with very little sense in it—

" Yambo Bana, here we are ;
Yambo Bana, this is war ;
Binderi Kisungu, white man's flag,
Mirambo ran like a bald-faced stag.
Hi! hi! hi! Ho! ho! ho! Lu! lu! lu!"

And so it went on, in the same silly manner and monotonous cadence, until all were wearied, and ceased with common consent.

In the afternoon, Sampson Jack and his party took their leave.

He willingly promised to look after Polly and treat her as a daughter.

Polly begged to be allowed to remain with Dick. This he would not permit.

" We have too many dangers to encounter, my dear," he said; " it is best for you to go with Captain Jack."

Giving her a kiss, he pushed her gently towards Alice, and the caravan started.

Shots were fired as usual, and each party seemed in the highest spirits.

Captain Vipond did not march till the following morning.

He made up his grievance with Dick, knowing that the latter was more popular with and more the master of the men than he was.

Dick received the honour of an invitation to dine with him in his tent.

Sangaru had been sent out to shoot some fresh meat, and an excellent meal was prepared.

Vipond had a few cases of French wines and spirits with him, and champagne was produced.

"You must not feel annoyed with me, Lightheart," said the captain.

"Why should I, sir?" replied Dick. "I had my way."

"Yes. I know, you saved my enemy Dugard from my vengeance."

"Because he had previously saved my life."

"I know nothing about that."

"Nor am I supposed to know anything about your rows, sir," said Dick. "When I agreed to travel with you, I did not bind myself body and soul."

"Certainly not," exclaimed Vipond, with a sigh. "It is a pity, though, that Dugard got away. I am as uneasy as ever now. Goodness only knows where my adventures will end."

"Let us push on to the interior of Africa at once," said Dick.

"As you please. I place everything in your hands."

"Mirambo is thoroughly beaten."

"Do you think so?" asked Vipond.

"Completely. He will not prevent us passing through his dominions."

"You will not betray me into Dugard's hands?" said Vipond.

An indignant flush spread itself over Dick's face.

"I don't know what I have ever said or done, Captain Vipond, that you should have such a bad opinion of me," he answered.

"Pardon me, I am weak and nervous."

"But that is no reason why you should suspect me."

"I cannot help it. You helped Dugard to escape; I am naturally suspicious. Forgive me if I have offended you."

"My dear sir," said Dick, "I would have saved your life under similar circumstances if I had the power. Be satisfied that I am not a traitor."

"I will," replied Vipond, drawing a deep breath of relief.

"Make your miserable life happy, and pass the bottle," said Dick, with a smile.

"Remember, I trust everything to you," replied Vipond.

"You can't do better," answered Dick;

"we shall push on past Unyanyembi tomorrow, and make for the shores of Lake Tanganyika. Who knows where I shall take you? To the middle of the earth, perhaps."

"I shall not mind, provided——"

"What? Do you mean if we have a return ticket?" asked Dick, with a smile.

"No. Provided Dugard cannot follow us."

It was in vain that Dick tried to make Crawley Vipond's mind dwell upon some other topic.

He was persuaded that Dugard would be the death of him some day.

It was impossible for him to shake off this all-engrossing belief.

Like a deer hunted by the hounds, his only wish and thought was escape from the enemy.

Early in the morning the camp was struck.

The professor pulled himself together, and recollected his character of a scientific man.

Still he said, "He was a Saxon. Poof!" as he watched the natives striking the tents.

Just as the long train was in the act of starting, Sangaru came up to Dick.

"Yambo, Kiboko Bana!" he exclaimed, "there is a camp follower, half English, half Arab, a mere boy, who wants to take service with us."

"Where is he from?" asked Dick.

"He says he has escaped from a caravan, the traders of which treated him badly. Shall he join?"

"Yes. I want a boy. Send him along," answered Dick.

It was not until the mid-day halt that Dick had an opportunity of noticing the lad.

He was dressed in the Arab costume, and wore more linen than a native, his body being scrupulously covered all over.

His face was dark, and he spoke broken English.

Dick had called for some water, and the Arab boy brought him some in a gourd.

"What's your name?" asked Dick.

"Hassan," replied the boy, in a nervous voice.

Dick thought he knew the inflection of that voice, but dismissed the idea from his mind as improbable

There was something, too, about those almost feminine features which attracted his attention.

"Be faithful to me, Hassan," he said, "and you won't find me a bad master."

"Me watch over you, sir, while you sleep," replied the boy.

"I don't want you to do that, but keep your eyes open, that's all."

"Me be your slave," said the boy, kneeling down at his feet.

Dick quickly raised him, and told him to go about his business.

"I hate slaves," he exclaimed; "do your duty, and I shall be satisfied."

The boy bent a tender, almost loving glance upon him, and joined the Pagazi who were preparing the mid-day meal.

Dick could not help thinking there was some mystery about the boy.

But he had so much to see to that the matter soon escaped from his memory.

The march recommenced.

At four o'clock by his chronometer they passed the smoking ruins of Yamwezi.

The old men, women, and children ran away from them as if they had been fiends.

A little further on the leader of the column came to a halt.

Sangaru ran back to Dick, gesticulating and making strange noises.

"Bana!" he cried, "come here. Look what is on that tree."

Dick hurried forward, followed by Messiter and Ted.

A horrible and ghastly sight met his gaze.

Hanging from a tree was the body of a white boy.

One look at the blackened and convulsed face showed him that it was Menzies.

The unhappy youth had been hung up to a branch by his neck, and was quite dead.

They never learnt the reason of Menzies' death, but it was supposed that Mirambo's men, actuated by superstitious motives, had insisted upon his execution.

A white sacrifice to their god was always highly esteemed by them.

Perhaps they thought that they would propitiate their deity by this act of cruelty.

At all events, there was the body swinging stiff and cold in the wind.

"He'd have done better to stay with us," said Messiter.

"It serves him right for deserting his friends," observed Ted. "What could he expect from such heathens?"

Dick turned away, ill at heart, from the sickening spectacle.

Ted began climbing the tree.

"What's your game?" asked Messiter.

"I'm only an odd boy, sir, but I've got my feelings," answered Ted, "and I can't see a Christian body hanging there for the birds to peck at. They've had an eye already."

It was too true.

A bird of prey had been at work, and the hollow cavern which had held the eye was gaping and gory.

Taking out his knife, Ted cut the rope.

"Below," he exclaimed, "look out."

The professor, who had come up to see what was the matter, was too late to benefit by the warning.

At his feet fell the dead body.

"Poof!" cried the horror-stricken professor, stepping back hurriedly; "do corpses grow on the trees in this strange country?"

"No, sir," said Dick; "it is Menzies, who has been murdered by those he chose for his friends."

"Dear me! He should not have fought against us. Poof! we are all Saxons."

"That's what we say, sir. He deserved his fate for his treachery," answered Dick.

The melancholy task of digging a grave was again gone through.

With a reverence that showed how deeply the boys felt this new shock, Menzies was laid in the silent grave.

Soon the spotted snake would glide over his rude tomb; the wild beast would roar and the beetle hum in the long grass.

No sister's or mother's hand would strew flowers upon the grave of the murdered boy, buried deep in the heart of an African forest.

No sympathetic tears would fall, and there his bones would moulder through the long years to come.

It was with a feeling of relief that Dick heard the natives preparing to renew the journey.

"Sofari, sofari, pakia," they shouted. "A journey, a journey to-day. Start."

Fresh dangers were before them, and who could tell what the morrow would bring forth?

They were pretty well seasoned to African travel now, and did not dread the fever as they had done.

Little time was lost. Captain Vipond kept continually saying—

"Push on, push on !"

He fancied that Dugard, more vindictive than ever, was at his heels.

For the wicked, it has been truly said, there is no peace.

CHAPTER LXIV.

SANGARU'S TREACHERY.

NO trading caravans go further than Ujiji as a rule.

Sangaru and his Pagazi had not agreed to go beyond that place.

They were not altogether satisfied.

Several of their number had fallen in the fight with Mirambo.

From Bagamoyo, their starting place, to Unyanyembi was nearly four hundred miles. It was customary to stop at Unyanyembi and make merry and rest for a few weeks.

But Vipond pushed on to Ujiji, on the banks of the Lake Tanganyika, without any delay.

The men grumbled.

When Dick heard them he threatened them with his revolver.

Still discontent existed amongst them.

They travelled as the bird flies, making an average of fifteen miles a day.

The distance in a straight line to Ujiji, the "place with the rum name," as Ted called it, was two hundred miles.

Making allowance for delays; crossing rivers, stopping to pay tribute, etc., Dick hoped to do it in three weeks.

They passed through the territories of the Usagozi and other fierce tribes.

At length, according to Captain Vipond and the professor's reckoning, they were within thirty miles of Ujiji.

It was evening, and all within the precincts of the camp had gone to rest except the sentinels.

The watch was entrusted to Sangaru and his Pagazi.

Stars sprinkled the firmament, but there was no moon.

Dick had been asleep about a couple of hours when he awoke, feeling a soft pressure on his arm.

Starting up, he saw Hassan, the Arab boy.

"Sangaru gone with all Pagazi and baggage, Bana !" said the boy.

He spoke in a soft, low voice, so suggestive of that of a woman.

" Gone ?" repeated Dick.

" Yes, Bana, I woke up and found all gone."

" Curses on the rascals to leave us like this !" cried Dick, furiously.

" It's not too late to pursue."

" How do I know which way they have gone? Devil take the thieves !"

He looked around and saw that the camp was deserted.

Sangaru and his Pagazi had departed with all that was worth laying their hands on.

Most likely they were on their way back to Unyanyembi, the Tabora of the Arabs, with their plunder.

He instantly woke Captain Vipond, the professor, Ted, and Messiter.

They, with himself and Hassan, were the only ones left in the deserted encampment.

Rich bales of goods, rifles, powder, shot, provisions, were all gone.

Vipond was overwhelmed when he heard the news.

" I trusted to you," he said to Dick, with a reproachful glance.

" It's all my fault," answered Dick; " I ought not to have put faith in Sangaru."

" Poof !" said the professor, " there is nothing like a Saxon after all. Poof !"

" This is a nice state of things," remarked Messiter. " What have they left us ?"

An examination showed that, except a few cases of provisions and some powder and shot, they had been stripped of everything.

Their rifles were left because they

never slept without having them by their sides.

"It strikes me," said Ted, "we're up an almighty tall gum tree, and no ladder to get down with."

Dick blamed himself severely for not placing a white on guard.

Perhaps if he had the cowardly Pagazi would have murdered him.

"Say no more!" exclaimed Captain Vipond, kindly.

"Accidents will happen occasionally in the best regulated families," said the professor, adding his habitual "Poof!"

"I am very sorry, sir," replied Dick.

"Never mind; we must push on by ourselves to Ujiji, and trust to fortune."

"We've nothing much left to carry," said Messiter.

"I shall never see a native again without a shudder. What brutes they are," observed Messiter.

"Ah! my dear boy," said the professor, "you ought to be proud of being a Saxon. Poof! let us have some palm wine."

"It's all gone."

"What! nothing left to console ourselves with? Oh, the thieves! the villains!" cried the professor.

"You'll have to be sober now, sir, in spite of yourself," observed Dick.

"Poof! What can one do in a wretched country like this but drink?"

"We want your valuable scientific advice, sir, in this fix," answered Dick, "and I am very glad the spirit is gone, for you've been more or less drunk for two months."

"This is an insult, Lightheart. Poof!"

"It's true. Stop the lush and you'll be all right; turn in again now, sir, and I'll watch. To-morrow you shall give us the benefit of your experience and scientific attainments."

"Ah! well, you are only a boy; I forgive you," said the professor. "Was I not a boy myself once? Poof!"

The wholesale desertion of the hired carriers and soldiers is no new experience with African travellers.

Burton, Speke, Grant, Stanley, Livingstone, have all had to put up with it.

Soon the members of the little party were asleep again.

Dick was the solitary exception.

Biting his lips he walked up and down, his rifle resting in the hollow of his arm.

He was furious with himself for letting the thief Sangaru have so good a chance.

A little way off he beheld the Arab boy on the watch.

Approaching him, he said—

"Hassan, why do you not sleep?"

"I am helping you to watch," answered the boy.

"Why should you do so?"

"I would die for you, and the Pagazi may return to kill you."

"Not they; I'll bet they are too cowardly for that," answered Dick.

"Perhaps."

"What am I to you, Hassan, that you should take such an interest in me?" asked Dick, looking strangely at the pretty face.

The boy made no answer.

"You remind me strongly of someone I have seen before," he continued, "though I cannot tell where. Go to sleep, child."

The boy bestowed an affectionate glance upon him, and wrapping himself up in his blanket, to protect his body from the night dews, obeyed his orders.

But had he watched him closely, he would have found that he did not close his eyes all night.

His hand was ever on his gun, and he peered steadily into the darkness.

There was something remarkable in the Arab boy's attachment to Dick.

The next day they started again, but without a guide their course was at once perilous and difficult.

For ten days they continued to journey.

Long before this they ought to have come to the Tanganyika Lake.

But it was clear they had lost their way.

At length they were delighted at the end of a long day's march to see a large sheet of water stretched out before them.

Their provisions were nearly exhausted, and they had been dependent for some time for food upon the fresh meat killed by their rifles.

Without cloth or beads they could not have gone much further.

Some petty chief would have made them prisoners, and perhaps killed them.

They rushed to the lake, and eagerly drank its sweet water.

Suddenly the measured fall of oars in a boat fell upon their ears.

Coming round a small, jutting rock was a canoe, with eight rowers.

At the helm sat a middle-sized, thin, browned man.

But the head was of the Caucasian type, and at once he was recognised as an Englishman.

Seeing the travellers, this man gave orders to his men to put the boat about, and run into the land.

He stepped ashore. Dick advanced to meet him, hat in hand.

There was something about the face that reminded him of portraits he had seen at home of the greatest African explorer.

"Have I the honour of speaking to Dr. Livingstone?" he asked.

"That is my name," replied the little bronzed man.

Dick's heart beat wildly in his bosom.

"Then I am in the presence," he said, "of one of the pluckiest and greatest of men of modern times."

"Don't praise me; I don't like it; in fact, I'm not used to it out here," answered the doctor.

A pleasant smile stole over his features, at once so firm, so frank, and so genial.

"Is this your party?" inquired the doctor.

"It is."

"How on earth did you get here without Pagazi and baggage?"

"We had heaps of both, but they have all cut and run a week or two ago," exclaimed Dick.

"And what was your object in coming here?"

"Adventure and a desire to find and relieve you."

"Thank you very much," said the doctor, kindly, "but I am all right now, thanks to Mr. Stanley, who has given me all I want."

"Indeed!"

"Oh, yes. I am quite set up now. Stanley came out from the *New York Herald*, you know. Fine fellows, the Americans."

"I have always thought so," said Dick.

"It seems to me," said the doctor, with another of his dry smiles, "that I am more likely to relieve you."

"We're not proud, I can tell you," answered Dick.

"Introduce me to your friends and let us have a quiet chat. It is tea-time, and if I am not mistaken you have a freshly-killed antelope there."

"It fell by my rifle half an hour ago," replied Dick.

"Bravo! We shall have a feast, I can see," said Livingstone.

Dick led the doctor to his party, and they were introduced, feeling very proud to be in the presence of such an illustrious man.

The native rowers came out of the boat, and produced everything required for making tea.

Messiter and Ted cut up the antelope.

A fire was lighted, and in less than an hour a tea fit for a king was ready.

CHAPTER LXV.

THE MEETING BY THE LAKE.

THIS was the first and only time that Dick had the pleasure of conversing with Dr. Livingstone, but the remembrance of the evening they passed together was never effaced from his mind.

The party had wandered far out of their way. Instead of going towards Ujiji, they had gone into Northern Watuta, and were not far from Mwezi's capital.

Livingstone was well supplied with stores, and had about a dozen men with him.

He generously gave Dick as much as he could spare, and advised him to go to Ujiji, and wait there until he could get fresh supplies from the coast.

This could be done by sending natives to Bagamoyo, with orders on the merchants at Zanzibar.

And as both Dick and Vipond had left money there, it was not likely their orders would not be attended to.

Livingstone was going to the copper mines of Katanga, and from there to the underground houses of Rua, where the people live under the earth.

The evening passed very pleasantly.

The doctor was charmed with Dick's spirit of adventure, and said—

"While English boys think as you do, we need not despair of finding men to take my place when I have done what little I can."

"I wish I could have done something for you, sir," replied Dick.

"It is all done."

"I know that, but at school I used to think of coming here to find you."

"Well, you have found me," said the doctor, smiling.

"But I am poor, and have lost all through those rascally Pagazis. Will you take me with you?"

"No, my boy," answered Livingstone; "stick to your own friends. In a year's time, or a year and a half, I shall be back again at Ujiji, please God, and if you are still in this African maze, we shall meet again."

"At all events you will give me credit for trying to bring you something," said Dick.

"Of course I will. You are a fine, brave, noble-hearted boy. Now, you see, I am flattering you," said the doctor.

At daybreak everyone rose, and Livingstone took his departure.

He had given the professor instructions which way to go to reach Ujiji, and supplied various little things which he thought they might find useful.

"Poof!" said the professor, "that is what I call a great man."

"It is something to say we have met him in Africa," remarked Messiter.

"He is as kind as he is great," said Dick; "see what he has given us out of his own slender store."

The sun was high in the heavens when they were ready to start.

Their stores had to be divided into parcels for each to carry his share.

All this took some time.

When they were about to start, the Arab boy came up to Dick and said—

"Natives on the lake, Bana."

Dick looked and saw three men in a boat.

"Here's luck," he said, "if we can only get that ship, we can go by water to Ujiji."

"Let's pot them," said Messiter.

The professor looked through a telescope.

"Only three of them," he remarked.

"But there may be a lot behind," said Ted.

"I don't like killing even niggers in cold blood. Poof! I am a Saxon," continued the professor.

"Nonsense!" cried Captain Vipond, who was standing by. "We want that boat, don't we?"

"Yes, sir," replied Dick.

"Very well, we must have it, Lightheart. Messiter, prepare to fire after me."

The unsuspecting natives came close in shore.

Captain Vipond fired, and the bow oar came down.

Messiter lowered his rifle.

"Fire, fire!" exclaimed Vipond, angrily.

"No, I shan't," answered Messiter; "they've done nothing to us."

"Fire, Lightheart," continued Vipond; "this boy is a fool."

"Not much," exclaimed Dick. "Harry's no fool. It is too much like murder to kill them when they've no quarrel with us."

Vipond uttered a curse and seized Ted's gun, which he discharged.

The stroke oar fell mortally wounded.

Alarmed at the sudden death of his companions, the steerer jumped overboard, and swam to land, and disappeared in a thicket.

"Ted," said Vipond.

"Sir."

"Swim to the boat and paddle her in."

Ted very soon had his clothes off, and plunged into the lake.

The boat was not more than a couple of dozen yards distant.

Swimming to the boat, he climbed in, but found it too big and unwieldy for him to manage by himself.

"Mr. Vipond, sir," he exclaimed.

"What is it?" answered the captain.

"Send the Arab boy to help me. It wants two for this ship."

"Hassan," said Vipond, "take off your clothes and go and help Ted."

"I can't," replied the boy, shrinking back.

"What are you afraid of?"

"Crocodiles."

"Humbug," said Vipond; "if there were any, they would have attacked Ted. Go along."

Hassan showed no signs of obeying.

Captain Vipond broke a stick down from a tree and held it over him.

As usual, he was sullen, savage, and ferocious.

"Strip!" he cried.

"Oh, Bana," exclaimed the poor Arab boy, "protect me!"

"Don't be foolish," replied Dick. "Do as he tells you. There is nothing unreasonable in it."

"I can't," was the reply.

"Why not?"

Captain Vipond did not give him time to reply, for he brought the swish down sharply over his shoulders.

A sharp cry of pain broke from him.

"Don't hurt the lad," said Dick.

"I will be obeyed," said the captain.

"Still you need not be brutal."

The soft blue eyes looked up so beseechingly into Dick's, that the latter snatched the swish out of Vipond's hand.

"Oh," said Vipond, "if you are going to be master, and thwart me at every turn, I can't help it."

"Let me talk to him," said Dick.

Vipond shrugged his shoulders and stood still.

"Perhaps," he said, "by this waste of time we shall have Mwezi's people down upon us. One nigger has escaped, as you know, thanks to your mistaken ideas of humanity."

"Can you swim?" asked Dick.

"Yes," said the boy; "I learnt at Brighton."

Dick burst into a loud laugh.

"That's either a thundering big lie or——"

He paused and looked hard at Hassan.

The boy crouched at his feet, and seemed overwhelmed at having allowed the fact to escape.

Captain Vipond, always of a suspicious nature, advanced and said—

"There is some imposture here."

At the same time he seized the boy's turban and snatched it from his head.

There was a cry of astonishment.

Long, silky hair escaped from its confinement and streamed down as far as the waist.

"Who are you?" asked Vipond.

"Why," said Dick, "it's Polly. It must be. Say, Polly, is it you?"

The Arab boy was detected.

It was Polly, who had assumed this disguise to be near Dick, who was the only friend she had left in the world.

"Yes," she answered, "forgive me, oh, forgive me, for coming after you, but I was so wretched and lonely that I did not know what to do."

"I placed you with friends."

"To me they were strangers. Tell me you will not be angry with me," she continued, her eyes swimming with tears.

"Not I."

"You will not send me away to die in the forest?"

"Is it likely?"

"I only wanted to be near you and Messiter, and wait upon you," she said.

"My dear Polly," said Dick, "I'm glad we have found you out, because we can treat you as a lady should be treated, though we are not such swells as we were when we started."

"Oh, don't mind me. Anything is good enough for me so long as I may stay with you."

Captain Vipond looked on curiously.

"I must apologize, ma'am," he said, "for striking you just now."

"Don't mention it," she said.

"I thought you were one of those lazy, obstinate Arabs, with whom you can do nothing without the stick."

Dick took Polly's arm and led her a little on one side.

The professor looked after them and grunted—

"So she's a woman. Poof!" he cried. "What were we about not to know it? It's a strange country where women dress up as boys. Poof!"

CHAPTER LXVI.

THE UNKNOWN RIVER.

DICK was somewhat embarrassed at discovering Polly as he had done.

"You little rascal," he said to her, "what do you mean by it?"

"I couldn't help it," she answered; "you would not let me come with you. My poor husband and father were both dead, and——"

Here the tears fell afresh.

"Don't cry," interrupted Dick; "I'll take as much care of you as I can, Poll, but I'm afraid you'll have to continue to dress like a boy, for we have no girl's clothes to give you."

"Never mind that. I don't care for anything, so long as I am with you once more," she answered.

Dick stooped over and kissed her.

Her eyes shone so brightly, and she looked quite pleased and happy again.

"You won't drive me away from you?" she continued, earnestly.

"Not likely."

Messiter came up.

"What have I done that you won't speak to me, Mrs. Snarley?" he said.

"Oh, Harry," she answered, "how formal you are."

"Shall I call you Polly?"

"Always."

They shook hands, and watched Ted, who was gradually getting the boat to shore.

At last he succeeded in his efforts.

It was a strongly-made canoe, capable of holding a dozen, with stores.

Ted had heard and seen what had taken place on shore.

His astonishment was unbounded.

"Well, I'm blowed!" he exclaimed. "Fancy it's being Miss Polly. I'm only an odd boy, but, hang it all, I've got my feelings!"

Suddenly the professor extended his arm.

"Look out!" he cried. "I may be wrong, but there is something very unlike a Saxon coming towards us. Poof!"

Dick followed the direction indicated with his eyes.

He saw a tall, handsome native, who was making signs of submission.

"Halt!" he exclaimed.

The man stopped, seeing a revolver levelled at his head.

"No shoot, sir!" he ejaculated. "Me peaceful native."

"What do you want?"

"Me Mabruki. One Captain Speke's men, and me be good guide."

"Come nearer," said Dick.

The man approached, bowing to the ground every now and then, and appearing very humble and submissive.

"How did you know we were here?" asked Dick.

"Me meet the great master who row up the lake."

"Livingstone?"

"Yes, sir. He send me on to you."

This was rather an improbable story; but as they wanted a guide, Dick did not stay to cross-examine him.

"Can you guide us to Ujiji?" he asked.

"Think so, sir; me try any way."

"What do you say, Captain Vipond?" cried Dick; "shall we engage the fellow?"

"Yes," answered Vipond; "we can shoot him through the head at the first sign of treachery."

"Very well," said Dick; "you may consider yourself engaged, Mab—what did you say your ugly name was?"

"Mabruki, Bana."

"All right; help the boy to put the things in the boat, and let us see what stuff you're made of."

Mabruki set to work with a will.

In half an hour all was in readiness for a start.

Dick, with Mabruki's help, constructed an awning out of some tent canvas to keep the sun off the stern of the boat.

There were but two oars.

It was impossible for Europeans to labour long in the burning sun.

So to simplify matters a mast was made and a sail set.

"We are not in a hurry," remarked

Dick, "and we may just as well take it easy."

It was an intense relief to glide smoothly over the surface of the silver lake after their many weeks' weary tramp.

A feeling of perfect happiness and contentment stole over them.

They let Mabruki take the helm, and as they knew nothing of the way, trusted implicitly to him.

But Dick watched him very closely.

He was prepared to send a bullet through his skull on the slightest provocation.

When travelling in a strange and savage country, with enemies on all sides, and death threatening you in a dozen different forms, you get to hold human life very cheaply indeed.

At each halt they caught fish of a palatable kind, which was a very welcome addition to their larder.

On the third day, when Ted was unpacking a bale of goods to get at something he wanted, a roll of newspapers fell out.

"What have you got there, Ted?" cried Dick.

"Papers, sir."

"English?"

"Yes, sir. I remember now that Dr. Livingstone gave them to me as he was going away, and I suppose they got packed up by mistake."

"You lubber," exclaimed Dick, "I've a good mind to rope's end you?"

"What for?" asked Ted.

"Why, we haven't seen a newspaper for goodness knows how long. Hand them over."

The papers were about a dozen in number, and everyone scrambled for a copy.

The doctor had received them with the supplies brought him from the escort.

It was quite a treat to get hold of them.

Even Captain Vipond put aside his gloominess, and eagerly looked at the printed sheet.

"Here's something about you, Lightheart," exclaimed Vipond.

"Where, sir?"

"In the *Times*. Shall I read it?"

"Please," said Dick, looking up, astonished.

Captain Vipond read a paragraph in the advertising columns. It ran thus—

"£100 REWARD.

"WHEREAS a young gentleman named Richard Lightheart has mysteriously disappeared from Harrow House School, at Brighton, this sum will be gladly paid by his sorrowing relatives to anyone who will give information of a satisfactory nature respecting him. He is supposed to have gone away with a friend named Messiter. Description——"

"Never mind that, sir," said Dick; "we shouldn't answer the description now, burnt as we are with the sun, and our clothes torn and ragged."

"It's odd," said Messiter, "that they should put that in. We wrote home and sent the letters by a passing ship."

"Perhaps it was lost; they evidently could not have received them," replied Vipond.

"I'm sorry for that," said Dick.

"They will be all the more pleased when we turn up," remarked Messiter.

"Is there anything about me, sir?" asked Ted.

Everybody laughed.

"Who'd take any trouble about a swab like you?" answered Vipond.

"Thank you, sir. I'm an odd boy, but I've got my feelings," replied Ted, putting his hands in his pockets and walking up and down.

"Here's a paragraph about Mr. Crab," cried the captain.

"Indeed," said the professor, puffing himself up, "I thought a distinguished man like myself could not be long removed from civilisation without being missed."

"Shall I read it?"

"By all means."

"We fear," ran the paragraph in question, "that the vessel in which Professor Crab, the secretary to the Society for the Exploration of the Unknown Parts of the World, sailed, has been lost.

"However, it is a consolation to reflect that Professor Crab was a much overrated man, and will not be missed in the world of science, which he has never adorned."

"Poof!" cried the professor, "that is written by some enemy."

"They give it you straight, sir," said Dick, smiling.

"I'll astonish them when I do get back," he answered.

Some hours were pleasantly passed in reading the papers.

News from home is always welcome when we are far, far away.

During the night the wind rose.

It was blowing hard when the boat started in the morning, and dark, heavy clouds scudded over the face of the horizon.

The strange guide, however, remained at his post, and spoke not a word to anyone.

For some hours the boat flew before a fierce gale.

Her course was so swift, that it was evident she was in the drift of a current.

This became apparent when, towards noon, they found themselves between the banks of a wide river.

"What river is this, and where are we going?" asked the professor.

The strange guide shook his head.

They were flowing swiftly along the tide of an unknown river.

As soon as possible Dick stopped the boat, and landed.

The party camped for the night on the bank.

In the morning, Dick held what he called a council of war, at which were present, himself, Messiter, and Sampson Jack.

Dick was sick and tired of African exploration already.

The country was uninteresting, and full of deadly peril.

Mr. Snarley's death affected him greatly, and he wanted to go home, but on his way he thought he would visit the diamond fields of South Africa.

After a long consultation, it was decided to break up the camp.

They all started for the coast.

Before they had gone a dozen miles, they were attacked by the natives.

A desperate conflict ensued, in which they were victorious, though the battle cost them dear.

Vipond, Dugard, and Menzies were shot dead, also Sangaru.

The remainder of the journey was devoid of interest—they reached Zanzibar in safety.

Here, Ted, Polly, and Alice determined to stay with Sampson Jack, so that Dick and Messiter went on alone by the first steamer to South Africa.

They travelled to the diamond mines, where they joined a party employed by an English nobleman, Lord Tregannon.

Dick was lucky enough to find a big diamond.

The manager of the camp was a man who had acquired the soubriquet of Champagne Charley.

The fellow was a rascal, who one day decamped with an accomplice named Corker, stealing Dick's big diamond and several others.

Dick was asleep in his tent, when the thief took his diamond from his coat-pocket.

A noise awoke him, and he ran out just in time to see the man on horseback, with Corker on another horse by his side.

He had his revolver in his hand, and fired. Corker was hit, but did not fall from the saddle. The rascals escaped.

There was nothing more to be done that night. In the morning Dick told Lord Tregannon and Messiter that he meant to pursue the thieves.

They tried to dissuade him, in vain; he started, though he had small hopes of being successful in his search.

After several hours' wandering, he got lost.

Hoping to attract attention, he fired his pistol.

Presently, a boy tending sheep for a boer came up, and conducted him to the farm.

On the way, Dick told him all, and Tommy Begg. the boy, said there were two men in his master's barn, one wounded.

CHAPTER LXVII.

THE FIGHT IN THE BARN.

A QUARTER of an hour's walk brought Dick to the boer's holding.

At the rear of the low-built, white-washed house, was the stock-yard, in which were some cattle, and behind that again was a barn.

A small window without any glass in it tempted him to look through, which he was able to do by standing on tiptoe.

The sound of voices fell upon his ears.

On a heap of rough straw lay a man, whom he at once recognised as Corker, and he seemed to be in great pain.

It was this man that he had shot.

Champagne Charley was sitting by his side, smoking a short pipe.

"What are you growling at, you old fool?" exclaimed Charley. "Ain't I done the best I can for you?"

"No, you haven't, if it comes to that," said Corker. "I've got a bullet in me, and am bleeding to death. You've bandag'd it up, but you ain't a doctor. Why don'e you go and get one?"

"How the devil can I?" answered Charley. "There ain't such a thing to be had in these parts. One or two up at the fields knows a thing or two about doctoring—that's true enough; but it's as much as my life's worth to venture up there after shooting little Bourgain and the baron. They'd string me up high enough, mate."

"Ain't my life worth nothing?" asked Corker.

"It may be to you, but it ain't to me," replied Charley, brutally.

"Then I shall die."

"Can't you die peaceably? What do you want to make a fuss about it for? I'll see the last of you," said Charley.

"Ah, my boy, wait till your turn comes. You won't take it so easy," sighed Corker.

"I can afford to wait, old pal," said Charley. "My time ain't up yet. I mean to have my fling in England. I've got the diamonds I stole from Bourgain when the bar was on fire, and even you don't know where I've got them. You'd like to split on me if you did, wouldn't you?"

"Curse you!" said Corker. "I've come out here for something. Can't you save my life, you cold-blooded brute?"

"No, and I wouldn't if I could," said Charley, frankly. "If that bullet had not caught you, I should have given you something before we got to the west. You know too much for me, and if you don't make haste and die, I shall have to knock you over the head. It isn't safe for me to stop here to see you kick."

Dick could see the wretched man shiver in a sort of convulsion, as if even he was horrified at such fiendish behaviour on the part of the man he looked upon as a friend.

"What's the use of waiting?" cried Charley. "I'll see what you've got in your pockets. Be still, or I'll brain you."

Corker, wounded as he was, tried to make some resistance, and begged imploringly that he would not rob him; but Charley had no mercy, and would not pay any heed to his prayer.

Finding that his victim had strength enough left to be noisy, he raised a heavy stick he had with him, and struck him twice on the head.

Corker laid perfectly still after this, and did not utter a word.

The wretch proceeded to rifle his pockets and transfer the contents to his own, seeming, from the smile that flitted across his features, to be well satisfied with his plunder.

Dick's blood boiled in his veins at witnessing this outrage on a wounded and dying man.

He had been powerless to stop it, but at least he could avenge him; and stalking noiselessly up to the barn door, he opened it and went in.

But gently as he had come in, Charley's watchful ears heard a slight creaking of the barn door.

In an instant he was on his feet and facing Dick.

Both fired at the same time, but such was the hurry and uncertainty of the moment that neither of the shots took effect.

Relying upon his superior strength, Champagne Charley rushed upon Dick, thinking it better to close with him at once.

With a pistol the boy was a match for the man.

But, body to body, the chances were in favour of the heavier and stronger of the two.

They rocked to and fro, falling on the ground, rolling over and over, getting up again, and hugging one another with the same cruel purpose, which seemed to be to crush the life out.

Dick was tall and well-built for his age, and might have had a chance of conquering the bully, had not his foot slipped.

Down he went with a crash which knocked all the breath out of him, and caused his head to bang against the earth till stars danced before his eyes.

"It's all over now," he thought to himself, as he saw Charley feeling for his knife.

Shutting his eyes, he tried to think of home, but he could not fix his mind.

He fancied the gleaming knife was being brandished before his face, and the idea so horrified him that he made a terrible effort to rise, which, to his surprise, was completely successful.

The movement was so sudden that Charley, who had taken one hand off him to hold the knife with which he was going to cut his throat, was thrown backwards.

Instantly Dick threw himself upon him, and presented the muzzle of a pistol at his ear.

Charley was so surprised at the sudden change of affairs that he could not move nor speak.

The knife dropped from his palsied hand, and he glared up in Dick's face as hopelessly as the lad had gazed into his but a moment before.

Disarming the ruffian, Dick made his arms fast behind him with a halter, and satisfying himself that he couldn't escape, went into the yard and saddled one of the boer's horses.

Champagne Charley had recovered himself as Dick returned, and was sitting up, not far from the dead body of Corker.

"What are you doin' of, tying my hands?" he asked. "Is this here a lark, or what?"

"You won't find it much of a lark when I get you back to the fields," replied Dick; "but stir your stumps, or I'll have to make you."

"Come, now, don't be hard on a cove," whined Charley. "Blest if you ain't like a shadder, followin' chaps about. Didn't I spare your life just now when I'd got you down, and might have cut your throat as clean as a whistle?"

"Don't tell me any lies, you murdering son of a gun," said Dick; "get up and tell me where you've put the diamonds you robbed Bourgain of."

Charley with some difficulty rose to his feet, and a malicious grin came over his features.

"You'd like to know all about them di'monds, wouldn't you, now?" he said, "specially the big un as you dug out. That one's worth a mint of money. It would set a chap up for life."

"Where have you put them?" asked Dick.

"That's telling. You let me go, and I'll give up the stone. It ain't about me. It's put away safe. Even he"—he pointed to Corker with a shudder—"didn't know nothin' about it."

"Diamond or no diamond," said Dick, resolutely, "you've got to have your neck stretched, so come along to camp. If you won't give me the stone, I must go without it, but I value justice more than wealth."

"Think of it, my lad," said Charley, clinging to this as to his last hope; "you'll be rich if you let me run, and you've nothing to gain by my death. Don't you be a fool. I'm the only one who can put you on to the diamond."

A shock head darkened the little window.

"Yah! yah! yah!"

Dick looked up and saw Tommy Begg.

"Ain't he been a-kidding you," said Tommy, "a-saying as nobody knew where he put the diamonds. I know. I seed him."

The fellow turned pale.

"Curse you!" he cried; "Be off, or I'll——"

"No, you won't, cocky," said Tommy; "he's got you made safe, and there's another of 'em outside; I've guided him here. You didn't think I was piping you off, when you id the stones. Yah! yah!"

"'WHY, IT'S POLLY! IT MUST BE. SAY, POLLY, IS IT YOU?' SAID DICK."—(See page 203.)

Dick compelled Charley to quit the barn, and outside they were joined by Lord Tregannon, who had come across Tommy, and after asking him a few questions, had got him to guide him to the farm, fearing that Dick alone might get into trouble.

"There's the prisoner," said Dick, as he tied him to one of the stirrup irons, "and he doesn't go out of my sight till he's hanged. Where's Tommy?"

"Here I am," answered the boy, who had been into the barn, and came out carrying a thick cane in his hand "Look what I've got. It don't seem very valuable, do it?"

"No. I can't say it does," replied Dick.

"Ain't it, though? Yah! yah! yah! You don't know nothing about it. He does, though. Look at him grindin' of his teeth as if he was fit to eat me."

Tommy pointed derisively to Champagne Charley, who was furious with passion, which increased as the lad's "Yah! yah! yah! rang out on the crisp air.

CHAPTER LXVIII.

FRESH PERILS.

THE fierce rage and the frantic struggles of Charley were ludicrous to witness.

He dragged the stirrup, trying to get at the lad, until he irritated the horse and made him kick.

"Oh, you young imp," he cried; "you've been a-spying and a-prying; I'll break your bones if I can only get hold of you."

But Tommy kept out of his way.

"You can't do it, yah!" he exclaimed. "Who cares for you? Dry up, you one-horse duffer. Yah! yah! I'm safe enough, and I'll split on you, there. Yah! yah! yah!"

Charley danced and swore like a Pagan.

Dick had taken the cane from Tommy, and was holding it up doubtingly.

"What's this got to do with the diamonds?" he asked.

"It's got all to do with them."

"How?"

"Cos its 'oller," said Tommy.

"Oh, you viper! you wenermous young serpint!" roared Charley.

"Don't you see," continued Tommy, "that it's got a cork shoved in the top?"

"Yes," said Dick.

"Well, you draw that out; the diamonds is in the 'oller of the cane. I see him put 'em in. I had my 'ead at the winder, but he didn't twig me."

"I'll brain you," cried Charley, trying again to get at him.

"You would if you could, but you can't, old pal," answered Tommy, putting his tongue in his cheek. "Ain't you bottled up nice? Yah! yah!"

Dick lost no time in removing the cork from the top of the cane, and taking off his hat, he allowed the precious stones which Charley had stolen from Bourgain to fall into it.

Amongst them was the big diamond he had found and which had afterwards been given to him.

Lord Tregannon bent over him.

"I congratulate you on your discovery," he said.

"Thank you," replied Dick. "I think we've got the best of him now."

Suddenly they were aroused from the contemplation of the diamonds by loud cries from Tommy.

"Look out! He's off! Oh, the clever beggar! He'd get out of Newgate. Stop 'im! Hi! hi! yah! yah! What are you up to?"

Tregannon and Dick looked up.

To their surprise, Charley had contrived to get on the horse's back, bound as his hands were.

He held the bridle in his teeth, and sticking his knees well into the sides, was urging the animal forward at a gallop.

It was a desperate venture.

If the horse stumbled, and he fell off, he would break his neck; but the rascal argued that he was sure to be hung if he stopped, and it was better to run any risk than to neglect any chance, however forlorn, which offered.

Dick and Tregannon fired their pistols.

But Charley had cleared the straw-yard, and had passed out of the gate.

Bang!

Bang!

He went on unharmed, the bullets falling short of the horse, which was plunging madly on.

"He'll come to grief," said Dick; "surely he cannot stick on with his hands tied."

"I don't know that," replied Tregannon; "when a man's life's at stake, he finds himself capable of doing things he would shrink from with horror at other times."

"He's a clever devil, anyhow. Well, we've got the diamonds, that's one comfort; let him go. The rope's made for him, I expect, and he'll swing sooner or later. Tommy, you follow him up as well as you can, and if he falls off, let me know."

Tommy nodded, and started off at his best pace after Charley, who was disappearing in the distance.

At such a pace did he go, that his body was but a faint speck on the horizon.

Dick returned the stones to the hollow of the cane, and replaced the cork, thinking they could not have a better receptacle for the present.

Then he beckoned Tregannon into the barn, and pointed out the body of Corker.

"Do you know him?"

Tregannon shook his head, but he examined his pockets, and found some letters, which he read attentively.

"It is as I thought," he said; "this wretch is an agent of my younger brother, who has sent him out here to murder me."

"Horrible," replied Dick.

"Isn't it dreadful to think that a brother can be so base? When I get to England I shall prove his villany to him, and give him a few hundreds to go abroad with. I'll not have him in the same country with me. I wouldn't have believed it, though, if I hadn't seen it in black and white."

Dick said nothing, as the subject was a painful one.

Before they returned to camp, they found the boer, to whom they related what had happened, and he assisted them to bury the body of Corker under a tree.

Then they partook of some refreshment which the hospitable farmer pressed upon them, and wended their way back to camp across the pleasant prairie.

Dick asked his companion whether he might keep all the stones that Charley had stolen from Bourgain, and Tregannon replied that, as Bourgain had no relations, he might as well have them as anyone else.

The value of the plunder came to several thousand pounds.

Determined to give them up if anyone had a better claim to them, Dick trudged along with the precious stick in his hand, until they came up with Tommy and his sheep.

As they expected, he had been unable to overtake Charley, but he had found the horse, which came limping back towards the farm as if it had been hurt by a fall.

What had become of the murderer they could not tell.

Dick thanked Tommy very heartily for the good service he had rendered them, and wished him every prosperity in the land of his adoption.

It was drawing towards evening when they arrived at the camp, and they found that Mr. Barker had been buried that day.

Messiter listened with interest to the account of their adventures, and was glad that, though the thief and murderer had escaped, he had not got off with his plunder.

Tregannon did not scruple to ask Dick for a dozen diamonds of small size, which he sold to pay expenses to Port Elizabeth.

The next morning they bade adieu to the fields, and took passage in a waggon which was returning to coast, it being their intention to engage berths in the first steamship going from Algoa Bay to England.

The boys' hearts beat wildly at the prospect of once more seeing their native land.

They had gone through their share of dangers and adventures during the time they had been away from school.

As day by day they drew nearer the coast, their delight increased.

They would soon see their friends and relations again, and be able to spin such yarns as few lads of their age could honestly do.

When within a week's journey of Port Elizabeth, they encamped in a wide and barren country.

The oxen cropped the stunted grass.

The drivers drew water from a small, muddy stream, and the passengers cooked such provisions as they had left.

The drivers informed the passengers that there had been some robberies on the road lately, about the spot where they were, and advised them to be careful.

"I shouldn't wonder," said Messiter, " if it's that fellow, Charley. He'd make his way to the coast, and you may bet he means having that big diamond of yours, Dick."

" Not he," answered Dick.

" There is some sense in what Messiter says," said Lord Tregannon ; " you know what an unscrupulous ruffian the villain is."

" I think he's broken his neck by this time," said Dick ; " anyhow, he'd be afraid to venture near us, because we know too much about him."

" Will you take a fool's advice ?" said Messiter."

" Yours, do you mean ?"

" Yes—mine."

" I can't tell, till I hear what it is."

" Remove the diamonds out of the hollow cane, and put them in the lining of your hat, or the toe of your boot if it's big enough. If Charley should be lurking about, he'll try and have the cane, thinking the stones are there."

" There is some sense in that," said Dick. " Tell you what I'll do. I've got a little bag, and I'll put them in that, and hang it round my neck."

He lost no time in doing as he said, and the big diamond, with a couple of dozen others, whose ineffectual fire paled before that of the monster, was hung safely round his neck.

" Now," he said, laughing, " they must have my life to get at my property."

" I've got an interest in the diamonds, too. You'll give me half-a-dozen to make presents when we get home?" asked Messiter.

" Of course I will, Harry. You shall take your pick, only I must keep the big one."

" For whom ?"

" I thought of mother, but on second thoughts it shall go to Henrietta, because then I shall have it again when we're married," said Dick.

" Oh, you artful old Jew," laughed Messiter.

" Nothing like looking after number one," said Dick, joining in the merriment. " What would my governor do for me? I'll lay anything he'll be awfully rusty when we get back, and call me all the scamps he can lay his tongue to."

" Well," said Lord Tregannon, " you have been a scapegrace from what you have yourself told me."

" Good job too. I like it," replied Dick.

" Never mind," continued Tregannon ; " if your governor kicks you out, come to me. You shall never want a home or a fiver, either of you, while I live. I'm not a half-and-half sort of friend. You'll find I go the whole hog or none."

Dick thanked him for the offer, but declared that he would never be dependent upon anyone.

Rather would he work for a living.

He was young and strong, and did not fear the world.

Night came and he crept into the waggon, and threw himself down in a sheltered corner.

Messiter was near him, and he was soon fast asleep.

It might have been about midnight when he felt someone touch his arm, and at the same time a heavy breathing was audible, close to his face.

" Don't, Harry," he said, half asleep, " keep on your own side."

After this all was still, and he went to sleep again with the impression that Messiter had a very bad nightmare, and was touching him with his arms or legs.

Then he had a dream.

He fancied that Charley was kneeling upon his breast and suffocating him with his weight ; he could see the fierce eyes glaring down upon him like burning coals, and held over his head was a cruel-looking, murderous knife.

" Help ! help !" he screamed, as he got into a sitting position.

He looked about him in the imperfect light, and saw a human form crawling past the bodies of the sleeping passengers.

Feeling for the cane which he had put by his side, he found it was gone.

Then he had no doubt that Charley had

crept into the waggon and stolen it, not knowing that the diamonds had only that day been removed.

Without hesitation, Dick drew his pistol and fired.

But the creeping form at that moment reached the end of the waggon, and slipped down on the ground.

The shot roused the occupants of the waggon, who started up with oaths and curses.

Dick explained that a thief had been robbing him.

No one but Messiter and Tregannon believed him.

The others abused him for an idiot, and told him not to be a fool and wake them again, or they'd know the reason why.

Dick got up and looked about him, though his search was unsuccessful.

"Anyhow he'll be sold," he muttered. "It was lucky indeed that I put the diamonds in the bag. What a lark it will be when he comes to take the cork out of the cane."

He continued walking about on the watch till the morning. There was no more sleep for him that night.

But his watch was undisturbed by any incident.

Charley—if indeed it was he—had made tracks with surprising celerity.

CHAPTER LXIX.

"WHAT A PRETTY SAILOR BOY," SAID THE WOMAN.

NOTHING of any importance happened during the remainder of the journey, and the " cow chariot," or bullock waggon, reached Port Elizabeth in safety.

Dick sold a couple of diamonds for a hundred pounds, which he divided between himself and his friends.

The first thing after this that occupied their minds was to go to a ready-made clothes store, and buy a new rig-out.

Very smart they looked in their midshipmen's dress, as they strolled about the town to show themselves.

Tregannon was at the hotel where they were stopping, writing letters for England, which were to go by the mail steamer, and inform the agents to the Tregannon estates that he was coming home to claim the title and the property.

"What are those things in that window," said Messiter.

"Yankee knuckle-dusters," replied Dick, looking at some bands of iron with holes in them to fit on the fingers, " have you never seen one before?"

"No. Have you?"

"Oh, yes. Lots of times. They're stunning things for a row, though it isn't fair to use them unless you're set on by half a dozen. One of those fitted on the right hand would soon settle a crowd. I'll buy one."

He went into the shop, and for three-and-sixpence purchased a knuckle-duster, which he put on his hand.

They proceeded to stroll along, looking in the shop-windows, and passing the time away as well as they could.

The steamer they intended to go by was called the " Patagonia," and she was expected to call at Algoa Bay in three or four days.

They had engaged berths at the office of the company's agent.

Coming down towards the shipping quarter again, a woman who was flashily dressed looked in Dick's face.

"You'll know me again, I hope," said Dick.

"What a pretty sailor boy," said the woman.

"Yes," said Dick, "I'm generally considered wonderfully good-looking for my age. It's a way I've got, though the African sun's browned me a little."

"Won't you stand me a glass of wine?" continued the woman, who was tall and handsome, though dissipation had left its mark upon her.

She was not more than five-and-twenty, and her dress , if " loud," was expressive and well chosen.

"Half a dozen, if you like. Where shall we go?"

"Oh, in here. It looks as good as any

other," said the woman, indicating a sailor's drinking bar.

"What's your name?" asked Dick.

"Call me Fanny."

"All right, Fanny. Come along. You're kind and I'm grateful. We ought not to drink in the middle of the day. It's naughty, you know."

"But it's nice," said the woman.

Messiter pulled Dick by the sleeve.

"Don't go in that place with that woman," he whispered.

"Why not?"

"I can see a villanous-looking lot of fellows inside."

"Well, what then?"

"Charley might be amongst them."

"Go and put your boots on," replied Dick sarcastically. "Charley wouldn't dare to show up in Port Elizabeth while I'm here."

"I don't know so much about that. A fellow like Charley isn't very particular what he does or where he goes to," replied Messiter.

"Perhaps it's a plant. Is that what you mean?"

"Yes."

"Humbug. You'll yet funky of your own shadow next," said Dick.

The woman could not hear this conversation, but she guessed its purport.

"What is your friend saying?" she inquired.

"He says you're a darling," said Dick.

"Oh, no. He did not say that. I can see from the expression of his face that his remark was not so complimentary."

"Never mind him, Fanny."

"But I do mind him. He's a surly, ill-tempered fellow. Let him go home."

"You hear, Harry," said Dick.

"I do," replied Messiter, "and I daresay she wouldn't mind me being out of the way, but I shan't leave my friend, so she needn't flatter herself."

"Who are you calling she?" said the woman. "I'm a lady."

"So I should think," exclaimed Messiter, grinning.

"Don't you cheek me, young tar-pot," said Fanny, her manner changing at once, and showing that if she could be soft when she liked, it was her nature to be a bully.

"I am not aware that I did," exclaimed Messiter.

"Well, you'll have bad luck if you do. I'll limb you. I don't let men cheek me, and I'm sure I'm not going to be sauced by boys."

"I for one don't want to have anything to do with you, and if Dick will be advised by me, he'll stroll on."

"He's got a mind of his own, I suppose. Are you paid so much a day for looking after him?" sneered Fanny.

Messiter offered her a shilling.

"Here's the price of two glasses of wine," he said, "go and lush it out."

"Drink at your expense? Not I," cried Fanny, knocking up his hand, and sending the money flying into the gutter.

"That's stupid. You'll want it some of these days."

"You aggravating little swab," exclaimed Fanny, "I'll get my husband to give you a rope's ending."

"Which of them?" asked Messiter.

This was too much for the woman, who lost her temper, and rushed at Messiter.

He ran away as hard as he could, but Fanny gave chase, Messiter doubling every now and then, and stopping to say something which increased her anger.

Dick laughed till his sides ached.

"Go it, Fanny," he said, "you'll win yet. You're bound to catch him, and when you do, give it him hot."

At length Messiter's foot slipped, and Fanny, seizing him by the hair, pulled him up, and boxed his ears.

"There," she said, that will teach you not to be insolent to a lady again."

Messiter took it very good humouredly, knowing he could not strike a woman back again.

"You should have told me, and then I should have known you were a lady," he said, picking up his cap.

"Now you can go home," continued Fanny, "we don't want you."

"Dick," said Messiter.

"What?"

"Are you off your chump? What can you see in the woman to go and treat her, after——"

"I shan't be a minute," answered Dick, interrupting him. "You know I promised to stand a drink, and I don't like to look mean."

"All right. I shan't come in, but I'm not far off, mind, if I'm wanted," replied Messiter.

The woman took Dick's arm, and dragged him forcibly away in the direction of the drinking bar, which was one of the lowest in appearance that can be imagined.

It was dirty and dingy, reeking with the smell of spilled liquors, and evidently frequented by the lowest specimens of the sailors of all nations, whose ships happened to be lying in harbour.

There were about half-a-dozen men in the bar when Dick entered.

He saw at once that he was an object of general attention.

If ever there was a murderous cut-throat-looking crowd, he was in one now.

But he only intended to pay for a glass of wine for the woman, and then go away.

He had the precious bag of diamonds round his neck, and he knew it was imprudent to venture into dangerous company.

All the stories he had heard of robberies in low drinking dens came into his mind, and he wished himself out again.

"What will you have?" he said, "sherry?"

"Thank you, that will do," replied Fanny.

While he was paying for the wine, a man emerged from a side room, and striding up to him, said—

"What are you doing with my wife?"

Dick slipped his hand into his pocket and put on his knuckle-duster.

"If the lady is your wife," he said, "there is no harm done. She asked for a glass of wine, and I have given it her."

"I'll teach you not to pick up married women," cried the fellow.

"I apologize," said Dick; "it shan't occur again."

"No, I'll take my oath it doesn't," said the husband.

At the same moment he struck Dick in the face, but as he drew back the clenched fist only grazed his forehead.

In an instant Dick's hand was out of his pocket, and a crushing blow sent him reeling against the wall, with one side of his face smashed in.

"He's got a knuckle-duster," cried the lookers-on, shrinking back.

"The coward! down with him!" exclaimed a voice, which to his surprise Dick recognised as that of Champagne Charley.

This miscreant emerged from the same room which had sheltered the husband.

Dick saw now that the whole thing had been arranged between them, and that the woman had been sent out to bring him in for the purpose of robbery.

He attempted to retreat to the door.

Several men interposed to stop him, and a general rush was made upon him.

Though he struck out freely, he was grasped from behind, and Charley hissed in his ear—

"The diamonds. Where are they? Give them up and save your life."

CHAPTER LXX.

THE SHARK'S PREY.

IN reply to Champagne Charley's whispered request, Dick said "Never!"

"You won't give 'em up?" exclaimed Charley.

"No. I haven't got them."

"Who then?"

"The baron," answered Dick.

"It's a lie. The young swab's got 'em somewhere about him, I'll swear," said the woman.

Half a dozen hands had seized Dick.

He was being pulled about more than he liked, and had no chance.

"Curse you," cried Charley, "I'll shake the liver out of you if you don't speak."

Dick's only reply was to make a fearfull effort to escape.

Charley had his knuckles inside his coat collar, and a sudden wrench burst the button off his shirt.

The bag of diamonds round his neck was disclosed to view.

A cry of joy broke from Charley.

It was echoed by the surrounding ruffians.

"It's here," exclaimed Charley, "I've got it."

He tore the bag off Dick's neck.

"Chuck him out. He's no good now," he cried.

One glance at the contents of the bag satisfied Charley that he had got the prize he was longing for.

"Better knock him on the head," said a tall, brutal man.

"No, no, let him go," said the woman. "He is too young and good-looking to die. I didn't bring him in to be slaughtered."

"Chuck him outside, I say," cried Charley, "and make tracks the back way. Here's a sparkler worth a hundred quid for you blokes to divide amongst you."

"Where's my share?" asked the woman.

"There's one for you, Fan; a reg'lar beauty."

"So it is," she cried, eagerly seizing the stone that Champagne Charley gave her.

Two men dragged Dick to the door and threw him out into the street.

He fell into Messiter's arms, half-fainting, and looking more dead than alive.

"What's up?" asked Messiter.

"I've been robbed," gasped Dick.

"Lost the diamonds?"

"Yes."

"By Jove, here's a go. What did I tell you?"

"Let's go home. I'll lean on you; perhaps the baron will tell us what to do," said Dick, feebly.

"You'll never speak to strange women again, I should think," remarked Messiter.

Dick shook his head.

They returned to their hotel, and told Tregannon what had happened.

He was much annoyed, and communicated with the authorities, who made a search for the thieves, but without avail.

Nothing could be seen of Charley or his accomplices.

It could not be helped.

They were unable to stay in Port Elizabeth on the off chance of recovering the stones.

The ship in which they had engaged a passage, was to sail in two days.

So they put all their traps on board, and embarked.

It was a steamer, which was to convey them to England, and though saddened by the loss of the diamonds, they all looked forward with delight to reaching their loved country once more.

As soon as the steam was up, and the vessel fairly out at sea, Dick, who had been drinking bottled beer down in the steward's cabin, went on deck.

He was soon in conversation with the captain, a portly man, who had a great respect for those who were going home with diamonds in their pockets.

Sometimes he had one or two small ones given him.

"Had good luck, sir?" he said to Dick.

"Yes and no, captain," replied Dick.

Captain Bunting stared.

"The fact is," continued Dick, "that my party and I have been very successful, but just before sailing, I got robbed in a drinking bar."

"And now you've got nothing to show."

"Not a grain of dust."

"Who robbed you?"

"A wild and daring fellow, a murderer and a thief, to my certain knowledge," said Dick.

Suddenly a man carrying a bucket passed by.

Dick looked at him, and he looked at Dick.

"Captain," said Dick, "is that a new hand?"

"Yes, shipped just as we were on the point of starting."

"Are you sure?"

"Of course; he was hard up, and I told him he might work out his passage."

"He is the man who robbed me."

"The devil!" cried Captain Bunting.

"I'll swear he's Champagne Charley; call him up."

Dick's heart beat wildly.

"Hi! you green hand. Come here," shouted the captain.

Reluctantly the man approached.

"So, Mr. Champagne Charley," said Dick, "I've spotted you at last."

The man glanced defiance at him.

"You did't expect to find me on board this ship, eh? You thought I should be hunting for you in the town; ain't you preciously sold, Charley?"

"I don't know what you mean," said the man.

Dick ran at him, and striking him with his fist, knocked him down.

"That's what I mean, murderer and thief!" he cried.

He knelt on his breast, and began to tear his clothes open, looking for the diamonds.

"I want my property, and I'm going to have it, that's what I mean," answered Dick.

"Leave go," cried Charley.

"I shall have you hanged for the murder of Corker up near New Rush, that's what I mean."

"Get up, will you?"

"Give me the diamonds."

"I ain't got 'em," replied Charley.

Dick's hand touched something sewn in the lining of the fellow's trousers.

He could not mistake the feel of the diamonds.

There they were securely hidden between the outside white duck and the lining inside.

"Ha!" cried Dick; "here they are."

The captain approached, and asked Dick if he wanted any assistance.

"Put this man in irons," replied Dick; "I'll hold you harmless."

"By ——, you don't," said Charley; "I'm not going to swing, and if I can't have the sparklers, curse me if anyone else shall."

He made a prodigious effort, and threw off Dick, who fell sprawling on his back.

Then, with the light of madness in his eyes, the desperate ruffian sprang over the ship's side into the sea.

"By Jove," cried Dick, recovering himself, "he's overboard."

"Man over," roared the captain; "ease her—stop her—back astarn."

Instantly those in the engine-room stopped the way of the vessel.

Dick eagerly watched the form of Charley.

All at once he uttered a cry.

"Look, look! a shark!" he cried.

Darting through the clear water was a huge shark, which had espied his prey.

Charley saw it too.

"Help!" he cried, in a frenzy of despair.

The steamer, being backed, was nearing him.

"Lower a boat," shouted the captain.

This was done.

Dick was one of the first to jump into it.

They neared the floating man, who had no difficulty in keeping himself above water.

"Help, help!" he shrieked; "can't you see the darned shark? Pick me up. I'll come back; hanging's better than—oh! help me!"

There was a slight foaming of the water as the voracious animal dashed straight at its prey.

An awful shriek of agony rose from Charley as the shark turned on its back, and opening its huge jaws, made a bite at him.

"Leg gone, by the hookey," said the boatswain.

"Which leg, bo'sun?" asked Dick, eagerly.

"Don't matter much which, I should think."

"It does; it does."

"Right leg, then," answered the boatswain.

"Devil seize that shark and fly away with him," said Dick, in a tone of vexation.

"What for?"

"He stole my diamonds, and sewed them in his trousers of his right leg, and now they're gone for ever in the shark's belly."

They picked up the wounded man, who had tinged the sea with his fast-flowing blood.

It was clear he could not live much longer.

By the time he reached the deck he had lost consciousness, and never rallying, sank rapidly, until at sunset he died.

Dick and his friends did not feel much shocked, as the villain deserved his fate, but they were annoyed at losing the diamonds again in so strange a manner.

The night passed, and so did the following day.

Dick was ready to cry at times.

"Why didn't that humbugging shark take the other leg?" he said.

"The brute might have had the whole body if he'd only left the breeches," remarked Messiter.

"That's a 'cute shark," said Tregannon. "He knows his way about."

"By George, I'm that wild," replied Dick, "I could cut my ears off, and throw them to a dog."

The man who had just been relieved at the wheel passed them, and stopping before Dick, said, "There's a shark following the ship, sir."

"What sort of a shark?"

"Oh! a good big one."

"Let's ask the captain if we may try to catch him," said Messiter.

"Oh, yes; he'll have no objection," replied Tregannon; "I'll go and speak to him."

Captain Bunting willingly acceded to the request, and a hook was baited with a piece of pork.

The engines were slowed, and the strong line thrown overboard.

The shark at once seized the bait.

A dozen men hauled in the rope, and the animal was brought on deck.

He was despatched with a hatchet.

"Cut him open," said Tregannon, "and let's see if he's got anything inside him."

"Not much, I think, sir," replied the boatswain; "he looks uncommon lean and hungry."

Knives being procured, his belly was opened, and to the surprise of everyone, a leg of a man was discovered.

Dick seized it eagerly.

"This is wonderful," he cried; "it's Champagne Charley's leg, and here are my diamonds.   Hurrah!"

"Hurrah!" rejoined Messiter.

The men took up the cheer, and the shouts redoubled when Dick ripped up the lining, and the diamonds fell on the deck.

Only a few of the smaller ones had been taken away.

Charley had reserved the bulk of the property for himself, and was going to England to enjoy his ill-gotten spoil.

Dick promised the sailors fifty pounds between them on their arrival in London.

He gave the captain a diamond, and became the most popular man aboard.

"My luck's in again," he said, delightedly. "Who'd have thought that we should have caught the identical shark that snapped off that scoundrel Charley's leg?"

He carefully put the diamonds away, and never parted with them day or night.

At length the ship, after a prosperous voyage, ran up the Thames, and landed Dick, Messiter, and Tregannon at Gravesend.

Tregannon took leave of his young friends, having to go to London to claim his title and estates.

He promised to come down to Dick's father in a few days.

So Dick and Messiter took the train to the South Coast, and as the evening fell, were at the rectory.

It would be difficult to describe the joy with which they were received.

Messiter stayed that night at the rector's, and the next day went to his friends, Dick having given him half a dozen splendid diamonds.

Dick's sister Emily telegraphed to Henrietta that the Scapegrace had come back, and invited her to come and stay with them.

The invitation was accepted.

Mr. and Mrs. Lightheart were so pleased to see their son again, that they freely forgave him all the trouble he had caused them.

Dick gave away diamonds right and left.

But he kept the biggest one of all for Henrietta.

His old schoolmaster came over from Brighton to see him.

His adventures were listened to with wrapt attention.

"What a man he's grown," said Mrs. Lightheart, admiringly.

"I hope his good qualities have grown in proportion to his body," remarked Mr. Lightheart.

Henrietta had grown a tall, handsome girl, and she was overjoyed to see her sweetheart again, and to find that in all his wanderings he had not forgotten her. When he gave her the diamond, she said—

"Oh! Dick, what a beauty."

"Take care of it, darling," said Dick, "it's worth a lump of money, and it will do to start in life, when we're married."

The Reverend Mr. Lightheart overheard this remark.

"Married!" he said, "who is talking of marriage?"

Dick turned round and saw his father.

CHAPTER XCI.

CONCLUSION.

"IN another year, father, we shall be big enough," said Dick, "to get married."

"Don't talk nonsense, sir," said his father, "you will have to work."

"What for?"

"Because I say so. You have had enough play, and I mean to put you in the City."

"I didn't bargain for that," said Dick, looking rather sheepish.

"My dear boy," continued Mr. Lightheart, "what I say is for your good you are only seventeen."

"Isn't that old enough to marry?" asked Dick.

"No. I will not give my consent until you are of age."

"Henrietta is a little older, and she is willing to be my wife," said Dick.

He put his arm round her waist, and looked up lovingly in her face.

"Miss Henrietta's father and I are in perfect accord in this matter; by all means engage yourselves, but you must not think of marrying for some time."

"I might as well have stopped in Africa," said Dick.

"On the contrary, you are better here."

"I can't see it."

"You must strive to make yourself a respectable citizen, and forget all your vagabondizing, and show yourself to be a worthy member of the community."

"Perhaps your papa is right, Dick, dearest," said Henrietta.

"I don't know so much about that."

"We shall often see one another, and we can write."

"I don't know that I shall like City life," said Dick.

"Have you any ambition?" asked his father.

"For what?"

"To be a great man—say a distinguished member of the church."

"No. I'll never be a parson."

"A barrister, then, perhaps a judge."

"I hate the law."

"A doctor?"

"Can't stand physic."

"A soldier?" said his father.

"I have seen enough of fighting."

"What do you say to a sailor's life? Not that I recommend it."

"I've been mast-headed and flogged and ben-cooped," exclaimed Dick, with a shake of the head. "No more sea for me."

"A merchant, then, with ships sailing to all parts of the world."

"That's better. Sampson Jack's a merchant. I shouldn't mind that. I like dealing," exclaimed Dick.

"A merchant be it, then. That you shall have some means of getting a living I am determined, for I will have no son of mine brought up to lead an idle life."

"Well, Harry, dear," said Dick, "you must wait, and I must work, I suppose."

He heaved a sigh.

"And work hard too," said his father. "I will at once see about getting you into an office, and the sooner you get rid of all the impressions your wandering life has given you the better."

Then it was settled that Dick Lightheart should go into a merchant's counting house in London and attend strictly to business.

Henrietta's good sense saw the folly of two very young people marrying on nothing but a diamond, which would soon be spent in housekeeping expenses and dress.

Messiter had also received a lecture from his friends, and he was told that he, too, must work.

He asked Mr. Lightheart if he would try to get him in the same office as Dick.

"I will try," said the parson.

"We shall both be so grateful, sir, if you can manage it," asked Messiter and Dick, in the same breath.

Their friend of the diamond diggings soon established his rights.

His wicked brother commited suicide directly he heard of his return, such was his terror and remorse.

Lord Tregannon, now a well-dressed and polished gentleman, paid Dick his promised visit.

He highly approved of Mr. Lightheart's plan of making Dick work.

"In me your son has always got a firm and sincere friend," he said, "and no one will be more pleased to see him get on."

"He will succeed, my lord, if he keeps out of scrapes," answered Mr. Lightheart.

"That's just what I'm afraid I can't do," said Dick, to himself. "I was born to get into scrapes, and I shall be as bad in the City, I'll bet, as I was at school."

A few days after this conversation, the reverend gentleman received a letter from town, informing him that the senior partner in the mercantile firm in which he proposed to place his son, would run down to Brighton.

If the young men could make it convenient to come over, he should be glad to see them·

"This is Mr. Golding, senior," said the parson.

"What is the name of the firm?" asked Dick.

"Golding Brothers. The senior partner is a working man, and a very strict disciplinarian. The younger one is represented to me as being much easier to deal with."

"I know who I shall like best," exclaimed Dick.

"And I, too," said Messiter.

"The Mr. Golding, junior, I presume," exclaimed Mr. Lightheart, senior, with a smile.

"Exactly," answered Dick. "I never get on well with fellows who want too much kootooing."

"You must remember that he will be your employer, and that to be dismissed from a City firm with a bad character will be your ruin."

"Don't croak," said Dick. "I haven't done anything wrong yet."

"I trust you never will. You ought to have plenty of experience by this time. However, we will say no more about that."

Dick breathed a sigh of relief.

He thought he was in for one of his father's lectures, which were as long as a sermon, and not half so interesting.

"If you like to have the dog-cart, James will drive you over to Brighton. Mr. Golding is staying at the Bedford Hotel."

"I don't want James; I'll drive myself," said Dick. "You needn't fear our coming to grief. It looks like being a kid again to have a servant sent to look after us."

Lord Tregannon had returned to town, or he would have accompanied them.

The following day saw them start early for Brighton.

Putting up the trap at some stables near the Old Steyne, they walked, arm in arm, along Castle Square, and on to the Parade.

"It seems a jolly long time since we were at school here," remarked Messiter.

"And yet," said Dick, "the place is not altered in the least; that is the best of Brighton, it never changes."

"They've built an aquarium, though; let's have a look at it."

"I think we had best go to the hotel, and see old Golding."

Messiter made no objection.

They walked up to the hotel, and on inquiring for Mr. Golding, were told that he had just stepped out, but was not expected to be gone more than a quarter of an hour.

The young gentlemen could wait in his room if they liked.

Agreeing to this, they were shown into a handsome room.

The door was closed, and they were left to themselves.

Dick walked critically round.

"I say," he said, "he's a bit of a swell, he wears patent leather boots."

"Here's the varnish for them," said Messiter, holding up a bottle.

"Let's apply it inside. What a lark," cried Dick, taking the bottle.

He emptied its contents into the boots, and adding a little water out of a flower vase, stirred up the delightful compound with the end of the poker.

"It'll all spurt up when he goes to put them on, and won't he look comical. Oh my!" he exclaimed.

"Holler, boys," cried Messiter, delightedly, "here's another guy. But I say, Dick."

"What?"

"We are going to be good, you know,

and not lose our characters on any account."

"Perhaps we shan't be found out."

Finding no more mischief ready to his hand, Dick grew tired of waiting, and began to whistle.

"Let's cut it," he said. "I want to have a look round."

"And come back here?"

"Yes. It's no good waiting for the old buffer."

Accordingly they put on their hats, and, leaving word in the hall that they would return, they once more sought the Parade.

One rather lumpy old gentleman, with a cross-looking, commanding sort of face, was stretched on the pebbles near the bathing machines.

As Dick passed behind him he touched his hat with his stick, and the wind carried it off towards the sea.

The old gentleman sprang up.

Seeing Dick, he said—

"Boy, go and fetch my hat."

"Did you speak to me?"

"Yes, my lad."

"Perhaps you will be more respectful next time. I am not in the habit of being talked to in that way."

The old gentleman's face grew red.

"I want my hat," he exclaimed.

"Then you'd better go and fetch it."

"Come, come, don't be foolish. I shall complain to your employer if you're insolent."

"Haven't got one."

"Come, I'll give you sixpence to get my hat; see, it is on the edge of the waves already. I can't run; I've got a touch of the gout this morning."

"That's more civil," said Dick, "and I don't mind if I do oblige you this once; only——"

"What?" demanded the old gentleman.

"Don't let it happen again."

Dick ran after the hat.

As he took it up he scooped a couple of handfuls of fine sand into the crown.

Running back, he clapped it on its owner's head.

"There you are, old cock," he said.

"Bother the boy," cried the gentleman. "That's not the way."

He lifted it up, and the sand streamed down over his eyes and into the nape of his neck, from whence it ran down his back, creating a most unpleasant sensation.

He felt as if he had just had his hair cut.

"Confound the young rascal! Pish! splutter! pish! I've got my mouth full of sand. Deuce take him!" he exclaimed. "I'll thrash him! I'll cane him within an inch of his life."

"You've got to spell 'able' first," answered Dick; "and this will teach you to be more civil to young people in future, you old bully."

The gentleman foamed at the mouth with rage, but the boys walked coolly away, and he could not do anything to them.

They had not gone far before a man, dressed in a suit of shepherd's plaid, and smoking a big cigar, stopped before them, with his hands in his pockets.

Jerking his finger in the direction of the old gentleman, he exclaimed—

"What's up? Got a fit?"

An idea struck Dick.

"No," he answered, in a whisper. "I recognised him."

"What?"

"Don't howl," replied Dick. "I tell you I twigged him, but I don't want to make a song about it."

It happened that a few days before an elderly man of high respectability had been tried and acquitted for a most atrocious murder.

Public opinion ran very strongly against the old man of high respectability, and it was pretty generally believed that the had foully murdered a young girl under shocking circumstances.

The name of the accused was Verinder Hutchins.

The trial was even then in everyone's mouth, and the public felt very strongly against the accused, who was said to have got off by the skill of his counsel and the skin of his teeth.

"Who do you mean?" asked the stranger.

Dick's mysterious manner impressed him very much.

"You won't blab?" asked Dick.

"May I be everlastingly blessed if——"

"That'll do. It's Verinder Hutchins, the Melham murderer."

"Nonsense!"

"It is. I was on the prosecution. I am a lawyer's clerk, and was in court all day. I tell you it's Verinder Hutchins, who killed the girl, and got off because he'd got lots of coin."

"Thank you," said the stranger.

Dick and Messiter strolled on a little further.

They saw the man in the check suit talk to several others.

The fact was he had come down from London for the day, with a number of others, to see Brighton, and have a look at the octopus in the aquarium.

He told his friends about Verinder Hutchins.

They crowded round the old gentleman and stared at him.

Presently murmurs arose.

Hisses followed.

"Oh, the brute! the wretch! to murder the poor girl," said the female portion of the excursionists.

"I'd like to lynch the fellow," exclaimed one of the men.

The old gentleman, seeing that he was the centre of observation for a noisy crowd, looked up.

"He's got murder in his heyes," said a woman.

"Look at his bloodthirsty mouth. I never saw such lips," remarked another.

"The willin!" observed a third excursionist, with a vengeful shutting of the hands, "I should like to limb him."

Dick kept in the back-ground, but he was not idle.

"If he is a murderer," he said, "remember the jury did not find him guilty."

"Never mind, he did it," replied a man.

"Don't throw stones at him," cried Dick.

The hint was acted upon.

A shower of stones fell upon the old gentleman, who pale with fear and rage rose from the beach, and hobbled away with the aid of a stick.

Fortunately the victim of the practical joke saw a policeman.

"Hi, constable," he said.

"What is it, sir?"

"Protect me from this mob, and ask them what they mean by their conduct. Look at my eye. It has been struck by a stone. I am sore all over. Hark at

their yells. There must be some awful mistake. Do they take me for the member for the borough?"

The constable approached the man in the plaid suit.

"What's all this 'ere?" asked the officer.

"What is it? Why, it's murder."

"Murder?"

"Yes, that old bloke's Verinder Hutchins, who got off for killing the girl."

"Who told you so?"

"That young chap over there," said the man in the plaid suit.

The constable returned to the gentleman, and related what he had been told.

"Are you Verinder Hutchins, the supposed murderer?" he asked.

"God bless the man, no," cried the gentleman, in astonishment. "It must be the mischief of that youth. I see him dodging behind a bathing machine."

"Better get back to your hotel, sir," said the constable.

"I will. Keep the mob back, and I will reward you if you come to the 'Bedford' and ask for——"

The name was inaudible, and the crowd began to yell again furiously.

The constable assured the crowd that they were mistaken, and caused them to remain where they were, while their victim went across the road, and entered the hotel.

"What a lark," said Dick. "We've had it out of the old boy."

"Serve him right for his cheek," said Messiter.

"Now for Mr. Golding. I'm peckish, and perhaps he'll ask us to lunch."

"He will if he's a good sort," answered Messiter.

They leisurely walked to the "Bedford," and went to the room where they had waited for the great merchant.

The door was open.

A great uproar was proceeding from within, and the bell was being violently pulled.

"You scoundrels!" cried an angry voice, "what have you done? I shall be poisoned. I'm smothered, ugh! ugh! Bah! devil take you all. Hi! help, hi!"

The boys looked into the room.

An elderly gentleman was standing with a boot half on and half off.

A black, slimy, sticky fluid had come out of the boot and splashed all over him.

His face was spotted and smeared with it, and it ran down his fat cheeks in an inky stream, on to his shirt collar and front.

Old Golding had changed his boots.

Dick and Messiter entered the room with a couple of servants, who, by the aid of soap, water, and a towel, enabled him to see a little.

His eyes fell upon Dick and his friend.

The recognition was mutual.

In Mr. Golding they saw the object of their morning's persecution upon the beach.

"Slope, Harry," exclaimed Dick; "we must cut our stick."

"Right. We've put our foot in it," added Messiter.

Hastily leaving the room, they went to the stables, and getting out their trap, drove home.

Their hope was that Mr. Golding would not find out who they were.

In this expectation they were greatly mistaken.

The merchant's first question to the servants was—

"Who were those boys?"

"Two young gentlemen from Hayward's Heath to see you, sir," was the reply.

"Their names?"

"Mr. Lightheart and Mr. Messiter," replied the servant.

"Order me a carriage to go to Hayward's Heath," he said.

Meanwhile the lads reached the rectory.

"Well," said Mr. Lightheart, "seen your future governor?"

"Oh, yes," said Dick, promptly.

"What do you think of him?"

"Nice sort of man. Very."

Wishing to avoid a long conversation, the boys recollected an engagement they had to play a game at cricket.

While in the midst of this interesting game, a servant came down.

"You're wanted, Master Richard," he said.

"Who by?"

"Mr. Verinder Hutchins has come over from Brighton."

The bat dropped from Dick's hand.

"Scissors!" he ejaculated, "that ball's taken my middle wicket, and I'm bowled out as clean as a whistle."

Dick sought the house, and hearing voices in the drawing room, stopped to listen.

"I tell you, sir, the young imp filled my ears and mouth and back with small sand; he had me hooted and chased for a supposed murderer, and he nearly blinded me with a fœtid mixture he put in my boots," said a voice.

"Very sorry to hear it, I'm sure," replied Mr. Lightheart.

"Sir," cried the voice of Mr. Golding, "that boy of yours will come to a bad end."

"I sincerely trust not, sir."

"But I say he will, sir."

Dick pushed open the door, and entered, looking very penitent.

"Here he is," cried the merchant.

"Mr. Golding," began Dick.

"You young rascal!"

"Will you hear me? I did not know it was you when I sanded your nut."

"Did what, sir?" roared Mr. Golding, excitedly.

"When I put the sand in your goss," answered Dick.

"Eh?"

"In your hat, I mean, nor did I know who you were when I put the vulgarians on to you as Verinder, and I beg to apologize."

"How about the blacking in my boots?" asked Mr. Golding, triumphantly.

"Oh, as to the varnish in the crab shells, that was an oversight. I can't say more than I'm very sorry, and it shan't occur again. You riled me at first by telling me to pick up your hat, as if I was a beggar."

"Forgive him this time, sir," said Mr. Lightheart.

"Well, well, say no more about it; there is my hand," replied the merchant, who was a good-hearted man after all.

"Thank you," said Dick, grasping it warmly.

"But," cried Mr. Golding, "when you come into the City, I'll dismiss you at a day's notice, if I catch you at any of your pranks."

Mr. Golding stopped to dinner, and over the port laughed heartily at Dick's jokes.

As for Dick, he told Messiter that he considered they were very well out of the mess.

*   *   *   *   *

We now conclude the adventures of the Scapegrace at Sea.

We must leave Dick Lightheart to go up to London, and start in the world of commerce with his friend Messiter.

In our next number we shall commence our volatile young hero's extraordinary adventures in the great City of London, and those who have followed his course so far, will, we trust, be happy to continue the acquaintance of

THE SCAPEGRACE OF LONDON.

www.ingramcontent.com/pod-product-compliance
Lightning Source LLC
Chambersburg PA
CBHW080822250626
47160CB00008B/2833